Children of the Water

Rita Redswood

ISBN-10: 1980952418
ISBN-13: 978-1980952411

Acknowledgements

Thank you to everyone who has supported my work throughout the creation of this book. I would also like to thank especially my good friend Pat for her invaluable feedback and suggestions on this book.

Chapter One: Village by the Ruins

Thick grey clouds loomed overhead while waves crashed against the bottom of a cliff. Jagged rocks traveled upwards and led to a small village. A wooden fence blocked the village from the cliff's edge as a stone path split the village in two. Some gulls rested on the rocks and others sat upon the fence. Their noise was drowned out by the chatter of people during market hours.

Businesses had their doors opens, and those inside enjoyed the cool ocean breeze that swept through their shops and homes. Those who weren't working stayed inside or shopped for goods. Children helped their parents indoor or with their business as others played games.

A game of ball was presently taking place between five children. The soft red sphere was being kicked around on one of the open spots of dark green grass. One of the players, a girl by the name of Margaret, kicked the ball too hard, and it rolled out onto the street. "I'll retrieve it!" called out another girl by the name of Odette.

"No, stop! Odette, come back!" Thomas, a seven-year-old boy, shouted. He had run after a rogue ball once, and it had led him to the ruins by the village. His curiosity had taken over, and he had peered at them. The boy had seen something standing in the ruins, and he had quickly darted off. All of his parents' tales were true, and he had been lucky, but Odette might not possess such fortune. Before he could stop her, the six-year-old abandoned her friends and gave chase. Thomas wasn't going to go after her; he was too terrified to do so.

"She's a goner," Margaret muttered and shook her head. Like Thomas, she wasn't going to race after Odette. Her parents' tales of the ruins kept her far away from them. A ball wasn't that important to her.

"Maybe, she'll get lucky. The monster might not grab her."

"Right, Thomas." She rolled her eyes and went back to the others. "I like her, but I like me more." She started to laugh once more with the other children. Reluctantly, Thomas faced away from her and followed Margaret.

Odette's long, light blonde hair bounced up and down while her little feet carried her forward. As the ball rolled down the street, she desperately tried to catch up, but the street, going away from the village, sloped downward. Things weren't made easier by some of the stones sticking out of the path. She had to be careful not to trip on one.

Once the street stopped its slope, the ball continued to travel fast, but it slowed down in time. Finally, Odette reached the ball and picked it up. During her pursuit, however, she hadn't noticed how far she had gone. The sounds of the waves, markets, birds and children were quieter, and she was left with the chilling atmosphere of the ruins by the village.

Steadily, she turned to them. Her parents had told her to never glance at them, or she would see a monster there. In fact, all parents told their children to be scared of the ruins. That if they were to look into the eyes of the monster, they would be taken and would disappear from the world forever.

The tales also scared off attackers. Their village of Watergrove was never invaded since people feared the ruins. It wasn't just children that were taken. Occasionally, an adult would apparently catch the eyes of the monster and be found dead the next morning.

None of the villagers, though, tried to dispose of the ruins. Despite them losing a child or an adult once in awhile, more lives were saved by the terror of the ruins. Since invaders didn't dare come near them, the village was able to thrive. Even though the ruins decreased traders significantly, the village was able to support itself on its crops and the sea's food.

Despite the stories, Odette peered at them. It was a child's curiosity, and part of her wanted to meet the monster. She wanted to know what happened to the missing children, and she wished to understand why the adults would be killed.

How could looking at something cause such problems? It didn't make sense to her, and her parents would only warn her to quell her questions. If they didn't answer her, she would seek out the source since she had the opportunity.

Maybe, it was because she didn't wish to believe that such a creature could exist. Perhaps, her curiosity sprouted because she desired to hear what the monster had to say for itself. Slowly, she took more steps towards them.

Stone pillars leaned against each other while rubble was spread out around the area. Pools of water collected around parts of the ruins while dark green grass and mud covered the rest of the vicinity. When she stood at the edge of the ruins, she searched for eyes staring back.

Instead of seeing eyes, she heard a splash to her left. She darted her gaze that way and saw something run past. It looked like a person, but she wasn't sure. Odette followed the direction that they seemed to go in. Another splash caught her attention. This time, it was closer and more in front of her.

Staring out ahead, she froze. Dark blue eyes locked onto her gaze. Those eyes had no pupils, and both the sclera and iris were blue. The eyes belonged to a boy of about her age. Short, messy and ink-colored black locks rested atop his head while his skin was a medium blue. A black cloth shirt and pants covered his form, but his feet were bare.

She dropped the ball and took a step forward. Odette ignored her name being called by her parents. Rather, she listened to her name now being whispered to her as she took another step forward. The boy remained in the same place, waiting for her. A gentle smile graced his lips.

Before she could take another step, she was pulled back, and her face was pressed against the chest of her father. Neither of the adults looked out towards the ruins but, purposefully, turned their backs to them. Odette struggled in her father's grip, wanting to see the boy again. She pushed her small hands against his chest and managed to look over his right shoulder.

To her disappointment, the boy was gone, but she saw ripples in the nearby pool. She had seen the supposed monster and found out that it was only a boy about her age. If only she had learned his name. "Father, put me down! Put me down!" she cried out, beating her tiny fists against him. "I want to see him!"

"I'm sorry, Odette, but you're not allowed to go near him. You shouldn't have come here in the first place. We had warned you." Her father started to walk back to the village with her mother after the woman had picked up the red ball.

"But, the ball ..."

"Catching a ball isn't important. Even still, you could've looked away from the ruins, but you hadn't." Her father wasn't going to be easy on her. She had broken a vital rule, but he was thankful that they had caught her in time. Now, they had to make sure that she never went near the ruins again.

Realizing that her parents weren't going to put her down, she kicked and screamed the entire way. She could still hear the boy's whispering of her name in her head. Odette wanted to ask him so many questions.

As they neared her parents' house, she cried out in vain, "Father! Mother! Please!"

"No, Odette. You must forget the monster." Her father held onto her tighter when she squirmed more in his arms. "And, we're going to ensure that." The girl's brown eyes went wide before she shouted even louder. Both her parents ignored her protests and brought her into their house.

From that day on, she couldn't forget about the boy, and she was punished for it. Her parents had sealed her in her room. The only time her door had been opened was for food and cleaning. Many times, she had tried to escape. With each of her efforts, however, her room became more of a prison.

Windows were sealed shut and boarded up. Her door bore several locks, and her three meals were brought all at once. Cleaning of her wash basin and emptying of her chamber pot were done when her empty plates were taken away. For her entertainment, books, parchment, ink and quills were delivered, but that was all.

Despite all of that, she still tried to escape. She refused to stay in her room for her whole life, so she developed escape plans and hid them in certain places. When an opportunity presented itself, she executed one, but it always failed. One day, she called out to her parents. They stood on the other side of her door and listened. Odette asked why they kept her locked up when she was past the age of a child.

“Once a child sees the eyes of the monster, they are forever under the creature’s spell. And, we know that you’re still attempting to go back to the ruins,” her father replied in a scolding manner towards the end.

“This is the only way to protect you,” her mother tried to reassure.

They left her alone after that. Things seemed hopeless for her, but she attempted to escape every now and then. Each time, someone managed to catch her before she broke free. It was either one of her parents or the maid, and it didn’t help that the three would change their schedules on her so that she wouldn’t be able to determine when they weren’t walking the halls.

During that time, the boy waited for her to return. He traveled to the edge of the ruins that faced the village. The male would listen for rumors on what had happened to his chosen. When he had learned that she was locked within her home, he had felt a rush of anger enter him.

Sadly, he couldn’t leave the ruins. It would mean death for him; he needed to be near water. As the years passed and he grew older, he had trouble resisting the urge to travel to the village. He needed his chosen soon. Otherwise, his purpose in life would be forfeit, and he would die a disgrace to his parents.

He remembered the appearance of her parents, though, and he would try to lure them into the ruins. Unfortunately, they kept their distance and never peered over into them. His blood boiled with rage as he wasn’t able to get his hands on her. The male remembered his chosen’s beautiful brown eyes, which had been filled with curiosity and wonder. She hadn’t looked at him in fear or disgust; she had been searching for him.

Other children before her had peered into the ruins, but he hadn’t chosen them. For when they had met his gaze, he had spotted the fear easily. They would be bent to his will, but they would never understand their purpose; they would never fully accept him since they would only follow out of terror. Then, he had met his chosen, and she had stolen his heart.

Now, he needed her back. She was supposed to go with him on that day all those years ago, but her parents had stopped her before she had stepped too far into the ruins. They had kept her from him, yet she was his.

On a particular day, however, he felt a surge rush through his heart. His dark blue eyes glanced to the village, and he knew that it was his last year to act. He pushed back his locks and stood up, for he wasn't going to wait until the last moment. Tonight, he would retrieve her.

Chapter Two: Night Whispers

Knees to her chest, she rested her head on them and breathed out and in slowly. It was Odette's eighteenth birthday, yet, for the entire day, she had been locked away in her room. During the day, she had been treated the same as well, and she had figured that her parents might've forgotten about it. After all the years of locking her away, it wouldn't surprise her.

Throughout the day, however, she did hear her name being called by that gentle, enchanting voice. Over the years, she had noted that the boy's voice grew with age and sounded like the voice of a young man. It would make sense for the boy to grow older as well since he did look human in some ways. She wondered how he appeared now.

Deciding to pick herself up, she headed over to one of the windows in her room. The whispering was growing more frequent and louder, and there was clear urgency to the male's voice. She wanted to escape, but going through the halls proved fruitless. Still, the windows didn't provide an easy route either.

She pressed her hands to the glass and looked to the boards. It had been too long since she last gazed at the sky. Odette desired those boards gone. When she stared at the wood longer, she noted the rot on them. The boards had been up since she was a child, and the moisture in the sea air had made the wood weaker over the years. There was also the rain that had come about once or twice a week.

If she broke the glass, she could charge at the boards and possibly break through them. Of course, she was two stories up, so it would be best to have something to prevent her fall. She would have plenty of time to prepare since the maid had made her last stop for the day.

While she began her operation, the male in the ruins stood at the edge of them. He needed pools of water nearby to live; he required his feet to be in water at all times. Moisture in the air or rain wouldn't suffice.

If there were puddles, he could hop from one to the other, but the downward slope of the village street prevented that. There were also the small spaces in between the stones of the street. That allowed the water to be absorbed by the dirt below, hence the grasses that would grow between the stones, and that only made water collections harder to form.

How was he supposed to travel to her? He had increased the times that he had called her name and the volume of those whispers, but that had served him no benefit. The male could risk travel to the village, but he didn't know how long he would last before he collapsed to the ground and died.

He paced around in the water, trying to come up with something. One way or another, he would have her tonight. There was the benefit that he knew which house was hers. Those villagers did gossip about her family, and how the boards on her house looked unseemly. Clasping his hands behind his back, he stared back out at the village. If he could transport the water in some way, he might have a chance to make it to her.

Unfortunately, there wasn't a water carrying device in the ruins. Hearing wheels on the stone street, he turned towards the sound and watched a late night cart come down the street. A draft horse led the wagon and its rider. On a rare occasion, there would be traders who would stay all day and leave in the night.

Focusing on the wagon part, a smirk began to form on his lips. Quickly, he made his way over to the cart. The rider obviously took the tales of the ruins lightly since he rode close to them. He could survive long enough to step out of the pools for a few moments. When he reached the wagon and its rider, he leapt from the waters and crashed against the rider.

The male was about to emit a yell, and the horse began to panic. Knowing that he had to act fast, he sunk his sharp teeth into the neck of the rider since it was the easiest place to strike. When the rider started to go limp, the male got to his feet and spit out the blood.

Swiftly, he grabbed the reins on the horse and pulled both the horse and wagon towards the ruins. The horse resisted, leaving him no choice but to calm it down. His energy was rapidly depleting, however. He forced himself to stay out a little longer until he soothed the horse. About a minute passed before he managed to lead the horse and wagon into the ruins.

When his feet touched the cooling waters of one of the pools, he let out a sigh of relief. He could feel his life returning to him. Now, he merely had to lead the horse farther in. Once at one of the deeper pools, he helped the horse swim through it by supporting the weight of the wagon as it went under. The horse managed to swim across and exit the pool.

With it back on solid ground, it struggled with the weight of the wagon, but the male helped push it out and onto the earth as well. Stepping on the edge of the pool, he grinned at seeing the wagon filled with water. Water was leaking out from some spots, but if he made a quick trip into the village and back, he would be fine. He hoisted himself up into the back and pulled up the hood of his black cloak.

Soaking in the water, he grabbed the reigns and guided the horse out of the ruins. His wagon did look odd, especially since some would've just seen the same one leaving the village. Still, the evening had grown darker, and more clouds had rolled in. Another storm was on its way, and most would be huddled up in their homes. If it did rain, it would help to refill his wagon.

Odette had managed to tear up her bed sheets and form a rope out of them. She had tied one end to one of the bedposts while she had her right hand gripped tightly on the other end. Keeping her hold on the rope, she picked up the metal chamber pot with both hands and chucked it at the stained glass. The glass shattered, and the pot rolled away from the crash.

Thankfully, her parents had bought her good leather boots, and she hoped that the glass wouldn't break through the bottoms of them. She heard footsteps rushing towards her room as she took some steps back. When the locks on her door were being unlocked, she charged forward and tightened her hold on the makeshift rope.

As her door opened, she leapt through the window and towards the rotted boards. She shielded her head with her arms and closed her eyes while the wood broke under her weight. The wood scratched against her arms, and she could hear it ripping through parts of her dress. Odette just hoped that it didn't tear through the cloth rope.

Soon, however, she felt droplets of water fall upon her skin while the smell of rain filled her nose. A smile painted itself across her lips. After twelve years, she was finally outside again. She felt the rope go rigid as it stretched to its full length. Opening her eyes, she noticed that she was hanging a few feet above the ground.

A loud ripping noise resonated, and she looked up; the rope was tearing. She dropped herself to the ground while the rope fell soon after. Glancing to her window, she saw the faces of her parents and the maid staring at her. They quickly vanished, and she knew that she had to run for it.

Taking no more time, she darted towards the ruins but halted her movement soon after. A horse filled her vision before the rider of the wagon pulled back on the reins and eased the animal. She took no time and went to rush past. Odette stopped again, however, when she heard her name being called. That familiar voice, it couldn't have been.

Turning to them, she saw a blue hand being held out to her. It really was him! She could hear her parents and the maid shouting out her name. With no hesitation, she took the hand and allowed herself to be pulled up. Water splashed around her before she found herself in a pool of the liquid. The male speedily steered the wagon around and signaled the horse to run towards the ruins.

The action sent her flying back and into the water more. She pushed herself up on her elbows and coughed out some of the water. Her gaze fell on the back of the cloaked male while many questions filled her mind. The girl had so much to ask him, but she understood that it wasn't the time for it. Once they reached the ruins, she could make her inquiries.

Positioning herself on her knees, she noted that her arms were bleeding some. "Um, excuse me, but shouldn't we get out of the water. I think that some of my blood may have run into it."

"It's not a problem. I'll fix your wounds when we get to the ruins," he answered, continuing to stare out ahead and guide the horse.

Her voice got stuck in her throat upon hearing him. It was the first time that she had heard him say something more than her name. His voice was truly mesmerizing. To her ears, it felt like running one's hands through cool waters, and that soft embrace, after a warm summer's day, made her voice melt in her mouth while her heart skipped a beat.

It seemed so illogical to be ensnared by someone's voice, but she wasn't able to help it. Hearing his voice directly instead of indirectly through whispers in her head lulled her into an overwhelming sense of peace. She couldn't even hear the yells of her parents and the maid anymore. Her attention was solely on him.

Chapter Three: Beneath the Pools

Near the ruins, there was a bump in the road. She was thrown upwards before she impacted the bottom of the wagon again. Water splashed all around her, and she was getting tired of getting soaked. She coughed out some more water before she peered over the edge of the wagon. They were entering the ruins.

Sitting up a bit straighter, she rested her hands on the edge of the wagon and looked out over it. She couldn't see out too far since the moon and stars were partially blocked out by the storm. Only thin rays of the lights broke through the thick storm clouds. The rain continued to pour down on them, but her companion didn't seem to mind at all. Then again, he was the one who brought a wagon full of water in the first place.

Once they were a safe distance from the road and far into the ruins, he stopped the wagon and hopped down into a pool of water. He went into another before detaching the horse from the cart. "You're free to go," he said, quietly, to the animal. The male hit the horse hard on its side, and it ran off.

He watched it dart away until he turned his attention back to her. The male stood closer to one of the beams of moonlight. His hands reached up to his cloak hood, and he steadily pulled it down. Long, ink-black locks fell past his past shoulders while the rest of his hair was secured behind his back. Prominent brows, in the same hue as his locks, complimented his dark blue eyes. A small smile fell upon his lips while a chiseled jaw line made him all the more attractive.

The black cloak cascaded down his broad shoulders and down his left arm as he held his hand out to her. She was embarrassed to take it; she was ashamed of her appearance. Her long, light blonde hair was tangled, her dress torn and her arms scratched. Overall, she was a mess.

He was stunning in his appearance, and she wished to hide in the shadows. Even though the rain plastered strands of his hair to his face, he held an otherworldly handsomeness to him. Heat had invaded her cheeks the moment that he had pulled down his hood. "Odette, come. Take my hand. You'll catch a cold if we don't get you out of the rain." His gentle smile remained on his lips.

With some hesitation, she reached forward and took his hand. She stood up carefully in the water and walked towards him, her heart hammering in her chest. When she stepped out of the back of the wagon, he released her hand and rested both of his on her waist.

More heat flooded her cheeks, and she thought that they would burst. He lifted her up and then down before he set her gently on the ground. The male took her right hand in his left again before he faced the pool. She summoned up her courage, however, and tugged back on him. "Wait, I need to ask you some questions."

Glancing over his left shoulder, he answered, "They can wait until we get you out of this weather, and we get those scratches taken care of."

Being bold, she shook her head. It was hard to resist that harmonious voice of his, but she forced herself to. "At least, answer one of them," she murmured, meeting his gaze. She nearly got lost in his dark blue eyes, and she quickly looked away.

Facing her some more now, she heard him sigh, but he remained quiet. She figured that he was agreeing to her request. "Will you tell me your name before we go any further?"

"I suppose that's fair." To her surprise, she watched him kneel on his right leg and place his right hand over his heart. He dipped his head before he met her gaze once more. "The name that I was given at birth is Tarhuinn, my chosen."

Chosen? She didn't know what he meant by that, but she wished that he would stop bowing before her. Odette had never been given such treatment before, and she didn't know how to handle it. To make matters worse, her knees desired to collapse after he had utilized the nickname. It was as if her whole body wished to fall forward and into him.

Seeming to notice her condition, he swiftly stood up and rested his right hand on her shoulder to support her. "Come. I'll take you somewhere that'll allow you a peaceful slumber." She couldn't resist his offer.

He faced away from her and headed further into the pool of water. Their two hands were still intertwined while they went deeper into the liquid. She didn't understand how it was better than staying in the rain, though.

At a certain point, she could tell that the water went deeper than she could imagine. They stood on the edge of the dark depths, and he squeezed her hand in reassurance. "Trust me," he whispered soothingly to her, and she couldn't even utter any protest. She nodded her head before she felt water surround her.

Before her mind could process what was happening, her face was pressed to his chest. His feet kicked in the water at an inhuman speed, and his arms were wrapped around her torso. Odette didn't know how much longer she would be able to hold her breath, and she gripped his cloak.

Lungs crying out for oxygen, she tightened her hold on him and shut her eyes tight. As consciousness slipped from her, air greeted her deprived lungs. She coughed several times as she did her best to draw in the air. Her breathing was ragged as she was lifted and set down upon smooth rock. Dull light made itself apparent when she opened her brown eyes and wiped the water from her face.

Odette found herself in what appeared to be a cave. There were passageways to her left and right. Iron lanterns hung from the ceiling and gave off the faint light. In front of her stood Tarhuinn, but she noticed that he was standing on a rock ledge in the water. Did he need to be in water to survive?

Her eyes did another scan of the area, and she saw that there were water walkways alongside the stone paths. Looking back to him, she jumped some since he had moved closer to her. A light chuckle hit her ears, and she was instantly reminded of relieving ocean waves. "Forgive me. I didn't mean to startle you. Follow me, and I'll take you to our room."

Freezing, she stared at him, and she felt her whole face burning. "Wh-what?" she stuttered out as her ears began to heat up as well.

"Well, I suppose that you don't want to return to the surface and back to the village," he remarked, confusion written on his face. There was also a hint of warning in his voice as if she was to say the wrong answer, she would be silenced. It was intimidating, and she shook her head rapidly. "I'm pleased to hear that. Now, come along."

Picking herself up to her feet, she trailed behind him on the stone path. She could hear the water sloshing around in her boots, and she made a mental note to take them off soon. Still, she didn't think that he understood the problem at hand. Odette barely knew the male, and they were already sharing a room. Of course, she had been hearing him call her name for twelve years, which led to another question. How was he able to whisper her name to her like that? There were just so many questions, and even more sprouted as the evening carried on.

Eventually, they faced a stone wall; however, there was a door in the water path. He took off a chain necklace, which had a key on the end. The male inserted it into the lock and stepped aside, motioning for her to go first. She jumped into the water, and he helped to balance her. Odette thanked him before she headed inside.

When she saw a stone floor again, she climbed up and surveyed the room. It was an interesting space to say the least. The water path encircled the perimeter of the room, eventually flowing into the rock walls and taking a hidden path. Another water path, in the center of the room, flowed into the main one.

In the middle of the center path, a peculiar bed rested. Its right side was flat and adorned with pillows and blankets. On the left, the bed was slanted downward so that water lapped against the base. A mere pillow lay at the top, and it didn't slide down due to a thin rock shelf below it.

Moving her gaze over to the right-hand side of the room, she saw a three-drawer dresser and cupboard with toiletries. A little ways away from it was a room carved out in the stone, with a wooden door that blocked what was inside. She assumed it to be a restroom. Next to the door was a bathtub carved out of the stone, and a waterfall flowed into it before the stream of water traveled under the wall and disappeared.

Hearing movement behind her, she saw Tarhuinn walk with ease through the water and into the main path. He sat upon the non-slanted bed, dipping his feet in the water, and began to untie his cloak. "There are medical supplies in that cupboard over there. Will you grab them and bring them to me? I'll tend to your wounds, then," he stated, peering up at her. A smirk touched his lips. "Or, do you wish to watch me undress?"

"N-no, I'm go-going," she replied quickly, her words stumbling in the process. A light laugh escaped his lips as she ran over to the cupboard, jumping over the water path in the process. She opened the cupboard door, and her fingers fumbled to pick up the bandages and what she assumed to be salve. Returning to him, he signaled for her to take a seat next to him. She did so as he cast his cloak onto the slanted bed. He took her right arm in his hands and began to work.

Keeping her gaze slightly off of him, Odette bit her bottom lip. He cleaned her arm with some of the water from the constantly flowing stream before he massaged the salve into her arm. Every few moments, a soft moan of pleasure desired to escape her lips.

To be honest, she wasn't expecting such treatment on her eighteenth birthday, but she wasn't complaining either. The worrying part was that she barely knew anything about the man. Forcing herself to speak, she questioned, "Tarhuinn, how were you able to whisper my name over all of those years?"

He kept working as he responded, "You're my chosen. For my kind, our chosens can hear us whispering their name in their heads. If I tried to do the same with someone other than you, it wouldn't work. It's just part of my kind's nature."

"Do you mind explaining more to me about your kind and this chosen concept?" she inquired as her legs felt weak once again.

Now wrapping up her right arm, he tied the bandages off before he hopped into the water and indicated for her to move over some. She did so, and he sat back on the bed. While he worked on her left arm, he mentioned, "There's a lot to know about my kind, and I can't explain it all in one sitting."

"Well, what about ..." she stopped herself, not knowing if it would be rude to question him on that.

"What about? Please, continue your thought, Odette."

"Your voice," she finished. He halted his work and locked his gaze with hers. She flinched some and scooted away slightly from him. It was as if he dared her to go on and explain. Maybe, it was a topic not meant to be discussed, but, to be fair, he did ask for her to proceed.

"Does it not please you?" His dark blue orbs narrowed, and she felt slightly threatened under his sharp gaze. "If doesn't, I'll correct the problem."

That made her even more nervous. He made it sound like he could change his voice in a matter of seconds. Or, perhaps, fixing the issue had something to do with her. Whatever the case, she felt that she needed to say something soon, or something would go terribly wrong.

"No, it's not that. Your voice is very calming to listen to," she complimented, noting that his expression visibly relaxed. "I merely wished to know why it sounds so mesmerizing. I've never heard someone have such a voice before."

At that, he chuckled some. "I'm honored to hear such flattery, but it's just my regular voice." He let out a few more quiet laughs before he tended to her left arm once more. Tarhuinn pulled her closer to him again to be able to work better on it.

Something didn't add up with his statement, though. A few moments ago, he mentioned that he could correct the error. Could he train his voice that quickly? Or, would it have really meant that something would be done to her? Was it actually his regular voice, or was there a deeper explanation behind it? Her mind swirled with various theories, and she understood that she should've forced him to answer her questions before coming to his home. Then again, she was eager to get away from her parents and the maid.

"There, your arms are all bandaged. You should get changed. A needle and thread are in the dresser if your clothes need to be adjusted."

His voice broke through her thoughts, and she merely nodded. "What about your clothes, though? Or, do you only have those?" she inquired, glancing over his black pants and black cloth shirt.

Another laugh escaped his lips. "If you look to left side of your bed, you'll see a drawer carved into the stone bed. That's where I keep my clothing items. Now, go change into some dry clothes."

Taking the bandages and salve, she hopped off the bed and onto the solid ground. As she made her way over to the dresser, she stopped and looked back to him. When he noted her gaze, he gave her a questioning gaze. "Is something wrong, Odette?"

"Well, you never answered my question about this chosen concept of yours," she muttered, noticing how before he had diverted her attention from it in a way.

"We'll discuss it tomorrow when I give you a tour of our home," he answered, his hands gripping at his shirt and pulling it off.

Instantly, she looked away from him, feeling her cheeks warm up. He didn't expect her to change in front of him like that, did he? Well, there was that room behind the wooden door. She would just switch clothes in there. She went over to the dresser and opened the top drawer, finding undergarments and nightwear. Still, she wanted to know about the title as soon as possible, but if he did tell her tomorrow about the chosen term, she supposed that it would be alright.

She picked out a simple blue nightshirt and underwear along with a blue nightgown. Odette grabbed the thread and needle too. Closing the drawer, she headed over to the closed off area and opened the door. A loud splash sounded, and she found herself in another pool of water. To her left was bench carved out of stone with a hole in the middle. A constant stream of water flowed down the slanted stone beneath the hole.

"Odette, why are you changing in the restroom?"

Not looking back to him, she called out, "I'm not undressing in front of you!"

"It's odd for you to change where the toilet is, though. Come on out, and I promise that I won't look."

Peeking over at him, she noted that he had already changed. She breathed a sigh of relief and stepped out of the room. After she closed the door, she pouted. "Well, turn away, then," she huffed before she saw him smirk and roll his eyes.

With him facing away from her, she swiftly switched into the new clothes. They were somewhat loose, so she took the needle and thread and adjusted the clothes. When completed, she put the thread and needle away before she held onto her old ones. "What should I do with these?"

He looked at her once again. "Set them on the ground, and we'll take them to the washing room tomorrow. Now, let's get some sleep. You look exhausted, my chosen."

There was that nickname again. Her legs felt feeble once more, and she practically dropped the clothes to the ground. He held out his right hand, and she clasped her left around it. She almost fell into him, but he caught her and lifted her into his arms. Tarhuinn carried her to the bed and set her upon it.

Clutching at his beige nightshirt, she ended up leaning her head against his chest even as he placed her on the bed. Her cheeks burned, but she merely wished to rest against him. It didn't make sense since she hardly knew him, but her body had a mind of its own. Like earlier, that name had some sort of effect on her. Was that why he was pushing the explanation until tomorrow; was he stalling?

Fingers combed through her hair while he whispered for her to rest in that enchanting voice of his. Her fingers grew slack, and she closed her eyes. Soon, she was fast asleep against him. The male noted her state and smirked. He picked her up again and walked to the right side of her bed. After he pulled back the sheets, he laid her down and tucked her in.

Twelve years had gone by, and he finally had her. He ran his fingers through her soft locks and across her jaw line. Resting his right thumb on her lips, he gripped her chin with his other fingers. Tarhuinn moved his thumb down slightly and leaned forward. Her supple lips molded against his perfectly. If she were awake, it would've been more delightful.

Originally, he had planned to kiss her tomorrow, but he couldn't resist how tempting they looked. When he pulled away, he licked his lips and watched her shift some in her sleep. Forcing himself to look away, he walked around the room and blew out the lanterns before he lied down on the smooth stone.

Only having his eyelids closed for a few moments it seemed, he heard her move around on her bed more. He thought little of it until she rolled off and onto him. Startled, he opened his eyes and was relieved to see that her head had landed on his pillow. Her steady breathing and closed eyes told him that she remained asleep. A small smile stretched across his lips. "I'll let you sleep on my bed if you want," he whispered as he pulled her close to him and shut his eyes once more.

Tomorrow, he would explain her purpose to her, and she would accept. He would make sure that she would agree. After all, she was his chosen, and he loved her.

Chapter Four: Some Clarity

Dull lantern light flickered across the room again, and the sound of running water pressed on. Odette rolled onto her left side and stretched her arms out some as if attempting to cuddle with the sheets. To the girl's disappointment, she found no soft fabric to greet her. Rather, her hands were met by the cold stone. The discomfort caused her to steadily open her brown eyes.

Upon doing so, she was met by a stone wall and drawer. She glanced up only a little to see her bed slightly above her, which meant that she still had the habit of rolling off of the bed. At least, she hadn't tumbled into the water. Moving onto her back, she noted that Tarhuinn wasn't there, which was a relief. It would've been embarrassing to wake up next to him.

Sitting up, she found that she could only do so steadily. Her limbs were sore from sleeping on the stone, and she wondered how he tolerated such a bed. Still, where had he gone off to? After she rubbed her eyes some, she glanced around the room.

When her gaze met the bathtub, heat flooded her cheeks, and she grabbed the sheet off of her bed to cover her face. A little warning would've been nice. Luckily, in her quick stare, she had only seen his bare shoulders and the top part of his chest.

"You're certainly shy, Odette," came his voice in between soft laughs.

"Well, forgive me, but unmarried people in my village typically don't take baths in the same room! Or, at least that's what I was taught!" she shouted out. She didn't mean to, but her bashfulness was currently dominating her speech.

She heard a splash and footsteps progressing towards her in the water. Tensing, she didn't dare uncover her face. "Well despite me finding your reaction cute, you're in the way of my clothing drawer. You can either move onto your bed or let me pick you up and move you." Her cheeks burned at the mental image of the second option, and she pulled the sheet away some to climb back onto her bed.

Facing away from him, she clutched at the sheet as he opened his drawer. “Let me know when you’re finished,” she murmured, hearing another laugh from him.

“Of course, but do you plan to bathe this morning?”

“Yes, but only once you leave the room. Unlike you, I have a sense of privacy.”

“I’ve noticed, but there’s something wrong with your plan,” he voiced as the sound of footsteps filled the room again. She shut her eyes tight and cursed in her head. He was definitely coming her way, and he hadn’t told her that he was changed yet. Hands rested on her shoulders, and cool breath blew onto her face. It smelled of soothing mint. “You can open your eyes, Odette. I’ve already changed.”

Hesitantly, she did so and tried to keep the heat away from her cheeks, but he was so close. She could feel her heartbeat increasing. Odette backed away some or tried to, but his grip on her tightened. “Wh-what’s this issue in m-my plan?” she questioned, looking down and refusing to meet his stare.

“It’s simple. This is our room, and you can’t force me to leave. What if I wish to stay and watch you bathe?” he breathed out, moving his face closer to hers.

Face and ears igniting, she turned her head away. She knew that if she looked into his eyes, she wouldn’t even be able to utter a counter. His captivating voice was drawing her in too much. “Th-then, you’re a p-pervert, and I-I’ll f-find a wa-way t-to ki-kick you ou-out,” she managed to argue.

A series of light laughs left his lips while he pulled away and stood up straight again. “You don’t sound too convincing, but I’ll let you off for now. You take a bath, and I’ll prepare some breakfast for us. I should be about twenty minutes. That should be more than enough time for you.”

She kept her gaze off of him until she heard him start to leave. Watching him, she noted that he had on a loose black jacket, a long purple shirt and black pants. It was a surprise to see the color purple on him as that color was exceptionally rare to view on an individual. Was he royalty of some sort? She pushed the thought aside, though, once he left the room.

Quickly, she stood up from her seat and attended to her morning routine. When she took her bath, though, it was odd since there was no soap. Instead, she found a bottle that smelled of mixed fragrances. She couldn't compare it to anything that she had smelled before; she could only tell that it was sweet. There was another bottle that smelled of pine. Odette decided to use the sweeter scent.

After she left the bath, she made her way carefully across the stone floor, not wishing to slip and fall. Reaching the dresser, she grabbed a new change of undergarments before she opened the second drawer. Simple blue, black, grey and purple dresses were in there. Her hands went over to the purple fabric, and she was tempted to wear it, but it seemed too important for her. She was intimidated by the color, and the power that was usually associated with it.

She picked out a simple corset grey dress. Slipping it on, she tied up the front and noted how her long-sleeve, black undershirt was quite visible due to the dress's short sleeves. Still, he wouldn't be able to see anything revealing. She smoothed out the skirt of the dress and did note that it went just below her knees. If anyone in her village were to spot her, they would consider her dress to be scandalous, but it made sense due to the water paths that she would have to occasionally walk in.

The door to the room opened soon after she had changed. Tarhuinn came in and shut the door behind him with his right foot. In his hands was a metal tray with two bowls, spoons and glasses. He walked up to the edge of the water near where she was at. While he set the tray down, she laid her nightgown on top of the dresser and added her other undergarments to the pile of clothes from yesterday.

He seated himself on the edge of the solid ground, keeping his feet in the water, and motioned for her to take a seat next to him. Doing so, she glanced to the food and noted scrambled eggs mixed in with chopped potatoes and peppers. There was also a glass of what looked like some sort of juice. The light pink color confused her, and she furrowed her brows. She picked up one of the glasses and peered at it for a bit longer. "What's this? I've never seen this color of juice before."

"It's grapefruit juice. I added sugar to it so that it wouldn't be so bitter."

"Grapefruit? I've never seen a grape this color," she mentioned, giving him a skeptical look. "Are you sure that you know what a grape is?"

An amused smile crossed his lips as he rolled his eyes. "Just try it, and I'll show you what the fruit looks like on the tour today. It's a type of citrus."

"That name still doesn't make sense to me," she muttered before she drank a small sip. She made a sour face, not expecting the bitter taste, but the sugar definitely helped. Odette didn't dislike it, though. "Thank you for making breakfast, but how are you getting this food let alone everything else here?"

"There's a central trading site for my kind. In that area is a chart for what one or multiple item(s) is/are worth. Still, I only go there for thread, fabric or fully produced clothes and a few others things. I produce my own food, salves, dyes, etc. since I specialize in growing crops."

That would explain how he had managed to get the purple dye. Despite it interesting that he grew his own food and such, she was more curious about the chosen business. To her, that seemed more pressing, and she was getting distracted again. Somehow, he kept managing to draw her attention away from the things that she originally desired to understand. If he didn't explain it to her today, she would pester him about it or try to.

His personality did seem to have moments where he looked like he was about to snap at her. She set down her glass and picked up the bowl and fork. Odette found the food to be delicious, and she finished it within a matter of minutes. It was also because she wished to satisfy her curiosity. Picking up her glass again, she swirled the drink around and questioned, "Will I be able to visit this trading site in the future?"

Silence answered her, and she peered over to him. She had asked merely to bring up conversation between them since she could feel his stare on her. Besides, she desired to learn more about her whereabouts and his kind. Now, she was worried that her question had angered him.

"No, you're not allowed to go there," he answered, placing his finished food down. "There'll be no argument on that. You're to remain in our home only. You have much to learn, and you won't have time to go there."

Seeing his hardened gaze, she looked back to her drink and took a sip. She was going to point out that visiting there would be learning, but she feared what he would do. "I'm sorry for asking," she mumbled, hoping that would get him to relax his expression. Out of the corners of her eyes, she noticed that it did. Regardless, the more time she spent with him, the more she realized that something was off.

Chapter Five: Walk in the Water

When breakfast finished, Tarhuinn led her out of the room and guided her to the washroom for her clothes. She merely set them in the space while he placed his in another pile. He mentioned that they would get to them later in the day.

Afterwards, he guided her to the kitchen where they both washed their dishes. Like the washroom, it looked pretty similar to her past home's kitchen. Throughout all of the rooms, though, were water paths for Tarhuinn while there were ground paths for her.

That was another peculiar detail about the house. The two different paths made it seem like it was common for a human to be with his kind. She didn't ask him if that was the case, but she did store the curiosity away. "So, where to next?" she questioned after the dishes were cleaned, dried and put away.

"I'll take you to the farming area, and you can see what a grapefruit is," he mentioned, chuckling towards the end.

She pouted and crossed her arms. "No need to make fun of me for it," she mumbled, following him out of the room and down the hallway again.

"I wasn't making fun. I thought that your reaction was cute."

A light dash of heat invaded her cheeks, but she was happy that she didn't have to make eye contact with him. Odette stuck out her tongue without him noticing. She giggled quietly to herself when she completed the action successfully.

They reached an archway, and she walked past him and peeked into the area beyond. The room was huge. It was about half the size of her small village. She whistled some, noting that not only were there various plants but also there were chickens, a rooster, rabbits and goats. "How do you manage to take care of all of this?" she asked in wonder, going over to the rabbit pen and crouching down to pet a short-haired grey one.

"Before I took my bath this morning, I had woken up a few hours before and came to tend to all of this. It's quite easy when you've been working this for most of your life. Of course, the first couple of years weren't easy. That's to be expected, however, when you're only two."

Her hand froze as she glanced over to him in shock. "You were only two when you were started all of this?! What kind of two-year-old were you?!"

Laughing some, he walked over to her and took a seat beside her. He picked up the bunny that she had been petting and set it on his lap. While he petted its ears, he explained, "For my kind, we mature very quickly. After a few months, we're able to speak. At the age of one, we're already helping our parents with chores around the house. When we're one and a half, we are taught reading and writing. Once at two, we take care of everything in the household."

Mouth agape, she couldn't believe what she was hearing. She couldn't even really remember what she did as a two-year-old, yet here he was running a miniature farm. "I j-just don't k-know what to s-say. I'm impressed," she spoke, shock causing her to stutter some. "What about your parents?"

He placed the bunny back in the pen and stood up, holding out his right hand to her. She took it and was brought to her feet. Was that another question that she wasn't supposed to inquire about? Tarhuinn met her gaze. "They passed away after I turned two."

There was something in his gaze that unsettled her some. Yes, there was a hint of sadness in his dark blue eyes, but he was completely calm at the same time as though he expected them to die when he had become that age. His hand suddenly felt unwelcoming, and she went to pull away from him, but he held onto her. "Odette, there's no need to worry. My parents' death was a hardship for me to deal with, but I learned to move on. I apologize if my tone sounded odd given the topic. I didn't mean to frighten you. Please, forgive me."

Tarhuinn dipped his head a little, and she relaxed. His last statement sounded more like a command, yet her mind dispelled the thought. Instead, she felt her heart skip a beat. Steadily, she took a few steps towards him and, hesitantly, placed her right hand on his cheek. "It's alright. I ... overreacted." She really hoped that was the case.

Looking up, he locked his gaze with hers, and she felt heat consume her cheeks. She went to remove her hand, but he reached up and held it there. “That’s very kind of you to say. Thank you, Odette,” he whispered out, moving his lips closer to hers.

If certain travelers told the truth about those legendary volcanoes, her face certainly felt like one. Swiftly, she moved her head back. “Weren’t you going to show me those grapefruits,” she chuckled out nervously. It felt like her heart might beat out of her chest.

Stopping, he quirked an eyebrow and smirked slightly. “Yes, I believe that I was going to do that.” He stood back up fully and released his hold on her. “Follow me,” he mentioned while she mentally breathed a sigh of relief.

Catching up to him, she noted that they halted soon after. In front of her was a massive tree with large green leaves. He pointed to some of the yellow fruits. “When you cut one open, you’ll see a very light pink color inside. These are white grapefruits. There are also pink and red ones.”

Odette peered up at the tree and noticed how they were clustered together. “I guess that I can understand why they’re called grapefruit now,” she muttered before her eyes turned to one of the light sources for the room. A window was carved into the stone wall.

It brought intrigue to her since she didn’t exactly know where she was. Odette walked around him and headed towards it. When she reached it, she saw the latch. “Can I open this?”

Coming up beside her, he leaned against the wall and nodded. Excitement brewed up inside her as she undid the latch and opened up the circular window. A cool breeze greeted her, but it was the breathtaking view that captured her attention. They were in the mountains near to her village. The ruins blocked passage to them, and she now knew why; the mountains were his kind’s home.

Resting her arms on the window's ledge, she let the cool breeze blow against her face while her eyes watched the grey storm clouds roll overhead. Some light shone through and highlighted a massive lake at the base of the mountains. The breeze blew in the smell of pine. She wished just to rest there since it was so soothing.

Once she stepped back from the stunning view, she glanced up and noted windows in the ceiling. She could spot more clouds. It looked like it would rain soon. "How often does the rain come here?" she asked, closing the window.

"About six times a week. That's why we're able to have so much water flow through these mountains, and why we're able to inhabit it."

"I'm guessing that it would be too much to ask to go outside and walk around."

"Correct. Like before, you're to remain only in our home."

"I thought so," she sighed out before continuing, "but are you going to tell me about this chosen business, or is there still more to this tour?"

"There's just the library, and we'll discuss that matter there. Come along," he voiced, pushing himself off of the wall and exiting the area with her.

Trailing behind him a little, she thought back to the view outside of the window. If she could, she would love to explore that terrain. Having been locked in a single room for most of her life caused her to want adventure. She thought that talking to the male in front of her would allow that, but she was now trapped in a home. At least, the window wasn't boarded up, and she had quite a bit of space to move around in.

Arriving at the library, they walked under the archway and headed into a circular room. Books covered the walls while a desk was in the center. A wooden chair rested behind it as two others were in front. Above was a large circular window. Due to the clouds above, a lantern rested on the table for better light in the room. Tarhuinn took a seat in the chair behind the desk.

After she sat across from him, she observed him lean forward and intertwine his fingers. "The concept of the chosen for my kind is a simple one, but a heavy responsibility comes with it as does with most important roles. I'll start off with the basic meaning behind it, however. Our chosens are our mates."

She didn't know if he expected her to gasp or faint or something of that nature, but she remained quiet. It probably should've been more shocking, but, given how her stay was going so far, it made some sense. Him whispering her name for twelve years, changing in front of her, taking a bath in front of her, etc., it all pointed to something other than him rescuing her from her parents just for the sake of being a kind person. Still, it was better than remaining in that room in her parents' house.

Odette reassured herself that the mate thing might not even be that bad. The term mate might mean something completely different to him. Such a thought caused her to nervously chuckle in her head. "So, what tasks fall under this role?" she asked, somehow managing to keep her voice steady.

"Over the next few months, you'll learn to help me with the small farm, and you'll study in here about my kind and our culture. This will prepare you for the end of those few months. From there, we'll be married, and you'll bear me a child."

There went her hope of mate implying something else. How could he say something like that so casually, though? She could already fill warmth rising in her cheeks. "Wait, but I barely even know you. Whispering to me for twelve years doesn't count as really knowing the other person."

"That's why those few months are there too. We'll get to know each other better."

"Don't I get a choice in this matter? You're not asking for some small thing here."

A frown appeared on his lips, and he leaned back in his chair. With his right hand, he rubbed his temple and muttered, "This is why I wish that I could've brought you in sooner. Things would've been so much simpler."

Offended, she sat up in her chair straighter and tightened her fingers around her dress skirt. “What’s that supposed to mean?! Is that so you could condition me into a willing wife who would do anything that you commanded?!” She didn’t mean to shout, but she couldn’t help it. What he had said had crossed the line for her.

“Don’t raise your voice at me, Odette.” His gaze locked with hers, and his eyes dared her to speak out again.

Almost she apologized, but she pushed his still soothing voice away. “Fine, let’s say that I agree to this, and we have a child. Are we to raise them how you were brought up?”

His gaze still wasn’t pleasant to look at, but he relaxed slightly. “Yes, and once the child turns two, we’ll die. The child will then take over the household.”

Freezing, she just stared at him, and her mouth gaped open some. How could he be so casual about that? Is that what his parents had taught him? She closed her mouth and tried to suppress her anger. “Not only does your kind take human children to inculcate them easily into your culture but also you expect them to hand their lives willingly over for your kind. And, you expect me to readily agree to all of this? Why can’t you mate with your own kind?”

“Our young need human life energy for their first two years of life. Without it, they die, and it can only be life energy from their human parent. Otherwise, death still happens for them. The kelremm then kills themselves to be with their partner. This is why a chosen is so important. They bring life to our kind where we would otherwise become extinct.”

“And, you thought that you could just claim me as yours and take away my future?!” she yelled, standing up from her chair and slamming her hands down on the desk.

Glancing up to her, it was evident that he was having trouble controlling his own temper. “Back when we first met as children, you didn’t look at me with fear or disgust. I only saw curiosity and wonder in your eyes. That drew me to you, and I decided to make you my chosen.”

“That doesn’t give you the right to take away my life, Tarhuinn!” she exclaimed before she spun on her heel and walked out of the library.

"Odette, come back here and sit down!" he yelled after her.

Covering her ears, she did her best to ignore his voice. She increased her pace and headed down the hallway to their room. The hallway happened to have a side path leading off of it, and she might be able to find an escape. Odette could've tried the window in the farm area, but it was a long drop from it to solid ground since it was cut right on a sheer mountain wall.

When she saw the turn, she darted down the new path and saw large double doors ahead of her. She could hear him whispering her name in her head, and she desired it to stop. Odette could feel her body wanting to turn back and go to him, but she forced herself to continue onward. It was slowing her pace, though. The doors were so close, however, and she wouldn't stop.

Upon reaching them, she uncovered her ears and threw her hands at the door handles. She pushed and tugged before she found them to be locked. Of course, they would be. Tarhuinn wouldn't give her easy access to an escape. Odette heard footsteps nearing. He hadn't reached the path yet, so she might be able to try for that pool of water they had entered through.

Without a second thought, she covered her ears and raced towards it. On the way, the male had nearly grabbed her, but she managed to dodge him. A low growl escaped his lips, but she didn't care; she wished to get out. Even with her ears covered, she still heard those two words quite clearly. "My chosen," her legs felt weak again, "you will stop right there."

How she wanted to move forward and fight back, but she couldn't find the energy to. She felt like falling forward and waiting for him to come to her. Splashes of water sounded closer, and arms wrapped around her waist. Her back pressed against his chest. His breath tickled her neck and sent a chill down her spine. "Tarhuinn, let me go!"

"No, you're mine, and you'll learn to accept that. I thought that you would run back to me, realizing your mistake, but it looks like I was wrong. Don't make me command you again, Odette."

"Maybe, you should've kept some of the information to yourself, then."

"It's not in my nature to lie to you about such a matter. Now, we'll head back to the library, and you'll begin your studying."

Her hands pushed against his arms in a last ditch effort at resistance. She wouldn't accept his fate for her so easily. If only his voice wasn't so beautiful, she wouldn't have as much of a problem. That was probably why they had such voices so that their mates couldn't get away from them. When he picked her up bridal style, she shoved her hands against his chest to try to get him to put her down. He merely ignored her and headed down the water path back to the library.

Tarhuinn had expected her reaction to the news to be somewhat shocked but not for her to run away. It was proof that it was easier to bring a partner back when they were younger. Her parents had ruined that for them, and, now, she was having trouble seeing the loveliness behind her duty to him.

It pained him to watch her speed off like that. His chosen, the love of his life, had tried to get away. Didn't she understand that he had been waiting for her for twelve years? Couldn't she acknowledge how lonely he had been for that time? Most kelremm would attain their chosen when their chosen was in the age range of six to eight. He had been struck with misfortune, and part of him wished to return to the ruins to get back at her parents.

Feeling her struggle against him, he tightened his hold on her and made it back to the library. He set her down on the chair which he had been sitting on and grabbed a book from the shelf. After he placed it in front of her, he took a seat opposite from her. "You'll start with a simple book of our history. You should find it interesting."

"And if I don't?" she asked harshly, and he could tell that she was testing out if she could bolt for it again.

"That's your decision. Whether you like it or not, you'll complete it and move onto your next book. I'll answer your questions if you have any that pertain to the book."

"So, you're going to be my personal guard dog."

"I'd prefer not to be compared to a dog, but I won't be leaving you alone, especially after that stunt you just pulled." He received a scoff before he observed her begin to open and read the text. His chosen wasn't going to make their relationship easy, but he would have her in the end.

Chapter Six: Partner in a Deal

What felt like hours passed, but Odette didn't want evening to fall. It was still awhile off, but she had no desire to share a room with the man sitting across from her. She had last night, and that had been embarrassing. Now, she couldn't really look at him without wanting to slap some sense into him. She hadn't even been reading the book that much; her mind kept going to solutions on how to solve her present problem.

There was the chance that actually reading would give her that knowledge, but she couldn't put her mind to it. Resting her arms on the desk, she laid her head over them and the book. A groan escaped her. She wished that she had never seen him that day out in the ruins, but she just had to search for the supposed monster.

"This will only take more time if you procrastinate," the male voiced as the sound of him flipping a page in his own book hit her ears.

"That reminds me. Why do we have to go through this process so quickly? I'm still not agreeing to it, but this time frame seems short to me," she mentioned, lifting her head up a little to look at him.

"It would've been longer had your parents not taken you from me."

"Well, why not wait five years until we have a child? Why can't I enjoy my life a little more?"

"The latest that you can have a child with me is when you're eighteen. Any later and our child will drain the entirety of your life energy before they turn two."

"And, how do you know all of this? Have you tested this out?"

"You would learn this information from that book in front of you. By you asking me, it shows me that you're not even trying to read it."

"Then, tell me how you knew me to be eighteen. I don't remember informing you that I was six back then."

"When our chosen turns eighteen, it feels like a wave washes over our chest. It warns us that our chosen has one year left to bear us a child. Again, you would find this in that book."

"Well, maybe, I don't want to read. I'm tired of being cooped up somewhere like one of your farm animals. I want to explore the mountains that we're in and enjoy the sights that life has to offer."

"You would insult me by comparing my treatment of you to that of an animal?" he asked, snapping his book shut and standing from his chair. "Your behavior today is reprehensible, and you're testing my patience."

"It's not my fault that you're getting mad by me simply stating the truth. You bring me here, lock me up and tell me that I'm supposed to give you a child. Afterwards, I'm to forfeit my life willingly like I was merely breeding stock. I don't care if you kill yourself when I die. That's a whole another issue. I merely want to live my life, and if I do have a child, I want to spend more than just two years with them. Wouldn't you like to spend more time with your child? And, wouldn't you have wished for more time with your parents?"

"Yes, I would've liked to have more time with my parents. And, yes, I would like to be with my child longer, but kelremm die with their partners. It's how things work in our world."

"Why, though? That seems a little harsh to me."

"Your question would be answered if you read like I told you to."

"You can't just throw my questions to the wind by telling me to read a book. That demonstrates to me how much you blindly trust a text. There is one important detail which I noticed about this book; there's no author. Who wrote this, and why does your kind trust it so much? That's what I would like to know. Who's the one that has been conditioning all of you to practice such things? Where did you even get this book?"

"Each kelremm home has a copy of it. It's been passed down through each generation. I'm not certain how old that book is, but it's what we follow," he answered, his right hand clenched around the binding of his book.

"But, you don't even know who wrote this! For all you know, some kelremm could've written this as a cruel practical joke and had copies of it made and distributed. And, don't get pissed off at me for pointing that out. There's no author on this book, so the possibilities are endless."

"Odette, don't you dare tell me that my culture is a mere joke! It isn't!" he shouted and slammed the book on the desk as if to frighten her.

She knew that she should probably be quiet for now, but she couldn't help it. He was telling her to practice traditions where the origins of them were questionable. "How do you know? Do you know the author and the validity of their account of your history? Are there other books to support the text written in this one?"

Seeing him raise his right hand, she flinched and shut her eyes. Thankfully, she felt no impact. She opened her eyes slowly and saw him bring his hand back to his side. He met her gaze, and she moved back in her seat some. It was intimidating, and she glanced to the side.

"Odette, look at me," he spoke softly, though; she could tell that he was holding back his exasperation.

Hesitantly, she did so, and his gaze softened. Her heart skipped a beat, but she angrily told herself to get a hold of it. She couldn't let him sway her; she had to keep up her fighting spirit. "What?" she muttered, attempting to keep her voice from sounding softer.

"We'll make a deal. If I can show to you well-founded evidence of my culture's ways, you'll accept them. If I can't find this, we'll search for the true answers. In both cases, though, you'll remain by my side. I refuse to let you go, for I won't let anyone else have you. Will you agree?"

"And if I don't agree?"

"Then, we'll go back to the original plan of me forcing you to accept my culture. I'd rather not take that route, but I'll do so if you cause me to."

"You won't tamper with the information?"

"No, and if you suspect me of unfair play, you can call me out on it. I'll admit to cheating, and we'll search for answers outside of these books. I'll take you beyond the walls of my home and past the mountains if we have to. We're both risking a lot on this agreement. I might be giving up my chance to have a child with you if it takes too long to find these answers."

"I understand. I'll agree to those conditions. Thank you for giving my concerns a chance."

“I’d rather not argue with you,” he simply answered, relaxing some and moving over to the bookshelf. “I still expect you to marry me, however. If you win, I’d rather not travel outside my home without people knowing that you’re mine.”

Some heat hit her cheeks, and she briefly glanced over to him. Luckily, his back was facing her. She turned away from him soon after and mumbled, “Right now, I’m not promising that I’ll become your wife. Despite this agreement, I’m still mad at you for earlier today.”

“As am I. I’m not fond of you running away from me, and you should know that I’ll catch you each time that you try to get away.”

“I won’t run as long as this deal is in place. Can you promise not to call me by my chosen, though? I rather like having the ability to use my legs at my free will.”

To this, she heard one of his melodic chuckles. In some respects, however, it was worrying. It was like he considered it a ridiculous request to make. “Odette, I’ll call you what I wish. Besides, I rather like you falling into my arms each time. Even though you say that you won’t dart off, those two words will guarantee that you don’t. Besides, it makes you dependent on me.”

“You’re a real gem,” she grumbled, turning her attention to the book in front of her and lazily flipping a page of it. She hated how small the text was. It made the book look all the less inviting.

“I do like to keep up my physical appearance for you.”

Rolling her eyes, she rested her chin in the palm of her left hand. That was probably why he felt so keen on changing and bathing in front of her. Not that she would indulge him by staring at his body. When she recalled those incidents, heat filled her cheeks. She hated the effect that he had on her.

Chapter Seven: Key Findings

Two weeks had gone by, and the routine over those fourteen days had been similar. She had woken up with Tarhuinn in the morning, and he had shown her how to take care of certain things in the farm and had given her tasks to accomplish while he had taken care of the other things in there. It hadn't been too bad, and she had fun learning how to grow her own food. Holding a fluffy bunny had helped as well sometimes, though; he had reminded her not to get too attached.

The only problem in the farm had been when she had walked over to the window and had stared out at the scenery for too long. He had called her back in a near growl as though he had expected her to go leaping out into the air. She had quickly closed the window lest he had called her by his favorite nickname.

Besides tending to the farm with him, she had to go with him everywhere. When he had made breakfast, she had been standing close by or helping. She had liked cooking since she had never received the chance to do so back at her old home. The frustrating part had been that every day he had put her on stirring or mixing duty. He had never allowed her to go near a knife, stating that he couldn't risk her accidentally cutting herself.

When they had walked the halls, she had sometimes glanced towards the hall with the exit, which had resulted in him wrapping his right arm around her waist and pulling her close. She had told him that she wouldn't bolt for it if the deal was kept in place, but he obviously hadn't trust her. What had been worse was when they had been going to bed. Odette had lain in her bed each night only to feel him watching her until she had drifted off into sleep.

Aside from those things, they had been in the library. Tarhuinn had taken over the desk in the room, developing detailed proof for why his culture's practices were viable. She had been forced to read in the meantime.

So far, she had been introduced to the history of the markets and how the kelremm homes had been built. Since the parents died young and the house passed onto their only child, no new homes ever had needed to be constructed in the mountain.

Right now, though, she was sitting in the library with him. She hadn't been reading her work like she was supposed to, but she was more focused on him scribbling notes down on parchment. The desk looked a complete mess, but she assumed that Tarhuinn could care less about that. When she grew bored with observing him, she peered back down at her book.

A word hadn't sunk into her brain before she heard a book slam shut. She jolted in her seat and glanced back to the male in front of her. There was a pleased smile on his lips, and he met her gaze. Odette froze a bit. Her time was up. Today would decide her fate.

"What did you find?" she asked, scooting her chair closer to the desk and setting her book aside.

"I found several books that support the max age of the human partner being eighteen for both male and female. And, the books that have these supports do have authors. They're these five." He held up the five books and handed them over to her.

Looking them over, she did find an author's name in each. "What pages are the references on and what paragraphs?" After he gave her the page and paragraph numbers, she flipped through the texts and read over the designated areas. In each one, it was relatively the same. Here and there, a synonym of the word would be utilized. "Can I see the first book that you gave me?"

He grabbed it for her and turned to the proper page. After he handed it over, she noted not many differences between the no-author and author versions. All six seemed to support the same idea, but she looked over the no-author version again and read the specific section.

Should a child be conceived between a kelremm and their human partner when the human is beyond the of age eighteen, the child will still be born, but the child will drain the human parent of life energy before the child turns two. This will result in the child dying as well since they won't have the human parent's life energy for two full years.

It really was similar to the other versions. "There's no date of when the no-author version was written. Is it older than the five author versions, Tarhuinn?"

"Yes, it's said to be the first book written about our culture."

With that in mind, she figured that the author versions could've been written after more tests were done on the matter, or those authors were copying what was written in the no-author text. It could even be that all of the books were written by the same person, who just used aliases. Biting her bottom lip in concentration, Odette looked around the specific sections in each book and found something interesting. The no-author version had a different passage concerning the death of the human parent after the full two years.

Once the child turns two, they'll have acquired the necessary amount of human life energy to live without it. The human parent, not having their life energy anymore, will die on the child's second birthday. As is tradition, the kelremm partner will kill themselves to be with their deceased beloved, and the child will take over the home.

Concerning the author versions, they all said something similar, but there was one piece missing. For the second sentence in the passage, the phrase *not having their life energy anymore* was absent. There wasn't even a rewording of the phrase, and she pointed it out to Tarhuinn.

"Yes, I came across that difference myself and searched for any texts on why it was so. I managed to find three books that discuss their theories on that specific passage." He placed the three books in front of her. "The one to your far left goes into depth about how the author versions merely found that line to be unimportant. The book in the middle has a similar conclusion but is less in depth about it. As for the book to your far right, it brings another theory to the table.

"It suggests that the no-author version isn't reliable on the issue of the child's requirement for human life energy and that the other five are. It continues to argue that the no-author version should be wiped out entirely because it warns that other falsehoods may be present within the text. Granted, it praises the author versions on that particular issue. There's no other support for this theory, and, personally, I think that it shouldn't be trusted. Still, I thought that you should know of its existence."

"There were no theories on the author versions being the unreliable ones?"

"No. Why, are you suddenly supporting the book that's the foundation of our traditions?" he asked with a slight smirk.

"No, but it's an interesting distinction. What else did you find?"

"I've found accounts of couples who tried to go past the eighteen mark and accounts of kelremm partners trying to prevent their human partner from dying. None of them show positive results." He grabbed several books and opened them to specific pages. Tarhuinn pointed to the passages of the accounts, and she proceeded to study them.

In one of the cases, a female kelremm conceived her child when her male human partner was twenty two. The child was born but drained the life energy of its father only after a year and half. Both the father and child died while the mother was left to grieve for a few years before finding a new partner. She managed to, but she was harsher on her new partner, not wanting to experience the same thing again.

Her account of losing her first partner and child described how it seemed like she had part of her soul ripped from her being, and she had never recovered from it even after finding a new partner. It went into more detail on the issue, but Odette found it far too depressing to read any further. Odette even felt a few tears threaten to fall.

Going onto another account, it was just as distressing as the first, so she decided to read an account about a kelremm trying to save his dying partner. While the human partner taught her child the things he ought to know before he turned two, the kelremm spent his time crafting various drinks for his partner to try. Later in his research, he started adding his own blood to the mixture. The kelremm eventually became so obsessed with his work that he even tried to harm the child at one point in an attempt to put the child's blood into the mixture.

With the human partner realizing that enough was enough, she destroyed her partner's work and locked the kelremm in their bedroom. The library of their home grew to serve as the child's bedroom, and the child never saw his other parent. In the end, the human partner still died as did the kelremm partner. All of the account was written by the child of the two, and some parts went into thorough detail of how terrifying the experience was at times.

Closing the books, she handed them back. "I don't think that I need to read any more. Do you mind if I just look through everything you've gathered?"

"Well, I took notes for a reason, Odette." He indicated for her to take a seat on his chair, and she did so. After she pushed a few strands of hair behind her ears, she started to look through it all.

Despite the vast notes that he had taken, she knew inside that she wouldn't be able ever to accept having a child only to die when her child turned two. She made a deal, and she would stick to it if she lost, but she still had a chance to win the bet. Even though he had accumulated substantial evidence, her mind went back to that absent phrase in the five author versions. That had to be the key to living past the child's second birthday.

On top of that, she was reserved about marrying the man and bearing him a child. They had been living in the same house for two weeks, but she hadn't appreciated how restrictive he had been. Even with the deal in place, had she mentioned going beyond the house, he had appeared as though he would murder her if she spoke of it again.

Glancing over to Tarhuinn, she jumped a little as he was gazing directly at her. She gave a nervous smile before she returned to peer at the piece of parchment in front of her. Odette could feel his eyes on her still. Why did he just have to stare at her?

Muttering a few curses in her head, she pushed the piece of parchment aside. She had looked at enough notes, and she couldn't push her mind from that missing phrase. *Not having their life energy anymore*. What could it imply? Odette tapped her right fingers against the surface of the desk. Was there a way to get their life energy back? "I'm guessing that the authors of those five versions are deceased."

"Yes. Why, did you wish to visit them?" he asked, a warning look appearing in his blue orbs.

"Well, it would be nice to ask them why they had left the phrase out. Maybe, we ... I mean you could ask their successors and see if they know why."

"Kelremm usually don't invite other kelremm to their homes. We meet in the market area, and that's the extent."

"Then, you could find them there and ask them."

"All we know is the families' last names. It would be strange for me to ask around for specific people. Either you have met the kelremm before, or you haven't. If you haven't, you don't go searching for them. Despite trading my crops with other kelremm, I have never met anyone with those names. Why are you so obsessed with that phrase?"

"It might mean the difference between me living and dying in the next few years."

"You think that one line can invalidate all of my work?"

"I believe that it might save the human partner from dying when the child turns two. It might imply that there's a way for the human partner to get life energy back, which makes me suspicious as to why someone would want to leave it out. That's why it's important to find their successors."

"You're saying that there's a possibility that these five wished to keep the secret of a kelremm's human partner living longer to themselves? Why would they desire to do that? They would want their own human partners to live longer."

"Maybe, there's only a fixed quantity of whatever gives this extra life energy, and they wanted to keep it to themselves. It would also help if we knew who wrote the no-author version, but that's unlikely to happen."

"Odette, it might also be that they found that phrase to be insignificant. Those two books, which mentioned the same thing, might be right."

"It's still a possibility, Tarhuinn. I want to find out the solid reason for why it was left out."

"So, are you saying that I lost the deal, then?"

"No. Unfortunately, you found evidence that well proves why your culture is the way that it is. Those accounts that you gave were proof enough that the human partner will die when the child turns two, and it makes sense to teach the child everything about the household before the parents die. The whole eighteen age limit was also well supported. In those respects, I do accept your culture.

"It's just that this missing phrase's implication is too important to ignore. If there is a way for my life energy to be given back to me, we both can raise our child for longer. Wouldn't you prefer that?"

"I would, but ..."

Cutting him off, she continued, "But what? This possibility exists, and that's what matters. I'll marry you. I'll give you a child if that's what you want, but we still have time. Instead of having me cooped up here for the next months, we can see if this extra life energy exists. I'm still abiding by the deal and accepting your culture by doing this. I'm only seeking to improve it so that we may live longer."

"Are you, though? It's customary that the human partner remains here and learns over those few months. I suppose that I could search for the facts on this possibility, but it would be odd as I mentioned before."

"I've already learned enough about the farm. Besides, I can work with it more after we return from searching for the answers. With regards to learning about your kind and culture, I've read so much in the past weeks that I think it qualifies for enough. Additionally, I'll be learning as we seek the answers to this.

"I can read countless books, but I won't really learn everything about the culture unless I interact with it more. Meeting other kelremm can help with that learning experience, and I'll make sure to stay by your side. Please allow me this, Tarhuinn."

A heated gaze touched his eyes, but he seemed to be considering her words. "I'm not fond of the idea, and I've made that clear enough, but the possibility of you living longer is tempting. You promise, though, to marry me and have a child with me?"

"Yes, I promise."

"Fine since I'll trust your feeling on this left out phrase, I'll agree to search for answers on it. On one condition, though, and that condition is that you marry me before we head out. Otherwise, I'm not letting you leave even if you're with me."

She really didn't want to marry him right away. It would've happened eventually, but it was too quick. Then again, he probably wouldn't give her another option, and if she stalled for too long, he might revoke his offer. If that were to happen, she would never get out of their home, and she desired to explore the area around them. "Alright, you have another deal. When are we to be married?"

"A week from now," he answered, getting up from his chair. "Let's go get something to eat. We'll head to bed afterwards." He went over to her and held out his right hand to her.

Taking it, she let him pull her up. She would've walked without holding his hand, but she knew better than to pull away. Besides with all of the water paths in the library, it made walking around and through them easier. As they left the area, she asked, "Tarhuinn, would it be possible for me to wear pants and a shirt when we leave? It would be better for me to move around in since we don't know how far we'll have to travel."

"I suppose that I could trade for some when I go to request for an officiant. It would help if I took your measurements beforehand. You wouldn't mind, right?"

"Can I take my own measurements and tell you them?"

"I suppose that'll work as well. I'll get you loose fitting clothes, though. I don't need others eyeing you when we leave the house."

"Well, I wouldn't like tight fitting clothes, either. Besides, it'll be a nice break from these corseted dresses. I'm tired of being bound up like this," she muttered, pulling at the tight bodice of the dress.

"It's very flattering on you, but I wouldn't want others to see your curves. That's only for my eyes to view."

Heat dashed across her cheeks lightly, and she glanced away from him. That was a concern of hers, though. Would he try that after they were married and before they left? She hoped that wouldn't be the case. After all, she desired privacy for some time still. Not only that but also she didn't wish for the possibility to have a child in her womb while they were investigating.

Hopefully, Tarhuinn would respect her wishes. Pushing the heat away, she headed into the kitchen with him. Once again, she was assigned to the tasks that didn't include a knife. Regardless, she was thankful that she would get the opportunity to extend possibly her life.

Chapter Eight: Night Escape

Over the course of the next week, Odette had found her schedule to be rather typical. She had been expecting him to teach her the wedding customs, but he had merely explained that there were the vows and rings. Odette had figured, however, that she could make a few modifications; she was getting married only once.

She had stressed that they should at least have a wedding dinner for themselves and that he shouldn't see her the morning that they were married. He had agreed to prepare a dinner, but he hadn't seen the point in not seeing her right before the wedding. Odette had explained the purpose for it and the reality that it was because families didn't wish to have the groom walk out on the bride before they were married.

Since that wasn't an issue in their case, she had mentioned that it would make things more exciting. She had received a skeptical look as he had explained that they were getting married and that was thrilling enough. In the end, he hadn't budged on the issue.

It being the night before their marriage day, Odette waited for Tarhuinn to fall asleep. When she felt that he had, she sat up on her bed and glanced over to her dresser. She had decided to wear the purple dress. The dress was the most elegant out of the selection, but she was tempted to wear her traveling clothes to spite him for not agreeing to not see her tomorrow morning. Besides, the travel clothes were rather comfortable since they were a bit looser than the measurements that she had given him.

Turning her attention back to him, she glanced downwards and noted that he remained asleep. It was hard to tell since his long locks covered most of his face. Carefully, she placed her feet on his bed, reached over towards him and went for the chain around his neck. If he didn't have such long hair, it would've been easier to remove the necklace, but she would manage.

Once her hands were on the chain, she lifted it and moved his hair out of the way. There wasn't a real problem until she discovered that some strands were under his left arm. Muttering a few curses, she set the necklace back down on him and rolled him a bit from his side to his stomach. She grabbed all of his hair and lifted it before she moved him back to his original position.

Glad that he didn't wake up, she removed the necklace with the room key. Smiling, she picked up her nightgown some and stepped into the water. Honestly, she didn't think that would work so well. She would've definitely woken up if someone had done that to her.

When she was at the room door, she inserted the key and unlocked the door. Once she left the room, she locked the door behind her. If he awoke, he wouldn't be able to follow her. She wished for a little alone time before she married him. The only alone time which she had received was when he had left for the market, but he had only been gone for a short time.

Besides, it wasn't like she had the key to the entrance door, and she had learned that the pool they entered through would mean death for her. Tarhuinn had told her that unless she could hold her breath for fifteen minutes, she would drown. The only reason she had made it on her entry to his home was because of his quickened ability to swim in water, so there was no reason for him to worry.

Stepping onto the stone path, she headed for the farm area. Once there, she headed over to the animals and went to the rabbits first. She picked one up and set it on her lap. Its nose twitched some as it stood up on its hind legs and sniffed her. Odette brought her nose down to its small one and nuzzled the creature, which was thankful for the attention. One of the goats, though, came over and bleated.

A small laugh left her lips, and she set down the bunny. Going over to the goat, she petted its head while it nuzzled into her touch. The goat was the most affectionate out of the five and seemed to want attention whenever Tarhuinn or she went near the goats' pen. After she gave the animal a few more pets, she headed for the window.

Unlatching it, she leaned on the edge and glanced over the scenery. A light rain sprinkled down from the sky as a few beams of moonlight broke through the thick clouds. She could see parts of the lake below, and a slight chill ran up her spine at the cold night air. Despite that, she reached her right hand out and felt the rain hit her skin.

Keeping her hand out in the rain, she rested her head against her left arm. After tomorrow, her journey for answers might bring her to the lake out there, and she might be able to explore the mountain terrain around it. Such a thought excited her greatly. She would have to get married to gain that adventure, but she wouldn't be locked away anymore.

Odette caught a few more drops in her hand before she heard footsteps and light splashes of water behind her. Tensing, she pulled her hand back and looked behind her. Tarhuinn appeared less than pleased as he stopped a few feet from her. "Locking me in our room is quite uncalled for Odette. Did you think that I wouldn't have a spare?"

"Well, I knew that you would be angry," she murmured, peering down at her feet and avoiding his piercing gaze.

"Of course, I'm mad. I woke up to find you and my key gone. Not only that but you also locked the door on me. For all I knew, you could've been trying to find a way out or attempting to kill yourself. Now, tell me what you're doing by the window."

"I wanted some time to myself. You never give me any, and tonight is the last night that I'm single. And, it's relaxing in here."

"Oh, I'm not relaxing to be around?"

"Truthfully, no. Your voice is comforting at times, but I don't like you watching me constantly."

"That's your fault for running away that one time and now this. Such actions don't inspire trust."

"Neither do yours," she countered, meeting his dark blue orbs. Ire and sadness filled his eyes as he pushed back some of his locks. He walked towards her and only broke his gaze once he was next to her. Reaching over, he closed and latched the window. She remained quiet and watched him as she hoped that he wouldn't unleash that anger on her.

"I trust you enough to let you outside of my home. That should satisfy you. My watchfulness is to protect you. Maybe, that frustrates you, but I won't apologize for it. You'll be grateful for it when we leave the safety of my home. On this search, I don't know what we'll find, but I won't let anything take you from me. Do you understand, my chosen?"

"Yes," she responded even though she wanted to argue back, but she couldn't. He had used that nickname again, and she leaned towards him. Catching her, he held her up in his arms. Her hands clutched his nightshirt while she wished that she could overcome the effect. The male picked her up bridal style and began to head back to their room. "Tarhuinn ... can we stay here for a bit longer?"

Peering down at her, he seemed to debate her request before he took a seat by the edge of the water path. He placed her on his lap. "I suppose that it would be nice to enjoy this place before we set out," he remarked as he pulled some of her hair back.

Figuring that there would be no use in trying to get off of his lap, she leaned back against him to be more comfortable. "Is someone going to watch this place while we're gone?"

"Yes, I have a friend of mine who will be coming over."

"I thought that you didn't interact with other kelremm much except for market interactions."

"That's correct, but my friend is another crop grower like me. Over the years, we met each other on multiple accounts, and we eventually set up a schedule so that we would head to the market on the same days. When I requested an officiant for tomorrow, I asked her to watch over the place for us. She agreed to come over each day to take care of the farm until we return."

"What's this friend like?"

"You'll see her the day that we head out. It's strange, though, to have another kelremm come into my home. She found the request odd as well, but since we've been friends since we were little, she agreed."

"She doesn't find it weird that you're taking your partner outside of your home?"

"She does think it bizarre, but she knows that I must have a good reason for doing so. And, I do. If we do find a way to give life energy back to you, it'll make our lives better, and we can enjoy time with our child more. I also wish to make up for those years that were lost to us. Even if I'm hesitant about taking you beyond this house, I understand that we might have more time together. And, the longer I have you, the better."

Chapter Nine: Bonded by Metal

Waking up to the usual sound of running water, Odette sat up on her bed and glanced over shyly towards the bathtub. She breathed a sigh of relief when she didn't find Tarhuinn there. When she peered down to his bed, he wasn't there either; however, she did discover a note in his place.

I've placed some breakfast for you on top of your dresser, and I'll be waiting for you in the garden.

A small smile touched her lips. He had granted her wish of not viewing her the morning of their wedding. Placing the note down, she got off of the bed and proceeded to eat her breakfast. After finishing, she completed her morning routine and changed into some new undergarments along with the purple dress.

She tied up the corseted bodice in the front before she buttoned the two buttons by the neck. The collar and long sleeves covered her undershirt, but between the high collar and straight neckline was a gap, which exposed some of her skin. Down from the bodice, the dress flared out and went to her mid-calves. Its dark purple hue really was identical to the purple dying berries, which Tarhuinn had shown her a little over a week ago.

With the dress on, she brushed her hair once more and pushed some of the loose strands behind her ears. Hopefully, she looked suitable enough. Taking a deep breath and exhaling, she made her way out of the room with her dishes in hand. Her free hand clenched around the skirt of her dress, and she walked slowly on the stone path. Once or twice, her eyes darted to the entrance doors when she passed them. It would be a waste of effort to try and open them. Besides, she had promised Tarhuinn that she would marry him, and because of it, she would get to exit through those doors tomorrow.

Forcing herself past the hall, she made her way to the garden after she had dropped off the dishes in the kitchen basin. As she neared, it felt like her heart might beat out of her chest or come up her throat. Somehow, her steps became even slower. When she entered the garden, though, she paused for a moment.

Directing her gaze over to Tarhuinn, she saw that he wore a long sleeved purple shirt and black pants. She had seen him wear the outfit before, but the significance of the event caused heat to rise to her cheeks. To avoid tripping or some other embarrassing mistake, she focused her attention on the officiant. It was her first time seeing another kelremm, though; the male was quite shorter than Tarhuinn, but he looked close in age. His hair was much shorter as well, only reaching his jaw line, while his facial structure gave him more of a childish look.

Upon reaching them, she stood across from Tarhuinn and looked up to him. Her head only came to below his shoulders. She folded her hands in front of her and gripped her fingers as the vows were read; however, her hands were soon taken up by Tarhuinn's. Odette knew that they were trembling in his. Embarrassed, she glanced away, and she heard him say, "I do."

On her turn, she was silent for a moment before she stuttered the words out, "I-I d-do." After her words, Tarhuinn pulled two rings out of his right pants' pocket. He slipped the silver ring onto her left ring finger, and she noted that it had plant-like designs worked into the metal. She took his ring and slipped it onto his left ring finger.

The officiant proceeded to announce that the groom could kiss the bride. She felt his hands move from hers as his right arm wrapped around her waist and moved her close. Her hands ended up pressed to his chest as his lips met hers. His left fingers glided under her chin, and he deepened the kiss. By that point, her cheeks were quite warm, and it was even more embarrassing that another person was watching them.

A few minutes seemed to pass before he pulled away and left her breathless. Out of the corners of her eyes, she saw the officiant bow and close the book in his hands. Still holding onto her, Tarhuinn mentioned, "I'll show you out. Thank you for coming."

"Of course, I'm happy to be of service," the male spoke as Tarhuinn finally released her.

"Odette, stay here while I lead him out. I'll be back in a few minutes." She merely nodded her head and tried to get her pounding heart to calm down. They walked away and left the area, leaving her to grasp the reality of her situation.

Peering down at the ring on her finger, she traced over the design. Now it made sense why Tarhuinn had asked her ring size back when they had been taking her measurements for clothes. It was still strange to see a ring there. She couldn't go back in time, and, after their search, she would have a child with him. The implication of that made her cheeks burn. Her hands rose to her cheeks.

Pressing against her warm skin was the cool metal of the ring. It only further reminded her of her bond to Tarhuinn. To cool herself off, she walked over to the window and opened it. A cold mountain breeze blew through while rain descended from the sky. The heat in her cheeks started to dissipate, but her left fingers came up to touch her lips. She couldn't deny that she had enjoyed the kiss.

Splashes of water sounded behind her. Soon enough, hands wrapped around her waist, and he rested his chin on top of her head. "The dress does look stunning on you, Odette. I'm glad that you suggested that I wait to see you in it, but I was wondering if you would like a dance. The rain can be our music."

Turning around in his arms, she nodded lightly. A gentle smile overtook his lips as he stepped back some. Each of them placed their hands in the proper positions before he led her in a slow dance. The rain gave them a gentle and peaceful background noise while the cool breeze now made her move closer to Tarhuinn.

"What time will we be leaving tomorrow?" she asked quietly, glancing up to him a little.

"The usual time since that's when my friend will arrive," he responded, spinning her before bringing her back in softly. "I'll show her what needs to be done each morning, but it won't take long since she takes care of crops of her own. We'll head out to the market afterwards and trade for some traveling foods while we ask around for information on the five authors. Just be aware that we'll receive some rather odd stares."

"Stares aren't going to stop me from finding answers. My life is more important than the judgment of others. You shouldn't be pressured by them either."

Smiling softly, he leaned closer to her. "I suppose that's true. Your life is more important, and I'll protect you to the best of my ability when we leave." He placed his lips on hers once more and moved them away shortly after. "If someone insults you or makes you uncomfortable, let me know, and I'll deal with them."

Odette gave him a simple, shy nod, but she detected a tinge of madness in his voice in his second statement. She didn't know how he would handle them, but she thought that it would be best not to find out. "Shall we start preparing our dinner for later? It'll take awhile to make," she voiced, finding that it would do well to switch topics.

"Yes, that sounds like a good idea." He drew his hands back from her and closed the window. The sound of rain quieted down, and he wrapped his right arm around her waist. It made her walk down the water path with him, but she figured that it would be fine since it was their wedding day.

Entering the kitchen, they went to work on the grand meal. She plucked the feathers from a chicken that Tarhuinn had selected that morning while he cut the vegetables and herbs. During the process, she would occasionally glance over to see how he handled a knife. Every time she watched him, he worked the blade expertly.

His skill couldn't have developed from just working in the kitchen, though. No, he handled the blade as though he had been in combat multiple times before or at least trained to be in combat. It was reassuring to know that he could probably defend against an attack if they were to meet some threat during their search. She wished that she knew how to fight with a blade since it would be better if they could both fight. Right now, she wouldn't bring up the request as it might anger him, and she didn't want to get in an argument with him today.

She held off and finished with her work. From there, she was tasked with filling a pot full of water and starting the fire. Once the fire was ready, she hooked the pot over the flames. Tarhuinn sliced up the chicken before he added the meat, vegetables and herbs to the water. She tossed in some salt to the mixture.

With it cooking, she washed the dishes from the morning and the new ones. While Tarhuinn helped her, she paused for a moment. "What name did I take up?" she asked, realizing that his last name had never been given.

Laughing somewhat, he looked to her. "I forgot to tell you. How silly of me. Our last name is Marredon."

Chapter Ten: New World

Odette purposefully had eaten her dinner slow. She had wanted to stall since she hadn't known what Tarhuinn had planned for them that evening. The dinner itself had been quiet as she had been too focused on eating to converse with him, but she had felt his gaze on her. It had only made the situation worse.

When they had both finished, she had helped him with cleanup. Even on that, she had moved at a snail's pace. Once completed, Tarhuinn had signaled them to head to bed. She had merely nodded and had followed after him. Arriving at their shared room, she had paused by the doorway.

Resting his right hand on her shoulder, he had voiced, "Don't worry, Odette. I'm not going to rush into that with you. We still have time like you mentioned."

She had breathed a sigh of relief and had given him a quiet word of thanks. From there, they had prepared for bed before they had gone to sleep. Tarhuinn, though, had made her sleep on his bed that night. He had stated that he wouldn't hurry anything, but he had mentioned that he wanted to hold her close from now on. To that, she had agreed since he was her husband despite how odd it seemed to her.

Now, it being the next day, both were stocking their travel bags. Items to trade, their own food, clothing, medical and hygiene supplies and books were split into their two bags. Earlier that morning, however, she had noticed him putting on a leather belt which was armed with ten small steel daggers. His cloak covered the weapons belt, and she wondered if he would have to use any of those weapons. Maybe, over the course of the trip, she could convince him to let her have a try with one.

Completed with their packing, they headed towards the entrance doors to greet his friend. Personally, though, she was just excited that she would be able to go past those doors. Tarhuinn easily noted her eagerness, but he made her stand back some from the doors. "You'll get to see the rest of our world soon enough, Odette. Be patient for a little longer."

"Fine," she mumbled as she adjusted the string of her cloak. She once again had her boots on, and she made sure to stay out of the water with them on. Soggy boots would make traveling somewhat of a nuisance. The rest of her attire was rather comfortable also. Her blue cotton shirt hung loosely around her torso but still covered her undershirt completely, and her grey cotton pants allowed her easy maneuverability.

A knock on the doors caught their attention, and Tarhuinn opened them. "Nyclaya, thank you for coming," he greeted as they clasped wrists.

"Of course, I'm happy to help out a good friend. It's a good thing that we live close. Otherwise, the walk over here every day would get old fast. Now, where's this wife of yours?" she asked before she peeked around him. She grinned before she unclasped her hand and came over to Odette.

Seeing the female kelremm head directly for her, Odette took a step back and looked slightly concerned. The female kelremm was dressed in an interesting manner. She wore a blue leather armor corset along with black leather pants. Odette thought that the attire would be uncomfortable for working on crops, but she kept that opinion to herself.

Nyclaya's ink black hair was tied up high, allowing it to swish back and forth with each of her steps. Her eyes were very similar to Tarhuinn's, but they were a shade lighter. She stopped in front of Odette and stood at about the same height as the female human. The female kelremm held out her right hand. "It's nice to finally meet you, Odette. Tarhuinn spoke highly of you."

Hesitantly, Odette took her hand and shook it. Her eyes darted over to Tarhuinn, and he merely smiled to her. Averting her gaze back to Nyclaya, she responded, "It's nice to meet you too. Thank you for watching over the place while we're gone."

"You're quite welcome," she answered before she pulled her hand back and looked to her friend. "Well, show me what I need to do. I can tell that your wife is wishing to leave already."

Heat lightly rose to her cheeks in embarrassment. Was she really that obvious in front of a stranger? Glancing back to Tarhuinn, Odette saw him nod before he came over to them. "Yes, she is one for adventure much like yourself," the male answered to his friend. "Odette, come along, and we'll head out once we're done with the instructions."

Upon them completing the instructions for Nyclaya, they all headed back to the entrance doors. Odette wished to race through them, but Tarhuinn had his hands over the handles. "Bring me back anything interesting you find, and I'll add it to my collection," Nyclaya stated as her friend nodded and finally opened the entrance doors. He had given her a spare key already.

Odette ducked under Tarhuinn's arms and into the area beyond. A chuckle was heard from the female kelremm before the male waved and closed the doors behind him. Walking up behind his partner, he pulled the cloak over her head. "We don't need anyone seeing what you look like, especially if your theory about those five authors keeping the remedy to themselves is correct."

"What about you?" she asked as her gaze stayed on what was before her.

"Other kelremm will recognize my voice, so there'll be no point. That's why I also want you to speak as little as possible. Besides, kelremm never cover their faces from other kelremm. For you, it's fine since humans rarely come to the market."

"Won't they know that I'm your partner?"

"Yes, but if they can't pin your identity, it'll be harder to find you if something were to happen. Let's just hope that this journey remains civil."

"I agree. The less fights, the better." Her gaze still remained fixed on what she was looking upon. They were in a large circular room. Stone vases held fires within them and illuminated the tall cylinder room. She could see other doors like Tarhuinn's all around. Some were on higher levels while others were lower. There had to be at least fifty doors in the space. "Is this all of the kelremm?"

"No, there are two more complexes like this, but even then, there aren't many of us. Let's head down," he suggested, already walking on ahead.

The sound of water echoed all around them as cascades of water gushed down some of the room's sides. Water paths were all around for the kelremm while small stone paths accompanied them. Looking down, she saw how much darker it got towards the bottom, but she could spot small fires.

Both of them reached a large path that spiraled down towards the base. Water ran down in a steady flow, and it seemed like one would have to slide down. "Is that the only way down?" she asked, concerned.

"No, there is another method, but this way is quicker. There are also ladders, but, normally, those are used only to climb back up. If you're worried, you can sit on my lap while we go down. I promise that you'll be safe, though; you may want to put your boots in your pack."

Tempted, she wanted to ask Tarhuinn if they could use the ladders, but she didn't want to spend forever climbing down. She had never been on a ladder before, and she wondered if it would be more dangerous than the slide. "Fine, I'll trust you," she commented before she took off her boots and socks. After she placed them in her pack, she glanced over to the male. "Alright, I'm ready."

He proceeded to sit down and motion her onto his lap. Doing as he instructed, she got on and felt him press her to his chest. His arms wrapped tightly around her waist while he scooted forward. Before she could back out of the situation, they were speeding down the path. She found herself hanging onto his arms for dear life, and she shut her eyes tight. Eventually, though, she opened them and saw the floors fly by.

Wind raced past, and water splashed up onto their faces. The feeling was actually exhilarating once she pushed her worry aside. It was soon over, however, and they raced into a shallow pool of water. Her lower half was soaked completely, but, at least, she wouldn't have to walk with wet boots. As he got up and lifted her up with him, she peered out ahead of them. Tarhuinn pulled her hood up quickly while she was amazed by the activity before her.

It was a small market, but she could see trades happening already. At the front of the market, there was a large sign dictating what could be traded for what. She did a quick glance of it before she looked to the tents ahead.

Small fires lit up the place, and she saw a staircase beyond the market. Beyond that was a large pool of water. The light barely touched that area, however, and she was slightly terrified that their travels would lead them in that direction.

Stepping out of the water, she seated herself on the ground, dried off her feet, rolled up her pants and put her socks and shoes back on. Once finished, she stood back up only to have Tarhuinn pull her close to him. His left hand intertwined with her right, and he kept a strong grip on her. Thankfully, it wasn't enough to hurt her.

Walking into the market, she glanced around at the various goods being traded, but she couldn't make eye contact with any of the traders. It was frustrating to say the least that she always had to keep her head downturned. Eventually, they stopped, and she glanced over the various dried foods up for trade. Tarhuinn pulled out some of their items and began to collect what they would need for travel if they did have to journey far.

"I never thought that you would bring your partner out here, Tarhuinn. You're usually the more protective out of any of us," spoke the man trading the dried foods.

"We decided to do some traveling before settling down in the house. I'm still keeping her close, but we're curious about some individuals. I haven't heard of their last names before, and I was wondering if you would know something, Carratus."

"I would ask if you drank too much last night, but you don't purchase alcohol. Regardless, maybe, I know something. Who are you looking for?"

"Their last names are Tergii, Amtoma, Bimaa, Rocean and Alpontus."

"I've heard of them but probably from the same location as you. They're the authors of those five books. That's all I have on them, but why would you be searching for them?"

"My wife has some questions for them. She's very persistent on knowing more about our culture. I thought that I would indulge her. I know that it's strange to ask, but I couldn't deny her such a request. She made a very convincing argument."

"She must have," Carratus muttered, glancing to her. She kept her gaze down and acted like she was incredibly shy. "Hmm, well, I know of someone that might know a little bit more about them or at least some of them. I wish that my wife was as interested in our history. She read the books, but she stated that she never wanted to read them again. Anyway, you'll want to talk to Delnella. She should be here today."

"She's one of the metal workers correct?" He received a nod from Carratus. "Alright, thank you. I wish your wife, son and you well." After receiving a word of thanks from the dried foods trader, they headed off in the direction of Delnella.

Speaking softly, Odette asked, "Tarhuinn, how old is his son?"

"He'll be a year old in two weeks."

"Then, we still have plenty of time to help them."

"First, we're extending your life. You're my priority. The others will come afterwards. I would like to save everyone, but that might not be realistic. So, I'm making no promises to anyone except to you. If a life-prolonging elixir exists, I promise to extend your life first. And, you've already made it clear that you wish to live longer. Otherwise, we wouldn't be here. I'm not letting you die so easily now."

A small smile touched her lips, but she did wonder if the possible solution would help out more couples than just them. Still, he was right. She did wish to survive longer, and that was her goal, but it would be nice to give that opportunity to others if they could.

They stopped in front of a female kelremm, who was on the outskirts of the small market and sitting in a pool of water. Her ink black hair went down to her jaw and had some natural curls to it while her eyes were somehow a darker blue than Tarhuinn's. They were like a night sky on a moonless evening. A simple black cloth shirt and pants covered her form while a blue apron decorated her form also. On a blanket in front of her were kitchen utensils, weapons and jewelry.

Tarhuinn pulled her a bit behind him so that the female kelremm couldn't see her face. "Delnella, correct?"

"Yes, what can I help you with?" she questioned, glancing slightly over to Odette's partially hidden form.

"I've heard that you may know something about certain kelremm: Tergii, Amtoma, Bimaa, Rocean and Alpontus."

"Besides them being authors, I know a few things but only about Tergii and Bimaa. Why do you ask? Or, is your partner the curious one?"

Tightening his grip on Odette, he responded, "My wife wishes to learn more about our culture. I thought that it was a reasonable request after she made a sound argument. Will you tell us what you know about them? My wife would ask, but she's exceptionally shy."

"If she's the one who wishes to understand, she should be the one to ask me for the information. If she's looking for Tergii and Bimaa, she'll need to improve her confidence. Bring her forward if she wants to learn what I have." Tarhuinn tensed, and a scowl rested on his countenance. "Perhaps, she really isn't shy, but you're worried that I'll harm her. I have no intention of doing so. Nor, will I tell anyone that you two asked me about these authors. I'll swear on my life if that makes you more comfortable in letting me speak to her."

"They're dangerous people, then?" he asked, hiding Odette more behind him.

"They're ones who aren't known well, but that is all I'll say until she asks me herself."

Squeezing his left hand, Odette tried to signal that it would be alright. His glare met her gaze, but she forced herself to stare back at him. She wanted answers, and she wouldn't let his over-protectiveness get in the way. If she had to listen to a lecture later, that would be fine, but the female kelremm might be their only lead on the authors. Risk was going to play a part in their journey at some point, and it decided to reveal itself early. "Let me speak to her. Please," she whispered.

Reluctance was evident on his expression as was concern and slight anger. With a heavy sigh, he brought her forward and pulled his hand away from hers. "Speak as softly as you can."

Positioning herself on her knees, she made herself comfortable in front of Delnella. A smile overtook the kelremm's face. "I congratulate you on getting him to cooperate. Then again, I imagine that you're the only one who can sway him like that. Now, why do you wish to know about them?"

Slightly embarrassed, she murmured, "I want to understand their wording in their books."

"I suspect that there is more to it than that, but I won't press you. That information is your business with them. As for what I have on Tergii and Bimaa, I've heard that they live past all three complexes and that they're intimidating to even gaze upon. They only make their presence known if they require something from someone, and that something is usually details on the kelremm population. The two also only ask for this information from those who have partners close to dying."

"How did you hear about this?" Odette inquired as her theory about the five only grew darker.

"Since I work in the metal trade, I go in search sometimes for rare metals or jewels to decorate my more delicate metalwork. On these travels, I come across interesting news."

"Did you hear these details directly from the two authors? Were you there when they asked for this information?"

"I'll only say that I've heard of this. You understand, though, that their behavior is suspicious and that they could be quite dangerous if approached."

"Yes, but do you happen to know anything more on their location, or how we get beyond the three complexes?"

"Your partner should be able to guide you to the outskirts of our homes. All kelremm are taught the way."

"Thank you for your help. Is there anything that we can do to repay you?"

"No, I'm close to dying, but you should be careful. You still have at least a few years ahead of you. I would recommend you to spend them wisely, but you seem to consider this the smart course of action."

"I do," she uttered before she stood to her feet. "Thank you again." She received a nod from the female kelremm before she turned to Tarhuinn. Swiftly, he took up her right hand once more and walked off with her. To her displeasure, they were heading towards the poorly lit pool of water.

Chapter Eleven: Advance into Darkness

They stood at the top of the staircase, and she looked out to the dark waters beyond. It unnerved her that she couldn't see even a little past the surface of the water. The calmness of the pool was also unsettling. She felt like something would leap out and pull them under. Instinctively, she tightened her hand around his. "You've been through this area before, right?" she asked, glancing up towards him some.

"Yes but only once," he answered, taking some steps down the stairs, while water ran down them. "You don't need to worry. Nothing in these waters will harm you."

"So, there is something in there?" Worry and slight panic were evident in Odette's voice while her mind started to imagine something horrid. "What's in there, then?"

"Water pixies, though, they rarely make an appearance to us kelremm. They might come out to see you, however, since they barely get to glance upon humans. And if for some reason they try to harm you, I'll make sure that they receive the message to stand down."

"I guess that's not so bad, then." She felt a little more relieved, but, personally, she didn't want them to come up and out of the water. If they did, something unwanted could occur, and she understood that Tarhuinn meant his threat. After seeing him handle a knife, she didn't desire to know what kind of carnage he could bring upon the pixies.

Reaching the end of the steps, the water lapped up against the bottom one. For a moment, she was concerned that they would have to swim across, but she saw a few boats stationed nearby. Tarhuinn let go of her and brought one over to them. As he crouched, he held the boat steady so that she could step in. Once she was in, he seated himself sideways. The one side of the boat was completely flat and more like a raft, which allowed him to place his feet and lower legs in the water.

"Alright, hand me the paddle," he instructed, holding his hands out. She did so, and they started off.

"Are you going to be able to see alright? The light's only getting dimmer."

"Yes, I made it across before. Remember? When it becomes pitch black, though, remain calm. My eyes can see in the dark since kelremm sometimes need to swim in dark waters like this. If you hear any other sounds besides my breathing and rowing, it's the pixies."

"Okay, I trust you," she answered as they went closer towards the unlit maw of the cave. When it did become pitch black, she tensed and clenched her hands around the fabric of her cloak. She made herself focus on the sound of the paddle moving through the water and closed her eyes. Odette told herself that they would be out of the area soon enough.

Feeling something brush across her right arm, she jumped and nearly lost her balance on the boat. She regained her balance, opened her eyes and rubbed her arm. When she felt something touch her left knee, her heart almost leaped out of her chest until she realized that it was a hand. "Are you alright, Odette?"

Glad that it was just Tarhuinn, she replied, "Yes, but something went across my arm. Was it one of the pixies?"

"Yes, it was. They're moving around us at the moment. Right now, they're all under the water again, but they might pop out more. If one strikes at you, let me know immediately. Otherwise, try to remain still. I don't want you to fall in the water."

"I understand." Frankly, though, she wondered if it really was a pixie. It felt slimy. Luckily, there was no residue, but she didn't expect pixies to be like that. Perhaps, he was lying to her about what it was so that she would remain relaxed. Unfortunately, she felt it again but on her left arm, but her attention turned to her lap. She focused on the area and hesitantly moved her right hand forward.

The slimy texture greeted her hand, and she pulled it back immediately. A quiet chuckle filled the area, and it reminded her of ripples on water. Whatever was on her lap started to advance towards her. Leaning back, she rested her hands on the sides of the boat to maintain her balance. It continued and moved onto her midsection. She could still hear the paddle in the water, though. That meant that the thing on her wasn't a threat yet.

How she wished to be able to see, though. Soon, the thing was at her collarbone, and its slimy hands pressed against her skin. At least, she assumed them to be hands. Biting her lower lip, she closed her eyes again and could feel her hands trembling some. The hands pressed against her cheeks while another chuckle left its mouth.

"You're a pretty one. No wonder your mate is giving us such warning looks," it spoke out. The voice sounded feminine, but she couldn't tell that well. Every time a word left its mouth, she thought that she had heard a drop of water. It moved closer to her left ear and whispered, "You should be careful. He bears the gaze of someone who wouldn't feel any remorse for killing another. Your mate is frightening."

Swiftly, it moved away from her as though it had only been a slight breeze. She sat back up and heard light splashes of water before it went nearly silent again. Her eyes desperately sought out something in the darkness, but even her hands weren't visible to her. Intertwining them, she tried to calm herself down.

"They're gone," Tarhuinn spoke as he reached over and rested his left hand over hers. "They shouldn't make another appearance, but what did that one pixie tell you? I didn't like how close she was to you."

"She murmured that you're terrifying." Of course, she wouldn't say the rest of what the pixie had told her. She was still processing it herself, and she was trying not to display her concern. Maybe, it was the creature only messing with her, but she thought that she had heard genuine fear in the pixie's voice. Already, though, she suspected that Tarhuinn was capable of something horrendous, but to hear another confirm it with such a tone caused an unpleasant chill to run up her spine.

"And, do you agree?"

An answer didn't leave her lips immediately. "You scare me sometimes."

"I'm only like that occasionally because I wish to protect you. You're the most precious thing to me in the world." His hand tightened over hers. "Keep that in mind and trust me to keep you safe."

Giving no verbal answer, she nodded and kept her gaze downcast. His hand moved away, and the paddle continued its movement. She held her hands in a greater grip. Tarhuinn's words soothed her, but her mind told her to preserve caution. He was her husband, but she felt that she would have to keep an eye on him.

In time, the darkness started to fade. Up ahead was a lit passage. The torches were over small stone paths that had water flowing down the middle of them. Water poured over the edges and created small waterfalls. They were a little ways off from reaching the tunnel, but she was happy that she could see the scenery around her better.

Stalagmites and stalactites met each other in some places while stalactites dominated the roof of the cave. They were quite beautiful, but picturing one of the structures falling on them wasn't a pleasant image. She doubted that they would, though. Her eyes glanced back the way they came, and she thought that she had seen something jump out of the water and stare at her. It was probably one of the pixies, or she hoped that was the case.

Diverting her attention away from that area, she looked back to the tunnel. "Will we be arriving at one of the other complexes soon, then?"

"We won't arrive until tomorrow. There's some distance to walk after we get off of this boat. We'll have to make camp tonight unless you would prefer to keep going."

"No, I think that we should rest. If we encounter the two authors and they're really dangerous, we should have our full energy on hand. Besides, I've never camped before. It sounds like it could be fun."

"You're really an adventure seeker," he muttered with a small smile.

Hearing him, she pouted. "Well, you weren't the one locked in a room for twelve years. I lost so much of my life, and I want to get it back. This is making up for that. Despite how you were in the beginning, you're now letting me experience a whole new world, and I'm grateful for that.

"I would've never dreamt to be in an area like this, but here I am. Granted, the darkness was worrying, but it's gone now. And, unpleasant things are part of a journey. I just hope that there aren't too many disagreeable things left."

"If there are, I'll deal with them." He leaned over some and placed a soft kiss on the back of her left hand.

Chapter Twelve: Uncomfortable

Back on foot, Tarhuinn tied the boat to one of the nearby posts before he walked beside her in a stream of water. The torchlight illuminated the continuing abundance of stalagmites and stalactites while torches on some of the rock formations lit the room up more. Torches continued far down the area, which meant that they wouldn't have to travel in darkness again at the moment. "Who lights all of these?" Odette asked, hopping over a small stream of water.

"Someone from the next complex is sent down here to relight them every other day."

"And, these torches continue until we arrive there?"

"No. After another hour, we'll be using natural light to guide us through the cave."

Despite not having the comforting light of the torches, she was thankful that they would at least have some illumination. Hopefully, it would be enough so that she wouldn't have to rely on Tarhuinn's eyes again. She liked being able to see around her and know if something was about to sneak up on them. Odette jumped over the next small stream and peered at the path out ahead. Unfortunately, she would have a lot of streams to avoid.

On their way through the cave system, Tarhuinn offered to carry her on several occasions, but she denied all of them. She merely answered that she wanted to travel on her own feet and that she should get used to long distance exercise. A frown graced his lips, but he didn't argued on the topic.

By the time that they reached the end of the torches, though, she was exhausted. She rested her hands on her knees and looked out ahead. There were three openings in the cave wall to their left. Water gushed out, and she could hear the falling of water. If they were to continue directly forward, they would run into a dead end. Gazing to their right, she saw the path lead that way. The natural light continued on for some ways down the massive tunnel.

Refreshed, just by glancing at the water, she looked forward to taking a bath later. Right now, however, they had quite a bit of time ahead of them before night rolled around. Judging by the light's color, it had to be early in the afternoon. Then again, it might be a little misleading since there were probably clouds outside.

Whatever the case, they started down the trail again. Odette pushed herself to keep going even though she was tempted to take up Tarhuinn's offer of carrying her. She could tell that he was casting a glance her way every now and then, but she didn't meet it. If she did, he would probably convince her to let him pick her up.

As they went further, they snacked on some of the dried foods. She favored the dried apple chips, but she forced herself to stop eating them lest she eat all of them in one go. It wasn't until the light in the area turned duller and only small beams of moonlight reached them that they stopped. Odette collapsed to the ground, glad to be done for the day. Her hands went to her legs and soothed the sore muscles.

Tarhuinn set down his pack, and she took off hers before her hands continued to comfort her legs. The idea of jumping into the cool-looking water, though, sounded more relaxing. "Do you mind if I take a bath first?" She was also eager to take off her boots since her feet were desperate for a breather.

"No, you go ahead. Just stay close so that I can come to you if you need me. I won't look either if that's what you're wondering."

"Thank you." Despite him saying that he wouldn't peek at her, she headed behind a rock anyway and slipped out of her clothes. She pulled the sweet scented bath mixture out and headed into the water. It was cold to the touch, but her muscles relaxed into it. Soon enough, she was all the way in.

Ducking under the water, she made sure that her hair was soaked before she came back up and lathered it in the mixture. Once done with her hair, she moved onto her body. When she was finished, she went to change into a new set of undergarments and clothes, but she felt a tug on her right foot. She thought that she might have caught her foot on some plant, but it pulled on her again.

Panic beginning to set in, she peered down. Horror swept across her countenance as she saw countless little creatures around her. Their tiny, blue hands grabbed at her skin and continued to latch onto her. Where had they come from?! They hadn't been there when she had been bathing.

She tried to kick them off, but they wouldn't loosen their grip. Instead, they tugged harder, and strings of rubbery, blue hair secured around her skin. Odette didn't want to call Tarhuinn since she was still indecent, but she couldn't shake them off. When they gave another forceful pull, she lost her balance and fell towards the water. Pushing her embarrassment aside, she yelled, "Tarhuinn!"

Before she went under, she heard footsteps rushing over. The creatures dragged her towards the deeper water, and she thrashed her right foot around. They wouldn't come off. Sharp teeth gleamed under beams of light breaking through the water. Their beady, blue eyes stared at her in hunger. More swam up from the depths and dominated her other leg.

Her hands battled against the water as she tried to get back to the surface. More of the things came to her arms and hands and forced them down. A few made their way to her face. They opened their mouths and looked like they were about to attack her, but a splash sounded from the surface. Two powerful arms wrapped around her waist. Tarhuinn began to pull her upwards against the creatures. When they tried to grab at him, a warning growl emitted from his throat, and they backed off.

They reached the surface, and he carried her out. If it weren't for her adrenaline, her cheeks would be on fire. She peered up at him, but his gaze was looking straight ahead. Tarhuinn set her down far from the water and handed her cloak to her. When she had it wrapped around her form, she glanced up to him. "Thank you. I didn't see them until they already had their grip on me."

Looking to her now, a displeased expression painted him. "It would've taken several tugs for those tenlites to pull you under. Why hadn't you called me sooner?"

"I had been trying to get them off myself. I had thought that I could handle them. Besides, I hadn't ..."

Cutting her off, he barked out, "You hadn't wanted me to see you nude?" She gave a small nod. "Had I purposefully looked at you? No, I hadn't. Even if I had caught a glimpse, it had vanished from my mind because I had been more focused on your safety.

"Because of your hesitation, you could've gotten yourself killed. I could've lost you!" He combed his left fingers through his locks. "Just get dressed for now. I'll take care of those vermin in case they try to come back. I expect you not to go near the water until I come back. Understand?"

"Yes," she mumbled, clutching the cloak around her form. She didn't meet his gaze, but she peered to her right foot. There were small bruises forming there. Honestly, though, she was more worried about Tarhuinn's mood. Hopefully, he would come back and be somewhat agreeable. Otherwise, she might get more than a lecture.

A loud splash sounded, and she took that as her cue to get changed. As she did so, she glanced to the water multiple times and recalled how the blue squid humanoids had grinned at her. She was just happy that she hadn't discovered where they had wanted to take her.

It took some time after she finished changing for Tarhuinn to return. She became slightly concerned, but when she saw him come out of the water, she scooted back from him. A few tiny tentacles also rose to the surface, and she could only imagine the damage under the surface. "I'm going to bathe a little more upstream now. You're coming with me. There shouldn't be any more unexpected guests this evening."

Knowing that arguing would only make things worse, she picked up her things and went up beside him. She made sure to stay in pace with him. Tarhuinn grabbed his things as they passed by their camp. Odette assumed that they were moving their camp up too. "Are those creatures typical in these waters?" she inquired quietly.

"Yes, but not at this time of year. As far as I know, they're only supposed to be out in the summer. It's autumn. Usually, they're closer to the next complex. Something must've pushed them down this way. If something up ahead is too dangerous, we're not continuing."

"What?! But ..." she went silent when he peered back at her. She gulped and cast her gaze downwards. Despite his threatening gaze, she decided that if something like that were to happen, she would find a way to move on. Right now, though, she wouldn't worry about it; she would focus on not angering him more. He was already in a foul mood.

Tarhuinn dropped his things and started to take off his clothes without any warning. She quietly squeaked and turned her back to him. Seating herself, she set her own pack down and placed her dirty clothes to the side. "Can I wash these while you're bathing," she questioned, holding them up some.

"Yes, but stay close to the edge of the water."

Having no intention of going back into the liquid, she moved over and tended to her clothes. She made sure not to look to her left and focused on her work. The young woman also paid attention to what was under the water and near her. Odette didn't need to get dragged in again by those tenlites. One time was enough for her.

Chapter Thirteen: Close at Camp

Drying her clothes out on the smooth stone, she brought her knees up to her chest and waited for Tarhuinn to finish bathing. Her eyes focused back on where the tenlites had attacked. Had she called out a second later, she might've been dead. She wondered if there would be any more creatures like that, and she wished that Tarhuinn would give her one of his daggers. It wouldn't be too effective underwater, but it was something.

At the moment, though, she knew that it wasn't the right time to ask. He was most likely still mad at her, and she now desired that they hadn't stopped for camp. Resting her forehead on her knees, she sighed against her skin. What if some more dangerous foe came upon them? Tarhuinn already mentioned that they would turn back around and go home, but she didn't want that.

She would make sure that they would press forward, but how could she defend herself? Tarhuinn would protect her, yet he had set a limit to their journey. If she could learn how to fight, Tarhuinn could focus on himself, and they might be able to fight off something more threatening if it did appear.

Footsteps and splashes of water caused her to pay attention to her surroundings again, but she kept her forehead where it was. Something was draped around her shoulders before she felt an arm wrap around her waist. Within moments, she was pulled towards what she could only presume was Tarhuinn. Her head ended up being pressed against his right shoulder, and warmth grew in her cheeks.

His hold tightened, and his other hand grabbed her. She was turned from her side to sit directly in front of him on his lap. In the process, she fell forward a little and ended up pressing her hands and head to his chest. Her cheeks became hotter, and she was glad that her face was hidden.

"I told you that I would hold you closer, but I would like you to look at me. I'm your husband; you shouldn't feel embarrassed by this, but it's cute that you do." His left hand came up and started to stroke her hair. "Or, is it that you're worried that I'm still frustrated at you? Well, I am. Your shyness is adorable to an extent, but there's no place for it when you're in danger. In fact, you're lucky that I don't force you to bathe with me from now on."

Fire seemed to explode in her cheeks, but her worry caused her to look up at him. "You w-wouldn't ac-actually d-do th-that; wo-would you?" she stuttered out, trying to push the warmth in her cheeks away.

"Only if you wait to shout to me again," he responded, bringing his left fingers to rest under her chin. "It may seem like a punishment, but it's because it'll elicit you to act in a safer fashion. Besides, you may change your mind later and willingly want to take a bath with me."

Not being able to maintain her gaze with him anymore, she looked to her left and pulled her chin away from him. "Can you let me off of your lap now? You're going to get my boots wet," she mumbled since she couldn't find another excuse at the moment. After all, he was sitting in such a way that his feet were in a small stream that ran down the smooth surface of the stone.

A chuckle left his lips, and he moved his left hand back down to her waist. Instead of letting her go, he leaned back and pulled her down with him. Caught off guard, she ended up face-planting onto his chest while his left arm secured itself around her waist. She looked up some and saw his other hand pull his cloak from out under him before he laid it over them.

"Your boots won't get wet if you lay on me. Now, let's get some sleep for the evening," he uttered, though; it sounded more like a command. The previous night, she had agreed to let him hold her close, so she didn't argue back now. To her relief, he seemed to be cooling down from his ill mood, and, hopefully, that mood would be gone in the morning.

Slowly waking up, she shifted a bit and found herself to be moving. Confused, she opened her eyes. She took in her surroundings only to find that Tarhuinn was carrying her bridal style. Torches were back on the cave walls, and he must've traveled some ways. "You can set me down now."

"No, I'm carrying you the rest of the way. Besides, the path right now is only water, and I do believe that you didn't desire for your boots to get wet."

As if to prove him wrong, she looked downwards. Unfortunately, there was no accompanying stone path. She pursed her lips before she crossed her arms over her chest. "Why didn't you wake me up? I'm sure that the entire path hasn't been water for the whole time."

"No, it hasn't, but you looked rather comfortable against my chest. I didn't wish to disturb you. And, I don't have to worry about something attacking you this way."

"What if something attacks you? Didn't you mention that the tenlites were closer to the next complex? What if not all of them moved downstream? You can't very well defend yourself while holding onto me."

"That's where you're wrong, Odette. I'm quite capable of fighting without the use of my arms."

Huffing, she glanced ahead. He would probably only set her down when they got to the next complex, but whatever pushed the tenlites downstream might be directly up ahead. If that were the case and it was too risky, she would have to force her way out of his arms. She wouldn't focus too much on that possibility, however. There might be another reason for the tenlites' movement. "Tarhuinn, how much longer until we reach the next complex?"

"Once we get out of this waterway, we have to go across another cave room. Past that, we'll be there, and we're nearly out of this tunnel."

True to his word, they reached the end of the waterway soon after. The room following was just like the one that they had camped in, but torches lit the space instead of natural light. It made the area more ominous, and she couldn't see far down into the water. Tarhuinn, however, stayed close to the stones but still in the water, not minding the lesser visibility of the area. Then again, he could see when there was no visibility at all for her.

When a splash was heard up ahead, she instinctively pressed more into him. Her eyes searched the area out ahead, and she spotted something moving in the water. Another splash sounded but closer. Worryingly, a fourth came from behind them. It sounded like they were surrounded by whatever was in the water.

Peering down, she saw a form swimming a few feet away from them. Two more could be seen from her perspective. They looked to be bigger than the tenlites. "What are those?" she questioned, wishing that he would set her down and on a stone far from them. Or, maybe, she could take one of his daggers.

"I'm not certain yet. If it's what I think it is, then they shouldn't be here, but their presence would explain why the tenlites were further down in the cave. Perhaps, I better put you down."

Back on her feet, Tarhuinn motioned her to move back on the stones some more. He walked deeper into the water and removed a dagger from his belt. She noted that one of the fishes' shadows swum quickly at him. It remained under the water, and Tarhuinn threw the dagger swiftly. Despite the fast moving target, the dagger pierced the fish. The other two attacked, and a similar fate awaited them.

He retrieved his daggers and pulled the fish out of the water. Grey scales coated their bodies, and white, lifeless eyes stared back. Rows of razor sharp teeth were housed in their mouths, and they were about the length of her arm. "These fish prey on anything smaller than them and occasionally kelremm and humans. They were probably terrorizing the tenlites and got them to move. The question is why they're in these waters."

"Someone in the next complex might know," she suggested, keeping her distance from the water still.

Wiping the blood from his dagger and sheathing it, he nodded. "We'll bring these fish with us and trade them. Someone who trades fish there regularly will probably know the reason. Plus, we should fill up on more supplies. After the third complex, we'll have to rely on what we have and what we find on our own. Now, let's move along before more of these come."

Agreeing with him, she made her way across the stones, but she was mindful whenever she had to cross a stream. She noted that Tarhuinn was watching her carefully. As they went along, she inquired, "Where did you learn to throw a dagger like that?"

"I taught myself. While I was waiting for you, I would practice in case I had to take you out of that village by force."

"I didn't see any daggers on you that night, though."

"My shirt was covering them at the time. You looked away when I was taking it off and changing," he responded, laughing a little at the memory.

Pouting, she turned her eyes ahead. If she hadn't escaped from her home at that time, he would've most likely tried to kill anyone in his path or at least tried to. Thankfully, they were on the same side.

Chapter Fourteen: Second Arrival

Entering the second complex, it was much like the one where they lived. The market place, however, was somewhat different. Instead of tents and blankets, there were stone stands. Pools of water rested behind each stand, and the typical stone path and water paths were present.

Her cloak's hood was up again, and Tarhuinn's left hand was intertwined with her right. Like before, he kept her close, and she was forced to keep her gaze downcast. After they were done with their journey, she would be thankful that she would no longer have to wear a hood over her head in public. Or at least, she assumed that would be the case.

Reaching one of the fish traders, Tarhuinn rested one of the fish on the stone counter. Odette caught a surprised look on the trader's face. He reached his hands out to the fish and picked it up to examine it. "You caught one of the escaped gnashers. We tried to get them all back, but some got out into the water system. You have my thanks. In repayment for this, I'll give you an extra one of whatever you want. Of course, you can hold onto your other two gnashers; you caught them after all."

"That's very kind of you. We actually wished to know why they were in the water. The tenlites had been pushed further away from here because of them. And, some dried fish would be welcome," Tarhuinn responded, holding onto the other two.

After the trader gave Tarhuinn the wrapped up dried fish, he placed them in his pack and thanked the trader again before heading off with her. "We solved that mystery quite fast," she remarked quietly.

"Yes, I'm sure that you're just happy that we don't have to stop our journey."

She gave a small nod, and she was also glad that she wouldn't have to fight him off to continue. Even if she had somehow managed to get out of his grasp, she understood that he would come after her, and she probably wouldn't make it far. All the water that was around did give him the upper hand. Luckily, she wouldn't have to worry about that now.

They proceeded to trade the other two gnashers for dried goods. They also bought a few fresh foods to eat that day. Sitting by the edge of the market, she draped her feet over the edge of a small cliff. Water flowed over it from the water path and into the large pool of water below. Thankfully, their path ahead didn't require them to cross the pool on a boat.

Nibbling on her piece of freshly baked sweet bread, she glanced over to the narrow stone and water path that went along the side of the water. From her current view, it looked stable enough, but it sloped upwards. As for illumination, there were a few torches lighting it, but she couldn't see beyond that. She hoped that more light would be provided along the way. Otherwise, she would be holding onto Tarhuinn for dear life.

"Is it about the same distance to the next compound?" she questioned after swallowing a bite.

"It's going to be a little longer to the next one. The distance is the same, but most of the walk there is uphill. The third complex is apparently at one of the highest points of these mountains. Right now, we're more towards the base. That's why there are so many torches down here. Kelremm don't want to put windows down this low because unwanted visitors may decide to come in."

"What about the openings back in that room where the tenlites were?"

"Those are fine since they're small enough and have rushing water flowing out of them. No human would be able to withstand the current at those points."

"I'm glad that we don't live in this complex, then. I like having the window in the farm room."

"So, I've noticed," he replied, bearing a gentle smile. "I'm just glad that you never decided to jump out of it. You had worried me a few times." His smile had fallen as he took a bite of his own bread.

"I would never leap out of the window. I promised you that I would give you a child, and, right now, I'm putting all my effort into finding a way to live longer. I'm not going to let my life fade so easily. I want to explore those forests below our home, not fall upon them."

Finishing his bread, he patted his hands against his pants and held out his left hand. "Are you ready to head off, then? We should try to make it to the next cave room before evening. I'm guessing that it's early afternoon right now."

Popping the last piece of her bread into her mouth, she took his hand and allowed him to lift her up. From there, they made their way over to the path. Once they stood before it, she looked upwards and didn't like how steep it was. There were even small stone steps to help keep her on it. She couldn't imagine walking up the water section of it, but at least the water path was next to the wall. For her, she would have to walk right on the edge. Not to mention that closer to the top, there was barely any lighting.

Tarhuinn let go of her hand and rested it on her shoulder. "While we travel up, you can hold onto me as much as you need. I'm not too pleased that you have to walk so close to the edge either, but I'll make sure that you don't fall. And if we take longer than expected to reach the next room, so be it. Your safety comes first."

"Thanks," she muttered as he walked to the other side of her. She reached her left hand and clutched at his upper right arm. Once she had a firm grip, she started to advance up while Tarhuinn carried along at her pace. Only when she got the hang of it, did she start to walk faster.

That didn't too last long, however, as her legs were starting to get tired. They were only about a fourth of the way up, but her calves were screaming at her to stop. She knew, though, that she might not be able to continue if she halted for long. Odette was tempted to ask him to carry her, but she didn't think that he would be able to support their combined weight on the water path. The water was running down the slope rather quickly, and, despite his stoic expression, she could tell that he was having a hard time with ascending.

Telling herself that she could rest later, she forced her legs to carry on. Instead of focusing on how much of the road was left, she counted down her steps. She had started at the number of a thousand since she had no idea how many she would have to make. Hopefully, though, it wouldn't be that many.

Making it three-fourths of the way up, she was practically cheering in her head, but her slight moment of happiness dissipated. Her right foot slipped on one of the stones, and her balance lost itself. Immediately, she gripped Tarhuinn's right arm to hold herself up. The sudden pull, however, caused him to slip back some.

With her source of stability gone, her balance disappeared again, and she toppled over the side. A scream escaped her. Tarhuinn came crashing down as well. His feet remained on the water path, but the rest of him was on the stone path and part of him was hanging off of the side. Odette was dangling. Her fingers dug into his arm to keep her hold on him, and she forced herself not to look down. She kept her gaze on him, but her fear remained present.

Due to the slope, Tarhuinn was starting to slide down. Swiftly, he unsheathed one of his daggers and plunged it into the rock. That halted the sliding, but his feet were barely in the water. His attention, though, was pinned on Odette.

"Hang on," he ordered, though; his voice sounded weak. Worried for both of them, she nodded and gripped at him harder. He slowly pulled her up while maintaining his grip on the dagger handle. To help him, she found some footing on the rock wall and was able to climb somewhat up. With one last tug, he brought her up and over onto his chest.

Breathing uneven, he moved his arm from her grip and wrapped it around her waist. His other hand remained around the dagger, but a relieved sigh escaped his lips. "Will you be able to get back on your feet?" he asked, after catching his breath.

"Yeah, I think so. What about you?"

"Yes, but I'll have to make it quick. Only one of my feet is in the water at the moment, and I can already feel the effects."

Hearing that, she immediately pushed her own tiredness away and signaled for him to let go of her. Steadily, he did so. She gripped his shirt as she put her feet back on the path. Once each foot was on one of the steps, she lifted herself up and stood.

With her off, he rolled onto his stomach and placed both feet back in the water. A pleased sigh left his mouth before he got back onto his own feet. He pulled the dagger out of the ground and sheathed it. “Hold onto my hand this time. It won’t surprise me as much if you happen to slip again.”

Bringing no argument, she intertwined her fingers tightly with his. Her heart was still beating like a horse running at full speed. “The next part after the cave room won’t be like this, will it?” she inquired as she kept her focus on the steps.

“No, we won’t be able to fall, but it still won’t be an easy trek.”

An exasperated groan exited her mouth, but she reminded herself that there would be a resting area soon. With rest, she could press on. Her mind needed to look past the arduous short term and to the comforts provided in the long term.

Chapter Fifteen: Ascension

After they had conquered the dangerous path and rested for a time in the next cave room, they made their way over to the next upward sloping road. Odette had wished to stay in the room longer since her legs didn't desire anymore climbing for the day. Besides, the cool shallow water that she had been dipping her feet in had been quite relaxing. Of course, Tarhuinn had kept a close eye on the water in case something was lurking in it. He had mentioned that there wouldn't be anything but harmless water plants at the bottom, but after the incident with the tenlites, he didn't let his guard down.

She peered up at the long, stone staircase; she couldn't even see the end of it. It was as though she was facing a staircase that led to the stars. Spiraling upwards, cascades of water poured down. Natural light flowed down the center space, but she couldn't see what was allowing it in. Despite its illumination, it was still dark where they were at.

"I thought that you stated that we wouldn't be able to fall," she voiced, craning her neck to try and see the top somehow.

"We won't. The stairs are wide, and we would only fall if we walked too close to the edge, which would be foolish on our part. We may walk side by side and still have plenty of distance between us and the edge. In that respect, we can't fall."

"How long is this staircase?"

"We'll reach the top when it's well into the night. As you can see from the light coming in, it's near dusk."

A groan parted from her lips. Her legs wanted to collapse then and there. They were so sore, and she didn't know if they could last for several more hours. She had received her rest, but her determination from before wasn't as strong. Odette took off her boots and socks even though she had just put them back on, placing them into her pack. Reluctantly, she stepped onto the first step and began to make her way up. Tarhuinn maintained his pace with hers and grabbed her left hand in his right. His hold helped her stay stable on the slippery stairs.

As they ascended, she could feel her legs yelling in protest, and each step became more difficult than the next. To get her mind off of her current condition, she asked, "Tarhuinn, what were your parents like if you'll allow me to know?" Water splashed against the stone, and the chaotic sound contradicted their quiet steps.

"My father had the same hair color as me and dark blue eyes. His hair traveled to his chest and was always in a side braid. My mother, who was about the same height as my father, had red hair and dark brown eyes. Her wavy hair traveled to about her jaw.

"Personality wise, my father and my mother were alike in their calmness. Both were wonderful teachers and knew how to keep me engaged in my learning. They maintained my interest so much that I would often fall asleep in the library or in the farm room. They didn't mind me staying up late into the evening with my studies, and I have a feeling that it was because they enjoyed their nightly activities."

Some heat fell upon her cheeks, and she wondered if he would be like that when they returned back to the house. The thought caused even more warmth to flood her face, and she tried to shoo the images away, but it did bring another question to mind. "If they were active in that regard, what stopped them from having more children? And, wouldn't that create a problem since a human's life energy can only support one kelremm child?"

"Only one child is possible between a kelremm and a human. Regardless of the human's gender, the process of the child taking the human's life energy makes the human partner infertile."

"And, what if more than one child is born at once?"

He didn't answer immediately, and a disturbed expression crossed his countenance. "There have been no reports of that ever happening. It's theorized that the children somehow know that after their birth only one of them can be supported by their human parent. So, it's been suggested that one of them consumes the other or others in the womb."

Her feet stopped, and she stared straight ahead. It didn't bother her too much that she wouldn't be able to have more than one child, but the other part made her sick. The imagery in her mind wasn't pleasant, and she hoped that such a thing wouldn't happen. If the extra life energy source existed and if she had more than one child in her womb, perhaps, it wouldn't come to that. Maybe, with it, she would also be able to have more than one child. Still, what if Tarhuinn had a sibling, but he had to eat them to survive?

The thought caused her to feel a little dizzy, and the exhaustion from all of the climbing wasn't helping either. Unfortunately, her legs began to wobble, and she leaned over to her left. Tarhuinn quickly caught her. His hands pressed against her upper arms to keep her standing. Before he could ask anything, she inquired, "Do you think that you had a sibling?"

"I'm not sure. If I did have one, I apparently did what I had to do to survive. If I hadn't acted, they would be in my place. Again, this is assuming that those theories are correct, Odette. I know that it isn't pleasant to think about or picture. For right now, focus on getting to the next complex."

Giving a weak nod, she pushed against him and managed to get her legs back to normal. They still had a long climb ahead of them, and her negative thoughts were only slowing them down. She decided to discuss a different topic to get her mind more away from the previous conversation. "Tarhuinn, do you know what's beyond the third complex?"

"I recall viewing a large pool of water but nothing else. I'm not quite sure where Tergii and Bimaa would go off to, but there might be a passageway underneath the water's surface. If so, we'll have to figure out a way to keep our supplies dry unless we come across them there. Some of the residents are bound to know of them, though, or at least have seen them."

"If we have to travel underwater, what if the passage is too long for me even with your quick swimming?"

"If I feel like it'll be too dangerous for you, we'll head back. There might be another way. I don't know, but I won't let you drown. Should we meet them there and they grow hostile, I'll make sure that no harm comes to you."

"Wouldn't it be better if you taught me how to fight? That way, I could defend myself and be more useful in combat. Right now, I really only know that the sharp end will stab them."

"I'd rather you depend on me for protection."

"I doubt that's the only reason. You're worried that I may injure myself with it on accident or that I might try to fight against you if you pull me back from this journey. In simple terms, you don't trust me with a blade, but what if we're surrounded? Could you realistically defend me and take on a group of people? Even with your skill, one of them would be bound to get to me before you could fully stop all of them."

"There will only be two of them if they attack. I can handle that."

"What if some of the other residents in the area attack because they see you as a threat? Or, what if they're more than what they seem? Who knows what they're truly capable of. You keep saying that you'll protect me, but who's going to protect you? You're not invincible. And if you die, then I'll probably fall soon after if I can't defend myself. Your work will have been for nothing, and you would fail in what you keep telling me. If you really wish to protect me, teach me how to use a blade."

His hand tightened around hers some more, but she didn't shrink away from her stance. Either he was going to reject the idea or he was frustrated at seeing her point on the matter. "Before the third complex, there's a small cave room. We can train there, but I'm only teaching you the basics. If you want to learn anything else, it'll have to be self taught."

Their hands disconnected for a short bit to avoid walking through one of the waterfalls. At the news, though, she practically threw her hands up into the air but reminded herself not to jump. She would most likely slip if she did. Tumbling down the steps would probably mean death for her. When they reconnected hands, she exclaimed, "Thank you! I'll be careful when using it!" In the process of her jubilation, she ended up hugging him with her free arm.

Surprised, Tarhuinn glanced down to her and wrapped his free arm around her waist. A small smile graced his lips, though; he was concerned about the consequences of his decision. If there were a point where they had to turn back, his training might come back to bite him. He knew that she wouldn't kill him, but it would be harder to restrain her. For now, he would enjoy her embrace, and the current peace on their journey.

As they progressed farther up the staircase, Odette realized that it was getting colder. Not only that but it was also getting harder to breathe. She found herself resting more against Tarhuinn, and she could even hear his difficulty with breathing. The light of moon became brighter while the darker depths disappeared behind them.

Taking several more steps, they faced a waterfall that covered the entirety of the next few steps. They didn't wish to get their supplies wet, but there was no other way up. Tarhuinn instructed her to take off her cloak and put it in her pack before handing the pack to him. It made sense to keep one article of clothing at least somewhat dry.

Once she had done so and he had done the same, Tarhuinn moved closer to the edge of the stairs. He leaned a bit into his left side and craned his neck to look beyond the waterfall. Concerned that he may slip and fall, she went over to him carefully and held onto his right arm. An appreciative smile crossed his lips, but he assured her that he would be fine. Regardless of his reassurance, she kept her hold on him. If he did happen to fall, though, they probably would both go tumbling down. There was no way that she had the upper body strength to bring him back up.

His focus, however, turned back to the stairs past the cascade of water. Swinging his left arm a few times, he released the pack in his hands and tossed it to the stairs beyond. It made contact with the stairs and slid a bit on them but otherwise stayed. He took her pack next and did the same. The bottom of the packs would get soaked, but if they hurried, the contents inside wouldn't get wet too badly.

He moved away from the edge, and she let go of him and walked back herself. She inwardly sighed in relief that they were no longer near that long drop down. Tarhuinn took up her left hand again and advanced with her up the steps. Odette felt the frigid water coat her person, and she wished to dart back the way they came. Already, she was shivering. Her hand instinctively tightened around his in order to find a source of warmth.

When they moved past the fall of water, Tarhuinn let go of her and picked up their packs. He set them on a rock that was sticking slightly out of the stone wall. His right hand motioned her to come over, and she gave no argument. Her dry cloak was in there after all.

Rubbing her hands against her arms, she watched him pull out the cloak and hold it out to her. She took it as though it was the most precious gem in the world. Putting it over cold and wet clothes, however, wouldn't do her too much good. "Tarhuinn, do you mind facing the other way?"

For a moment, he was confused by the request, but that puzzlement vanished quickly. "Of course, you might want to do the same, then, unless you want to watch me change." Heat hit her cheeks, and she shook her head. A soft chuckle reached her ears, which caused her to pout some. Turning from him, she hung her cloak on the jutting out rock until she had her wet clothes off.

She set them aside on the rock and grabbed her cloak. She kept her underclothes on since she could tolerate them being wet. It was either that or climbing the rest of the way nude under her cloak. The second option didn't seem like a swell one.

After wringing her hair out, she tied her cloak around her. She held it tightly to her body and announced that she was done. Tarhuinn finished shortly after her before he handed her pack to her. Odette slipped it through her arms and onto her back slowly since she didn't want the cloak to open accidentally on her. "What are we going to do with our wet clothes?"

"We'll have to carry them in our free hands. Once we get to the next room, we can let them dry out properly," he answered, picking up his own in his left hand while his right hand intertwined with her left.

There was the option to put them in her pack, but everything else would get wet. That would defeat the purpose of Tarhuinn having thrown the packs in the first place. She took them up in her right hand, managed to hold her cloak closed and continued up the many steps with him.

It still wasn't easy to breathe, and the cold air was only making their wet forms worse. If she caught a cold, she wouldn't be surprised. Hopefully, they would be able to form a fire in the next room. Her body was also finding the option of cuddling up to Tarhuinn a must. The idea was embarrassing, but he would probably hold her close when they slept regardless.

By the time that they reached the top, she was somewhat dry. Her hair was a little wet, and her underclothes were nearly done with drying. The ones in her hands were wetter but would hopefully dry with the night. Cold surrounded them, however, but at least they didn't have to walk up stairs anymore. She finally felt like she could catch her breath some.

Her eyes glanced up to the stone roof. There was a small hole in the ceiling, which permitted the moonlight to come in. Storm clouds would occasionally float by, explaining the instances where the stairwell grew dark. White flecks fell in through the hole, and she recognized it as snow. Tarhuinn did mention that the third complex was at one of the highest points of the mountains.

Directing her gaze to the stone path and water path that were ahead, she slowly turned around. With all of their climbing today, she wondered if she would be able to train with him tomorrow. "It won't be too long to this cave room, right?" she asked, slouching over some due to her energy depletion.

"It'll only take a couple of minutes. And then, you'll be able to rest."

"Will we be able to have a fire?"

"We can try and see if we can make one," he responded, moving his right hand to her waist and pulling her close. She nearly wanted to stop there and snuggle into him. Odette forced herself to keep moving with him, though.

Reaching the cave room, she noticed that the water path flowed into a larger stream and went across the entire room. The rest of the room had jagged stones jutting out of the ground while there were a few smooth spots. At the end of the room, a tunnel presumably led to the next complex.

Odette's focus shifted away from it and to one of the smooth spots. Tarhuinn seemed to notice her gaze and began to progress over to it with her. She used the last of her energy to increase their pace. Once there, she pulled away from him and collapsed onto the smooth stone. Unfortunately, there was no wood around, so a fire was out of the question. The only illumination in the space was the light that fell in through the small opening at the top of the room. A pile of snow lay directly under it.

The opening allowed the cold night air in too. She pulled her cloak around her tighter while she laid out her clothes next to her. Tarhuinn did the same with his clothes, but he was sitting closer to the water. He positioned her closer to him and rewrapped his right arm around her waist. The male proceeded to reach into his pack, and he retrieved some dried meat for them. Odette gratefully took a slice and began to take small bites before she finished it.

"Odette, for sleeping arrangements tonight, it might be better if we use our cloaks as blankets."

"I was already planning on using mine as one."

"No, I mean combining them so that we sleep together in a makeshift bed."

Almost dropping a new piece of meat, she moved away from him. "But my clothes aren't dry yet, and I don't have a nightgown with me." Her one hand tightened around her cloak.

"I won't look at you, but it would keep us warmer through the night."

That might be true, but she would only have her underclothes on. She could feel the heat in her cheeks, and she scooted away from him more. Odette checked her clothes again, but they remained somewhat wet.

Still, she didn't go away from them. It was as though she was trying to convince herself that staring at them would make them dry faster. Granted, she did desire to cuddle up to him but not without her cloak wrapped around her.

Frustrated that they weren't dry, she peeked over her left shoulder at him and speedily looked away. He had already untied his and was laying it on the stone ground. She pulled her cloak hood over her head to hide her burning cheeks. Odette was soon tugged back, however, and onto his cloak. His hands slipped over her shoulders and towards the bow on her cloak.

Before he could untie it, she rested her hands over his and tried to get them off. That failed, and soon the cloak was slipping down her shoulders. She squeaked in embarrassment, going to grab it back, but he took it off and turned away from her.

"Now, lay down. I'm not looking at you; I just want to keep you warm." Peeking over to him, she noted her cloak resting partially over him. Hesitantly, she laid herself down as she realized that he wasn't going to budge on the issue. Odette draped part of the cloak over her and mentioned that she was covered. He rolled over and faced her before he brought her to his chest.

Chapter Sixteen: Instruction

Waking up, Odette groaned a bit in her sleep and was already able to feel the soreness in her legs. It didn't help that they had slept on stone. There was a cloak there, but it didn't add too much comfort. Admittedly, the only real comfort that she had was from Tarhuinn, who was providing her much needed warmth. Maybe, they would find something in the short distance from the cave room to the third complex and trade it for warmer clothes.

Her cold body only pressed more against him, and her tired mind didn't consider how embarrassing it was. It wasn't until she opened her eyes and noted how close her face was to his bare chest that heat swept over her cheeks. She glanced up to his face, seeing his eyes still closed. His breathing seemed steady also.

Looking forward again, the warmth remained in her cheeks, but she didn't look away. He was asleep, so she could admire his well-toned chest. Besides, he was her husband, so it wasn't like she was being weird. Gently, she ran her right fingers down his chest and occasionally peered up to see if he had awoken. Since he hadn't, she continued and stopped right above his naval. She went to draw her hand back up, but a hand caught her wrist.

Hesitantly, she glanced towards his face and noticed that his eyes were still shut. An amused smirk painted his lips as he brought her hand up towards them. He placed a light kiss on the back of it. "If you wished to feel my chest, Odette, all you had to do was ask. I do enjoy the feeling of your delicate fingers running along my skin. We're in an unfair predicament, though."

Before she could respond, he opened his eyes and abruptly sat up while he placed his hands on her hips. She cried out, startled, and discovered herself to be on his lap. The cloak fell down around them. Instantly, she tried to get it back, but Tarhuinn wrapped his right arm around her waist and held her to him. His left hand went under the fabric of her undershirt as it began to travel slowly upwards.

A chill ran up her spine while her cheeks felt like they were on fire. "Tar-tarhuinn, what a-are you d-doing?" she stuttered, pushing her hands against his chest.

"Giving my wife my affection. Is that wrong of me?" He leaned his face closer to hers.

She was about to argue, but her words were cut off. Lips rested against her own. Her eyes widened for a moment as he tilted his head a little to deepen the kiss. His hand pressed more into her bare back, and she had to reach up to grab the front of her shirt since it was riding up some. Soon, though, she gave into the kiss.

One hand stayed on her shirt while the other rested against his chest. His lips slowly trailed away and down towards the right side of her neck. He placed feather-light kisses down her exposed skin. Hitting her soft spot, she unintentionally let out a light moan. Tarhuinn paused for a moment before he brought his lips to the area again.

Biting and sucking at the area, he took his time in leaving a mark there. That earned him a series of light moans from his partner, who leaned her head on his right shoulder and rested her hands on his upper arms. Her shirt had ridden up a little more than expected, but she barely noticed due to her mind going into almost a daze.

Lips trailing down from the spot when he finished, he placed soft kisses along her shoulder before he started on marking her again. His hands moved up to her shirt sleeves. Steadily, they pulled down on the fabric. Her shirt began to lower, but it reached too low of a point for her. Odette managed to get a hold of her mind again and pushed against him roughly.

The action caught him off guard, causing his hands to slide from her upper arms. She fell backwards and landed on her bottom. Her hands supported her in a sitting position, but she speedily sat up and pulled her shirt sleeves back up. There was a small tear in the middle. If she had waited a few more moments, she might've been more exposed to him than her liking.

Even at the moment, she didn't like sitting by him in only her undergarments. Her mind had lost itself in pleasure, and she could feel the two bruises starting to form. Swiftly, she grabbed her cloak before she wrapped it around her form. She couldn't meet his gaze nor could she even glance his way. Despite the frigid air, she felt warm. Her left fingers traveled up to the marks on her skin, feeling a few scratch marks from his teeth there. They didn't seem to be bleeding, however.

Going over to her and lifting her chin up, she tensed against his touch and held the cloak tighter. Her eyes looked to her left. "Odette, I apologize. I was getting carried away."

Shaking her head, she mumbled, "I was ... enjoying it too ..., but I should've stopped you sooner. I was only ... encouraging you." Hesitantly, she met his gaze. She examined his dark blue eyes before she trailed her gaze to his lips. Odette leaned forward a bit and pecked him lightly there. Shyly, she pulled back and added, "I want to wait longer before we go to that step. So, for now, let's start the training."

Receiving a nod from him, he let go of her and got to his feet. He headed over to his clothes, and she did the same, though; walking was painful. Her legs protested against every step. Odette wondered if she would be able to properly train. She remained quiet, however, on her legs' condition since it might be the only training opportunity that she would ever get from him.

Done with changing, she was glad to have her dry clothes on again. Tarhuinn, fully clothed, handed her some dried fruit and one of the bread rolls. He had an identical breakfast, and they still had two bread rolls left. When they finished eating, they glanced around and figured that the smooth spot that they were on would suffice.

Unsheathing one of his ten daggers, he closed the distance between them and told her to hold out her hands. She did so before he placed the blade onto them. The small weapon weighed more than she expected, but she would get used to it with time. Odette switched it to her right hand while she looked to him for instruction.

"We'll begin with holding techniques. First, we'll start with three forward grips. Right now, you're utilizing a forward grip called a hammer. Now, a forward grip is when your little finger opposes the blade. As for the hammer technique, your fingers are curled around the underside of the dagger, and your thumb is also around the handle while touching your forefinger.

"If I move your thumb to the spine of the handle, this is called a saber. A problem with this grip is the gap between your forefinger and thumb, making the grip not as stable. Should I move your thumb to the side of the blade, this is a modified saber. The clear issue here, especially with this small blade, is that your thumb can slide downwards and get injured on the blade during an attack.

"Concerning a reverse grip, it's when the thumb opposes the blade." He moved the blade in her hand until she was holding it in one of the positions. "Now with a one-sided blade, you could have the blade facing in or out, however; you're working with a dual bladed dagger. With this in mind, the blade will be facing both directions. Since this is the case, you might be striking towards yourself due to an in-strike, moving the enemy closer to you. There are also some unusual grips, but I want you to focus on these. Do you have any questions?"

"No, I think that I understand it all."

"In that case, I want you to rest your legs before carrying on. During this, I'll call out the four grip techniques, and you'll show me what they look like. In addition, I want you to practice with both hands. This'll give you an advantage over an opponent. Once I feel that you're ready, I'll have you practice each."

Complying, she took a seat on the stone floor. Her legs were grateful for the action, and she started with the blade in her right. He took a seat across from her and began to call out the grips. Even after she had them all memorized, he continued the process.

She figured that he was testing her ability to switch between the grips quickly. On a few times, she would nearly drop the blade, but she was getting the hang of it. Occasionally, he did have to step in and catch the blade so that she wouldn't accidentally harm herself.

"All right, I think that's enough. It'll take practice for you to be quicker, but that's good for a beginner. We'll move onto striking now."

"What about throwing the daggers?"

"You don't need to worry about that. If we can fight from long range, I'll be attacking. Remember, I'm only teaching you this in case we're surrounded." Standing to his feet, he held out his right hand, and she took it. He lifted her up before she placed the blade in her right hand again to begin with.

"Hold the blade in a hammer grip." She followed his instruction. Walking over to her, he began to give instruction on the various strikes that she could deliver with such a grip. When they finished those, he moved onto the next style and did the same.

Chapter Seventeen: Onto the Third

Both of her arms were exhausted when they completed the training. Tarhuinn had her practice the strikes countless times to guarantee that she would know what to do when she had the knife in a certain grip. She had never fought against him even though she tried to convince him that it would be good practice for her. He had merely answered that he could never strike a blade at his wife.

Instead, he had gone through the strikes, had given various scenarios and had asked her to perform the proper grip and strike. Once he had been pleased with her results, they had stopped. She had attempted to persuade him that an enemy would probably not follow a formulaic scenario, but one warning glance had told her to be satisfied.

Personally, she thought that he was refusing to teach her more because he didn't wish for her to learn his exact fighting moves. He didn't desire her to be able fight against him if he were to claim that it were too dangerous to move on ahead. Maybe, it really was because he didn't wish to strike at her, but she had a feeling that it was more than that. He might wish to have the upper hand over her. Not like he already did with that nickname, though.

He took his dagger back and sheathed it while she picked up her pack. With it resting on her back, she faced the tunnel ahead. Tarhuinn stepped up beside her before he intertwined his right fingers with her left. They moved on ahead, but Odette wanted to practice just a little bit more even with sore muscles. She supposed, though, that some training was better than no training.

As they went on ahead, only some morning light shone through the hole at the top. It barely broke through the thick storm clouds, which released snow down onto the mountains. The pile of it in the room had grown. With the continuation of autumn, it would only increase.

They passed from the room and into the tunnel, where the light decreased as they made their way down it. Eventually, Tarhuinn had to guide them since she could no longer see in the darkness. Her grip on him strengthened in fear that something would come out of the shadows. Thankfully, no such thing happened.

Up ahead, she heard voices, and it sounded as though trade was occurring. Light began to fill the tunnel again as the third complex unveiled itself. She pulled up her hood before she stepped out of the tunnel. Glancing around, she noted how the complex had fewer floors, but there were more homes on each floor.

Several stone pillars were spread throughout the center space. The market tents gathered around them. Beyond the marketplace, there was the huge body of water that Tarhuinn had mentioned. Nothing lay beyond it except the mountain wall. Despite the light coming in through the windows at the top of the complex, the water was like the darkness in the tunnel. There was no hope of viewing anything beyond the surface. They might not have to travel down there, however. Tergii and Bimaa might be in the complex, or there might be another way to reach their homes.

Focusing back on the kelremm in the area and seeing no humans about, she noted how much warmer everyone was dressed. They wore thick cloaks and more leather. Compared to them, Tarhuinn and she looked like they were dressed for summer. "Do you think that we'll be able to trade for some of those clothes?" she asked since the thicker cloak looked quite nice. Unfortunately, they hadn't found anything extra to trade from the cave room to the complex.

"We might be able to swap our current clothes for them, but I doubt it. Even when it's hotter up here, they'll still need thick clothes to stay warm. All of our clothes might fetch us one cloak. So, we'll most likely have to wear multiple layers from now on. Now, let's go search for the two authors. I don't see anyone standing at the doors of any of the houses, so they're probably not here."

Odette glanced over the area again. No one looked out of the ordinary. Perhaps, they would have to ask around, which would raise suspicion. "Are you going to be asking kelremm, then?"

"Yes, we'll need to trade to draw less attention to us. We could trade some of the dried fish for dried meat and fruits. Let's hope that the trader will know something."

Going over to one, Tarhuinn pulled out the fish and began the transaction with a female kelremm. After the exchange was complete, he asked about the two authors' last names. Both of them noticed that a frightened expression appeared on her countenance. "Why would you two wish to know about them? You're from another complex; you shouldn't involve yourselves since they never visit the other ones."

"We have some questions for them. That's all. Why are you so terrified of them?" Tarhuinn inquired, his hand tightening around Odette's.

"I've never talked to them personally, but others have. All of those kelremm have partners that are close to dying. That's concerning in its own right. The two usually ask about the population, making sure that there are no anomalies. They always walk away after that or so I've been told."

"Wouldn't they need to visit other complexes to know the true population?"

"That's the odd part. Those that they have spoken with have asked the same question, but both of them state that they have it covered. Rumors have spread that they have spies in the other complexes or that they have some quicker way to get to the other two complexes."

"Do you think that they'll be coming today for a visit?"

"No, they came a few weeks ago. So, they probably won't come back for awhile now."

"What about their appearances? Or, where do they go when they leave?"

"Both of them have white cloaks that blend in with the snow outside. Tergii has a shaven head and eyes that are a very light blue. As for Bimaa, she has long straight locks that descend to her knees. Her eyes are a medium blue. Both of them are about your height. Granted, they always look the same as though it's been the same people all along, not their descendents who happen to look identical.

"As for where they go, there's an abandoned home on the first level. It's closest to the pool of water. The doors aren't locked, and almost all of us have searched the place. We can never find how they get out, but there's a secret passage somewhere in there."

"Thank you. It has been most kind of you to share this information. It must be odd, though, that we're asking. I'm curious to know why you're being so accommodating to us."

"It's strange since it concerns those two, but someone needs to have the courage to talk to them when it's not on their terms. All of us here are scared of them, and we wish that they would stop coming. It's also bizarre that they don't live in the complexes, and if they do, their location has never been learned."

"Well, thank you again. We'll be on our way," Tarhuinn stated, clasping his left hand with her left. He pulled away and started to walk towards the house with Odette. When they stood before the door, neither of them entered

"Do you think that it's a trap?" Odette questioned quietly as she found the kelremm's eagerness to tell them information suspect.

"It could be. The two authors might've told everyone to lead curious travelers to this place. We could be ambushed upon entering. Everything she told us could be questionable, but if the part about the spies is true, we'll need to be extra careful. Before we even came here, they might've been on our tails or still are."

"Do you think that she tampered with the food that she traded with us?"

"No, I asked her about them after we already had traded goods. Besides, she looked genuinely terrified at my question. Unless she's good at acting, we should be fine on the food. And, I picked out the food from her stand. She would either have to be a mind reader, which isn't possible among our kind, or she would have had to poison all of her food.

"Also, her expression would tell us that no one had informed her about us. That is again if she wasn't acting. Overall, we were given a lot of information, and we shouldn't let fear of not knowing what is true and what isn't consume our minds.

"Still, it would seem that your theory about possibly being able to replenish one's life energy might be true if these two are the original authors and not their descendents. For right now, we'll go into this home and search for the secret passage. If we get attacked, I'll defend us to the best of my ability."

Odette took a deep breath in and exhaled as he slowly opened the double doors. The home was rather dark, but the light from the center of the complex flooded down the hallway some. She could easily see the dust floating in the air.

They both walked in further, and Tarhuinn closed the doors behind them. It became dark in the passage, and she moved closer to the water path that he was on. He probably had closed the doors so that they would know if anyone came in from behind them, but she hoped that they would find a light source soon.

Traveling down the hallway, she trusted Tarhuinn to guide them through the house since it was now pitch black in the place. She knew that he would stop if he saw anything odd lying around. As they made their way down and took a left turn, he told her to step a little to her right to avoid some stones on the ground. After she passed them, he increased his pace a little. They took a right turn next, and he stopped. "I'm going to let go of your hand for a moment, Odette. Just remain where you are."

Reluctantly, she agreed. She intertwined her fingers together before she fiddled with the fabric of her cloak. "What are you doing?" she asked to hear his voice. The surrounding darkness kept her imagination on high, so knowing that he was still there would help.

"I'm going to try to light the fireplace in here. We can then light the lanterns using this. It might take awhile, but I'm sure that no one will mind us spending the day and possibly the evening in here." He grabbed the firesteel and chert, and the fire was soon lit. Placing the items down, he stood up and glanced over the kitchen.

Odette was just happy that she could see in the place. "Tarhuinn, how could a kelremm house become abandoned? Your population seems to be quite stable according to you. And, there doesn't seem to be conflict between the three complexes. And, I haven't seen anyone who looks ill."

"Illness does strike us occasionally, but we have tougher bodies than humans. If a human partner takes ill, it becomes a community matter, and the complex works to form a cure. The same happens if a kelremm falls ill, but again that rarely happens. So, I doubt that was the reason for this abandoned house. Perhaps, it was built to be specifically abandoned so that the authors would have a secret way out."

"Then, why furnish it? There are still pots and pans in here and a ready supply of wood."

"It might be an elaborate illusion to make it seem like it was abandoned. We could go back out and ask one of the wood traders. It might be that they supply wood to this house since the other trader mentioned that almost everyone has explored this place."

"That's something that I've been wondering. How is wood supplied to the complexes? Your ceilings aren't high enough for pine trees, yet there seems no way to go outside except for that water passage you used to take me to our home."

"Kelremm used to have to bring in cut-up trees from outside the mountain, but that was rather risky due to unwanted humans possibly spotting us. So over the years, we developed a new kind of tree. We took the shortest of the trees and bred them together. Eventually, we were successful in getting a tree to be a little over my height. This allows the trees to be grown in kelremm homes."

"That must've taken years, though."

"According to history, it took many generations of kelremm, but the amount of years still seems to fall short. Some have just stated that we always have had the trees in the mountains and that the history is a fabled myth. Others have mentioned that magic may be at work, but a mage has never crossed paths with our kind. Or if they have, there have been no records of it."

"Maybe, that's where this possible extra life energy is coming from. A mage might be involved. Perhaps, mages have been interacting with your kind all of these years, but it's been hidden from the general population. Those five authors might not only have been trying to keep this source of life energy a secret but also their knowledge of kelremm dealings with a mage or mages. That would garner the reason to make this house seem like it was abandoned."

"That could very well be the case. It would explain why these five authors took out that phrase in that line. We won't know until we find them, though. So, let's begin lighting the lanterns and searching. Who knows how long it'll take us to find the secret passage."

"Right, I don't want to be in this house for too long, especially if spies are around and they know about our inquiries," she responded as he grabbed one of the lanterns from the kitchen walls. He lit the candle within before the two of them joined hands and made their way throughout the house.

As they went around and lit the candles, she did wonder who was replacing the candles. It was far too weird. Maybe, it was one of the kelremm from the complex, or Tergii and Bimaa restored them to keep up the grand illusion of things. At least with the light, they could finally begin a decent search for the hidden passage.

They started with the bedroom since they had lighted the lanterns in that room last. Dust had gathered like in the other rooms, though; there was more in the space than the hallways. Maybe, the kelremm from the complex thought not to search too far in.

When they had finished with the room, every section had been looked through. Both of them even tested the walls and floors. Tarhuinn had managed to reach certain parts of the ceiling by standing on the bed. Nothing popped up. "No kelremm have magic, right?" she questioned, thinking that there might be a magic seal involved.

"Correct. If they have magic, they either gained it by some forbidden means, or they made sure that no other kelremm would have magic. Still, it's unlikely, but we don't know exactly what we're dealing with. My knowledge of my kind might not even be correct when concerning those five."

"Could they possibly bring a mage with them and have the mage wait in the house until they return?"

"Yes, that's a possibility. We shouldn't dwell on that, though. If that's the case, however, then we can't move on. I have no magic, and as far as I know, you don't either."

"I know for certain that I don't have any. Otherwise, I would've escaped my room back in my parents' house a long time ago. In the end, it worked out since we're now exploring. I doubt that we would've done this if I had come to you sooner."

"That's true. Then again, I would've had for certain more years with you. This is all riding on chance."

"But things keep pointing to my theory," she commented as they left the bedroom and headed to the laundry area next. A sigh escaped his lips as he nodded in response, and a triumphant smile graced her lips. On their way, though, she noted the pool of water off to the side. "Do you think that pool could lead to where Tergii and Bimaa went off to?"

"It's a possibility, but I'd rather not travel down some abandoned water tunnel unless we have to. We'll check the rest of the house first. If we can't discover anything, then we'll test out that way."

Agreeing to that plan, they continued through the other rooms. The laundry, kitchen and library provided nothing. They even tested all of the books on the shelves. Several hours had passed by that point. Neither knew what time it was, but they decided to take a short break and eat something. Chewing on a dried apricot, she looked over the library once more. Unlike back in their home, there was no window in the ceiling. Only more lanterns lit the room.

The books were back on the shelves, but she had been hoping that there would be a book-lever activation. Those seemed too obvious, though, since they were always mentioned in tales of mystery. Hopping off of the desk, she landed on the stone and stretched a little. Tarhuinn had finished eating, and they went off to their last location, which happened to be a room with the shorter pines.

No lanterns were in the space. Only a large window in the far left wall provided light into the area. The room did answer the question of where the wood was coming from, though; it raised the question of whether Tergii and Bimaa took care of the trees themselves.

From the large window, they could see that it was late afternoon, but that light barely penetrated the trees in the center. It was amazing that they still grew so well. They must've come from some variant of pine that could tolerate partial sunlight. Something could very well be hiding within the trees. Both of them shared a similar thought, and Tarhuinn made sure that he had a tight grip on her.

Advancing into the trees, they watched carefully around them. They would need to use the afternoon sun to their advantage. Thankfully, not too many clouds seemed to be blocking it at the moment. Occasionally, they stopped a few times since one of them thought that they had heard something. It turned out that it was only their imagination getting the best of them. At least, that was the conclusion that they made.

They remained wary, however. As the light from the sun grew dimmer, they found themselves still examining the trees. By now, they weren't able to see much in the center. "We'll need to go back and grab a lantern. Then, we can come into here again. We don't want to be caught in here in the dark," Tarhuinn advised. The idea sounded like a good plan to her, and they headed back to the library to grab one. It was odd, however, that it appeared darker farther down in the house. It looked as though the lanterns had been blown out.

Her whole body went tense, and her eyes stayed pinned to the hallway. Tarhuinn had grabbed the lantern by that point, but he quickly noticed her fearful expression. His gaze turned to the darker hall. Immediately, he ordered in a quiet voice, "Odette, we need to get back into the forest room and do so swiftly."

She only nodded her head slightly as they rushed over. Something zipped through the air, however, and soared right between them. Had she taken another step forward, she would've been dead. Her heart rate increased while her grip on his hand tightened. An arrow lodged itself into the stone wall to the right of them.

Tarhuinn pulled her forward before he swept her into his arms. He wasted no time in dashing towards the trees. Another arrow flew by, nearly striking him. Footsteps started to run down the hall, but Odette didn't look. She trusted Tarhuinn to get them to the room in time.

Seeing their attacker would possibly induce more panic. To try and calm her racing heart, she went over the grips and strikes in her mind. Hopefully, there wasn't more than one attacker, but she would prepare herself regardless.

Making it to the forest room, Tarhuinn ran into the small woods a little ways. He hid the lantern behind one of the trees, but its warming glow remained readily visible. Tarhuinn ran out of the woods and towards the left wall of the entrance. After he set her down, he motioned for her to press herself up against the wall as he did the same.

In the blink of one's eyes, he unsheathed a dagger and had it at the ready. She upturned her gaze to his. An uneasy chill ran up her spine. He intended to kill the person in one swift strike. His expression held no mercy, and it seemed like he would attack her if she spoke to him. There was no doubt that he was consumed by murderous rage.

Hesitantly, she reached out her right hand to try and ease him, but approaching footsteps caused her to withdraw it. The point of an arrow made its presence known first as well as a medium blue hand. It looked fixed on the light behind the one tree. Slow and careful footsteps advanced. When the kelremm walked fully into the room, Tarhuinn remained deadly silent.

While the attacker continued forward, Tarhuinn crept up behind him. His steps matched the steps of the attacker so that his movements in the water wouldn't be detected. To Odette, it was both horrifying and thrilling to observe. It terrified her because she realized how easily her husband could sneak up on her if she was ever required to make the journey on her own; however, it was exciting because she could watch and learn. Unintentionally, he was giving her another lesson in combat.

The attacker was a few steps from the lantern. He was about to discover that they weren't hiding there. When he moved his next foot forward, Tarhuinn closed the distance and brought down his blade to strike. His blade almost made it into the male's heart if it weren't for the male acting on a split second. Bringing up his bow, he blocked the attack, but his weapon was ruined in the process. With a broken bow, he tossed it aside and gripped onto the arrow to defend himself.

Not fazed, Tarhuinn swept his left arm against the shaft of the arrow. Effectively knocking the weapon from the male's hands, he struck again with the dagger. Odette had barely caught him moving from a reverse grip to a forward hammer grip due to the quickness of the switch. The blade went to swipe across the attacker's chest as the attacker went to jump back. His footing betrayed him, however, and he collided with the base of the water path.

Water splashed around while the rest of his arrows left the quiver and flowed down the path. The attacker's arms drew across his chest and face before he curled his form up to better protect himself. "Wait! Please! I'll leave you two alone and won't come back; I swear!"

Swiftly, Tarhuinn reached down, tossed away the dagger that was strapped to the male's right leg and lifted the male by the front of his shirt. He slammed the attacker against the nearest tree. Pine needles scratched at the skin of the male and Tarhuinn's left arm.

"Like I would believe that, you worthless piece of trash. You nearly killed my wife! That action is only forgivable by death. You're lucky that I intend to give you a swift one but only if you answer my questions. Otherwise, I'll hold you out of the water so that your energy depletes itself before dipping you back in so that you can experience more than one cut from my blades."

"I'll answer your questions, but, please, they made me do it! I didn't have a choice! I'm the best fighter in this complex, so I was chosen recently to take care of questioners. If I had refused, my wife and newborn daughter would've been killed. You would've done the same if you were in my position."

"No, I wouldn't have. I would've killed the people trying to force me into such a situation."

"Well, maybe you could do it, but I hadn't been able to, and I still don't possess the strength for that. Please let me return to them. My best hope for them now is to prepare myself for when Tergii and Bimaa return. Otherwise, they'll die. Even if you kill me, they'll be killed to make an example."

"Why would they kill off a kelremm if they seemingly care so much about the population?"

Due to his feet barely touching the water, he drew a labored breath and took some time before he answered. Tarhuinn lowered him just a little more. "They would kill my daughter because they can easily replace one kelremm. At least, they claim that they can. Now promise me that you won't kill me if I continue to answer."

"You're in no position to order me around," Tarhuinn mentioned, his voice dripping with venom. A hand steadily rested on the upper part of his left arm. He only glanced for a second her way before he stared back at the defeated attacker. "Odette, step back. I don't want you too close to him."

"I think that you need to calm down, Tarhuinn. If he tries to attack again, you can easily take him out. You know that as well as I, especially since he has no weapons on him. I'm not pleased about him trying to kill us, but he was protecting his family. If you look closely enough, you can tell that he's being genuine."

"He attacked you, Odette! He needs to be killed for that!" Tarhuinn barked out, his hand now traveling up to the male's neck. "Now, stand back and let me continue."

"No, I'm not going to. You're losing control of yourself, and you're about to make a huge mistake. Think of it this way. If you kill him, his family will be put in more harm's way, and you'll have possibly the rest of this complex angered at you. More of them will come so that their loved ones aren't killed. If you keep him alive, perhaps, he'll be given a second chance. If that's the case, he'll come after us, but we know how he fights. We'll know the threat that targets us."

"That's assuming that he gets a second chance. Besides, don't you find it strange that Tergii and Bimaa are supposedly making these threats, but no other kelremm has come to this man's aid? If one kelremm is threatened, the complex reacts and does their best to help them. So, why was he seemingly thrown into the position of a sacrifice?"

At a loss for words, she glanced to the restrained male to urge him to defend himself. He got the hint and countered, "You don't understand. Two people may seem easy to beat, but even with your skill, I doubt that you could take them on. Those two have control over magic. They would wipe out at least half of us before we would be able effectively to wound them."

"What do you mean that they have control over magic?!" Tarhuinn shouted, slamming the male against the tree trunk once more.

A pained grunt left the male's lips. He coughed a few times before he spoke again. "They don't have magic themselves, but they have control over a mage. I don't know the characteristics of the mage, but they had the mage give us an example of their magic. The flames could've killed ten of us at once, and there are rumors that the mage has lived for centuries. Both the first and second complexes are lucky that they aren't close to those two. None of you have had to live in fear of their visits!"

Odette noted that Tarhuinn's gaze relaxed by a mere fraction, but he still intended to murder the male in front of him. "Tarhuinn, set him down, and we'll continue questioning him. I don't think that he's making this up. Will you please listen to me?"

In response, his hand now latched around the male's neck. He increased his grip before letting go of him. "You better answer everything truthfully, or I won't even consider my wife's suggestion of sparing you." A swift nod from the male was given to Tarhuinn. "Now, why would Tergii and Bimaa want anyone asking about them dead? Why would they instill such fear in all of you? It's completely unheard of for kelremm to do such things."

Taking a deep breath and exhaling, the male remained terrified. "I'm not certain why they take such actions. There are rumors, however. Some kelremm here think that they have found the secret to eternal youth and that we've been encountering the original authors rather than their descendents."

"We heard that same rumor from the trader," Odette voiced to Tarhuinn, who nodded in response and kept his gaze on the male.

"And, I'm presuming that no one has verified this rumor because it's too dangerous to ask Tergii and Bimaa," Tarhuinn pointed out as the scared male nodded. "And, how many questioners were there before us? Who before you did they send on the task of killing them?"

"There weren't many. You two are the first that any of us have seen. In the past, it is said that there were a total of four others, but you understand that most of our kind don't question the texts in our homes. Even we here don't question the books, but that's mainly because we're too afraid to, especially if it regards the five authors' texts. As for who was given the task before me, it was my father. He's the one who taught me how to use a bow and a little bit about a blade."

"I wonder if they were going to ask the same question as us," Odette muttered more to herself than to her partner. Looking to male, she asked, "Were those four killed, then?"

"Two of them were, but, apparently, the other two vanished in this house like the authors. They must've been killed along the way, though, since Tergii and Bimaa still visit us."

"That means that it's possible to find the secret passage without magic. And, you don't know where the passage is?" Tarhuinn questioned, his voice still anything but pleasant towards the male.

"No, I swear that I don't. None of us in this complex do. Even if we did, we wouldn't go down there. We know what we're dealing with, and we don't invite an early death to our homes."

"What about their ways to know about the other complexes? Do you know anything more about these spies or other passages?"

"No, I only know of the rumors that have spread among us. If that's all, may I please go now?"

Maintaining a look of hatred, Tarhuinn switched the dagger in his hand to hold it by the blade. He swiftly lifted the male up and pushed him away. With the attacker's back towards him, Tarhuinn reacted swiftly and brought the handle of the blade down against the back of the male's head. The sound of the blow made it seem like he had killed the male, but Odette noted that he was still breathing.

"He'll survive, but we can't have him running off before we find this entrance. I want to be out of here when he wakes back up. Otherwise, the rest of the complex might be on us, and, soon, they'll probably be wondering what's taking him so long," Tarhuinn explained as he picked up the male. After he had placed the male out of the forest and partially in the water path towards the entrance to the room, he came back and picked up their lantern. "Let's hurry and check these trees."

Stepping over the male, she made no argument and followed beside her partner. Odette did keep herself on alert, however, in case someone else decided to strike at them that evening. In a worst case scenario, they could always run for the window and head outside, but the climate out there wouldn't be too forgiving. A shiver ran up her spine just thinking about the biting cold.

Her attention, though, snapped back to the task at hand. That option wouldn't happen as long as they found the secret passage in time. They moved between the trees, and she would have to push back branches most of the time so that she wouldn't get too severely scratched by the needles. When they reached the center of the small woods, they spent more time on each tree since it was harder to see.

The current tree was being examined thoroughly and more so than the others. Tarhuinn pushed back some of the grass and tapped at the trunk more. A smirk pulled at his lips as he hit it harder. With the impact, even she could hear that the trunk was hollow. She reached her hands out to the needles and noted that they felt softer.

Standing up, Tarhuinn motioned for her to step back. As she did so, he reached his hands past the smooth needles and gripped the trunk. He tried to move it to the left, then the right. Both times, nothing happened, so he attempted to push it backwards, and, lastly, he pulled it towards him. A rumbling sound echoed throughout the room as the beds of trees started to move closer to each other. The water path that Tarhuinn was standing in grew bigger until the ground beneath him began to lower.

He took a couple of steps back while the descending ground revealed a passageway. Stone stairs spiraled downwards as the water trailed over them. Odette proceeded to take off her boots and socks. The cold water wouldn't feel welcoming on her feet, but her dry socks and boots would greet her on the next stone path. She placed them in her pack and stepped into the water.

About to take a step forward, she was tugged back. "Odette, I would pull us out of this, but we're far too deep in already. We'll most likely have someone trying to kill us from now on. The option to go back home and back out isn't possible anymore. To keep you safe, I won't tolerate you questioning me if I'm about to kill someone. You made a good point about me not ending his life, but I won't spare another no matter your argument.

"Hopefully, it won't be another kelremm forced into the position, but if we keep sparing them, there will be more out there to murder us. I'm not going to allow your life to be put on the line because of someone trying to gain sympathy. Tell me that you understand before we move on."

Finding the request or more like demand quite strict, she responded, "I don't think..."

"Tell me that you understand, Odette." His voice grew lower and nearly went into a growl. A warning look crossed his countenance. If she refused again, he would most likely use the nickname on her even though it would be foolish to weaken her when enemies could be on their tails. They would both need to be on their feet if they wished to deal with the authors, but his request was asking for too much. How could she even pretend to agree with that?

"I understand, but I don't agree with it. If you saw how you looked back there, you would comprehend where I'm coming from. You had lost control of yourself and weren't thinking straight. How can I agree to hand the reigns over to you after witnessing that display?"

"I was protecting you. That's what matters. That man had threatened your life. I was going to have him pay the proper price. In the end, though, I let him go because you reasoned with me. That was a onetime happening. The next person that comes after us most likely won't be him. I even doubt that it'll be someone from this complex since he was their best fighter.

"No, the next person will most likely be one of these spies or someone with more fighting experience. If we let someone like that go, we'll be putting ourselves under more risk. Maybe, you'll come up with a good reason to spare them, but my reason to kill them will be better because you'll be safer that way."

"How can you be sure of that? You're letting your emotions gain control of you. Saving them might be the better option. It might be more beneficial to us. If you throw my opinion out of the equation, you're losing a valuable perspective. Have trust in my word, not just yours."

"Yet, you don't trust my decisions."

"I might agree with you on some points. What I'm saying is that when I don't, I want you to hear me out. That's all I'm asking for. Whether you follow it or not is up to you. Please, give me that much. You've already limited how much you'll teach me on combat, so don't try to restrict my speech too."

An irritated sigh left his lips as he combed his right fingers through his locks. "So if I decide to kill an opponent even if you advise me not to, you won't intervene?"

"I ... yes. I just want you to hear my opinion. Beyond that, I'll let you make the choice." It wasn't the best of deals, but at least she had persuaded him not to silence her on such matters.

"Then, I'll agree," he uttered, turning to face her completely. He placed his right fingers under her chin and lifted her head up. His gaze softened a little. "I just don't want anyone to take you away from me again. The time with your parents was enough, and I don't wish to experience that again. I'll do what I have to in order to keep you by my side. Whenever I act out, it's only for you and your safety."

Grabbing his right hand, she moved it to her left cheek and rested against it. There was some heat to her cheeks at her action, but it would help calm him down more. “I know. I just don’t desire for you to lose yourself in frenzy. For right now, though, let’s head down those steps. Like you mentioned, we need to go before more come tonight.”

A soft kiss was placed on her forehead as he intertwined his hand with hers. Pulling away, he held the lantern up in his free hand and descended the steps with her. She tugged the lever and closed the entrance behind them.

Chapter Eighteen: Warmth before the Storm

Reaching the bottom of the stairwell, they were greeted by a long hallway; however, they could see a wooden door at the end of it. Pale light peeked through the cracks, and a cool breeze broke through. Odette hugged her cloak tighter around her and made a mental note to put on a second layer if they were to go outside. Thankfully, though, her feet were no longer in the cold water. She didn't know how Tarhuinn could tolerate it so well, but she supposed that kelremm were less sensitive to the cold since they had to be in water all of the time.

As they made their way down the path, they noted that there was a small room off to the side. There was a slanted bed for a kelremm, and there was a regular bed too. A wooden table and chairs were in the middle of the room while a small kitchen area and fireplace were against the back wall. The only strange part about the room was that it was covered in dust and cobwebs. "Why would they leave the room in this state? Wouldn't it be useful to utilize?" she asked, stepping in a little further.

"They might have better accommodations nearby, or they use this room as a trap if someone manages to find the secret entrance. I don't know the extents of magic, so this room could very well be laced with many traps for intruders. I say that we leave this room alone and camp somewhere else for the night. Right here, we're quite exposed, and I'd rather have the upper hand when we confront them."

Despite his plan sounding like the wiser choice, it was hard to give up a bed and warm fire when it was freezing. Maybe, that's what Tergii and Bimaa suspected, though. She reluctantly agreed. "Just let me put on another layer first. It's too cold for me to be wearing only this." In the end, they both pulled out dry clothes from their packs and put them over the ones that they were wearing.

Already, she felt warmer but not by much. She really wished that they would've been able to get one of the thicker cloaks, but it was no use dwelling on them. After she put on her socks and tied up her boots, she glanced around the room another time. "Even if it's enchanted, do you think that they left something in here that might give us a clue to their homes?"

"I doubt it, and I don't think that we should try to open any of those cabinets or drawers. We'll need to hope that whatever lies beyond that door will give us a clue. Otherwise, we're going to have to decide our next direction on guessing work, and we have a limited food supply unless we can find more along the way, so wandering around might ensure us an early death."

"We'll figure it out. We made it this far, and I already made a promise with you. I intend not to break it. We'll survive the journey and the encounter with these authors. If we worry about all of the negatives, we'll be weighed down by them and not find the answers."

A small smile touched his lips. "I suppose that you're right." He took up her right hand and headed towards the door before he reached for the door handle and pulled. When that didn't work, he pushed. That still did nothing. There was no keyhole for the door, but the door seemed to be locked. Frustrated, Tarhuinn released her hand and put more of his weight into it. Unfortunately, that achieved fruitless results. "It looks like we might have to force the door down."

"But, it might be enchanted. There's no place for a lock, yet it won't budge. I think that breaking it open would bode very ill for us. There has to be another way to open it," she mentioned as her eyes looked for anything that might help them. When she peered downwards, she squinted some and moved back her feet. There was something carved into the stone.

Squatting down, she examined the words. They were somewhat confusing, but they did give a way to open the door before them. "We need to find something of the door's master. At least, that's what this message says."

Glancing down and reading it, Tarhuinn remarked, "Those may be fake instructions, but it's unfortunately the only thing that we can go on. But, we don't even know this door's master. Nor, do we probably have something that belongs to them." He walked back towards the room. "We'll have to look over this area after all and hope to find something that'll work."

"Right," she answered before standing up and going after him. They investigated the room, though, cautiously. Drawers were taken out and cabinets opened. Bed sheets were pulled off while the mattress was flipped. Even the old ashes in the fireplace were searched. When none of those places produced anything, they were irritated and exhausted.

It was well into the night. They hadn't eaten much, and sleep was demanding attention. Figuring that by now the furniture was safe to interact with, Odette plopped herself down onto the old mattress. She rested her head and back against the stone wall while Tarhuinn grabbed the old pieces of firewood and tossed them into the fire. He was anxious to light it, but she assured him that they would most likely be fine.

With great hesitation, he grabbed the firesteel and small piece of chert. Striking it, a spark flew onto the old wood. Flames grew, warmth began to envelope the room and nothing struck out at them. A relieved sigh escaped his lips before he rested himself on the slanted bed. He rested his chin in the palms of his hands. "Perhaps, we're going about this the wrong way. Maybe, it's something much simpler than what we're thinking of."

"What are you proposing?"

"We need to give the door something of its master's. Well, we could presume that whoever created that door also created this room. So, everything in this room would belong to that master. We could bring the door one of the drawers. If that doesn't work, the door itself is something that its master owned. I overlooked it before because it seemed too easy, but, with our present luck, we might as well try it."

"I agree, but if it works, can we still enjoy the fire for a little bit more? I know that isn't wise, but we just lit it, and we might not get another fire for awhile."

"We'll stay a little bit longer, but we'll leave before it goes out. Starting it might have not done anything, but a spell may react when it dies. I don't want us to be caught in that if it does."

"I understand. Let's test out your plan and go from there." She got up from the bed and grabbed one of the drawers. Tarhuinn took it from her before they headed back to the door.

Holding it up before the wooden object, he stated, "I have brought you something of your master's." Instantly, the drawer was blown from his hands and impacted the stone behind them. It broke into several pieces while some of the wood floated down the water path and beyond the door. Since that didn't work, he announced, "Then, you yourself are something of your master's." That time, the force attacked him directly.

"Tarhuinn!" she shouted before she darted over to him. Crouching besides him, she grabbed his right forearm and helped him to sit up. "Are you alright?"

"I'm fine, Odette. Looks like we'll need to test something else out, though," he muttered, getting to his feet and bringing her up with him. He headed back to the small room with her, and they retook their seats. She was tempted to fall asleep on the bed, however.

Forcing herself to keep her eyes open, she thought over the message again. "Maybe, it means something directly from its master. Like a hair sample."

"If that's the case, Odette, we'll be lucky if we can find such a thing."

"Not necessarily, this master probably lived here as you suggested. Everyone sheds hair, so we might find an old strand around here somewhere. It'll be hard to locate if there is one, but it's the best that we can do at the moment. I'm not giving up."

"Then, let's continue searching. We might've missed something." Getting up from his seat, he groaned a bit and drew his right hand to his back. Before she could ask, he spoke, "I'm fine. My back will just be sore for a little while. I should be fine later in the day tomorrow or sooner."

Giving a hesitant nod, she turned away from him and began to look for something from the door's master. They searched the same places again but more thoroughly. Her attention went back to the bed. She checked the sheets before she flipped over the mattress once more. Odette squinted and crouched.

Extending out her right index finger and thumb, she pulled something off. It was a long grey hair. Neither of them had such a color nor did supposedly Tergii or Bimaa. There was a possibility that it might be the mage that was traveling with them, but it could also be the door's master's hair. She held it up and turned to her partner. "I think that I might've found our way out of here."

A small smile tugged at Tarhuinn's lips, and he let out a sigh of relief. "Thank goodness." He took her hand, and they made their way back to the door.

Standing in front of it, she stepped in front of her husband. She refused to let Tarhuinn present the hair. "Let me. You don't need to be in worse pain." He was about to speak, but she shook her head. "No, I don't want to hear it. I'll be fine." Reluctantly, he agreed, but he stood behind her in case the force shot out at them. Holding the hair to the door, she inquired, "Does this belong to your master?" No force came at them. Instead, the door slowly creaked open.

Chapter Nineteen: Snow Covered

On the other side of the door, the water path flowed into a larger stream. Snow covered the ground and fallen tree branches while the pines blocked out some of the night sky. The clouds overhead did well to hide most of the moon, giving them little light to go by. "I guess that we follow the stream," she muttered, not wishing to talk loudly in case there was some dangerous animal nearby or something else. Or, maybe, they would get lucky, and they would find the homes to be quite close to their current location. "Unless kelremm can walk in the snow," she continued softly.

"No, it may be another form of water, but it's not enough for a kelremm. The water has to be in liquid form. The only issue that concerns me is this mage. What if the mage could form a temporary stream to guide them to somewhere else?"

"Wouldn't that leave some effect on the terrain?"

"Yes, but it's been a few weeks since they've been here. More snow might've covered their tracks, but again that's just an overly cautious solution. If it's the case, we won't find out unless we camp out here, and I personally don't want to be so exposed in these woods."

"Then, let's follow the stream down some and set up a camp for us. We both need rest if we're to continue tomorrow." She received a simple nod from him, and they let the stream guide them. Odette hopped onto the snow covered ground and was doing her best to avoid snapping any dried wood. Alerting something out there wouldn't do either of them any good. Her mind wasn't helping either since her imagination was recalling tales from childhood.

There was the tale of the snow pixies, who would lure humans into their homes at night. They would promise eternal gifts of warmth and food to lost souls. Once the human had walked into their snowy cave, they would be killed and served as a feast for the hungry creatures. It was a gruesome tale, but parents told it so that their children wouldn't wander off into the snow. She only hoped that it was a story and not based on an actual account. Of course, she wouldn't follow a snow pixie anywhere.

Once they couldn't see the wooden door, they stopped. "We should be safe here for the night, but we should try to gather some of the twigs and needles to make a dry bed for ourselves. We can lay one of our cloaks over them, and we should do so under those branches. If it snows while we sleep, we'll want some cover for ourselves."

Agreeing with him, she started to brush away the snow in the area. Her hands weren't too fond of the work, but they would enjoy the warmer bed and makeshift blankets later. Of course, she didn't back too far into the woods because of her own fear and Tarhuinn telling her where to stop. If something were to surprise them and catch her, he wouldn't be able to make it far. Thankfully, he handed her one of his daggers for protection against such a happening.

It felt comforting to have a weapon concealed safely on her. He had detached the sheath as well from the belt so that she could store it in one of her boots. She had placed it on the outer side of her right leg in such a manner that it wouldn't bother her too much when moving around. Granted, it still took some time getting used to it, yet it reminded her that if something did attack, she would be ready.

When they had cleared away the snow, they put more nearby twigs and needles onto the bed. It would be softer than the stone that they had been sleeping on previously. If only it wasn't so cold. Once it was finished, she reluctantly took off her cloak and laid it over the bed. Tarhuinn took off his as they both lied down. He draped it over them and allowed her to rest her head on his chest. Since they were out in the open, they had agreed to take shifts. For tonight, he would watch first.

Due to her exhaustion, she fell asleep rather quickly. Tarhuinn combed his right fingers through her light blonde locks, a light smile on his lips while he did so. He was quite pleased that she was growing accustomed to him, yet she still became embarrassed about things that a husband and wife would normally do. It was adorable.

In some respects, he was grateful that she had convinced him to go on their journey. Not only would he possibly get more time with her but also he loved the expressions that she would bear. He had been smirking when they traveled through the area with the water pixies. Fear had been evident on her facial features, and she had understood that she could only rely on him for safety.

During her training session, she bore a look of determination, which he now admired. It had worried him at first, thinking that she might use it against him. After her guarantee that she would keep her promise to him, however, he knew that it would only serve him positively.

Before they had left the secret passage, she had even displayed a clear worry for his health. If they didn't have a limited supply of medical supplies, he would've had her rub salve on his back just so that he could feel her delicate hands glide over his skin. His memories of their last kiss filled his mind, and he instinctively trailed his fingers over to where his marks were. He pulled back at her shirts. A smirk tugged at his lips upon seeing them. When they healed, he would make sure to place another two on her.

His thoughts were pulled from such desires when a nearby snap alerted him. Carefully, he moved Odette off of him and rested her head on the bed. He sat up and had his left hand on one of his daggers. Tarhuinn glanced behind him and to where the sound came from. Peeking out from behind the tree were two glowing eyes. They reminded him of a pale full moon, but he made sure not to be distracted by them for long.

The creature began to advance slowly. Little white hands grasped the side of the tree trunk as thin strands of white hair fell down from its sickly looking head. Its parched lips parted to let a thin snake's tongue slither out. It moved its hands from the trunk to the ground, and its white tail carried it quicker across the snowy floor.

Tarhuinn unsheathed a dagger, preparing for its strike. It stopped a few feet away and raised its hands. "I don't wisssh to harm you. I only wisssh for a piece of that human there. A few ssstrandsss of her hair will do. They look ssso yummy. I haven't had human hair in ssso long. I'll leave you be otherwissse."

"Are there more of you nearby?" he asked, not letting up his grip on the blade.

"No, thisss isss my territory. If you go down further, you'll encounter more of usss, but we only come out at night. We mean no trouble, except to asssk of sssome deliciousss hair. It's nice to sssee human hair rather than jussst kelremm hair."

He didn't care for how the creature was looking at Odette, but he controlled himself not to strike. Who knew what he would alert if he did. Besides, the creature seemed to hold valuable information. "You've seen other kelremm out here? What did they look like?"

"I'll tell if you promissse me four ssstrandsss of her hair."

A glare set upon his countenance as his grip on the knife tightened more. He felt that he might crush the handle of the blade. "Fine," he practically spat out. Tarhuinn was disgusted with the trade, but the creature might know where Tergii and Bimaa went. "Now, answer my questions."

"I've ssseen three kelremm travel thisss part about once a month. They all wear white cloaksss, but the one unfortunately keepsss their head ssshaven. The other, with the hair to her kneesss, usssually sssuppliesss me with a few ssstrandsss. For the third, ssshe hasss jaw length hair and eyesss like the darkessst night sky. Unlike the firssst two, who are tall, she isss rather ssshort."

That was the same description that the trader had given them of Tergii and Bimaa. The third was presumably a mage, but this creature said that she was a kelremm. It wasn't possible for kelremm to have magic, though. At least, there were no accounts of such a thing. Had the members of the third complex known the mage to be a kelremm and just didn't tell him. Was that a secret they were forced to keep? Right now, it just wasn't adding up. "Did this third one cast magic at any point?"

"I'll need two more ssstrandss."

Almost, he lashed out at the creature. He glanced to Odette and found her to be asleep still. She had curled up into a ball to keep herself probably warmer. "Fine, you have a deal," he growled out as he motioned the creature to continue.

"I have heard the third dissscusss magic with the other two, but I have never ssseen her cassst any."

Tarhuinn reluctantly reached over to his beloved and held onto six of her strands. The creature didn't deserve to touch any strand of her beautiful hair, but the consequence of breaking the promise might put her into more danger. That, he couldn't have, so he plucked them from her head.

She shifted quite a bit in her sleep. He handed the six strands over to the creature, who took them eagerly. It slithered back into the forest while Odette rolled onto her stomach to get comfortable. Tarhuinn moved her to lie on his lap as he remained sitting up and alert for more things roaming in the night.

Chapter Twenty: A Strike of a Smile

Night rolled along, and Tarhuinn didn't wake her up yet. He would give her a little more time to sleep. Besides, he enjoyed watching her sleep even though he was exhausted himself. There was also the issue of the third kelremm. It would make sense if a kelremm mated with a human mage for a mage kelremm to exist, but there were complexities with such a pairing. There were warnings in some of the books that a kelremm should avoid mating with a mage, and so no one to his knowledge had ever attempted such a pairing.

Still, evidence was pointing to the five authors already being questionable with regards to that missing phrase in their texts. If anyone had gone through with a pairing like that, it would probably be them. Perhaps, the warning had been created as a lie so that no other mage kelremm would be born, but it would be a gamble to make.

Should a kelremm mate with a human mage, there was a high chance that the child would be killed after birth due to the mage's magic counteracting the child's need for human life energy. The magic would protect its owner regardless of the owner's wishes. In the books, there was no measure written to take against the magic's protectiveness.

Thankfully, it was easy to tell a mage child from a regular child. The books told that a mage child would bear the mark of magic on a portion of their face until they reached the age of ten. That fact he knew to be at least partially true as he had seen such a child during his wait for his chosen. It had been on the child's left cheek, and he had seen the light blue mark when the child had turned to glance his way.

A shift on his lap, though, caused his focus to turn back to Odette. She had more of her torso on him, and both of her hands gripped at his pants' legs. There was a frown on her lips before she mumbled something in her sleep. Was she having a nightmare? To try and soothe her, he combed his right fingers through her locks and leaned down to her. He placed a chaste kiss on top of her head, which caused her to shift again.

She moved her head up some. Her eyes blinked open tiredly. "Tarhuinn? Is ..." She let out a small yawn, and he couldn't help but smile at how cute she looked. "Is it time for me to wake up?"

"No, you can rest a little longer. I just thought that you were having a nightmare."

"I was," she muttered, glancing away from him now. She could still picture the beginning of it, but, luckily, he had awakened her before it had really started. "To be honest, I'd rather get up now. I don't want to go back to it."

"What was it about?"

Odette shook her head. "I'll tell you later. Let's switch places for now. You need your rest too." She went to sit up but got pulled back down by him. He was lying on his right side and held her back to his chest. His warm breath hit the back of her neck, sending a chill up her spine and heat to her cheeks.

"In that case, I'll take my turn, but wake me if you need me or if you hear something moving about nearby." He relaxed against her and nuzzled his face into the left crook of her neck. Her cheeks warmed up more. Despite that, she hoped that she wouldn't fall back asleep. It would be easy to given how she was, and she doubted that Tarhuinn would let her go.

For the moment, though, she would probably be safe from the arms of sleep. Her nightmare's beginning played back in her mind. She could clearly see the fallen bodies as Tarhuinn stood in the middle of them. Crimson had decorated the blades of his daggers while his back had faced away from her. Even in her dream, she had understood that he was protecting her, but the sight before her had been terrifying.

When he had turned to her, she had noted the blood running down the corners of his mouth. A smile had crossed his lips while his sharper teeth had glistened with bits of red. His dark blue eyes had held an overly pleased look before he had begun to advance towards her. She had been awoken by that point, but the image of his face had been burned into her mind.

By that look alone, she had known that he had lost control of himself. Even if he had been protecting her, she had been worried about what he would do after the attackers had been disposed of. Her left fingers trailed up to her right shoulder. She slid them under her shirts and winced upon hitting the marks. Moving them more gently, she trailed over them.

His teeth had touched her skin there. A mental picture of his smile from the nightmare flashed in her mind. Quickly, she pulled his arms from her and rolled herself away. Getting to her feet, she darted over to the nearest tree and collapsed onto her knees. Her arms wrapped around her stomach as she hunched over and relieved the nausea.

Hands rested on the sides of her head. She practically jumped until she heard Tarhuinn saying that it was only him. His hands held back her hair before she ridded herself of another wave. It was humiliating to have him see her in her present state, but the image plagued her. The nausea continued a few more times before she just sat there and caught her breath.

"Come. Let's go clean you up," he voiced gently before helping her to her feet. She remained hunched a little bit as he walked her over to the water. Seating her down, he told her to rinse her mouth and drink some. He swiftly grabbed his pack and brought it over.

Kneeling beside her, he rummaged through it until he removed a small container. When he saw her sitting motionless, he set the container aside and grabbed a spare cloth. He dipped it into the water before he rested his free fingers under her chin. After he turned her to face him, he dabbed at her mouth and didn't speak; he allowed her to recompose herself.

Setting down the cloth, he asked, "Are you able to drink?" He received a light nod from her before she turned to the water and brought some of it to her lips. Only when she was finished did he rinse the cloth off. Once he placed the cloth aside, he opened the container and pulled out a mint leaf. "Here, chew on this. It'll help your stomach." She complied and took it. "Now, let us return to our bed, and you can tell me about your nightmare. I won't take no for answer as I'm assuming that it was the cause of this. Or, was it something else?"

"You're right. It was the nightmare," she admitted quietly, not meeting his gaze.

He got to his feet and lifted her up with him. Picking up the pack after putting the container back in, he brought her over to their bed. Once he placed the items down, he seated himself and placed her between his legs. Her back rested against his chest while his right arm wrapped gently around her waist. His left fingers intertwined with her left ones. "Tell me."

Hesitant, she remained quiet. How would he react to her nightmare? Would he grow angry at her for imagining him in such a light? She wanted to curl up into a ball and be alone for a bit. Tarhuinn wouldn't permit that, however, especially since they were in unknown territory.

"Odette, please tell me. I wish to know what troubles you."

"It was ... about you." She brought her knees closer to her chest and wished that his arm wasn't around her waist. "You had killed many kelremm and had this chilling smile on your lips." His hand tightened around hers for a brief second, but she could feel him tense against her back.

"And, this caused you to be sick?" His voice was calm, but there was an underlying tone present. She couldn't tell if it was hurt or anger. It might've been both.

"No. I looked at the ... marks that you had given me. An image of the contents on your teeth flashed through my mind, and I recalled your teeth gliding against my skin." She heard him sigh before his grip on her was released. Within moments, she was facing him. His hands rested on her cheeks while his eyes held clear pain in them.

"You wound me by thinking that I would sully your beautiful skin with the blood and flesh of others. I would make sure that I was clean before I touched you. Those marks upon your skin are my signs of affection for you, and no one will defile them. As for the nightmare, understand that I would never let my rage consume me to the point where I would come after you to kill you. I imagine that was your real fear for my smile. That fury will only be unleashed on others if they try to take you from me."

Giving him a weak nod, she pushed against his hands and rested her forehead on his chest. She heard the steady beat of his heart. It soothed her some, but his words were only somewhat comforting. No matter what he told her, he didn't have to see that smile upon his own face. He didn't know what he truly looked like when he became controlled by rage. Odette hoped that the oncoming day would draw her focus elsewhere. "You should get back to sleep, Tarhuinn. I'll be fine now."

"Are you certain?"

"Yes, thank you for your help earlier. I'll wake you when the sun rises." She received a disinclined nod from him, but he let her go. As she seated herself beside him, he lied down and went back to sleep. Odette brought her knees to her chest, allowing the gentle sound of the water to keep her mind at ease.

Chapter Twenty One: Upon a Rumored Tale

Dawn steadily came and met Odette's brown orbs. A smile rested on her lips as she could feel the beams break through some of the clouds and trees. They weren't too warm, but they were more welcoming than the arms of night. She loved how the light hit the running water and caused it to sparkle. The scenery took on a new, inviting life.

She turned to her partner, about to wake him up. An image from her nightmare flashed before her eyes, however, and she withdrew her hand back. A frown dominated her mouth until she pushed the picture away. Odette couldn't let that nightmare conquer her mind. For their journey, she needed to be comfortable around him. They were a team, and they would have to work together to get through whatever obstacles lied ahead.

Perhaps, one of them could go forward on their own. The journey would take longer, though, and nights would offer little sleep. Besides, he was her husband. She felt the ring around her finger to remind herself more. Despite being terrified of his violent side, she needed to trust him. Her nightmare was only putting doubt in her mind. It was just that, a nightmare and nothing else.

Reaching towards him again, she gently shook him. He shifted some in his sleep before he rolled onto his back and opened his eyes. His dark blues glanced up to her. A smile fell upon his lips. "Beautiful." Heat rose to her cheeks. It came even more so when his right hand rose to her left cheek and brushed against it. "This is one advantage to having our bed where the sun can reach. It highlights your beauty in an exceptional way, my ..."

Quickly, she threw her hands over his mouth. A questioning look crossed his eyes. Just as swiftly, she pulled back her hands and apologized. "Sorry, but thank you for the compliments. Still you shouldn't call me by that nickname now. We might have a long walk ahead of us."

A light chuckle escaped his lips as he sat up. It reminded her of smooth honey being poured into a warm winter drink. "Forgive me, I got ahead of myself. Now isn't the time for that."

"Tomorrow morning, I'm stealing my cloak back before you wake up," she mumbled before she got off of the makeshift bed and stood up. Another pleasing chuckle reached her ears. To get his mind off of such a thing, she asked, "Are we going to be eating while moving?"

"Yes, I think that staying here any longer would prove unwise. We may not be able to see that door, but we're still close enough to it. Let's put more distance between it and us." Standing up himself, he lifted up the cloaks and handed hers back to her.

Readily, she tied it around her and hugged it to her body after she draped the hood over her head, which finally had some protection against the biting cold. Tarhuinn did the same before they put on their packs and started to head down the stream more. He took out some dried apricots and meat. The taste of the seasoned meat almost caused her to gobble it down, but she forced herself to savor it. They probably wouldn't eat again until dusk.

The sun rose higher in the air as they continued downstream. She avoided the dried twigs and fallen branches. Her attention was also focused on their surroundings. Something could easily hide behind any of the many trees in the area. One of those things could be that snake creature that Tarhuinn told her about along the way. Thankfully, he mentioned that they only came out at night, but she kept herself alert regardless. There might be one who stayed out later to try and get some hair.

According to Tarhuinn, they weren't a real threat, but, in her opinion, it would be better to avoid them. Anything that saw them could always report their presence to another. It was relieving to know that they were headed down the right path, but the part about the third kelremm possibly being a mage was disconcerting. If the authors had found a way around the issue with a kelremm and human mage mating, then what other things had they discovered a solution to?

One thing after another seemed to be added to their list of concerns. At least, Tarhuinn understood that the five authors couldn't be trusted. The discovery only begged the question of what else in the texts was questionable or hiding some secret.

They halted their movement. Ahead of them was a fork in the stream. The trees blocked the view, so they couldn't tell if the two paths met up again. Movement behind one of the nearby stones caught Odette's attention. She stepped closer to her partner. Her gaze didn't shift from the rock. "Tarhuinn, there's something there," she warned, pointing to the place slightly.

Instantly, he went on alert. He grabbed her left arm and moved her to stand as close as she could without getting in the water. A blade rested in his left hand. Small translucent wings flicked out from the sides of the rock while a tiny head popped up. Long strands of white hair draped down, and skin as pale as the snow covered its body. Eyes, a very light blue and almost white, stared up at them.

Blood drained from Odette's face. It was a snow pixie; it had to be. The only strange thing was that it was out during the day, not night like in the tale. Maybe, it wasn't an accurate account. She would keep her distance, though, until she learned of the pixie's intentions.

"State what you want," Tarhuinn ordered as the pixie flew up from her hiding place.

"I saw your human and was interested. I've never seen one before, but I've heard tales of their appearance. She's prettier than I expected a female human to look like."

Tensing up more, Odette prepared herself to reach for the blade in her boot. Tarhuinn kept a firm grip on her while his gaze remained threatening. "Is that all? Or, is there something else?" he inquired, eyeing the pixie for a sign of attack.

"Well, I'm a guard to this part of the forest. We're not allowed to let unwanted visitors past. Technically, we're supposed to give a surprise ambush, but I couldn't help myself from spotting your human. Maybe, we can arrange something to permit you both passage. My king and queen would love to view a human. None have come through these parts in ages, or so my leaders tell me."

"And if we refuse?" he questioned, noting that Odette was eyeing her right boot like it was a prized jewel.

"In that case, I'll attack and so will the other pixies. You should know that we can be quite the killers when provoked. You might take out a good number of us, but, in the end, you'll both die. It'll be a slow, painful death. And, it would be a waste of a pretty human. Your other option is to follow me, and we can negotiate something. I can guarantee that if you come with me, neither of you will die by our attack."

If only Tarhuinn could walk in snow, they could get around the pixies. Of course, that would mean that it would be harder to find Tergii and Bimaa. She didn't want to go with the pixie. Maybe, they wouldn't be eaten, but she didn't think that the arrangement would be a completely positive one. "Who told you to block visitors? And, how do you distinguish between wanted and unwanted? What are you leaving out?" she asked, gaining the courage to talk to the creature.

A serious expression covered the pixie's countenance. "They're individuals who we despise but can't harm. If you come, your questions will be answered. Otherwise, you face our attack. Please, decide. I won't give you too much more time to choose."

Glancing up to him, she wanted to tell him not to consider. They should fight, but that was her fear talking. The gruesome tale was clouding her judgment. Another memory of the nightmare formed before her eyes. She saw that smile again. Odette clenched her hands and bit her bottom lip; she had to trust him. "I'll leave the decision to you, Tarhuinn."

Surprised, he swept his gaze over her. He saw how her hands trembled lightly and noticed how she looked to the pixie with terror. If he declined the offer, the pixies would strike. Realistically, he could handle a good number of them, but some would get past and reach Odette. She wasn't skilled enough to deal with a small, speedy opponent. To make matters worse, there would be well over one going after her.

Like with the snake, he was put into a situation that he despised. The pixie was obviously only interested in Odette. If it had merely been him, he would've been swarmed. That meant that whatever arrangement was made, it would probably only concern her. Her life was ensured not to be threatened by an attack, but she could live and still be injured.

Even though he would like to think that he could take on a whole colony of pixies, he knew that was an unrealistic assessment of himself. To keep her ultimately alive, he would have to surrender them both to the mercy of the creature before them. Sheathing his blade, he agreed. "We'll follow you to your king and queen under the condition that neither of us is harmed."

"There will be no conditions added. You follow, or you die."

Practically growling, he responded, "Fine. Lead the way." Back to being cheerful, the pixie nodded and signaled them to follow. As they ventured forward, more pixies made themselves known. The countless pairs of eyes observed them. Hopefully, they would both be alright.

Chapter Twenty Two: A Court with Pixies

Since they were heading onto the land that was between the two streams, Tarhuinn picked Odette up and carried her across. He also did so because it would be harder for the pixies to take her away from him. His secure grip didn't go unnoticed by her, but she didn't mind it. They had no idea what arrangement would be formed, and, among all of the snow pixies, she felt safer being held by him.

When they reached the land, there was a thin stream, which trickled from the center of the land. Tarhuinn walked one step at a time to keep his feet in the small path. Even then, his feet were nearly going out of the water. No doubt, escaping the pixies if need be would be all the harder.

She noticed small heads pop up from behind stones or out from the sides of trees. The sun reflected off of their snowflake-like veins, which covered all of their body except their face. They all glittered under the light, and only thin dried leaves, used as clothes, dampened the sparkle of their reflective skin.

At the center, the trees formed a circle, but the stream continued its straight path. White rose bushes surrounded the perimeter of the circle while at the very center was a single stone column. Twigs and branches wrapped around it. At the top, there were two thrones made out of twigs. Dried rose leaves served as cushions for the two royal pixies.

In the chair to her right sat the king. The snowflake-like veins were more intricate on him, and a dried leaf skirt wrapped around his hips, flowing down to barely touch his knees. Long white locks descended to his chest while a twig and leaf crown sat atop his head.

As for the queen, the dried leaves wrapped around her chest and descended down into a form fitting dress. Like the king, she bore a crown and had more detailed veins. Her hair fell past her hips. Both had large pale blue, nearly white, wings extending from their backs.

Their pixie guide bowed to her rulers before she pointed to Odette. “My king and queen, I have brought the unwanted visitors to us. As you can see, the one is a human. I thought that she might be of interest to you both.”

“Thank you, Ilexa. You may wait nearby to hear of our decision. A human is a rare treat for us,” the king voiced, his light blue eyes traveling from the pixie to Odette and Tarhuinn. “What a lovely match,” he mused as he sat a little straighter on his throne. “Still, you may set your partner down, kelremm. We’ll not steal her away from you.”

Tarhuinn didn’t listen. Letting out a light laugh, which gave off the image of snow’s first fall, the queen reassured, “We promise that we won’t harm your wife. We only wish for her to come closer so that we can see her.”

Odette rested her left hand on his shoulder. She gave him a simple nod to indicate that it would be best to listen even though she didn’t want to go anywhere near the pixie royals. If Tarhuinn disobeyed them again, though, their polite demeanors might fade.

Hesitantly, he put her on her feet on the snow. Slowly, she took careful steps towards the pair. To not cause insult, she bowed lightly to them. When she brought her head back up, the queen was directly in front of her. A frightened squeak left Odette’s lips as she jumped back some.

Another laugh exited the queen’s lips. “You bear such perseverance, yet you’re greatly terrified of my kind. Still, you stand before us. Is this because of that human’s tale? The one where we eat humans after bringing them to our caves? Do you see any caves around you?” A tiny grin was on her pale lips as she flew back over to her chair and seated herself once more.

“Well, yes, I’ve heard of it. And, there are no caves, but how do you know about that?”

“My king and I have been around a long time. That tale has existed nearly as long. It was spread by us after all and served to protect our kind. We whispered it into the ears of humans while they slept, and it eventually spread around until humans feared us. Stories are a useful weapon if you craft them as such.”

"You must have questions, though. As does your husband," the king pointed out, glancing between them. "We'll answer those inquiries upon forming an agreement for your passing. We know why you have come to this forest as some scouts of ours have informed us of the chat that your husband had last night with the haasna. So, you must know the danger that we're putting ourselves in for seeing you. You both should understand that your passage will come at a fair price and that it'll involve you, my dear." His attention locked onto Odette.

"What would you have me do?" she questioned, her mind coming up with a list of horrid things. Even if the pixies had made up that gruesome tale, it didn't mean that they weren't capable of other atrocious acts.

"You both have heard of the mage that travels with the two authors. This mage is a threat to my kind, and the only reason why my wife and I agreed to stop all unwanted visitors for those three. Their fire magic would wipe out my kind very easily. We could've moved, but this has been our home for centuries, and we won't abandon it because of those wretched three. By offering you passage, that mage will most likely kill some of my kind as punishment. So before they come back and discover our betrayal, we'll need protection from our own mage."

"I don't even know where a mage would be," answered Odette, wondering how she would accomplish what the king was implying.

"We've heard rumors of where one lives. We've never approached the place, though, because of these rumors. Down by the lake, there is a cabin. Smoke rises from the chimney every so often, indicating that someone does live there. As to who, we haven't checked," the king began before Tarhuinn cut him off.

"And, why haven't you checked? What do these rumors say?" His hands were resting near his dagger belt while his tone took on a hostile one. It looked as though he would pull Odette back and start attacking.

This time, the queen spoke. “We haven’t confirmed the person because the rumors speak ill of them. This mage is said to be unstable unless confronted by someone of his tastes. My husband and I prefer not to have our scouts killed if we can prevent it, so we have had them keep their distance and ask creatures in the nearby vicinity that have traveled closer to the cabin.

“This supposed mage moved in several months ago. The haasna that lives closest to the cabin tells us that this mage brings in a woman once every three weeks. She told our scouts that the mage comforts the woman for a time before he grows an appetite for them. I won’t go into the details that the haasna described, but this is why a human woman is important. Your looks are also a benefit to us.”

Blood drained from Odette’s face, and she felt like she might faint. “W-why would y-you w-want som-someone like th-that to pro-protect your k-kind?” she stuttered out as what they desired became very clear.

“And, how would you expect her to get that man over to your side?!” Tarhuinn shouted, stepping forward. “You’re condemning my wife to a terrible death! No less, you ask her to give herself over to this man before she’s murdered! I’ll not permit that!” He was by now directly in front of the king. A dagger was pointing between the king’s eyes, but the royal remained calm.

“If you try to strike me, you’ll be blinded before that blade leaves a mark on me. You may be skilled, but you shouldn’t underestimate a pixie king. Now, put down your blade, kelremm, before we attack. Your wife will be guaranteed a permanent meeting with death, then.”

“Your threat falls deaf upon my ears,” Tarhuinn growled, raising the blade.

Swiftly, Odette ran over to him and grasped his arm. “Tarhuinn, stop! Please! They’ve made it clear that this is the only way to get past them. If we fight, we’ll be killed. You saw how many of them there are.

"We can't take them all; you know that! So please, calm down. I don't like this plan, but we have to keep pushing forward. Like you stated before, we can't go back now. Tergii and Bimaa will have us one way or another unless we get to them and catch them off guard."

"I'll not have another man possibly touch you, Odette! That's unacceptable. You're mine. You're my wife. I won't listen to any more ridiculous proposals. Now, let go of me, my chosen!"

Her legs grew weak, and her body wished to fall against him. Odette lost her grip on him before she collapsed to the ground on her knees. She looked up to the pixie royals. Using all of her strength and fighting against the urge to agree with her partner, she told them, "Please, knock him out. He's not thinking rationally. Please, don't kill him."

An enraged expression fell on Tarhuinn's countenance. "You would break our agreement?" he asked in a harsh and hurt voice, but her words distracted him long enough. Before he could attack a single pixie, the queen blew a wind towards his face.

His dark blue eyes landed upon Odette. She couldn't meet fully his disappointed and pained gaze. He fell backwards and impacted the snow. The soft substance puffed up into the air as he grew unconscious. Thankfully, his feet remained in the water, and no further damage was done to him.

Unable to bring herself to her feet, Odette closed her eyes for a moment. She focused on regaining her breath and fought back the pain that swelled in her body. Going against him after the use of the nickname had been like jumping into a roaring fire. It bit at her skin before it traveled throughout her entire body. Odette brought her hands up to her arms. Her gaze focused on her unconscious partner.

He looked peaceful enough. His breath was steady, and the rage in his eyes was sealed off. One of his daggers lied nearby: a few centimeters from his fingers. Despite the quiet and calm that seemed to take over the area, she knew that the consequences of her actions would be great. When he woke up, a beast ensnared by the burning flames of outrage would most likely greet her.

Earlier that morning, he had explained to her that he wouldn't turn that fury onto her, but it was so easy to replace the image of the murdered kelremm in her dream with the pixies. It was simple to see him attack her with that sickening grin. Despite the horrific images piling in her mind, she knew that she had made the right decision. If he had attacked, they would both be dead or soon to be dead.

Perhaps, there would've been another way. They could've remained by the door and waited for Tergii and Bimaa; they could've planned a surprise attack and taken out the mage first before the mage could cast a counterattack. Tarhuinn, though, had to stay in the water. Due to that weakness, a sneak attack would be near impossible. The outcome would've probably been the same had he fought against the pixies.

Taking in a deep breath before exhaling, she clenched the fabric of her pants. She looked up to the pixie queen. "What exactly did you do to him?"

"I placed him into a winter's sleep. As the snow pixie queen, I'm gifted with such a power. I would've used it long ago on that mage with Tergii and Bimaa if it weren't for their magic's protection. But, don't worry; he'll awake by mid-afternoon, but we'll have him bound by then. We can't have him chasing after you in a rampage. As I'm sure you know, his temper will destroy you both if he isn't watched carefully."

"I'm aware of that," Odette answered, quietly. She received a nod from the queen before Tarhuinn's daggers were ordered to be removed from him. As the pixies undid his weapon's belt and picked up the lone dagger, she called out, "Wait! Let me take them with me. They might be useful against this mage."

The king gave her a look as though she were a foolish child. "You're to bring him back to us if he truly is a mage. You can't convince a mage to work for you at the point of a blade. You'll be killed before your blade ever reaches him. Besides, threatening him with death would be senseless. A dead mage will serve us no purpose against the other."

"It would only be meaningless if he were to discover that I had no choice in keeping him alive," Odette countered, finding an extra means of protection only a benefit to her mission.

"As soon as you mention that you want him to serve under us, he'll understand the situation. He'll understand that you made a deal with us. From that deal, he'll make the connection that we threatened your life and that your only option is to bring him to us. That's why should you ask him to come here at the end of a blade, you'll only end up killing yourself."

"If he'll understand that connection and he kills me, wouldn't he come after all of you next? You did mention that he was unstable if dealing with anyone outside of his tastes. He'll be quite angered if he learns that pixies sent me over."

"Perhaps, but would a man who seemingly can't handle interactions with anyone outside of his liking really travel out of his way to deal with pixies, who only sent him a beautiful young woman who has yet to consummate her marriage. If anything, the only one who'll anger him is you."

She froze and felt a light dose of heat hit her cheeks. "How did ..."

"Our scouts have told us of how easily you get embarrassed around your husband," the queen cut in. She flew gently over to her throne chair and seated herself. "Not to mention that you have innocence hidden behind that determination of yours. It's an innocence that can only be spotted in a virgin."

"How long were you watching us? I take it that Ilexa's greeting with us was actually planned too."

"We were watching you ever since you came through that door. Our scouts patrol this forest far and wide. If we were to only stay knowledgeable of this confined space of ours, we would be opening our arms wide to harm. That doesn't matter right now, though. What does matter is that we need a mage to fight against a mage, and you're our ticket to that. You fail, and you'll be probably killed by him. If you somehow escape, you can turn back the way you came or die by our hands.

"Your husband's life is also in your hands. If you fail and die, he'll try to kill us, which will cause us to kill him. If you fail and turn back the way you came, I doubt that your husband will walk away without spilling blood. Your best option is to succeed, and success should be your only worry right now.

"As my husband recommended, I suggest that you convince this mage by other means than threatening his life. Besides, you have a dagger on you already if you really desire to take that route. At least, I presume so since one is missing from your husband's collection."

Her hands tightened more around her pants. "Why would you even want a mage like that protecting you? I asked this before, and I still wish to know why."

"Protection is protection, and he's a means to fight those that we despise. My kind's lives are more important to me than judging a mage's choice for hobbies," the king responded.

"And if this man turns out not to be a mage? What then?"

"Then, you don't have to worry about convincing him. From that point, your objective should be to escape and turn back the way you came. If you try to proceed forward, we'll kill you. We'll promise you a quick death, though."

"So, my only option is to hope that this man is a mage and that I can convince him somehow. How do you expect me to do that if I can't use a knife?" she asked both royals. Odette knew the answer, but she was hoping that there would be some other option.

"We've hinted at that enough for you, my dear. Charm him well enough, and you may be able to persuade him to help us and not kill you. I would offer you some time before going to the cabin so that you could have a night with your husband, but your husband will probably still be unstable if we wake him. Not only that but also your innocence is an advantage in this task."

It seemed like her blood went still as her vain hope crashed into a sea of oblivion. The only thing that kept her from falling completely into the abyss was the reason for her journey. It was a fight to live longer. She couldn't let terror reign over her mind; she would find another solution, another way to convince the mage.

Picking herself up steadily, she forced herself to stand. Her mind begged her to go over to Tarhuinn and lie next to him until he woke up, but there wasn't time for that. If she remained when he woke up, she wouldn't be able to go through with the deal.

Staring to her left ring finger, she grasped the metal there. She slipped the ring off and held it out to the royals. "Will you two hold onto this ring for me? The mage doesn't need to see it. I know the story that I'm going to craft."

Getting up from her throne chair, the queen flew over and took the ring. She set it at the base of her chair. "We'll watch over it for you. Are you ready to leave, then? If so, we'll have some of our scouts guide you part of the way."

"Are you certain that he's there now?" Odette questioned, untying her cloak and dropping it to the ground. She couldn't have one for her plan. Her story needed to be as believable as she could make it.

"We've had our scouts watch this man ever since we've heard of his arrival. These scouts confirmed yesterday that smoke rises from the cabin's chimney," the king answered, looking to her fallen article of clothing. "Shall we watch over that as well?"

"Yes. Give it to my husband as a blanket to keep him warm. Now, how much time do you suppose I have before Tergii and Bimaa return this way?"

"Two to three weeks. If I were you, I would take only a week to settle this matter. You don't want to accomplish this task only to have Tergii and Bimaa return here. You'll want to be well on your way to their homes when they come back to our territory."

Agreeing with the king, she stated that she was ready to go. Several snow pixies flew over to her and signaled for her to follow. She gave one last look to Tarhuinn before she trailed behind the five pixies.

Chapter Twenty Three: Screeching Halt

As they traveled to the cabin, Odette wished that she had kept her cloak and had asked the pixies to bring it back to their home before they left her on her own. At the time, though, she had been more focused on making a convincing story for the mage. Keeping her hands under her armpits, she tried to keep herself as warm as possible, but it didn't help that the sun was blocked completely by storm clouds. To make matters worse, the smell of rain was becoming rather strong. Any moment, it would probably pour on them.

Her eyes pinned themselves to the pixies' wings. How she would give to have wings. Then, she could travel to Tergii's and Bimaa's home(s) without all of the trouble. Unluckily for her, she wasn't born into the graceful and delicate yet deadly fae race. Instead, she was reminded of the aching pain in her worn-out legs. It had to be at least noon or later, but she couldn't catch sight of the cabin. Realistically, though, they probably wouldn't reach the area until dusk.

Thankfully, she brought some of the dried food with her. It was just enough for one meal that day as she had left her pack behind as well since it wouldn't have served her well to be carrying a fully supplied pack into the mage's home. If the mage were to spot that, her story would be thrown to the wind. In order to best avoid any unwanted interactions between them, she couldn't let a piece in her story be questionable.

Plodding through the thick snow, she kept her gaze forward on the pixies. Around her was nothing of interest. There was the occasional sound of an animal, which would cause her to turn in that direction, but it would always go out of sight before she could examine what it had been. For all she knew, it was some strange creature like the haasna.

Since her surroundings gave her little distraction from the nipping cold, her mind turned to thoughts of her husband. Come mid-afternoon, he would be up and most likely furious. Odette was glad that she wouldn't have to face him then and there. She stood by her decision, but convincing him of it was another story.

Was she to be there, he would most likely use the nickname on her until she wouldn't be able to walk for days and/or speak any other word but to agree with him. She hoped that he wouldn't act out and try to murder a pixie on sight, but she understood that such a hope would probably fall flat the moment that he awoke.

A heavy sigh exited from her parted lips. Right now, she would be able to avoid his wrath, but she had to return to the snow pixie royals. There was also the fact that the supposed mage would be in tow if he really was a mage. She would be lucky if Tarhuinn didn't try to rip him to pieces.

If things didn't go as she planned them and she had to give more than she was comfortable with, there would be no possible way to persuade her husband to return to his senses. He would have to be left behind; she would have to entrust him to the pixies until she returned from the journey. That brought up another issue. Would the pixies even agree to watch over him if things took that route?

Hands moving out from their warm shelter, she combed them through her locks. A frown plastered itself on her lips. Odette wished to scream out her frustrations and kick the snow up into the air. Why did desiring more years on her life come at such risk? She wasn't asking for immortality; she just wanted to live longer. Even if it was by a couple of years, that would be satisfactory. It wasn't only that but also she would get to spend more time with her child that she had promised Tarhuinn. The child wouldn't be left alone at the age of two.

Then again, the extended life might not even exist, but it was likely. To keep herself from crashing, she reassured herself that Tergii and Bimaa would answer her questions. They would show her the life giving secret if it existed. There would be no other option. She was dealing with too many ridiculous things to go back empty-handed.

Fingers parting from her light blonde strands, she placed her hands back where there was more warmth. Her breath was clear before her eyes, and she tore her mind from the possible outcomes. There was only one suitable result. She would see to it that she received it.

~ ~ ~ ~ ~ ~ ~ ~ ~ ~ ~

It was most likely around mid-afternoon when the pixies offered Odette a break for her feet. Agreeing to take a short rest, she cleared away some of the snow at her feet before the pixies joined in and caused the snow there to disappear. It prevented her bottom from getting any wetter, and the branches above her did aid a little against the present rain.

Taking out her meal, she ate the food somewhat slowly to savor the taste. She didn't know how generous the supposed mage would be. There was also the issue of another woman already being in the man's home. If that were the case, the outcome would be unpredictable, and everything might go to ruin. "Do you five know if this man has brought in another woman already?" she asked to see if they would ease her mind on that potential problem.

One of the scouts turned to her and nodded. "The haasna that lives nearby mentioned to us that they haven't seen the latest woman moving around the home, but she confirmed that no new woman has been brought in."

"Has she been able to go into the house to learn what has become of the woman?"

"No, she said that it hasn't been necessary since she has enough hair at the moment to feed her hunger. She noted that the woman is probably dead, however, since she smelled fresh blood from within."

She bit into her dried cherry as a visible gulp went down her throat. Well, she most likely wouldn't have to encounter that issue, but she was worried about what she might end up eating that day. Odette forced her stomach to calm itself. Right now, she couldn't waste any food. It might be her last decent meal in awhile. For that swallow, she forced it down and took a minute to regain her appetite.

About to take another bite from the cheery, she stopped. It felt like something had pierced her head. At first, no pain was administered. Hesitantly, she ate the rest of her cherry and swallowed. After that swallow, though, the thing raced through her head again. If she had been standing, she would've been knocked to her feet. Her hands shot up to her ears as a third wave passed through.

Ringing echoed in her brain. She desperately sought to soothe the near numbing pain by means of covering her ears more, but the action did nothing. It felt like someone had shot multiple cannons near her ears and in her head. The sound was excruciating, and the pain was so agonizing that not even a scream left her lips. Her voice fell silent, but her lips were parted as though she was emitting an earsplitting cry.

All five pixies looked to her in worry, not knowing what was happening. Neither did she until she heard among the screeching her name being called. Tarhuinn was awake, and he was beyond inflamed. If only she could ask to him to stop. At any moment, it felt like crimson would run out of her ears.

Tears threatened to fall from the corners of her eyes. She continued to hold her hands to her ears while she curled up into a small ball. It made sense that he could turn an alluring call of her name into something deadly if he wished. After all, the nickname possessed a temporary damaging effect on her legs. His voice really was a double-edged sword.

Waves of immense agony kept swimming over her. Her body was wracked under the shrieks of her name. She soon began to convulse. Any snow was shoved aside against her violent movements. The cold's fangs were but a mere gnat to the suffering inflicted by his call. Odette thought that she would die right there. How she desired for it to end. Tears were now cascading down her chilled cheeks.

Vicious sobs were even made mute by the torment. The pixies gathered around her but not too close, for fear of getting harmed in the process. They were clueless as to what was causing her distress. A few thought that she might've been possessed somehow by a wrathful spirit. In a way, they were correct. Tarhuinn's cry for her was equivalent to that of a fabled beast of one's greatest nightmares.

There was a pause in the calls. Odette finally was able to take a steady breath. Her body still shook, but she breathed in and out slowly. She glanced to the terrified pixies around her. All she could do was breathe out, “My husband...”

Exhausted, her eyelids closed against her will. She had to get to the cabin, but her body refused to stand. Sleep’s fingers grasped at her upper arms and pulled her backwards into an unwilling embrace. The fingers refused to relax. Arms began to wrap around her before absolute darkness overtook her.

Immediately, one of the scouts nodded to their companions before they dashed off towards their king and queen. The other pixies tended to the unconscious human. They formed a perimeter around her and made sure that if any snow fall occurred that it wouldn’t cover her. None of them knew how long she would be out, but they would make certain that she reached the cabin alive.

Chapter Twenty Four: Smoke Filled Night

From the moment that he woke up, Tarhuinn had hoped that it had been some terrible dream and that his wife wasn't off to that supposed mage's cabin. His dark blue eyes had searched the pixie home for her, believing that she would appear if he had stared long enough. The icy bonds around his wrists and feet hadn't really been there. They had merely been fragments of his imagination. Odette hadn't broken her agreement with him.

All that had happened was that he had grown tired and passed out. His waking up eyes just hadn't noticed her yet. He had sat up straighter and had put his feet more into the thin stream. The royals, on their thrones, had stared down at him while the other pixies had seemed armed to the ready. It was then that his mind had realized the truth. She really had left him behind; she had ordered the royals to stop him.

Pain had erupted in his chest. He had brought his head to his bound hands. His mind hadn't been able to take it since his wife was off to some perverted, murderous and cannibalistic mage. Tarhuinn had begun to tremble while his fingers had grasped for his hair. She couldn't go there; she wouldn't travel there.

He had needed her to come back to him; he had needed to restrict her movements. Bonds should've been placed on her, not him. Having known that, he had resorted to that method; he had turned his charming call into something from one's nightmares. It was as though he had called upon the dead for service and had sent a reaper to claim her back.

The call had been so powerful, so terrifying, that it rang beyond just a connection between him and her. His lips had parted, but her name had never been heard by the pixies. All they had listened to was the unearthly wail of the male. They had all covered their ears and had used frost to help protect them from the deafening sound.

When the awful sound had finished, Tarhuinn had been at a loss of breath, and tears had been streaming down his face. He had never wished to use that against her; he had never thought that such a case would arise where he would need it. The effect of it on her was known to him, but he couldn't have her running off to danger like that.

He had his knees to his chest and his forehead resting on them. All he had desired was to have her back in his arms and to murder the pixies that had placed the horrid idea into her mind. The idea of that mage putting his filthy hands on her had made his blood boil. His fingers had twitched a little as they had itched to wrap themselves around the mage's neck. Both the mage and the pixies needed to die.

Hopefully, though, Odette would come back to him and not head to that cabin. She would realize her mistake; she would break his bonds and let him dispatch as many of the pixies that he could. His body now pulled itself closer together while his toes curled in the small stream. Despite his optimistic wishes, he could feel tears still run down his cheeks. "Odette, I want you back so much. Please, come back to me now. Please..." he whispered to himself countless times.

The pixies around him merely watched. They kept their distance, understanding that his current display would transform into pure murderous rage if they were to get too close. Both royals planned, though, that if he tried to release that cry again, they would freeze his mouth over. It would prevent them from hearing it. Unfortunately, the luxury wouldn't be extended to Odette; however, one of the scouts came plowing into the pixie home.

Nearly, they ran into the stone pillar. They bowed to their king and queen, explaining the situation. Tarhuinn peeked up from his position. A small smile formed on his lips. For now, he stalled her from reaching the cabin. When she awoke, she would hopefully make the right decision and come back to him.

Even with the news, however, he wished to be beside her. He should be there, holding her in his embrace. His lips should be administering delicate and sometimes rough kisses to her luxurious skin. Tarhuinn glanced to the extra cloak wrapped around his shoulders. The item should be with her. It should be protecting her from the cold. They both needed to be there with her.

Once the scout finished and took off, the royals peered down to him. He returned their gaze with a murderous one. The king and queen now understood that he would have to be knocked out should he try to call out to her again. It would interfere with her mission and reduce their chances of getting the mage on their side. Both royals broke their stare with their captive before they returned to other business. Tarhuinn looked back to his knees. His hands clenched as he continued his whisperings.

~ ~ ~ ~ ~ ~ ~ ~ ~ ~ ~

Her hands moved a little. She felt somewhat wet ground beneath her, and her clothes still weren't dry. A few droplets of rain fell upon her. Blinking her eyes opened, she found herself where she had been eating. The sky was dark as she could barely see around her.

Noting that she was awake, the scouts instantly turned to her and breathed a collective sigh of relief. They ushered her to get up as they wanted to return home before it became later in the night. She, however, couldn't just burst to her feet. Her body was sore from the previous torment. Odette positioned herself on her knees and hands. Slowly, she made her ascent.

Finally getting to her feet, her legs were unsteady. She almost fell back to the ground if it weren't for the pixies coming to her rescue. They held up her arms to the best of their abilities until she could regain some proper balance. When she felt that she was able to walk, she thanked them and signaled that they could let go. "Let's head to the cabin."

As they walked onward, somewhat steadily, she finished her meal from earlier. It sated her hunger for the time being and gave some of her energy back. Eventually, however, they were close to the lake. Just barely, she could spot the smoke rising from the cabin's chimney. The pixies wouldn't go further. Frankly, she didn't wish to either.

Summoning her courage, she pulled out her dagger from her boot and unsheathed it. The pixies looked to her questioningly, but she assured them that it was to make her narrative more believable. Before she dealt some of the blows, she tore her clothes up some. Once they looked untidy enough, she inhaled deeply and drew the blade across her arms and legs a couple of times. Tears formed in the corners of her eyes, but she reminded herself that the pain was nothing in comparison to Tarhuinn's calling for her. She bit her bottom lip until she was completed with the task.

Odette wiped the dagger clean on the snow. She kicked the snow until the red was buried beneath more snow. Satisfied with her work, she sheathed the dagger and placed it back on the outer side of her right boot. Taking a few steps forward, she glanced back to the pixies. They hovered in the air but offered no encouragement; they merely waited for her to enter the cabin. From there, it was entirely on her, so she faced the cabin once more.

Every step sounded in her ears. There was less snow now, but its crunching under her boots gave away her position. Trees were somewhat barren by the cabin, giving her little place to hide. Of course, she wasn't expected to keep herself from the eyes of the mage.

Getting closer, her hands tightened. She prepared her story in her mind. Her demeanor would have to change somewhat, but her fear, for once, would do her good. With her heart thumping louder in her chest, she stood several more steps towards the back of the cabin. There were no windows there luckily, but it meant a harder escape. Not that she could run away, though, if he were really a mage.

One deep inhale and exhale later, she was off. She ran the rest of the distance, falling at one point on purpose. Exposed tree branches scraped across her. Some of her cuts were rubbed against, causing a cry to emit itself from her lips. Good, she wanted to be heard. Odette picked herself up and peered over her left shoulder as though she was being pursued. In doing so, she noted that the pixies were distancing themselves farther from cabin.

Movement could be heard inside the cabin. She swallowed back her desire to run off in the opposite direction. Continuing to go forward, she raced to the wooden door. Firelight illuminated the inside of the home and showed her a brief view of the contents as she darted by the window. Odette brought her hands quickly to the doorknob and attempted to open the door. It being locked caused her to raise her right fist.

Banging on the wood, she called out for help and for the person inside to open up. “Please, he’s after me! Let me in! I need help!” she cried out in hysteria. In the back of her mind, she hoped that Tarhuinn would never learn of the story that would leave her lips that evening. She knew that it would send him even more into a raging frenzy.

Door opening slowly, she dashed forward. She was stopped by a solid wall as her hands reached up. Odette clutched at the green fabric of the male’s shirt. Her head buried itself into his chest. “Please, help! He’s after me; he’s going to kill me!” she cried out more while her voice was muffled by his shirt.

Sobs escaped her lips soon after. Tears accompanied in tow. They stained both her skin and his shirt. Arms slowly wrapped around her. A smooth voice, which reminded her of a soft, fleece blanket, spoke, “It’s alright. No one is going to harm you. Let’s bring you in from the cold night.”

Chapter Twenty Five: Masquerade

Sitting in a wooden chair, she held her hands to her eyes. The tears kept coming as she sat a little hunched over. She made her hands tremble. Her ears picked up the sound of the door closing and locking. Despite her show of despair, her mind couldn't help but wonder if she would ever get past that locked door with the supposed mage in tow.

Wood creaked under footsteps. Hands soon greeted hers, pulling them gently from her face. The male crouched in front of her and sent her a reassuring smile. He continued to hold onto her hands as his thumbs worked soothing circles into her skin. "Now, no one's going to harm you here. I want you to calm down and tell me who's coming after you."

Looking into his bright green eyes, she noticed that they only displayed kindness. If she didn't have a husband and hadn't known about his darker hobbies, she probably would've melted into his arms. She kept up her terror, however. Odette pulled her hands back from his timidly and curled up more on the chair. Frankly, it felt like he was assessing how well her skin would cook when he touched her. It only helped to fuel the inner fear within her.

She let out another sob before she took a deep breath and exhaled. "M-my h-husband, h-he thinks th-that I che-cheated on h-him. He-he's fur-furious and told m-me that h-he's goi-going to k-kill me." Her body shook more as the man stood back up and took a seat across from her.

"You look thoroughly exhausted. How long have you been running?"

Not meeting his gaze once more, she made a nervous glance to the window and door. When she turned back to him, he gave her a reassuring smile to continue on. She returned the gesture with a meek nod. "A f-few days, I man-managed to ge-get away on the fir-first and se-cond days, but h-he ca-caught up to m-me to-today. I s-stole his k-knife and f-fought him off but n-not be-before he had ad-administered th-these." Odette pointed to the various cuts on her. Only fear reigned in her eyes when she glanced upon them.

"And, do you think that he follows you still?"

Her body froze before she tightly wrapped her arms around her knees. “I h-hope n-not. I kn-knocked him out w-with his k-knife b-before plu-plunging it in h-his l-left sh-shoulder. I’m n-not s-sure if he’s st-still alive, b-but I didn’t w-wish to chance i-it. So, I con-continued to run. When I s-saw you-your h-home, I cou-couldn’t he-help but c-cry ou-out for a-aid. I’m s-so ter-terrified.”

Footsteps sounded once more. He held out his left hand. “Come on. Let’s get you cleaned up. You can tell me the rest once you’ve settled down.”

What he said sounded so close to what Tarhuinn had told her earlier that morning. They were both gentle in their words, but she could tell that Tarhuinn was genuine. This man, she could only guess that he was trying to spin the art of manipulation around her. She met his gaze with a fearful and doubtful one.

“Trust me. I’m not going to hurt you. I just wish to help.” He continued to hold his hand out. She gave him another questioning gaze before she hesitantly reached out and took his hand. Odette moved her feet off of the chair and back onto the ground. With a smile, he lifted her up and onto her feet.

His hand intertwined more firmly with hers. She figured that he meant it to be a calming gesture, but it felt different from Tarhuinn’s grip. Despite him trying to be kind, she could decipher that there was something more sinister to his hold. They walked into his bedroom before he sat her down on the plush bed. It seemed like a new set of sheets had been laid upon it. Besides the bed, she noted that there was only a wardrobe and a writing desk with a matching chair in the room.

He headed over to the desk and pulled out a red hair tie. The male tied up his shoulder-length, golden blonde locks before he sat beside her. Without warning, he reached for her left arm and started to tear at the fabric. Instantly, she pulled her arm back, but she winced in the process. She scooted farther away from him on the bed.

"I was just trying to get at your wounds better. If I tear the fabric, that'll allow me to do so." In response, she shook her head. A sigh escaped his lips. "Then, at least let me see your arm. The cuts on you need to be healed, or they could get infected." Cautiously, she gave him her arm. He pressed his hands to the wound before a pale red light emitted from them.

The man was indeed a mage. She could already feel the magic working its way around the cut and healing it. Despite her relief at him being one, she only appeared shocked. "You're, you're a mage!" she exclaimed, eyes widening as they glanced between him and her arm. An amused chuckle left his lips.

"Yes, I am. This is why you have nothing to fear if your husband finds you here. He won't be able to do a thing against me." He moved onto her next wound. "And, you're welcome to stay here until you feel safe enough to leave. I can't possibly send you back out there when such a man is on the loose."

As he was about to take up her next arm, she tugged it back. Distrust shadowed her gaze as she looked like she had just gained her courage back. She wiped at a few remaining tears while a frown fell upon her lips. "That's kind of you to say, but we're both strangers to the other. How could you let me stay here? And, how could I trust you not to try something? My husband told me things about your kind. That you trick people and use them to your own benefit."

"And, you would believe a man who doesn't trust your own word? Based on what you've told me about him so far, he seems to be the untrustworthy one. He's the one causing you pain, not me. I'm only trying to help you. Some mages can be rather fowl, but not all of us are. Please, let me aid you."

Another suspicious stare coated her eyes. She broke it soon after, looking down to her lap. "I suppose that you're right. He's a rather awful man." He reached over and grabbed her other arm to tend to the wounds. Odette didn't give protest that time. Of course, she wished to dash out of the home, but she forced herself to allow him to put his hands on her.

Shyly, she observed his actions and inspected his features. His facial structure portrayed him in a soft light as though he were meant to always laugh. It gave him a friendly air, but his sharp, bright green eyes contradicted that appearance. The well-groomed eyebrows above his keen eyes only strengthened that. As for his shoulders, they weren't as broad as Tarhuinn's, but they complimented his overall form. In some respects, it wasn't hard to see how the male could charm women and bring them back to his home.

"And, finished," he remarked before he moved away from her. He stood up from the bed and walked over to the wardrobe. "I'm sure that you wouldn't mind a change of clothes. Yours are quite ruined after all." When he didn't at first receive an answer, he looked over his left shoulder to her.

Her hands firmly clenched her pants. Odette met his stare before she peered over to the item of furniture. Regardless of the condition of her clothes, she didn't wish to wear anything from him. For the task, however, she acted hesitant, especially when he opened the wardrobe to reveal a few dresses. They were probably from his past victims. "And, why do you have women's clothing?" she asked, concern written all over her countenance.

"Ah, this must look quite mistrustful, but these are my sister's. She comes over for a visit once in awhile. She left some clothes of hers with me so that she could reduce her packing."

Distrust remained on her face. Some of those dresses were rather revealing. If her life weren't on the line, she would've commented on that fact. "And, she'll be fine with me wearing one of her dresses? You're already offering me a place to stay. I think that's enough kindness ..."

Catching onto her pause, he smiled a little. "It's Willem. Call me Will for short. And, it'll be fine. She's an understanding individual. I'm sure that she won't mind. You can go ahead and change. I'll be by the fireplace waiting for you with some tea."

"Thank you, then," she muttered, intertwining her fingers and staring back down to her lap. As he walked by, he placed a hand comfortingly over hers. He squeezed them a little before he left the room and closed the door behind him. With him gone, she let out a breath before she stood to her feet.

All of the dresses were floor length as they normally were. She had become accustomed to the ankle length ones back in their home. They allowed better maneuverability. One of the bothering things about his dresses, however, was the corseted tops that looked to be quite low. There were undershirts to go with them, but they were off-shoulder and did little to offset the low cut. Not only that but also the cotton fabric of the skirts was made quite thin. It wouldn't surprise her if one of the dresses was partially see-through.

Finding the thickest and most high cut dress, she changed out of her ripped clothes and into it. Personally, she wished to remain in her ruined clothes, but she didn't know what would happen if she came out of the room in them. She did keep on her own undershirt, which managed to hide her chest well where the other wouldn't have. Odette smoothed out the grey-blue skirt before she left the room.

Will was sitting in the seat he had taken up before. There was a tea kettle over the fire. He indicated for her to retake her seat, but she did happen to note that his eyes traveled to her chest area for a moment. A laugh escaped his lips, causing a light dose of heat to hit her cheeks. She sat down in a huff. After she crossed her arms, Odette asked, "What?"

"That undershirt looks rather odd with that dress, no?"

"Well, excuse me for wanting to be more covered, especially in winter," she countered, glancing away from him. If there was one thing that she wouldn't act about, it was her articles of clothing. For as long as she could prevent it, she would make sure that he wouldn't see too much of her. He was lucky right now that he could see her exposed arms. The less skin was all the better.

Odette didn't want to send the wrong message. She needed things to go smoothly on her end, but trying to win his sympathy towards her wouldn't be easy. The male's kindness was probably all an act on its own. If he got bored of her, he would reveal the fangs that he currently kept so well hidden. Still, she couldn't let too much of her actual personality come through.

She cast her gaze to the window. Outside, she couldn't see much due to the light's reflection on the glass, but she let fear glaze over her eyes. She tightened her fingers around the skirt more as she permitted a visible shiver to run up her spine.

His amused expression fell upon noting her state. "I see that you're still worried. It makes sense since it sounds like your husband truly meant his threat." He stood from his chair and headed into the next room where he pulled a blanket off of the bed. Returning, he set it upon her shoulders before he wrapped it around her. It was obvious that he had purposefully glided his fingers across her upper arms. She made it just as clear that she tensed under his touch.

Taking his seat once more, he continued, "Though, I would like to hear why your husband thinks that you cheated on him. That's quite an accusation to make."

Holding the blanket around her more, she permitted her bottom lip to quiver from terror. She acted as though she had seen the grim reaper himself ready to execute her. "H-he w-was..." Odette paused and swallowed to force away the stutter. "He was so angry when he returned home from his trip to town. I think that something went wrong with his business. Or, maybe, he didn't sell enough wood. I'm not sure; he never told me what had happened.

"When he asked me to follow him to the bedroom, I refused as I could tell what he wanted. I didn't think that ..." She looked down at her fingers and played with them some while a little bit of heat entered her cheeks. "I'm sorry ... it's just awkward to tell someone that I barely know this, but ..." she peered back up at him meekly before glancing back down, "I suppose that your generosity deserves an explanation." He gave no movement to protest, but when she looked up, she saw him giving her one of his reassuring smiles again.

Nodding in response, she continued. "I didn't think that it would be right to consummate our marriage when he was so enraged. He thought otherwise and grabbed me before he left these marks on my skin." Her fingers instinctively went up to the two bruises. "But, I managed to push him away and create some distance between us.

"My second rejection of him caused his fury to rise, and he started to yell that I had been cheating on him. He shouted that was why I had never accepted a proposal of his to be more intimate. When I tried to reason with him that wasn't the case, he lost it and started to threaten my life. From there, I tossed my wedding ring at him and bolted. I didn't have time to carry anything with me, except a few pieces of dried foods in our kitchen and the clothes on my back."

In response to her conclusion, the tea kettle made a high pitch screech. She jumped in her seat before her attention spun to the window and door. Will stood quickly and lifted the kettle off before he placed it on the fireplace mantel. "It's alright. It was just the tea kettle," he mentioned in a calming voice. Meeting his gaze, she nodded slowly before she relaxed.

Walking around the table, he opened a cupboard and pulled out some cups for them. Once the tea was poured and the loose leaves strained, he set the tea kettle down and handed a cup to her, but he didn't return to his seat right after. He stood in front of her before he wrapped his hands around hers. "I'm truly sorry to hear that your husband assumed such a dreadful thing." Will, gently and slowly, moved his hands away, which allowed his fingers to glide like light feathers over her skin. A small chill ran through her body, and she drew her hands closer to her chest.

As he headed back to his chair, he remarked, "I'm sure it's because you were waiting for that right moment. You didn't wish to give your innocence up until you found that perfect time. Am I correct?" He spun on his heel and took his seat again. His cup was soon in his hands before he took a cautious sip.

She could tell that he was trying to be understanding, but despite his considerate appearance, she saw for a second the monster within. It was as though she had seen Tarhuinn's smile from her nightmare, but the smile wasn't one of murderous intent. It displayed only a wild lust and gluttonous curiosity. In that instant, it felt like she was looking at some beast hiding in the shadows. That beast was waiting to come out and have a taste of the prey before him.

Despite the difficulty in doing so, she forced back the dread that had nearly dominated her countenance. Instead, she grew more embarrassed. "Well ... yes. I know that's childish, but I didn't want my memory of such an event to be a terrible one."

"That's not childish. It's actually quite understandable, but it begs the question of why not on your wedding night. Surely, that would've been a fond memory, or were you forced into the marriage with your husband? Of course, you don't have to answer. I'm diving into personal material after all."

Shaking her head lightly, she answered, "It's fine. It's nothing to hide. If I were to hide anything, it wouldn't be my wedding." She let out a light sigh while sorrow reigned in her brown eyes. "We never grew intimate on our wedding night because my husband's mother had been very ill. It was a miracle that she could make it to our wedding in the first place, but her illness finally took her on that day. My husband spent the night caring for her until she passed away. That night and the days following just never seemed to offer that ideal moment. I only wish that he hadn't taken to such an allegation against me. I had still cared for him, but after that display ..." Another shiver ran up her spine, and she curled up more on the chair as grief was replaced with terror.

"He did make a grave mistake. In his fit of anger, he let go of a beautiful woman. He accused you of something that you're clearly not capable of."

Staring up at him, she permitted her cheeks to warm up some, though; she desired to receive no compliment from him. She reminded herself that she had to maintain her act until she had him snared and ready to go to the pixies. Still, it was like the beast had shown more of itself. It was as though he was presenting a challenge to her on whether he could bed her or not.

It sickened her to her core, and she nearly called out for Tarhuinn. He was one man whom she wouldn't mind being killed by her husband. If things turned out well and their journey bore positive results, she wouldn't stop Tarhuinn from going after the man before her. Will was a true menace.

"Honestly, I hope that this man is dead. That way you can be free of him and find that perfect moment with someone more deserving of your love." Hearing that, she swiftly looked to the ground. She heard a cup being set down on the table a little harder than the past times as though he had finished his drink. Footsteps sounded before she saw his feet near her. "Forgive me. That was indecent of me to say."

A hand rested on top of her head. She kept her gaze off of him, moving her head away in her established shy manner. "Why don't you finish your tea? I'm going to head outside and take a bath. And, don't worry. I won't let that man come into my home if he's still alive." He gave her a gentle pat on the head before going into the bedroom, grabbing some clothes and heading outside.

With the door just there, it was tempting to bolt for it, but he most likely had spelled it in some fashion. Besides if she tried to leave, he would no doubt see her. Not to mention, there was only one other window besides the one by the main door. The bedroom window faced the lake also.

Sending constant reminders to herself that she couldn't leave yet, she turned her back to the door and faced the cup on the table. Personally, she was worried that he had done something to the tea. He drank from the same tea kettle, but, perhaps, he could've spelled it so that it would only affect her; however, she couldn't not drink and eat.

Starving herself would do her no good. She required her strength to win the battle. She wrapped her hands around the cup and brought it to her lips, taking careful sips. The mint tea did taste good, and there was nothing odd about it. Right now, she merely needed inwardly to celebrate since Will didn't seem to doubt her story.

Chapter Twenty Six: Delicate Flower

By the time that Will came back inside, her tea had been finished. She had remained on the chair and had huddled into the blanket, but she hadn't fallen asleep. Odette was far too worried to do so until he went to bed.

"You must be very tired ... Why, I don't believe that you've told me your name," he voiced, leaning against the doorframe to the bedroom.

Personally, she didn't wish to tell him, but would he catch on if she lied about it? Already, she was thinking too long on the request. She brushed it off as being hesitant and shy. She twiddled her fingers and kept her gaze on her hands. A light chuckle reached her ears. "If you don't desire to tell me, how about I give you a name? Besides if your husband is still out there, it wouldn't be wise to go around towns with your actual name."

He pushed himself off of the frame and moved a chair closer to her. Taking a seat directly in front of her, he leaned forward and rested his chin on his intertwined hands. Odette instinctively went to move back on her chair, but she was already pressed as far back as she could go. Mentally, she became annoyed. The man was invading her personal space. To top it off, it wasn't the first time either.

His gaze stayed fixed on her, however. Eventually, her brown orbs met his. A small grin pulled at his lips. "It'll be Bluebell. The color suits you, and you did ring for my assistance like a bell. Besides, sometimes the flower is associated with gratitude, and I'm sure that you're quite grateful for being allowed to stay here. It's perfect."

She didn't object the nickname, but it was because she wouldn't have to give him her real name. Still, he didn't know how wrong he was about her gratefulness. If she were grateful for anything, it was that she wasn't dead yet. The bluebell, though, had a meaning of constancy to it too. Odette wondered if he was again putting that to the challenge. Should her husband not be dead, which he definitely wasn't, would she remain faithful, or would she give herself over to the kind mage in the cabin?

There was that sadistic twinkle in his eyes for a split second before he stood up from his seat. "Well, what do you think? I can always shorten it to blue or bell if you would like. Of course, I might do that anyways." Remaining silent, she simply nodded. "Excellent. It's been a long night for us both, so why don't we head to bed?"

Instantly, she shook her head. "I'm comfortable on the chair. I can remain here for the night. This is your home. You should have your own bed, and I'm not sharing a bed with you. I appreciate your kindness, but I'm not comfortable with that."

"Truly, your husband lost a wonderful woman. Even after threatening your life, you still have some hope in your eyes that he'll take you back if he's alive. Such a devoted woman but I understand where you're coming from. We're new to each other, and it would be wrong to share a bed even if I wouldn't try anything on you. Still, I must insist that you take the bed. I can sleep on the ground during your stay."

Before she could answer, he took her hands and lifted her from the chair. She nearly cried out in protest, but the sound was muffled by his shirt. Her hands ended up pressed against his chest. Immediately, she pushed herself back as his hold on her disappeared. "I just want you to have a decent rest after your escape. Please, indulge me that much. I only wish to help."

Analyzing his gaze, she saw only kindness there again. She knew better, however. The man couldn't charm her into lowering her guard. Hesitantly, she took a step towards him before she went around him. "Thank you, then," she mumbled as she headed into the room and towards the bed. Once seated, she held the blanket out to him. "You'll need it more than me."

Another one of his soft smiles was sent her way. He gently took the blanket from her, but he didn't lie down immediately. Instead, he leaned downwards and pressed a light kiss to the back of her left hand. Out of surprise, heat lightly touched her cheeks as she drew her hand to her chest. His green eyes gleamed a bit in amusement. "Goodnight, Bluebell."

It felt like a wolf was staring her down with its teeth bared in a deadly grin. Once he lied down, she grew a bit more at ease. She moved closer to the window and took off her boots. Odette placed them on the window seal in such a way that the hidden knife wouldn't be seen. When she was satisfied with their position, she pulled the sheets over her form.

Resting her hands over her midsection, her eyes stared up at the wooden ceiling. They turned to their right some and out towards the night sky. Occasionally, she would catch a few stars being revealed by the rolling-by clouds. It was odd to think that last night she would've been cuddled up next to Tarhuinn. Now, she had a murderous mage as her companion. Her hands clutched at the sheets.

Admittedly, she missed having his protective form nearby, yet she desired to prove that she could handle a dangerous situation on her own. Of course, she was scared. Nerves were her best friend at the moment. When enough time seemed to pass, though, she cautiously peeked over the left side of the bed. Will was fast asleep or at least looked to be. Noting that, she forced herself to calm down and close her eyes.

~ ~ ~ ~ ~ ~ ~ ~ ~ ~ ~

Tarhuinn lifted his head when the scouts returned. His eyes searched through the night to see if Odette was behind them. Even as he heard the report that she had gone into the cabin, he kept his gaze pinned to the entrance. He couldn't believe it. Hadn't she realized her mistake? Why hadn't she turned back; why weren't her arms around him as she apologized for breaking their deal?

Dark blue eyes finally shifted back to the pixie royals. It was then that he finally noted the object at the base of the queen's throne. Breath caught in his throat. Why hadn't she taken her ring at least? Terrible theories seemed to swarm his mind. Shakily, he questioned the queen, "Why did my wife leave her ring?"

"She told us that she had a story formed for the mage and that he didn't need to view the ring," the queen answered truthfully. "Would you like to hold onto it?"

"Is that even a question?" he growled out as the sparks of a fire began to flicker to life. The queen didn't acknowledge his threatening gaze. She merely rose from her chair and picked up the ring. Her husband nearly stopped her, but she reassured him that she would be fine. Keeping her distance from the kelremm, she tossed the ring to him, and he managed to catch it with his bonded hands.

Returning to her chair, the queen made herself comfortable and was about to drift into sleep. With Tarhuinn's call, she would have to stay close by in case he attempted to perform it. Before she could fall asleep, Tarhuinn asked, "What were the story's details?"

The king responded, "She didn't relate them to us. We merely recommended that she use her beauty and innocence to her advantage. Perhaps, that's why she left the ring behind."

All appeared to freeze. Tarhuinn pressed his wrists against the ice bonds. The cold burned his skin, but he didn't care. His mind focused only on Odette. He couldn't let that mage have her. Dark blues focused in front of him but on nothing in particular. They were glazed over with the intent to hunt down and kill. Despite the most troubling look in his eyes, tears slipped down his cheeks.

None of the pixies flew to action yet, but they heard the sound of cracking ice. To their utter disbelief, Tarhuinn was breaking through his bonds. His gaze still was fixated on nothing in particular while his right fingers clenched around the ring as though it were his last hope. The kelremm's lips began to part slowly before the queen sprung into action.

Right before she could send him into sleep, his jaws opened wide. His sharp teeth revealed themselves before he snapped at the pixie. Instantly, she flew back with fright. Guards swiftly flew into action and attacked him on the back. A growl left his lips before he turned swiftly and swung his hands at them. When his gaze flew forward again, the queen managed to get him. Despite that, he went to enclose his jaws around her again.

Barely dodging, the queen zipped to her throne. The king rose from his and prepared himself for a full-on fight if the kelremm didn't calm down. Tarhuinn's lips started to part again, but sleep ensnared him. He collapsed onto the ground unconscious.

Pixies speedily committed to work. His bonds were strengthened before he was turned over to tend to the wounds on his back. All remained silent while that occurred.

The queen was recovering from shock. Her king rested his hands on her shoulders to soothe her. Both royals, though, kept their eyes pinned to Tarhuinn. If the human girl could get the mage back to them in a week's time or sooner, that would truly be the best since neither of them knew how much longer they could detain her husband without seriously harming him.

Chapter Twenty Seven: Cold yet Warm

Her right arm draped over her eyes, and her left hand clutched at the sheets, Odette was trying to block out the morning light. It streamed through the window as most of the cloud cover was at the top of the mountains. Down by the lake, it seemed more like a summer's day than an autumn one, but the cold still persisted. Groaning at the amount of light, she rolled onto her left side and pulled the sheets over her. Her eyes snapped open, though, upon hearing that particular laugh.

An entertained Will stood beside the bed. His hands rested on his hips before he crouched down in front of her. Instantly, she sat up and moved towards the window. It was a pity that she couldn't remain asleep longer, but she did have a job ahead of her. "Still shy around me? If you stay here longer, you'll get used to me. Regardless," he stood back up and opened the wardrobe, "you should go ahead and take a bath."

Offended, she crossed her arms and huffed. Quickly realizing his implication, he apologized. "Not that you smell but it might do you good after these past few days. The lake water is nice once it's heated a little."

It had been a few days since she had bathed, but she didn't want to be nude around him. "And, I take it that you'll be heating the water?" She received a nod, and, now, she definitely didn't wish to have one. Odette noted as well that he seemed to be taking out some attire for her.

When she noted the undershirt, nearly see-through underwear and questionable blue dress, she shook her head at him. "I'm not wearing those. I'll wash the clothes on me in the water while I take a bath. And, I don't need the water heated."

"I'm not going to stare at you, Bluebell. I'm just going to heat the water towards the shore of the lake and turn my back to you afterwards. With your husband possibly still out there, I'll need to remain outside, though. As for the clothes, suit yourself, but those will get worn out if you keep washing them every day. And, my sister wouldn't want her dress ruined. So at least change into the new dress."

She wanted to tell him that the dress wasn't his sister's, but if she said such a thing, she would be out in the open. Perhaps, it really was his sister's. If that were the case, she felt terrible for the girl that had to call the man a sibling. Fighting back the urge to punch him, she handed back the undergarments and took the dress with her. To her relief, she still had her own undershirt, which would offset the very low cut of the dress.

"Fine, but if I catch you peeking at me, you're going to regret it." She truly did mean that, but she said it in such a way as though she were a little girl scolding a cute tiny animal. It would put him off guard and give her the upper hand if she did have to attack so soon in the game.

Another light chuckle left his lips. "I'll keep that in mind," he answered playfully before he signaled for her to follow. Getting up from the bed, she grabbed her boots and trailed behind him. When they reached the water, she watched him place his hands over the surface of it. Once again, a pale red light emitted from his hands.

"Is your magic always that color?" she asked, wishing to learn a little more about how it worked. It wouldn't only help against him but also the other mage.

"No, it's only this color if I seek to use my magic to influence something. Last night, I wished to affect the healing rate of your wounds. Now, I desire to control the temperature of this small area of water. As long as I have a goal in mind and it deals with me impacting the nature of something, my magic will take this color."

"Are there limitations? Or, can you perform really anything with that?"

"Someone's certainly interested in magic? Weren't you worried that I would trick you last night and use you to my benefit?"

"Yes to both of those. Even if I'm still concerned about that, I want to learn how magic is used. I also want to make sure that you know what you're doing should my husband be alive and find me. If you don't want to tell me anymore, though, I understand. You might want to keep your trades of magic a secret."

"Well, I'll keep it simple. A mage does like to keep their abilities somewhat a mystery to those around them. Granted, I doubt that you'll ever pose a threat to me. You're much too kind for that, and you need my help. Still, I'll say that every aspect of magic has its limitations. I can't hold my hands out to the sky and influence the season to change to winter for example."

"How does that work with a small area of water, though? The heat will travel through the liquid, and I doubt that I'll feel any effect."

"That's a good point, but if I hold my hands here for long enough, the water will be warm enough for a time. That's why you'll need to take a quick bath unless you'd rather bathe in freezing water. And, on that note, don't swim out too far. Even I don't know what lies out in the middle of this lake. If something does brush against your legs this close to the shore, don't panic. Only harmless fish swim around this section."

Finishing up his work, he stepped back and indicated that it was ready for her. She thanked him but also gave him the signal to walk away and turn his back. He shook his head in amusement before doing just that. Once she made sure that he wasn't looking, she quickly slipped out of her clothes and bathed. The water was a nice temperature, but she could feel the heat disappearing already.

There was a clear problem with her undergarment washing plan, though. They would be washed, but they would be wet when put on. To top it off, she couldn't stay in the water and let them dry. Cursing at her own failure, she washed them. She would have to wear them wet; she refused to call him back over.

While she was bathing, Will had his arms crossed over his chest and stared out at the pine forest. A grin wouldn't leave his lips. He bit his lower lip sometimes to keep himself from laughing out loud. His glee extended from the fact that his flower would soon be realizing her mistake with her clothes. Any moment she would call him over, and he could catch a look at her more exposed form. Naturally, he would claim it as an accident. Her reluctance to wear the clothing that he desired on her would end up benefitting him in the end.

A yell and loud splash sounded, and he wondered what was going on back there. Being too curious, he turned. He did so in time to see her head come back up from the water. She was in a sitting position, most likely leaning on her arms for support. Water covered her chest and lower region, but her left leg was lifted into the air. Will caught sight of something slimy-looking attached to her leg.

The girl was about to lean forward to remove it until her eyes spotted him. Her eyes widened before she became rather embarrassed. “Turn around, you pervert!” It was as though the creature on her leg was no longer important; it could’ve been killing her, yet she no longer cared. It caused him to chuckle before he did as she requested.

Holding his hands up in surrender, he called back, “I heard your shout. I thought that you were in trouble.”

“I don’t care! If I had asked for your assistance, then you could’ve turned around. Unless I ask for it, don’t look my way! I have this handled,” she countered before he heard a loud huff of irritation from her.

That was definitely a reaction that he wasn’t expecting. Normally if something odd had grabbed to one of the girls, they had usually cried for his help. There was the occasional one that had run out of the water and into the cabin. It had been most entertaining. None of them had stayed in the water, however. Still, he had mentioned that the fish were harmless; he just always had withheld the fact that some of them were grabbers, but her behavior had been a first for him. Will wondered how many more surprises there would be from her.

As if to answer him, something smacked him in the back of the head. The impact caused him to nearly fall forward before he stabilized himself and heard something slip to the ground. Backing up a little, he picked up the clinglob. Its slimy, glob-like body clung to his hand, but it desperately wished for water.

Will broke into laughter before holding it up for her to see. "Thanks, Bluebell. You've caught us breakfast!" he called to her while looking to her in the process. He caught sight of her sitting fully up, but before he could see anything, another one collided with his face. The male fell backwards, but he continued to laugh after he removed the second clinglob.

"Stop being a pervert already, or I'll throw more at you!" she cried out as she lowered herself into the water. Only her head was above the water.

"Then, we'll have lunch and dinner," he answered back with a smirk. The girl grew frustrated before she looked ready to aim at him again. That time, he obliged her and moved his gaze elsewhere. If she kept up the unexpected behavior, he would keep her around a little bit longer.

Chapter Twenty Eight: Conversation's Clue

After she hurriedly left the water, she dressed herself, partially wet undergarments and all, and headed inside for a bit of warmth. Hearing her footsteps, Will stared to her once more while he bore an entertained grin. She pursed hers in response before she went inside. Odette noted that he had scanned over her dress rather slowly and obviously. If she had worn the undergarments that he had picked, she imagined that his gaze would've been longer.

That was another trait that she missed about Tarhuinn: his sense of decency. Whenever she would take a bath, he would look away and not turn around until she told him that she was ready. With the tenlite incident, he had kept his gaze forward, not looking at her exposed self. A frown worked its way on her lips before she took a seat at the table. Hearing the door open behind her, she returned it to her somewhat childish expression of contracted lips and raised nose.

A hand rested on top of her head before she felt her wet hair be ruffled a little. Instantly, she pulled away from him and tried to fix the damage, but more knots had already formed. Glaring at him in a non-threatening manner, she was about to speak before he voiced, "It's good to see that you're more relaxed today. I'd rather not have a lovely girl worried sick under my roof."

"Oh, so you like having other girls in that state here?" she questioned as she crossed her arms across her chest and acted like she had said the most clever thing in the world.

"Of course not," he replied, placing his right hand over his heart. He wore a hurt expression, though clearly fake, before he added, "I always make sure that a woman becomes satisfied if she enters my home."

"So, you've had other women stop by, then? Sounds like you're a popular man." She placed her chin in the palm of her right hand to get more comfortable. "Perhaps, I should take my leave so that I don't interrupt any future encounters of yours."

Laughing, he placed the two clinglobs on the preparation counter at the back of the room. He grabbed a knife and started on breakfast. "Oh, have I made you jealous already? If you're husband is still alive, he would be quite mad to hear that. Still, I'm flattered."

Rolling her eyes, she wished to remark about Tarhuinn. The mage before her had no idea what beast lied in wait for them. "I'm not jealous. I barely know you. All I've learned so far is that you're a confident mage and a pervert. You have some compassion for letting me stay here, but that gets overshadowed by the other two. Honestly, I'm worried about your sister. You must get some scolding from her if you frequent women so much."

"You certainly know how to deflate a man's hopes, Bluebell," he sighed before he stared back to her. He set down the knife and made his way over. She tensed as she watched him like a hawk. Will stopped a few feet from her. His right hand rested on his hip while his other hand covered part of his face. "Still, you have no idea the agony that my sister puts me through. The other women that come here are her friends, and when she brings them over, it's so exhausting."

He moved back from her before he collapsed onto his chair. Both his hands went to his face as he leaned forward. His fingers combed back until his golden blonde locks became somewhat disorderly. "Her friends demand so much when they come for a visit. It's hard to satisfy their appetite."

Despite his explanation to get around the truth of the matter, she felt that his lies were still built upon that truth. When she looked at it from that angle, it was hard to keep the heat away from her cheeks out of pure embarrassment. If she ever heard Tarhuinn say such things, she would probably die from the blood rushing to her face.

"For breakfast, lunch and dinner, they all command me to give them the best that I have. It drives a man to the brink of insanity to have such ordering women around."

She almost yelled at him to be quiet until she heard the second statement. Will had already gone down the path of insanity, but he knew how to control it. That was what made the man before her so terrifying. At any moment, he could let it loose and let it take over before pulling it back with exceptional skill.

Or, that seemed to be the case. How else would he be able to deceive so many women? Still, that wasn't the most disconcerting part. Did he truly have a sister or sisters for that matter? If so, where were they? Were they even alive?

"You'd think that they wouldn't mind delicious courses of fish for each meal. I live by a lake. What do they expect of me?"

The harmless finish to his otherwise potentially debauched remarks was almost like being hit by a massive wave. She was thankful, though, that it drained any possible heat from her cheeks. Odette could recompose herself. Unfortunately, the male before her wasn't so kind to let the opportunity before him slip away.

"For one so innocent, your mind certainly does travel to interesting places."

Like rain suddenly pouring down, the heat came back at full force. Tightening her hands around the skirt of her dress, she huffed and looked away. "You're the one who said it in such a questioning tone."

Chuckling loudly, he got up from his seat and went behind hers. Without any warning, he pushed the chair and her forward only to receive a yelp of surprise from her. He positioned her directly in front of the fireplace before he worked on getting it started.

Once it was, he rested both hands on his hips while a smirk graced his face. "Why don't I show you how delicious I can make a meal? I really did mean it about cooking for them. They really had such high expectancies. Perhaps, you'll be more pleased."

If it weren't for how he was standing, she might've taken him seriously, but she had a feeling that his words still had a dual meaning to them. There was that worrying gleam in his eyes again, but it vanished as he made his way back over to the fish. "Warm yourself by the fire while I prepare our meal. You need to dry off, or you'll become ill in this weather. Granted, I could always dry you off myself." He peered over his left shoulder with a playful smirk and winked.

"I'm perfectly fine by the fire," she remarked, sending a warning look his way. He shrugged as though she was missing out on some extravagant offer, but her attention turned back to the fire before her. At first, she had thought that he was going to toss her right in. Will probably could've if he had truly desired to. It didn't help that he had a well-built upper body. The muscles in his arms were rather noticeable with his short-sleeved, tan shirt on.

"Are we really going to eat those fish, though?" she asked, wondering how something that gross looking could ever taste delicious. Then again, the male before her ate humans, so who knew what quelled his hunger when he didn't have a ready supply of human. Of course, he might've stashed some away in a secret location in the cabin, but there was no odd smell about the place. At least, her nose couldn't detect any.

"Yes, it tastes like octopus if you've ever had any of that."

Having never tried octopus or seeing one for that matter, Odette was left with only her doubts about the disgusting looking fish. It honestly looked like someone had coughed up enough bile until it turned into a moldable glob. Once he prepared the food, he walked by with an empty pot and headed outside to retrieve water from the lake.

"Couldn't you use magic to fill the pot with water?"

"I could, but it's helpful to learn how to live without my magic all of the time. Not everyone across the lands is fond of mages," he called back before he continued on his way to the lake.

Such a statement was true enough. There were such individuals back in her village. No harm ever came to the mages that went through Watergrove, but it was clear that some wished to administer it to them. Right now, she desired to attack the mage she was with, but the deal with the pixies held her back. There was also the realistic truth that she couldn't take on a mage by brute force alone. Instead, she had to perform a dance of deception until she had him captivated and willing to do her bidding.

Her expression changed to one of curiosity when he came back inside. The door was shut again, but it did help to block out the cold. He placed the fish into the pot along with some herbs and seasoning before he set it on the hook above the fire. Will pulled his chair up next to hers afterwards, relaxing his arms over the back.

"Will since you're allowing me to stay here for a bit, can you tell me a little bit more about yourself? For example, what drew you to come and live all the way out here? Not many travel out this way unless they wish to take advantage of the abundant supply of wood. Besides, it'll make me feel better about staying here."

"Is that so? Well, I do aim to please. In that case, I suppose that I can relieve your curiosity and boost your trust of me. I came out here several months ago and found this abandoned cabin. I fixed it up and decided to call it home. As for why that is, it's because I couldn't tolerate things back in the villages and towns. It was too crowded for my liking. I like the freedom and quiet that this place provides."

A pleasant smell emanating from the pot, her stomach almost grumbled. Brown eyes trained on the food, she intertwined her fingers and rubbed her thumbs together. The warm flames sent a satisfying wave of warmth her way as she found that she could actually relate somewhat to what he had just told her. "I think that's also what drew me to my husband. He lived out in the woods, and it was quiet. My old home was so confining, and, with him, it was very freeing."

Tarhuinn didn't live out in the woods, but the rest was true in a way. Despite the troubling parts of the journey, she was experiencing more of the world. "Or, maybe, it was more curiosity that drew me to him. I had never lived out of a village setting before, and he seemed to offer something more thrilling in life. There was the chance to leap out and explore something new."

While explaining, however, she didn't notice the expression of fondness that began to paint her face. Odette didn't register that a few tears had begun to run down her cheeks. Sure, Tarhuinn had caused her immense pain from calling out to her and he was overprotective on an unhealthy level, but he had trusted her enough to take her out on their journey. He had given her a chance at adventure that she never would've had before, yet she had left him behind to the pixies.

Odette knew already that she had made the right decision. She had told herself beforehand. If she hadn't taken her present course, they would both be dead. It was simple, yet the image of Tarhuinn's countenance when she broke their agreement was difficult to handle. To him, it was like she had taken his own dagger and stabbed him in the back.

Resting on her left shoulder, a hand snapped her out of her memories. She now felt the tears on her face, and she quickly wiped them away. "I'm sorry. It's just that I wish this had never happened between us. Our marriage was doomed to fail, though, wasn't it? I was too much in a fantasy. I was looking for that perfect moment too much to realize that he just wanted me for my body in the end." A sob left her lips before she covered her eyes with her hands. Odette needed to get back into the game; she could only let so much truth slip. If too much came out into the open, the false pieces of the story would appear questionable.

Wood scraping against wood sounded before Will faced her. He rested both hands on her shoulders, sending her a sympathetic smile. "Your marriage from the beginning wasn't predestined to fall apart. Your husband made that decision a few nights ago. He's the one who destroyed your relationship by not having trust in you."

Pulling her hands away from her face, he set them on her lap before he wiped away her tears. At first, she leaned away from him, but when he persisted, she forced herself to relax. She didn't meet his gaze, though. Instead, she pretended to be shy. Her eyes turned to her left some while she bit her bottom lip to fight back another sob.

As he tended to her sorrow, Will was chuckling on the inside. It was obvious that the woman before him still cared for her husband deeply. There was just enough vulnerability there, however, that he could twist her to his liking. He could sink his fangs in steadily and let the poison corrupt her in such a way that she wouldn't notice until it was too late.

He was quite tempted, however, to reach over and nip at her flesh to have a taste. Unlike his past house guests, she had never been touched there before. Will could barely resist on finding out what her flesh's difference would be. Patience would be vital, though. If he rushed, he would spoil the exceptional prize before him. There was also the possibility that he would never have a house guest like her again, so he would savor her. Besides, she had amused him genuinely several times already. Her innocence really brought some interesting characteristics to the table.

Maybe tonight, he would steal something of hers. A small taste wouldn't hurt if she didn't notice. She was recovering for the moment, though. Sliding his hands away from her tantalizing skin, he sat up straight in his chair. "You did nothing wrong, Bluebell. Just remember that. You stayed loyal to your husband, but apparently that wasn't good enough for him."

Shifting her brown orbs over his way, she let a small smile grace her lips. "Thank you for the kind words ... I suppose that you're right. It's just hard to accept everything that's happened. I'm terrified of him, but I want to remedy things too. If he's alive and if I go back, though, I know that he'll kill me. The fantasy in my mind can no longer become a reality, yet it pains me to acknowledge that."

She clenched her hands around the skirt of her dress like so many times before. Will desired for her to tug a little harder so that the skirt would rise up a bit. His want remained only mental. Only a caring expression fell upon his face and eyes. "I would go search for your husband and learn of his state, but my fear is leaving you behind here. If he's alive, he could do some damage if he found this place and you inside. Hopefully, you understand that."

"I do. You're concerned for my health even though you've only known me for less than a day. I appreciate that very much."

Smiling gently, he nodded before he turned his chair back to the fire. He intertwined his fingers and rested his chin on his knuckles. "Your fantasy by the way," he looked over her way to make sure that her gaze was on him, and it was, "can still happen." Confusion flashed onto her countenance.

Will diverted his gaze more onto her. "Let's say that your husband is deceased; you can move on. You can find another love of your life. I believe that it's fair to say that your husband didn't deserve your affections. You shouldn't stay fixed on a man like that. For awhile, it might be hard to think like that, but I assure you that it'll be better for your health. You have your whole life ahead of you; don't waste it on him."

Silence was his answer, but he could tell that she was debating his words. That was all that he needed. He planted the seed, and he would have her soon. She would come over to him and care for him. Will had her in the proper mold; it simply needed to harden.

~~~~~~~~~~~

Lying on his back, he pretended to be asleep. Currently, some of the scouts were giving a report to their king and queen. He knew that they were talking about Odette and the mage. To his relief, it sounded like she hadn't given her name away. Instead, the mage took to calling her 'Bluebell.' It still bothered him immensely. If anyone were to compare her to a flower, it would be him, not some other male.
~~~~~~~~~~~

He was able to listen to the report calmly until the scouts mentioned that she had bathed in front of him. In an instant, he shot up and reached out to grab the nearest pixie. Cries sounded before they flew out of his reach. If he didn't have the bonds on, a good few of them would've been killed. "What do you mean that she bathed in front of him?!"

"It's exactly how it sounds, kelremm," the king answered calmly. "He was facing away from her a few times. Whenever he looked back her way, she would throw a fish at him. Apparently, she hasn't taken our advice to heart yet. Now, do you have to be put back to sleep, or will you remain at ease?"

The clarification did soothe him somewhat, but he would kill the mage when he had the chance. How dare he try to view Odette nude. The perverted b*stard would pay dearly. Moving into a sitting up position, Tarhuinn sat cross-legged before his stomach annoyingly rumbled. A mumble of irritation left his lips before he searched for one of their packs.

"Your food will be saved while you stay here. I've had some fish and rose petals prepared for you," the queen responded as some pixies swiftly placed a plate in front of him before they flew off.

"I won't eat that."

"Then, you'll starve. It'll be a shame if your wife returns only to find you dead because you wouldn't accept our hospitality," the king voiced in way to indicate that he was tired of Tarhuinn's behavior. When the kelremm still didn't eat, the king asked, "Should I have the plate taken away, then?"

Clenching his fingers, Tarhuinn pressed his lips into a thin line. He held back a remark before he brought the plate closer. Reluctantly, he began to eat. The pixies were inflaming him all the more. All he desired to do was go after Odette and murder the d*mned mage. If something were to happen to her, he would lose himself. There wouldn't be a point to him living. His twelve years of waiting would come to naught.

They had been married, however. That was something, and the ring beside him and the one on him reminded him of that. If she were killed and he gave completely into fury, at least they would've had that much. Hopefully, it wouldn't get to that point. He didn't wish to discover that she had been murdered in some brutal fashion. All he could do at the moment was hope and attempt to get out of his bonds. For that, he would have to eat the pixies' food.

Chapter Twenty Nine: Discovering a Reaction

His words would've been effective had her story really been completely true, but since it wasn't, it had the opposite effect. She did have her whole life ahead of her even if it was bound to be short with Tarhuinn. That was why she had started their mission: to live longer. Will's words only motivated her more to get him to travel to the pixies. Once the deal was made, Tarhuinn and she could move on. Tarhuinn most likely wouldn't walk out of the area without causing trouble, but she would convince him one way or another to let it go for the time being.

Perhaps, she would've had a much longer life had she never listened to Tarhuinn's calls and remained in her room, but she would've been locked away for it all. Could one really call that living? To her, her life now was the better alternative.

Looking to the mage before her, Odette nodded her head but continued to wear her saddened expression. "Thank you. I'll think on it." He responded with a warm smile before his attention returned to the cooking fish.

Getting up, he grabbed two bowls and spoons before he came back to the table. Soon enough, the soup was served. She thanked him for the meal, glad that it wasn't some suspicious meat. Odette wrapped her hands around the bowl at first to warm them up even more. When she took her first bite, she couldn't help the small smile that appeared on her lips. It tasted delicious. The eighteen-year-old found herself gobbling down the meal only to have a chuckle reach her ears.

Glancing out of the corners of her eyes, she noted Will quite amused. "I must say that I should've searched for you out in those woods if you like my cooking that much. It's a nice change from the complaints of my sister and her friends. Not to mention your difference in eating techniques."

Heat invaded her cheeks a little bit. She hadn't meant to be so obvious, but it really did taste amazing. Part of it could be, though, that she hadn't had a warm meal in several days. There was the bread, but it didn't compare. "Sorry, the running made me hungrier than I realized." Odette glanced down to the bowl, still embarrassed, and ate with her spoon more delicately.

"There's no reason to hold yourself back. Like I said, it's a welcome change. All of them would typically eat with a doubtful look on their faces and slowly as though they could make something better out of the resources around here. They were rather ungrateful."

Giving him a side glance, she analyzed his face as though she was seriously debating his words. She pressed her lips together before she looked back to the soup. In the next instant, she went back to her old eating style. Another chuckle hit her ears, but she took it as approval. So far, she seemed to only be on his good side unless everything he did he adjusted to his victim's personality.

Over the course of the meal, which was short-lived for her, she went back to asking various questions about him. They weren't anything serious since she wished to keep the conversation on less sensitive topics. Despite the simplicity of the questions, any information could be turned against him in one way or another. There was merely the issue of whether he was answering them truthfully or not. She tried to discern what information wasn't falsified, but it ended up bringing no success.

From the various questions, she learned things like his favorite color, food, season and activities. He happened to like the color green, but, on occasion, it would switch to blue. For food, he preferred meat, though; he didn't specify the type. His favorite season was winter since it made preserving foods easier. Will mentioned that he didn't have to use as much magic, which leaves him a little more energy for the day. As for activities, he preferred cooking and fishing.

Everything pointed to his hidden nature. The color green not so much, but she had a suspicion that he had said blue because she was wearing a blue dress. For the meat, it was most definitely human flesh, and preserving it was important. He couldn't let his house smell like rotting corpses. Concerning his activities, cooking was obvious enough, but fishing could also mean fishing for women. Or maybe, he also did like the regular sort of fishing.

"Maybe, you could show me how to fish, then. It might be a good skill for me when I decide to leave your hospitality."

Instead of answering her immediately, he began to laugh. At first, she thought the reason was because he had no intention of letting her leave until she remembered the bathing incident. "Bluebell, I think that you know how to fish well enough."

She puffed out her cheeks. Her arms crossed over her chest before she looked away from him. "You deserved every fish thrown at you. I probably should've chucked ten more at you. That would've kept you from looking for a long time."

Laughing some more, he agreed. "It surely would've, but do you honestly want to learn how to fish? It can be quite boring at times. There's a lot in this area, but many of them aren't as willing to be caught as the clinglob. Even then, clinglobs only like to attach themselves to smooth surfaces."

"Yes, it might not be fun all of the time, but it's a useful skill. I need to learn how to provide for myself if the situation asks for it. I'm not going to find a nearby cabin with a compassionate mage every time life brings its troubles."

An arrogant smirk touched his lips. "No, I suppose that you won't. I'm quite a host." He placed his knuckles on his hips and puffed out his chest. "This pose says it all." A laugh did escape her lips. Whether it was genuine or not, she couldn't tell. Not being able to determine its nature worried her, but she couldn't let that cloud her expression.

Dropping his stance, he wore a more caring countenance. "Of course if you ever find yourself in trouble again, you're more than welcome to come back here. My home will always be open to you, Bluebell." He stood up and grabbed both of their empty bowls. Will stood in front of her for a little longer than expected.

Inspecting his gaze, it almost seemed like he wished to kiss her, but he refrained and turned around. Thankful, she mentally sighed before her eyes followed his movement. "And, I appreciate that. I don't know where I'll go after this, so it's nice to know that I'll have a place to return to. Your sister and her friends wouldn't mind, though?"

He placed the dishes in the dish bucket. The sound of the wood bowls hitting each other resonated throughout the room. There was a long pause, which was odd. Will had talked about his sister and her friends before with no trouble. Now, it was as though she had said something that had greatly offended him. "I apologize if I had said something that I shouldn't have."

"No, you're fine. I was just remembering something." He picked up the bucket and walked by her. Will rested his left hand on her left shoulder. "There are some books in my room's desk. They're in the upper right hand drawer. You can grab them and entertain yourself for the day. I'm going to go wash these and do some work outside. We can fish tomorrow." With that, he headed out and closed the door behind him.

Whatever he had recalled, it would do her well to find out what it had been. Despite all the smiles and warm gestures he made, that beast always seemed to be lurking nearby since it had first made its appearance. Before he had left, however, it was gone. Maybe, he was faking it. To her, though, genuine grief had filled his gaze. It was as though the brightness in his green eyes had vanished completely. Then and there, the madness had entirely left him.

Odette needed to discover what had caused such a reaction. In that memory, she might find his true weakness. It might be terrible of her to exploit something like that, but she was dealing with a man who had taken advantage of multiple women. He had ended who knew how many lives and continued the practice with a monstrous grin. Will was only asking for something ill to happen to him.

The male's talk of his sister did raise suspicion. She was beginning to think that he might very well have or have had one. His sister might be the key to solving the time puzzle before her. Getting up and going into the next room over, she was tempted to explore his belongings, but she didn't know if he had spelled them in some way. If she touched certain ones, he might learn of it, so she refrained from curiosity.

There was a way to discover the male's secrets by merely talking to him. She was sure of it. Already, she had gotten quite far in less than a single day. If she continued on her current path, her reward would come shortly.

Opening the drawer that he had mentioned, she found two books inside. One was a book of children's tales. The other was a guide on what was edible in the wilderness, which would prove useful. Still, she picked up both and closed the drawer.

It would serve her well to switch between the two so that her mind could have a break from reading over a guidebook. Odette seated herself on the bed and lied back against the headboard. She set the books down, took off her boots, placed them in the same fashion as last night and pulled the covers over herself to keep warm before she opened the guidebook and began to read.

The remainder of the day was uneventful. Odette continued to read the two books while Will remained outside. He was probably at the back of the house because he wasn't anywhere near the lake. At least, that was the case until it was close to dusk. Perhaps, he had been in his secret holding area for his wicked appetite. If that place existed, she wanted to avoid it at all costs.

After a short stop at the lake shore, he came back into the house with two more clinglobs in hand. Closing the children's tales book, she was about to get up, but he walked into the room. "Hopefully, you hadn't been too bored in here."

"No, I enjoy reading. It's been awhile since I've just been able to sit down and read." That was somewhat true. Beforehand, she had been reading for research purposes. Today, had been more of enjoyment reading. "Still, I wouldn't think that you would own a fairytale book, but it was nice to read some of the old tales again."

"Well, that book is my sister's. Honestly, she leaves a lot of things behind it seems," he answered with a sigh before a shrug followed. It sounded, though, like he was holding something back. She questioned whether the original owner of the book was really his sister.

Getting to her feet, she grabbed the books and put them away. "Can I help with dinner? You made breakfast this morning, and I just sat by. I feel that I should be more helpful."

"I wouldn't mind the aid. Come along then, and I'll show you how to make some delicious soup." He turned on his heel and headed back into the kitchen. At the preparation counter, he set the fish down before he started to show her how to cut them. Will worked on the first and handed the knife to her for the second.

If she were committed to her old tactic of attacking him to convince him, she would've held the knife to his throat in an instant. Since that wasn't the case, she brought it to the fish. As she was cutting the clinglob, though, she could easily feel Will's stare on her. It was unsettling to say the least. Was he imagining her under the knife?

His left hand soon rested over her right. "That's enough ... Let's turn to seasoning now." Complying, she placed the knife down and looked over to him. There was the tiniest of grins on his lips. It appeared as though he had been chuckling madly to himself. It vanished soon after, but it reminded her that at any moment he could lash out at her. She could be his next meal within seconds.

Once everything for the meal was ready, Will grabbed the pot and went outside to fill it with water. From there, she placed the fish, seasonings and herbs into the pot before it was put over the fire. When the meal was finished, they both ate.

Light conversation greeted them along with the occasional lingering glance and dual meaning remark from him. Nothing of new information came to her ears, which was a disappointment. It appeared, though, that Will was purposely avoiding anything of that nature, meaning that the memory from before was possibly still haunting him.

Like the night before, he headed out to take his bath, though; he took the dishes and wash bucket also. She made her way into the bedroom, taking her boots off and putting them in the same place as last night. Odette pulled the covers over herself and kept her gaze on the ceiling. Were she to glance out the window, she would see something that she would rather evade.

She rolled onto her left side. Odette held the sheets closer for warmth, but her mind traveled to how Tarhuinn was holding up. It wasn't hard to imagine him causing trouble for the pixies. He probably already had tried to escape once or twice. At least, he had been prevented from calling out to her again.

Maybe, he understood that using such a tactic while she was so close to the mage was a poor idea. If she were to go into that state again, Will would find it more than suspicious. There was a chance that he didn't know what a kelremm was, but with Tergii and Bimaa's monthly trips she doubted it.

That was when she heard it. Her name was being lightly called. She recognized the soothing tone of his voice. Part of her wished to get up and go back to him, but the rest of her forced herself to stay put. Right now, she couldn't answer his call. He needed to accept that. Bringing the sheets closer, she shut her eyes and pictured his protective arms around her. The calming image nearly lulled her to sleep; however, the opening of a door brought her back to her senses.

Moving onto her back, she glanced over to see Will dressed in a simple green, long-sleeved shirt and brown pants. He smiled to her from the doorway before setting down the wash bucket and putting away the clean dishes. Once done, he came into the bedroom and made himself comfortable on the floor with the blanket. Will said goodnight to her before seemingly falling asleep; however, she stayed awake until she felt that he was really asleep. After rolling onto her left side and making a quick check on him, she was pleased enough and let the image of being in Tarhuinn's hold bring her into the folds of sleep.

A little bit of time passed before Will sat up from his position. Smirking, he got to his feet and quietly made his way back into the kitchen. He grabbed a clean knife before he came back into the room. When they had been preparing dinner, he had been quite tempted to slice the blade across a section of her skin, but he had resisted the urge. One of his grins hadn't been able to stay away, though. Luckily, it had faded away swiftly.

Carefully, he pulled the sheets from her clutches. A shiver ran up her form. Her hands reached out and grabbed onto his right pant leg. The smirk wouldn't leave his lips as he sat down on the bed and permitted her to hold onto him more. He moved the pillow aside, which permitted her to rest her head on his lap. His stunning prize's breathing remained steady.

Gently, he pushed aside some of her light blonde locks. His fingers glided across her right cheek before he moved them down to her lips. They were silken soft. He desired to bite at them gently before doing so roughly. To have her crimson life source run down his own lips nearly caused him to drop the knife in his left hand. He couldn't wake her, though.

Regaining his focus, he lifted her right hand and upturned her palm to him. Steadily, he drew the blade across her skin. She winced in her sleep, and he paused for a moment. When she calmed back down, he continued. Once finished, he licked the blade clean. The taste was as though someone had dipped a fresh cherry in the finest chocolate. If sweet bread were to be dipped in her blood, it would be absolutely divine.

Placing the knife to the side of him, he brought her palm to his lips. To keep himself from losing complete control, he allowed himself only one lick. As he dragged his tongue across, he healed her wound too. A groan exited her lips before she moved in her sleep. She rolled onto her stomach, and he let go of her hand. It was healed by then, but he couldn't keep his mind from how delicious the rest of her would taste. No doubt, he had to hold onto her for longer. His bluebell was something to be treasured.

Slipping away from her, he picked up the knife, put it away and lied back down. Tomorrow, though, he would have to work on his last catch to keep himself from moving along too quickly with his prize. They were to go fishing, however. Maybe, he whould get up earlier. As he made such plans, a grin plastered itself onto his lips before he drifted off into sleep himself.

Unaware to both of them, Tarhuinn was still awake. He sat upright in the pixies' home. The royals were asleep, but several guards kept watch on him. While he called his beloved's name, he focused the rest of his energy on his bonds. It would take awhile, but he would break them slowly so as not to draw attention to himself. His rage would channel itself steadily into the icy holds.

By the end of tomorrow, he would be free. The problem would be getting out of the area on the thin water path. First, though, he would have to dispatch the guards. Occasionally, to take a break from the bonds, he would watch his night guards' behavior. He studied every aspect of them to learn their weaknesses. It would be better to knock them unconscious than to kill them. If he were captured again, he would probably receive better treatment, which would lead to him having a higher chance of escaping again.

Sleep tried to claim him on multiple accounts, though. Eventually, it would ensnare him, but he forced himself to stay awake for as long as possible. Rain started to pour down with the passing of the night hours. The water felt luxurious across his skin and cleansed him of the past days' efforts. Both royals wouldn't allow him a bath since they knew better than to remove his bonds. Unfortunately, that wasn't the most humiliating thing out of his captive state. To have guards watch him relieve himself was something that irked him greatly.

Just the thought of it caused him to put a little too much energy into his work against the bonds. A crack was heard, but his gaze remained pinned on the pixie guards. He acted as though it was nothing and relaxed his hands and feet. Moving his gaze up to the sky, he let a few droplets fall into his mouth before he fell back. Tarhuinn told himself that tomorrow he would be free; he would be able to retrieve Odette.

Chapter Thirty: Falling Catch

For the first hour of morning, it was relatively similar to the previous one. Odette woke up, bathed, dressed in her own undergarments and a new dress, with it being an off-white color, and ate some breakfast. Like yesterday, the dish was created with clinglobs, though; it was cooked in a pan with vegetables.

During breakfast, however, she wasn't able to shake off an odd feeling. Her right hand felt strange since she had woken up. It was as though there should've been something there, but she wasn't able to see it. The sensation reminded her of when Will had healed her wounds upon first arriving there. Had he done something to her in sleep?

Towards the end of breakfast, a hand rested on her left shoulder. "Are you alright, Bluebell? You look troubled. Did you have a bad dream last night? You've been rather quiet this morning."

She knew very well that she had experienced no such thing. In fact, she had a simple yet pleasant dream. For the whole time, she had been resting against Tarhuinn. That fact couldn't slip past her lips. "Yes, and it would explain why I woke up with the sheets partially off and my pillow off to the side."

Removing his hand, he took the last bite of his meal. After he swallowed, he asked, "Are you willing to tell me what it was about? Your husband, perhaps?"

"Yes, he was chasing me again. I dreamt that I hadn't found this cabin and that he had recovered from the wound that I had given him. He charged after me, and I ran for the lake. Having nowhere else to go, I jumped in and started to swim across.

"He didn't go in the water himself. When I looked back, he was gone as was the shore. I was in an endless sea of water before something started to float up to the surface." She paused as though she couldn't say the next part. He motioned for her to go on. "And, it was a horribly mutilated body; it was your body, Will."

Fingers intertwining, she glanced over to him. His expression remained neutral before he smiled to her. He patted her on the head and stood to his feet. "If you're worried about your husband killing me, you shouldn't. I already told you that I'll be able to handle him. It's flattering to know that you're concerned about my safety, though."

A shy gaze crossed her face. It turned to her hands and stayed fixed there. "I feel that it's insulting to you. You've been so kind to me and promised to give me safety, yet I doubt your word as I'm sleeping in your very bed."

Picking up their dishes, he chuckled some. "Having someone apologize to me about dreaming about me is a new one. It doesn't bother me at all. You've only seen your husband fight, not me. You have no comparison to make. It would only be natural for you to assume that your husband could very well win against me. His actions probably overshadow my words at the moment." He sent her a charming smile. "Now, how about I make you forget about that nightmare by showing you how to fish?"

Smiling a little, she nodded. "Thank you. I would like that." He gave her another smile before he put the dishes in the wash bucket for now. When he returned to her, he held out his left hand. Hesitantly, she took it and allowed him to pull her up.

Leading her outside, he closed the door and gestured her to go towards the lake. "Head over while I get the supplies. I'll meet you there shortly." She complied while he headed off to the back of the cabin. If she tried to follow him, it would most likely result in her death. The supplies were probably near the entrance to some secret area of his. Odette didn't need to see the bodies to know what he was capable of.

As she stood by the lake's shore, she glanced out over the water. In the middle of the lake, she saw Will's body come up again. She knew that it was purely her imagination, but the way that his body looked could become a reality. Tarhuinn was more than able to perform such damage on another living being. The incident with the tenlites had proved that quite well.

Hugging her arms, her attention went back to the chilled air. She should've brought a blanket out with her. Her dress was barely doing anything against the cold. Despite the low cut of the dress, the skirt was a little thicker than the blue dress from yesterday. If it had been as thin as the blue one, it would've been see-through.

Footsteps sounded nearby once more, and Will returned with two fishing rods and some bait. He seemed to note her state before he set the items down and ran back into the house. A few moments later, he came back out with a blanket in hand. "Sorry about that. I should've known that this weather wouldn't suit you." Will draped the blanket over her shoulders and pulled it around her front. "Better?"

"Much. Thank you. I could've gone in, though."

He waved his hand dismissively. "Nonsense. I asked you to wait here without any real protection against the cold. Of course, I should've headed into my home and grabbed you one." To that, she gave a small smile in thanks.

He handed her a fishing rod with bait on the end. Standing close to the shore of the water, he demonstrated how to set the wired hook in the water. She followed his example. Soon enough, both of them were waiting patiently for a fish to bite. It was rather simple, but she needed to know how to make the tool. "Did you craft these poles, Will?"

"No, I bought them at the market in the village, which is a day's travel from here, but I do know how to make one. It might be hard for you to craft one, though, if you don't have the proper tools. The pole itself will need to be made out of wood. Preferably, you'll want one that bends well for when the fish pulls. We're surrounded by pine trees, however, so you'll want to break off a branch and trim it. It'll last some days before the wood dries out, but I would recommend using it only for small fish. Otherwise, your pole will have a high chance of snapping on you.

"As for the line itself, horse hair is common, but I haven't encountered too many wild horses out here. Then, there's the issue of getting the horse to lend you its hair. Normally, you could probably buy some off of someone in a market. You may have to use your own hair, which would take a lot more strands to have comparable thickness. For the hook, again you won't be able to purchase a hook in the middle of a forest. With that in mind, you'll want to find a small animal, kill it and carve one of its bones."

"Thank you. I'll keep that in mind." A light laugh left her lips. "I seem to be doing a lot of that recently, though. I think that you deserve an award for your hosting abilities."

Wearing a grin, he rested his right knuckles on his hip. If there were a boulder nearby, he would probably have a foot propped up on it. "I know; I'm …" He never got to finish his line of thought as something tugged on his fishing rod. The force caught him off guard, and, in the attempt to pull it back, he fell into the water.

His catch probably swam away in the process. As he sat up properly, he found a clinglob on his right hand. Covering her mouth with her free hand, Odette couldn't help but laugh. The incident was too amusing not to. "And, you said that I knew how to fish. I think that you're the better in this instance," she chuckled while he pursed his lips in annoyance.

Soon, though, a smirk covered them. "If that's the case, I need to show you how it's done, then." He swiftly reached over to her fishing pole, but she let it go in time. She jumped back just in case. A frown appeared on him as he took the clinglob off and placed it back in the water. Will crossed his arms over his chest. "I guess that you don't want to learn about fishing, then."

"Oh, I do, just not that method." She picked up her fishing rod and distanced herself from him a little. "Unlike you, I can't wave my hands around and heat myself up." Before he could speak, she continued, "And, I'm not letting you warm me up either, pervert."

"That's a shame." There was a playful grin on his lips before he picked himself up and dried himself off. He grabbed his fishing rod once more. "Getting that dress wet would be quite beneficial to me too."

Embarrassed, she crouched down and felt for a clinglob in the water. When something grabbed onto her hand, she smirked and lifted the fish out and threw it at him. He had been looking away, which allowed the fish to impact the side of his face. It fell back into the water, unharmed, and swam off swiftly. As for Will, he had lost his balance once more. Another splash sounded, leaving a victory smile on Odette's lips. "Serves you right."

"I really should keep my distance from you when we're near water," he mumbled, rubbing the right side of his face. "Otherwise, you might make the population of clinglobs here extinct." She rolled her eyes and focused on catching a different type of fish.

Over the course of the day, they moved out further since none of the fish were biting. Odette was convinced that only clinglobs lived by the lake shore. Now, they stood on some rocks that peeked out from the deeper water. The middle of the lake was far off, but if she fell in, there would probably be some good distance between the surface and floor of the lake. If the water was clearer, she would feel better about it, but she doubted that Will could influence the water to be so.

Seating herself on the rocks, she looked over to Will, who stood several feet away from her. She maintained a close eye on him in case he tried to push her in to get payback for earlier. He falling in, though, wasn't even her fault. Thankfully, he looked focused on fishing.

As silence was about to continue, she decided to take a risk. "Will, that book of children's tales ... was it really your sister's?"

Instead of one of his cheery responses, he asked in an unnerving calm voice, "What do you mean?"

"You said that it was your sister's, but when you mentioned that, you had a different tone in your voice. Usually, you're in a more optimistic mood when you talk about her despite all of the complaining her friends and she make about your food. For the book, you seemed like you had recalled something unpleasant." When he didn't answer but tightened his grip around the fishing rod, she quickly added, "I'm sorry. It's none of my business. My curiosity got the better of me."

Taking a seat himself, he shook his head. “It’s alright. I made myself too obvious. I should’ve known that you would’ve suspected something. There’s also the fact that you do observe me quite closely. You still don’t trust me. Then again, who would immediately trust a man out in the middle of the woods?” He pushed his left fingers back through his hair.

Meeting her gaze, he sent a small smile her way as if to say that he was alright. She wondered, though, if he was debating on killing her then and there. “The book ... wasn’t my sister’s. It belonged to a childhood friend of mine. Unfortunately, she passed away ten years ago in an ... accident.” As the word accident slipped past his lips, she noted pure rage burning in his eyes. It reminded her of Tarhuinn’s look whenever he became inflamed.

When it vanished, she responded softly, “I apologize for asking. That must’ve been rough on you.”

“It was,” he simply answered. “You didn’t know, though. There’s no need to apologize. I had you explain your rough marriage to me. It’s to be expected that I give you some more information about me.”

“Would you like me not to read the book again? I wouldn’t want to ruin something with a precious value to it.”

“No, I’d rather you utilize it. I haven’t read it in awhile, so it’s good to see it in use. I’m sure that my friend would’ve wished for that. Besides, I like you. I haven’t laughed like I’ve laughed with you in quite some time. For that reason, I’d like you to read it even more.”

His words took her a little off guard, and she didn’t know what to say. She didn’t like him back. If anything, she was merely happy that she had received more information from him. There was the possibility that it wasn’t true, but that angered gaze of his had suggested otherwise. To her, that had been no act, and something more than an accident must’ve happened to his childhood friend.

"Thank you, then." She fell silent afterwards. Out of the corners of her eyes, she still watched him. Since he was aware of her past observations, he probably could feel her current stare. His focus seemingly remained on the lake. Biting her lower lip, she didn't know whether she should say something else, but a tug on her fishing rod caught her full attention.

The supposed fish tugged harder, causing her to stand to her feet. It pulled more, and she planted her feet firmly on the rocks. She started to back up some, but the fish continued its fight to swim away. Swiftly, Will set his rod down and ran over. He stood behind her, resting his hands over hers and gripped the rod in the process. Will jerked his hands back with hers.

A trout was brought out of the water and landed on the rocks. Will gave her a congratulatory pat on the back before he crouched down and unhooked the fish. He kept it from hopping back into the water. "Looks like we have dinner now, but let's see if we can catch a few more," he voiced as his grin was back.

Odette remained hesitant, so she simply nodded in response. She grabbed another piece of bait from the bucket and attached it to the rod before she dipped the hook back in the water. After Will tossed the fish into an empty bucket for catches, he rested his right hand on her left upper arm. "Don't feel guilty about asking me that question. Let's just enjoy the rest of the day. We should be joyful; we have an amazing meal ahead of us."

"You're right." Bringing a smile to her lips, she exclaimed, "Let's see who can catch more fish! I've already bested you with one."

"Well, we still have most of the afternoon. I can still beat you."

No bets were placed, but they had forgotten about them in the first place. If anyone were to walk by, they would find two individuals glaring at the water and asking a fish to come. The competition became more of a waiting game and hoping that the fish would choose their hook over their competitor's.

It was odd, though, for Odette. She didn't think that she would end up in a friendly competition with a dangerous mage. There was also a genuine smile on her face since she was having fun. Will seemed to be in a similar condition. A grin covered his lips, and he kept chanting for the fish to choose his hook. He looked like a little kid, but she probably appeared the same.

Perhaps, it was similar to how he was with his childhood friend. If that were the case, she might have decent odds at persuading him to come with her. By Will permitting her to read that book further, it could mean that she was on the right path. The question remained of whether that was enough, however. If it wasn't, she would be at a loss, and she might have to go down that other route.

In the end, the score was three to two, with her in the lead. Setting the end of her rod down, she rested her right hand on her hip and smirked victoriously. "Looks like I win. And already, the apprentice has surpassed the master. I'm looking forward to this amazing fish dinner that you've promised."

"It would appear that I'll have to accept that." He picked up the fish and bait bucket. "I'll put everything inside. It looks like it's about to rain. You should head inside. Otherwise, that dress of yours might be too revealing for you."

Heat touched her cheeks as droplets of rain began to fell. Right now, it was a light sprinkle, but that could change shortly. She huffed and handed her rod to him roughly. "Pervert," she mumbled as she walked by. Odette was careful on the rocks, though, since she didn't desire to fall into the chilly water. His typical chuckle sounded, but she kept her gaze forward.

By the time that she reached the front door, it had begun to pour. Quickly, she went inside and shut the door. She pushed strands of her light blonde hair back before she placed some wood in the fireplace and started it. Will came in shortly after. Unlike her, though, he was soaked. He seemed pleased to have the fire going, but he headed into the bedroom. "Should I leave the door open for you?" he asked as he set the bucket of fish by the doorway.

Frowning, she countered, "Would you like to meet your dinner early?"

Holding his hands up in surrender, he laughed before he closed the door. She finished with the fire and seated herself in her regular chair. Odette would've brought the fish over to the counter, but she would keep to her prize. Besides, she didn't want to be anywhere near him when he had a knife in his hand. The dagger in her boot, however, did provide her some comfort.

Remembering the dagger did bring a frown to her lips. It reminded her that Tarhuinn was left in the pixie camp and probably worried sick about her, yet she had been laughing earlier that day. She was making jokes with a man that would eventually try to kill and eat her. Odette wished to return to her husband and apologize; she desired to tell him that she was laughing because some of events had been genuinely hilarious and not because she was growing closer to Will.

Her right hand reached down to her boot, and she patted the side of it lightly. Soon, she would be able to see him. The max time that she would allow herself to stay was a week, but she believed that it would be shorter than that. A couple more days and Will would hopefully be willing to come with her. "Just wait a little longer for me," she whispered as though Tarhuinn would hear her.

Chapter Thirty One: A Mark of Fear

After dinner was finished, she volunteered to wash the dishes since the rain had stopped. She mentioned that she was feeling a little more confident to go out on her own since it had been a few days now since the incident with her husband. Reluctantly, Will agreed, but he told her that he would be at the back of home, checking on a few things. Odette merely nodded as she had no desire to inquire about what those things were.

Once she headed out, she washed the dishes and took care of a few other nightly things. Just to relax in the cool night air a bit longer, though, she kept her hands in the water a little bit more. The water was quite cold without Will's magic, but it was somewhat refreshing. Despite its frigid temperature, it was soothing to have the water run over her skin. It reminded her a bit of how there would always be a constant flow of water back in Tarhuinn and her home.

The cold temperature, however, did get to her after several minutes. She pulled her hands out and wiped them on her dress's skirt. Odette picked up the bucket with the clean dishes before she headed back in. Will was still out, but she assumed that he had heard her close the door. After she placed the bucket on the ground and put the dishes away, she grabbed the blanket from the back of the chair and made her way into the bedroom.

Apparently, the blanket in her hands had been a spare as Will's other blanket was draped over the end of the bed, but she added it to the other one. The sheets were enough for her. Once she had her boots off and settled herself in, Will came inside, grabbed some clothes and went off to take his bath. Like before, she kept her gaze away from the window.

Unfortunately, she didn't hear Tarhuinn calling her name softly. It really did calm her nerves even if it could be turned into a painful weapon against her, but her eyes did close. Even though she did her best to keep herself awake, her body had other plans, and it won in the end.

Outside, Will walked into the lake up to his knee level and was pleased to find that she had gone inside already. There was some blood on his fingers after all. Even after eating a decent helping of trout, his craving for his bluebell hadn't vanished, so he had to have a small snack. Otherwise, he might've lost himself.

Splashing water onto his face and smoothing back his golden blonde locks, he wondered if he would be able to snatch another small taste. He did earn such a pleasure. After all, he had told her that he liked her, and he had meant it. Never had he done that before to one of his victims.

Not to mention that she also had discovered his lie about the one book. In the past, a couple of his victims had read over its pages, but they had never caught his lie when he told them of the original owner. If they had, they had never voiced it. That was probably part of the reason why he liked his bluebell more than the others. She had similar way of going about things like his childhood friend, or, at least, he imagined that his friend would've behaved like her if she had lived longer.

That might've been because he had spent too much time around one type of woman. He hadn't really interacted with a woman out of those features for awhile unless it was to buy supplies. Despite all of that, he would still have his bluebell. She would merely stay alive longer than the rest; he would give her that much.

Deciding to come out of the water, he walked onto the shore and dressed himself. He wrung out his hair before he stepped back into his home and locked the door. Will peeked into the bedroom and was glad to see her already asleep. To double check, he quietly stepped in and glided his fingers across her lips and down to her neck. She shifted some but otherwise made no other movement.

He went back into the kitchen and left his washed clothes on the mantel of the fireplace to dry. When he was about to grab a knife, however, he pulled his hand back as another idea came to his mind. Smirking, he turned on his heel and stepped softly into the room. He grabbed the dress and shirt's right sleeves to reveal the second mark on her. The bruise was getting lighter, but he had other plans for the time being.

Glancing over to the one on the side of her neck, he pressed his right middle and index fingers to the spot. She moaned slightly in her sleep, and he knew that she would be too sensitive there, so he went back to the shoulder mark. When he brought his fingers to that spot, she moaned but quieter than the first. If he were careful, he would be able to get away with his action there.

Gently, he rolled her from her left side and onto her back. Odette tried to move onto her right side, but he held her back. Her brows furrowed, but she didn't wake. She shifted slightly more before she settled down. He straddled her hips and leaned down until his lips touched the mark. Her husband was most likely dead, so he saw no reason for the deceased man's mark to be on her.

His hands pressed against the pillow and on either side of her head before he softly kissed the area. If she was awake, it would feel as though powdery snow brushed across her skin but left a warm touch behind. The kiss progressed to a rougher one as though the cold was finally nipping at her skin. When she went to move her shoulder away, he relaxed and carefully nudged it back against the bed.

As he waited for her to get comfortable again, he eyed the front of the corseted dress. He trailed his left fingers down the laced front, but he was tempted to untie the ribbon at the top. If she had been another one of his victims, the dress would've been off. In fact, that would've happened on the first or second night.

Bringing his fingers back up, he slid them along her exposed neck until his hand rested on the pillow again. By then, his lips were back on her shoulder. His teeth grazed her skin while he had a hard time keeping himself from biting her. The delicacy before him was too tempting. He pulled back a little and bit his bottom lip but didn't draw blood.

Analyzing her state, he wondered if he would be able to get away with it. Barely able to think on it, he leaned back down. He latched onto a small section of the mark before he sucked it between his teeth. As he reveled in the taste, he permitted his teeth to sink in too much.

Her sweet blood flowed into his mouth, and a moan of pleasure escaped him. Odette, however, groaned in her sleep before she tried to abruptly get her shoulder away from him. Swiftly, he let go and looked to her. She was beginning to get up. Wasting no time, he quickly pressed his right hand to the bleeding mark. As her eyes began to blink open, he healed it back to its previous state, pulled her sleeves back up, grabbed one of the blankets and made his way to the floor.

Draping the blanket over himself, he faced away from her. As he heard her sit up on the bed, he sucked on his bottom lip. The taste of her blood was still there, and it would be a pleasant treat to fall asleep to. He remained awake, however, until he heard her lay back down. Almost, he had revealed his true nature, but his reward was well worth it. With the delicious taste of her blood on his lips, he drifted off into the welcoming arms of sleep.

Regarding Odette, she had sat up on the bed in near panic. It had felt like something had pierced her shoulder. Her left hand had come up to the skin there. The sensation had been right where Tarhuinn had kissed her a few days ago. Brown orbs had gazed down at Will to see him asleep, but she had thought that she saw movement before she fully had awaken.

Removing her hand, she had examined the bruise there. It looked like it hadn't been touched, yet she had a similar feeling to that of her hand from when she had woken up in the morning. What had been occurring? Had Will truly been falling asleep, or had he been staying awake secretly until she had let sleep take over? Worry had gnawed at her as a shiver had run up her spine.

Hesitantly, she lied back down and turned over. She curled up some before she focused on the night sky outside. The young woman had trouble deciding whether she was progressing in her task. Her left hand went back to her right shoulder. Odette squeezed the area tightly as though that would bring Tarhuinn to her, though; an enraged husband wouldn't have been the most calming person. Like the previous night, she eased her scared self so that she could rest.

Currently, though, Tarhuinn was heading out of the pixie home with his guards. He had asked them if he could relieve himself, and they had complied. By now, his bonds were barely holding together. With one more tug, he would be free.

There were other pixies on guard. He could see some resting in bushes or in the higher regions of the pines. He didn't know how far he would get, but he would try his best to make it to the cabin. If he followed one of the streams, he was bound to reach it eventually. When the pixies stopped, he halted his movement as well and swiftly looked over their positions. Two snaps sounded before he began his escape.

Chapter Thirty Two: Runaway

Adrenaline coursed through him, and spears raced towards him. Tarhuinn focused on the pixie that had the weakest control of their weapon. As the spear was about to scrape past his left cheek, he grabbed it from the guard and twirled the small weapon around between his fingers. The tail and shaft of the spear hit the creature in the back of the head, knocking it to the snow below.

Several cuts were made across his arms, but he paid them no mind. Instead, he swiftly directed his attention to the remaining personal guards of his. Knowing their weak points, he hit them all before he knocked them unconscious. As the guards fell to the snow, the other pixies flew into action. He darted down the stream. If it were deeper, he would jump in and swim.

He could hear spears zipping past while metal being unsheathed rang in the air. His dark blue eyes didn't glance back once. Tarhuinn knew that he had at least a dozen pixies on his tail. It would only become more as the chase continued. The pixies didn't matter, though. Getting to Odette was what was important.

His feet pounded hard against the bottom of the stream as it intersected with another and led down the mountain's side. The droplets of rain only made his escape all the easier as they helped to deflect the spears some. By now, his hair tie was long lost. Soaked strands of long, ink-black hair clung to his face and arms. Small streaks of crimson trailed down his arms, but it was washed away as it came.

Odette's cloak had been abandoned in the camp when he had left the pixie home. Now, he let go of the one tied around his neck. It was slowing him down too much. He needed to be faster to reach his destination. Once off, the article of clothing flew back and blocked several pixies. They were pushed back until their weapons pierced the fabric, and they were able to carry on ahead.

The king and queen joined the pursuit. Forming a protective ring around the queen, the king and his personal guards charged ahead to get the queen close enough to the male kelremm without being harmed. They still couldn't catch up to him. Matters became worse when the stream took a steeper downward slope.

It only caused Tarhuinn to go faster. His feet nearly slid down the rocks under the running water. Surrounding pine trees blocked his view to both sides, but he knew that he still had a ways to go before he reached the cabin. The main concern for him was running out of stamina before getting to the structure.

Up ahead, tree branches hung over the stream. He ducked in time for them, but he heard several impacts behind him. Tarhuinn lowered himself another time as there were more branches. No more pixies collided into them. While the overhead branches had been a benefit to him, a problem was quickly approaching. Some of the pines' roots grew slightly into the stream.

Cursing, he pressed more on his feet before he jumped into the air and avoided the first of the roots. He had to make several more jumps before he crossed the rough patch of water. Finally, there was a clear space. For a split moment, he was able to see past the trees and spot the lake in the distance. It was nowhere close to him, and the stream was starting to have a flatter slope once again.

With all of the jumping, he had already been slowed down some. He would have to exert himself more, but the pixies managed to get closer. A few spears hit him, landing in his shoulders. Tarhuinn swiftly pulled them out as he noticed two large rocks up ahead in the middle of the stream. Reaching them, his feet left the water as he ran across them and leaped off towards the stream below.

Making contact with water again, he instantly became relieved. The pixies, though, decided upon a new course of action. Several guards threw off their armor and tossed aside their weapons. With that weight gone, they raced ahead and towards the water itself. Suddenly, the surface of the water started to freeze over. As for the fastest two of the team, they continued to dart through the air before they began to freeze the water ahead of him.

At his speed, Tarhuinn couldn't slow down fast enough. His shins rammed against it, and he tumbled to the water below. The kelremm's body crashed against the ice as he used his arms to protect his face. Water and ice splashed upwards while pixies surrounded him.

Refusing to lift his head out of the water, the pixies gathered on his sides and forcibly turned him over. Before he could attack any of them, the queen came forward and sent him into unconsciousness. The world slipped from his view. Before his eyes closed fully, tears trailed down the sides of his face. They weren't distinguishable from the falling rain, and they slipped into the stream unnoticed.

No shafts of morning light greeted him. Only droplets of rain fell upon him. Tarhuinn found himself lying on his back. Snow had been cleared around him so that he lied on a bed of twigs and dried leaves. His wrists were by the sides of his head. He couldn't move them as ice bonds held them to the ground. His legs were restrained against the floor too. Odette's cloak rested over his body as a blanket, but its absorption of the water only weighed him down more.

All of the cuts on him had been tended to, but he was glad to know that their wedding rings were still in his left pants pocket. He had placed them there as soon as the bonds had been off of him. Tarhuinn wished, though, that he had made it to her. His lips parted as he softly whispered her name, but he didn't have the strength to have her hear him.

Currently, the king was saying something to him, but he wasn't listening. He didn't care what left any of the pixies' mouths unless it was a report about his beloved. Turning his head, his eyes followed the path of the stream. His eyes wished to see her travel up it, but such a desire wasn't granted.

Even though he knew that it would most likely end in failure, he wanted to break out again. He desired to continue going after her. The odds didn't matter. His wife was in danger, and he would keep trying, yet his body felt like it was on the brink of death.

Lifting his head up gradually, he discovered the reason. The back of his heels were the only part of his feet in the water. His head fell back down. Their new tactic didn't matter. He would find a way to break free again. Odette would be back in his arms. That he was certain of.

~ ~ ~ ~ ~ ~ ~ ~ ~ ~ ~ ~

Rain against glass awoke her. Odette opened her eyes and sat up in the bed slowly. Throughout the whole night, she had fallen in and out of sleep. Exhaustion was evident in her eyes as she rubbed them to wake herself up more. Drawing her hands away, she stretched and looked down to the floor. Will was gone. She assumed him to be tending to his hobby.

Clothes were laid out on the bed for her. As usual, the more revealing undergarments were there also. Grabbing them, she placed them back in the wardrobe. On the bed was a green corset dress. The skirt was thin, but it had a higher top then the off-white dress on her. She picked it and her boots up before she walked to the main door.

Stepping outside, she wondered if she would be able to handle the lake water without Will's magic. It was raining but lightly, so she couldn't take a shower in the rain. He wasn't around, though. That was a benefit in its own right. She decided to go for it. Once she dealt with Will, she would have to get used to water that wasn't heated.

Slipping out of her clothes swiftly, she set the old and new clothing on the shore. She dipped her feet in. Immediately, she shivered, but she forced herself to travel in further. It would be a very quick bath. When she couldn't take the slow stepping in process, she jumped into the slightly further out water. Cold embraced her instantly before she came up to the surface.

Odette swam closer to the shore and hurried along with washing herself and her other clothing. As she was in the middle of doing so, Will walked out from the back. His eyes latched onto her before a look of panic crossed his face. "What are you doing, Bluebell?! I didn't heat the water! Are you mad?!" He started to dash towards her before heat rushed to her cheeks.

"I'm fine! Just turn around! I'll throw another fish at you!" When he didn't listen, she grabbed a clinglob that had just attached itself to her right leg and threw it at him. He caught it and dropped it back into the water.

"I'm merely going to heat the water for you," he reassured, but she distanced herself from him. Before she could get too far, he stepped into the water, reached out and grasped her right wrist. Her feet still touched the bottom, so she dug them into the soil. She felt a few clinglobs attach to her legs, and one stuck to her midsection, but she didn't budge.

"Bluebell, this is ridiculous. You shouldn't head out any further. We don't know what's out there." He tugged on her again, but she kept her feet planted where they were.

"Just heat the water like you said, and I'll come back," she argued as she resisted his pull on her again. Will was clearly annoyed, but she was ready to slap him if he tried to force her forward. An irritated mumble left him before she felt the water grow warm. Her body relaxed against it, and she accidentally lowered her guard.

With a rough tug, Will brought her closer. Odette fell forward, and she crashed against him. More warmth entered her cheeks since her face was pressed to his midsection. Her lower half was hidden, but if she backed up, her chest would be exposed. Will released his hold on her before he placed a hand on top of her head. "Finish your bath. Next time, wait for me. I can't have you getting sick on me."

Instantly, she sank into the water and covered her chest for extra precaution. She looked away from him as a glare settled on her countenance. "Can you just go now?" she asked harshly. He shook his head in amusement before he faced the opposite direction and went back inside.

Having completed her bathing and clothes washing, she swiftly changed and headed on in to dry off by the fire. Will had mixed the leftover trout in a fish soup with some vegetables and had it ready for them. Once breakfast was finished, they had decided to go fishing again.

For the moment, the light rainfall stopped, but there was wind in its place. Unfortunately, it wasn't the gentlest of winds either. Odette wished that she still had her traveling pants so that she didn't have to worry about the dress's skirt blowing around. It gave Will an unfair advantage in their fishing competition because one of her hands constantly had to push her skirt back down.

Even when she resorted to sitting on the rocks, her skirt wasn't cooperating. Odette also had the urge to knock Will straight into the water for all of his quiet chuckling. She ignored him, however, as she focused on her skirt. Resting her feet over the rod's end, she secured the pole while she worked on wrapping the dress skirt tightly around her legs. It appeared as though she was trying to create a mermaid tail with fabric.

Satisfied, she held onto the rod again with her hands. Today, she was even more determined to beat Will at fishing. Unlike yesterday, they had placed bets. If she won, he would tell her more about his past, but if he won, he would pick out her outfit and take her on an evening stroll. It sounded completely suspicious. When she had given him a questioning gaze, he had merely stated that he had wished to show her something spectacular. That answer hadn't aided her nerves in the slightest.

To ensure that she lived to see another day, she would do her best to win. Neither of them caught anything yet, though. The fight of patience nearly got to her on several instances, and she almost stormed off in frustration. Her life was on the line, but the fish refused to come.

A pout remained on her face until something tugged on the pole. Excitement raced through her veins and to her eyes. Odette jumped to her feet and positioned herself for the catch. While she paid attention to her own soon to be catch, a fish bit at Will's hook. Within moments of each other, they both caught one. Her joy dissipated to learn that the competition remained at a tie.

They unhooked the fish and dropped them in the bucket before they grabbed more bait. The fierce fight continued. Waiting for the next fish, she pictured the familiar gleam in Will's eyes when they had placed the bets. He had something horrid planned for her, and it wasn't just the fact that he might be able to put her in more revealing attire. Her heart tightened at the possibilities. Thankfully, it wasn't a reality yet.

The day wore on, and only one more fish had been caught. Unluckily for her, it was Will who had caught it, but the wind had settled down. Worryingly, though, large storm clouds were forming overhead. If Will were to win, she doubted that he would postpone his winnings for rain.

Thunder sounded, but she remained seated on the rocks. A storm wouldn't stop her either. Odette bit the left side of her bottom lip in frustration and concentration. She just couldn't lose. There was too much on the line.

Hair untied, it hid the side view of his face. Will couldn't keep a grin off of his lips. If her luck remained the way it currently was, he would win. He would finally be able to get her in a full outfit that he fancied, and he had the perfect one in mind. She would look splendid in it, though; he would have to provide her with a blanket on their trip into the mountains. His grin widened at the image that formed, and as the day passed, he almost let out an insane chuckle on several occasions. Still, she caught no more fish, but he would be fair and give her until dusk.

Rain started to fall while the thunder continued. The wind picked up once more but more violently. Despite all of that, Odette stayed seated until she jumped onto her feet suddenly. Her dress skirt blew forward, but she didn't bother with it. Against the rough wind, she stepped back as she pulled on the rod to get the fish out. With a final tug, she flung the fish out and caught it before it went flying back into the water. Nearly, she had lost her balance, but she had regained it in time. "Looks like we're back at a tie!" she exclaimed with a grin.

An impressed smile found its way onto his lips. While holding onto the pole, he clapped a bit. "Well done, Bluebell. That was most stunning. With how you were treating your skirt earlier, I thought that your attention would've been more on that."

Dropping the fish into the bucket, she smirked. "Like I'm going to let a piece of cloth interfere with me beating you." She faced away from him and seated herself once more, but she did wrap the skirt around her legs like before. He supposed that he couldn't claim victory yet. His grin maintained itself, though, as he faced the water. A challenge was always fun, and he would be sure to overcome the present one.

Despite the rain picking up in intensity, they remained outside. Wind blew hair into both of their faces, but neither let it bother them. Dusk would be upon them soon, and they didn't desire a tie. With the last beams of sunlight managing to break through some of the clouds, fish became a frequently spoken word along with cursing from both parties.

There was a loud cheer from one of them, though. A fish was ripped from the water and was unhooked before it was placed into the bucket. Outwardly, a sigh left the loser's lips, but the loser congratulated the winner regardless. Inwardly, the loser was terrified.

"We should head inside. We're both drenched. Besides, I want to take you on this evening walk as soon as possible. I think that you'll enjoy it," Will voiced as he took her fishing rod from her. She merely gave him a skeptical look before she went ahead of him. The temptation to run was strong, but if she made for an escape, all of her previous efforts would be for nothing.

Reminding herself of her end goal, she went inside the cabin and waited for him. She started up the fire and sat on the floor to warm up since she didn't wish to sit on a wet chair during dinner. When Will came back inside, he set the bucket of fish on the countertop before he motioned for her to follow him into the bedroom. Reluctantly, she did so.

Crossing her arms over her chest, she scowled at the clothes that he was choosing for her. He set them on the bed before he headed to leave the room. "I'll get dinner started unless you want to change together." As heat touched her cheeks, she picked up the pillow in the room and tossed it his way. He dodged before he closed the door after him.

A grumble left her lips as she went over to the pillow and set it back on the bed. Her brown eyes glanced down to the pile of clothes. Warm clothes did sound nice, but the ones in front of her looked like poison. She directed her gaze to the window, wanting to open it and run away. The urge to bolt out of the cabin kept coming back.

Clenching her fists, she told herself to remain brave. It was possible that he wouldn't attempt anything at his mystery location. That was a massive lie to herself, though. If she didn't get changed soon, however, he might come into the room to make sure that she fulfilled her end of the bargain. With immense dislike, she undressed herself and draped her old clothes over the back of the desk chair.

Nearly, she tore the dry clothes to shreds, but she took a deep breath and exhaled. After a couple more minutes of an inward struggle, she slipped on the revealing underclothes before she put on the light pink and white dress. Once it was tied up, she tried to pull the off-shoulder dress up more, but it remained in place. Grabbing a blanket, she wrapped it around her shoulders and held it to her chest, which was too exposed for her liking. She kept her boots on, figuring that they would dry quickly enough by the fire.

Leaving the bedroom and stepping into the kitchen, she immediately went for her chair before she wrapped the blanket tighter around her. Will turned around and wore an amused smile. "Well, I was going to grab you a blanket for the walk outside, but it looks like you beat me to it. Won't you let me see you without the blanket, though? I'm sure that the dress looks lovely on you."

"You're not charming this blanket off of me," she grumbled, clutching it in an even stronger grip. "So, why don't you go change? I thought that you wanted to go on this walk sooner rather than later."

“Yes, you’re right. Dinner will be ready soon after I’m done.” He walked away from the preparation area and into the bedroom. Once the door was closed, Odette relaxed a bit until her eyes fell upon the dress’s skirt. Her dress would be even more awful if it continued to rain outside. The skirt would become see-through, and her undergarments didn’t offer much coverage.

If Tarhuinn learned of the bet that she made with Will and that she had to wear such a dress for the mage, he would go into frenzy. He would attack Will on sight if he hadn’t planned to do so already. Knowing her husband, though, he would most likely wrap one of their cloaks around her for proper coverage. Hopefully, she would be back with him soon.

Chapter Thirty Three: Concealing Retreat

Dinner passed by slowly. Odette ate each bite steadily while Will finished rather quickly. It led to an awkward staring situation, but she pretended that she didn't know about it in the slightest. Unfortunately, she eventually finished her food. Will grabbed their plates, washed them and returned quite speedily. He bathed soon after, but that hadn't taken him too long either.

Before she knew it, they were already out of the cabin and making their way into the forest. She did walk at a slow pace, but it wasn't entirely on purpose. The snow was thick, and she kept sinking in some since there was no path carved out for them. It was also freezing. At least, the storm had stopped momentarily, but that didn't prevent her from clutching at the blanket around her shoulders. Odette even used part of it as a hood to keep her ears from getting too cold.

As for Will, he had on a long-sleeved brown tunic and black leather pants. Leather boots covered his feet while a green cloak without a hood was wrapped around him. She was tempted to steal the cloak from his shoulders. If he had a spare, he probably hadn't offered it because he wanted to view more of her.

Whatever the case, she forced herself to maintain some distance between them even though her body was telling her to huddle close to him for heat. If she submitted to such an urge, he would most likely take advantage of it within a heartbeat. She resorted to hugging the blanket closer. Occasionally, she would blow on her hands to keep them warm.

When at last they stopped, Will pushed back some pine branches and motioned for her to go ahead. She didn't desire to step in front of the male, but she didn't want to raise an alarm. Stepping forward, she found herself on a small hill which overlooked a barren patch in the forest. Down below was a small pond, and a tiny waterfall led into it.

Making her way down, she headed over to the water and glanced around. It was a secluded area no doubt, but if she needed to, she could push him into the water. That would give her a few seconds of an advantage. There wasn't anything else in sight that could be of use to her. Another problem was that there was no coverage if it started to pour down on them.

If only there were leaves large enough to be used as a miniature roof. She had heard stories of such things existing in warmer parts of the world, but no such thing had been traded up in the northern regions. Will walked up beside her with one of his cheery grins. "What do you think? Isn't it nice?"

"I suppose that it is if you needed a place to come and think, but what if it starts raining? I'm already freezing. I don't need to be soaked too."

Chuckling, he answered, "That's why you have a mage with you. I'll warm us both up while we're here. I just wanted to enjoy the night with you in one of my favorite spots."

"That's what I'm worried about. I'd rather be under sheets to stay warm than have you be that source of heat."

"I apologize that I didn't prepare a bed out here for us, but that's why I had you bring the blanket." Within a moment's notice, he snatched it from her shoulders and draped it over a patch of snow. He seated himself before she could take it back and proceeded to pull her down next to him. Having been caught off guard, she squeaked and collided into him.

Her hands landed on either side of his head while she ended up straddling his hips. Heat rapidly fell over her cheeks, and she went to get off of him, but his hands held onto her hips firmly. "Ah, this is quite a view. I knew that the dress would flatter you." A smirk fell over his lips before she roughly pushed herself upward. Instead of the desired result, her hands only sunk more into the snow below.

Odette's face landed right beside his head and pressed into the blanket. The chilly snow started to soak the fabric more, but that was the least of her concerns. When she tried to get up again, she was flipped onto her back and forced into the snow more. By now, the blanket was doing very little to keep them from the snow. Her brown eyes, though, stared wide at Will, but she managed to shout, "What do you think you're doing?! Get off of me!"

"I'll get off as soon as you answer some questions for me, Bluebell." There was that joyful smile on his lips, but the menace behind it was quite clear. "First, do you not find me attractive?"

Despite her nerves ringing alarm bells and the urge to cry for help, she replied, "Yes, you're attractive, but that doesn't mean that I like you in a romantic way. I'm not entering a romantic relationship with you."

"And, why is that? We're good around the other, and you've made me laugh like no other. I'll be honest, and it's probably already obvious. I want you to be mine. I do take good care of you, and I'll do so in the future too. Besides, I'm sure that you find my personality charming, and you just admitted to me being attractive. What's holding you back? Is it your husband? After the wound that you gave him, I doubt that he's alive. You really should feel no more commitment to him."

Going to move her hands to push him off of her, he gripped her wrists and shook his head in disappointment. "Remember, I won't get off until you answer me. I'm most curious, and I'm intrigued as well at how observant you are of me. It's like you know some forbidden secret. Maybe, that's what's keeping you from giving yourself over to me."

"I'm not going to have sexual relations with a man after a few days of knowing him. Nor will I do so unless I'm married to the man in question. You're nice company, but you're quickly ruining that image," she countered harshly. "There! I answered your questions. Now, get off of me, Will!"

"I never specified the amount of questions. So, here's another. Why are you so observant? Is that because you don't trust me, or is there something more?"

"Your actions now don't exactly inspire trust. As for why I'm observant, that is the reason. I told you what had happened, so you should understand why I'm so cautious." Her gaze hardened, and she desperately wanted to reach for her dagger to defend herself. "Besides, you already lied about your past once, and I expect that you've lied about it on other instances too."

Another chuckle left his lips as he sat up and brought her up onto his lap. His right hand clutched both of her wrists. Left fingers trailing her jaw line, he inquired, "Why are you so interested in my past? I doubt that the only reason is because I'm some man who lives in a secluded cabin. It's like you're trying to analyze what my weakness is. Perhaps, that's the real reason you're so watchful of me, but that raises another question. Why would you want to know my weakness? It definitely isn't to ensure that I become your lover. Is it possibly to have a willing puppet under your control?

"Then again, it might also raise your trust in me. It's wise to know about your partner before committing to them." His eyes gleamed as a grin took over his mouth. "How about I make an arrangement with you? I'll tell you about my past, and you give me a chance. You let me kiss you and cover these old marks of your husband's."

Gulping, she didn't desire to agree to that deal, but it might keep her alive. If she refused, he would probably ask more questions that would back her into a corner. She couldn't even reach the dagger at the moment. Still, she felt like she would really be betraying Tarhuinn if she agreed. Odette summoned her courage and shook her head. "No, I can't accept that. Please let me go, Will."

"You're really still in love with such a man?" He shook his head in amusement. "Unbelievable. He's most likely dead, and he threatened to kill you. Were you to go back to him, you would be killed. Even you understand this ... unless there's something missing in your story. Is there because I'm having a hard time believing this? Or, do you really want that perfect moment with him? I can give you a perfect moment within a heartbeat. I can make that fantasy of yours come true; he can't. He's already ruined his chance."

Against her better judgment, she mumbled, "No, you're wrong."

"I am? Before now, I have treated you well. I had made a perverted remark or gesture here and there, but I had never mistreated you. I have been a welcoming and kind host. I have joked with you, and I have laughed with you. You find me attractive, and you enjoy my company. What has this husband of yours done that makes him better than all of that? Make me understand."

Lips held tightly shut, she moved her face away from him and turned her gaze to her right and down. What was she to do? If she compared him to Tarhuinn, her story would fall apart, but it already was. Were she to live to tomorrow, she would be lucky.

"Is it because this husband is different from what you first had told me? I know that you aren't lying about having a husband. Your commitment to him is too obvious. It must be that you're hiding something from me, and I'd very much like to know what that is." He grabbed her chin and forced her to look at him. "Now, answer the question. It's a simple yes or no. And, don't lie to me. You're too vulnerable right now for you to hide the truth from me."

He was right. Her mind was too panicked. All she wanted to do was grab her weapon and make some effort to defend herself. Will had already made it quite clear, though, that he wouldn't let her go until she answered his questions. Odette forced herself to find the courage to speak, to utter at least something. Gulping, she replied, "... Yes, he is."

She didn't give him time to react, for she only had moments to spare. After the words left her lips, she drew her head back and brought it forward. Their foreheads collided, and a cry of pain left them both. Will, however, lost his grip on her.

Despite the sharp pain in her head, she pushed her hands against his chest hard, which allowed her to fall backwards. Her hands sunk into the soaked blanket and snow. The cold bit at her, but she dug her hands in further until she felt the solid ground beneath. Once discovered, she crawled backwards on her hands and created some much needed distance between them.

Her right hand flung to her boot and unsheathed the blade there. As Will locked his gaze with hers, she pushed herself to her feet. The dagger pointed towards him while her free hand was pressed against her forehead. "Oh, so you have been playing me this whole time? Do you wish to kill me, then? Or, is it something else that you want from a lonely mage in the woods?" he asked, getting to his feet and healing his forehead. "Then again, some of your actions were definitely genuine."

"I did laugh with you and become embarrassed, but that's it. There's nothing more to it. As for what I want from you, I want you to come with me to the pixies. You're to protect them." Her response was greeted with silence and an unreadable expression. Everything was falling in around her, and her plan in the end had resorted to threatening him with her dagger.

A grin began to form on Will's lips while his hands rested on his hips. "Is that so? So, the pixies sent you to me. And, that's why you were so observant of me and so doubtful of my words. They had told you about me." His grin grew wider, and it was as though all kindness had left him. He took a step towards her, and her grip on the knife tightened.

"Though, I do wonder what would cause you to make such a deal with them. Maybe, they spared you the details of what I do to my victims when their time expires. Even then, only someone mad would agree to enter my home willingly once the truth about my favorite treat is revealed. You must desperately want something from the pixies. Again, I question what that is." He came closer, and she backed away more, preparing herself for an attack from him.

Stopping, he brought his left hand up to his lips and tapped his index finger against them. "I'm also curious about how you intended to originally persuade me to come with you. Did you hope to learn about my past and find my weakness there? Did you think that you could turn my past against me by becoming a sympathetic maiden? Were you going to try and comfort me before you turned me into your friend?"

Seeing her bite her lower lip and the evident fear in her eyes, his eyes gleamed. "So, that was your plan." A loud chuckle left him before he burst into more laughter. His hands clutched his sides, but she knew better than to attack him then. He appeared vulnerable, but he was probably fully aware of her.

Regaining his composure, he stood upright and placed his hands back on his hips. "Unfortunately, Bluebell, that wouldn't have worked. Despite how different you are from my past victims, I still and will always consider you a prize for me to claim. Your natural kindness and innocence have led to some most amusing incidents with you, but they only would've extended your life with me, not saved it. The same goes for if you had comforted me once I had told you my past, but I see in your eyes that you're still curious about my childhood. So, I'll indulge you.

Will pointed his hands towards the ground and heated the nearby snow. It melted, and he dried the earth beneath it. Seating himself, he rested his chin in his right palm. His green eyes gazed up at her, but his new position didn't make him any less terrifying. If anything, he looked like a snake about to spring forward and sink his fangs into her flesh.

"When I had been seven, I had lost my mother to an unfortunate wagon accident. She had been leaving the house and had walked onto the street only for one to hit her before she could've done anything. Her injuries being healed wouldn't have achieved anything because her head had been crushed by the horse's hooves, and she had already been gone. I had been left with my two older sisters, who ordered me around as though I had been their servant.

"My only freedom from them had been when I went out for supplies. It had allowed me to spend some time with my good friend, Patricia. In our interactions, she had loaned me that book of children's tales. That had been a mistake as my sisters had found out. They had learned that she wasn't a mage, and they had decided that I could no longer interact with her. I had refused to listen and had continued to secretly meet with her.

"At age fourteen, somehow they had discovered that I was still meeting up with her. They had never disclosed to me how they had learned of our meetings, but I imagine that someone in the town had betrayed Patricia and me so that they could earn the favor of mages. Regardless, they had punished me by killing her in front of me.

"I hadn't been able to stop them because they had been more skilled at magic than me back then. Of course, they had made it look like an accident as though her balcony railing had become old and broken on her, sending her to the pavement below. In reality, they had used some wind to send her and the railing to the ground. Like my mother, a wagon had ensured her death.

"In repayment, I had killed my sisters that evening. I had waited until they were asleep before I had slipped a sleeping potion into their mouths. They had remained unconscious as I had dragged them down into the dining room. They had always demanded the best meals from me and had always burned my fingers if they hadn't been pleased, so I had decided to return the favor. I had made them the best meal possible by throwing them into the fireplace. They had considered themselves the best, and they had always ordered for the highest quality of ingredients."

Disturbed, Odette stepped back from him more. Her hands trembled, and she thought that he may charge at her. He remained in the same place, however, and the grin never left his lips. His tongue glided across his lips while only more madness entered his green eyes. The beast was finally coming fully out of the shadows.

"I must say, though, that they really hadn't been the best. They had tasted rather dreadful. It must've been the perfume that had been on them. Since I had thought that it was high time that I have the best food, I had gone in search of more.

"I had decided to find girls and later on women when I was older that were like my sisters. Tight and revealing dresses, hair done up in the latest trends, too much makeup, etc., you understand the picture. I had seduced them, brought them to my home and comforted them until I had grown bored of them.

"Then, I had tested out to see if they had tasted better than my sisters. None of them had. Even when I had moved out to the cabin because things were finally starting to get too risky in the town, I still hadn't been able to find one with a divine taste." Somehow, his eyes lit up more. "But, then you had come to my doorstep. And, you taste extraordinary, and I've only had a small sampling too."

Odette felt like she might be sick. How could she ever sympathize with a man who committed such treacheries? His sisters didn't sound like the best of people, but what he had done and continued to do was taking things too far. She had known of his cannibalistic nature beforehand, but his story made it all the more horrifying.

Will's anger at his sisters had developed into him truly loving the taste of human flesh. The man was terrifyingly beyond reason. Never had she wished to run so much; how was she to convince him to come with her to the pixies? There was also the nauseating fact that he had done something to her in her sleep. "What did you do?"

Laughing, he took his left index finger and pointed to the palm of his right hand. He proceeded to place his finger on his right shoulder. "I cut your hand and bit into your husband's mark. Your blood tastes truly phenomenal. I almost lost myself the other night."

The urge to expel the contents of her stomach grew stronger. It didn't help that terror laced her veins and made her desire to curl into a ball and pretend that her present situation wasn't a reality.

"Don't look so disgusted. You should be honored. After all, you're going to live longer than any of my other victims. I can't possibly kill someone as charming and delectable as you immediately. No, no, you'll be with me for at least year. I'm sure that you now understand that I really have no intention of going to these pixies. I'd rather just enjoy you."

It was a foolish action, but her fright had gotten the best of her. Her legs darted to her left. In that instant, it seemed like the only reasonable option. She wished to continue her journey and find the five authors, but she didn't know what to do against Will; however, her flight served her no benefit.

Air slammed against her, and she was thrown back into a nearby pine. Needles scratched her skin and tore her already revealing dress. By that point, the skirt was see-through from the snow soaking it, and the now falling rain only added to it. Quickly, though, she went to get to her feet and grab the dagger. A force of air hit her again and held her there. The blade was out of reach, but her attention turned to Will.

He stood a foot away from her. The male crouched in front of her and shook his head. "Running will do you no good. You should've considered that before dealing with a mage." He reached over and picked up the dagger before he grinned at the metal.

"Now, I'm going to tell you what's going to happen to you for the next year or so. I really want to watch the horror overtake you even more." Swiftly, he grabbed her wrists and pulled her to him so that she was on her knees. The dagger lay under her chin while her body shivered from the cold. Desperately, she desired to call out for Tarhuinn, but they were too far from the pixies' home. She was trapped, and any nearby pixies wouldn't lend her aid.

Even though she was kneeling in the snow, with no real protection against her skin, the metal of the dagger felt colder. With one swipe, she would be killed. She tensed under the dagger as it moved from her chin to her chest. Will began to tap it against the dress as if debating something, but his eyes never left hers. His grin never vanished from his face. Odette wished to close her eyes and think it all to be one nightmare. When she would open her eyes again, she would be back with Tarhuinn.

He twirled the blade between his fingers, permitting the sharp edges to cut through the fabric a little while also digging into her skin. She tried to pull back from him, but he drew the blade back and brought her closer. "Now, now, Bluebell, you know better than to try and get away," he chuckled out before he seated himself and placed her between his legs.

Will rested the dagger on the ground for the moment while he kept her wrists secure. With his free hand, he dragged his index finger across the small amount of blood on her chest before he licked it off his finger. "Delicious," he purred, not breaking eye contact with her. She desired to insult him endlessly, but she held her tongue. Angering him wouldn't be wise. Odette had to somehow push through the terror and find a solution.

A cry of surprise left her lips, however, when she was spun around. Her back faced him, and his right arm wrapped around her waist and secured her arms. His left hand smeared the crimson across her chest some. Will's lips rested near her left ear. Grazing his teeth across her helix, he whispered, "Here's the plan. Tonight, I'm going to take what your husband never did. I'm going to show you how well I can pleasure a woman."

His hand glided down from her chest. Blood sullied the white and pink fabric. Odette unintentionally pressed more into him as his hand moved past her navel. She squirmed against him, trying to get him to stop. "I'm going to make sure to taste your innocence." As his lips glided across her jaw, she couldn't hold it in anymore. Parting her lips, she went to scream. A hand covered her mouth swiftly. "I'll have none of that. The only screaming that I'll permit is when you're screaming my name in pleasure."

Her head shook against him, but she was thankful that the rain covered her tears. His hand pressed more against her and pushed her head into his chest more. In response, she opened her mouth and bit down hard on his skin. Will, however, only laughed. "I suppose that I can let you have a taste of me right now but only a little bit. I'll save you the rest for later." Bile rose up her throat, but she forced it back down. Unfortunately, the blood from his hand traveled down her throat too. She nearly choked on it, but, thankfully, he drew his hand away from her mouth.

Sliding his fingers under her chin, he turned her head towards him and smirked. "And after I've had my fill for tonight, I'll drag you back to my cabin. You won't be staying in my nice, comfortable room, however. Rather, I'll take you down to my lovely storage space. I'll..."

Before he could finish, she rammed her arms against the one around her waist. The collision caused his arm to loosen its hold for a moment, and she reached for the dagger. Her fingers had just reached the handle, but she was thrown back. Snow greeted all of her limbs, though; the feeling in them was lessening.

Heat, however, soon encompassed her body. Will intertwined his hands with hers while his knees straddled her hips. "Lucky you, I'm giving you warmth even when you've tried to attack me." Amusement fell upon his face. "I just can't have you dying from a cold." Getting to his feet, he lifted her up with him and pinned her to him.

Resting his chin on top of her head, he continued, "Once I have you in the storage area, I'll clear a table just for you and bind you to it. From there ... Well, you can imagine all of the things that will be done to you." He removed his chin from her and started to chuckle darkly. His lips moved to her right ear. "Shall I tell you what they are?"

Given no choice, he forced her to meet his gaze as he narrated only a few of his many plans. Her body seemed to go numb despite being warmer from his magic while her limbs wished to hang loosely. As for her countenance, it was the definition of dread. "Ah, there's the look that I want to see. It looks so beautiful upon your face. Unfortunately, I can't gaze at it for too long. I want to taste you now."

Odette couldn't react in time. Her body collided with the snow once more. Knowing what was coming; she rolled on her side and tried to extend out her hand towards the dagger. A foot kicked her onto her back. Will picked up the blade before he secured her to the ground again. While his left hand was around her wrists, his right trailed the dagger down the front of her dress.

Realizing that she couldn't free her hands, she resorted to trying to kick him off of her. He didn't budge, and she couldn't move too much under him lest the knife puncture her torso. Despite the miniscule likelihood of persuading him to stop, she had to attempt it. It was the only thing left to her.

"Please, let me go, Will! Please, get off of me! You're making a mistake. As soon as my husband finds out about this, you'll be killed before you can even blink! Please, let me go!"

The blade stopped above her dress skirt. His monstrous grin highlighted his lips. "Oh yes, I almost forgot. You never did tell me what he's really like, but I'll find out once I have you in safe storage. I'll have to kill him so that he doesn't cause a problem for me. I can't have him taking back his wife. I can't wait to see his expression once he learns what I've done to you. Maybe as a present to you both, I'll let the two of us dine upon him. That way you both can see each other again."

Holding back a violent sob, she managed to glare at him. It probably looked pathetic given how terrified she was, but it was all that she could muster. Still, the utter hopelessness of her situation was dawning upon her. She had nothing to bargain with. He was already going to take everything from her. As the dagger began to tear through the skirt of the dress, she exclaimed, "I'll tell you why I needed to get past the pixies! You said that you were curious!"

Halting the weapon, he smirked. "Bluebell if you're trying to get me to stop the inevitable, you should understand that nothing is going to work. I can learn of it afterwards."

Not listening to him, she shouted, "I know where a serum to eternal life is!"

Grin falling, he raised an eyebrow before he sat up. He brought her onto his lap and held her chin up with the tip of the blade. "Do you now? That's a most curious thing. Countless have sought after such a thing, and I would very much like it myself. Where is it?"

It was her turn to smirk. "I'll bring some back to you if you agree to my conditions."

"Well, I'd be lying if I said that I wasn't interested. How do I know that you're not lying about this?"

"Would I enter your cabin willingly if I didn't have such a good reason to do so? I risked everything so that I could get past the pixies and continue on my journey to reach it. In my opinion, the chance to live longer was worth the risk." Honestly, she wasn't sure of that herself anymore; she just desired to get away from the man in front of her.

"Name your terms, and I'll give it a quick consideration."

"You're not to ruin my innocence, you're to let me go, and you're to come with me and protect the pixies."

"And, why would the pixies need my protection?"

"Another mage has been giving them trouble. In order for them to let me passage, I need to bring back a mage to protect them against the other. If I hadn't agreed to bring you back, they would've killed me had I tried to go forward."

"I take it that they have an agreement with this other mage, but they're not on good terms with them either. Interesting, I have always wanted to sample a mage. Unfortunately, none have crossed my path yet. Probably the story of my sisters scared the others off. And, you're certain of where to go for this serum?"

"Yes," she answered resolutely. Of course, she didn't know the exact location, but she knew what steps to take to discover it. He didn't need that information, though. "Do we have a deal?"

"We do," he answered, but his grin returned. "After all, you never said that I couldn't take you later. Once you return with that bottle, I'll claim you as my prize, then. And, don't try to run off with it and not fulfill your promise. I'll hunt you down otherwise, and I'll make sure to give you even worse treatment. Like I said before, whatever you do will only delay your death by my hands, not save it. Do you understand?"

Giving a weak nod, she wished that she had thought of that flaw in her bargain beforehand. It was too late, but, in the future, she would have Tarhuinn by her side. She could go back to him.

Chapter Thirty Four: Unconscious Return

Stepping back from her and standing, he examined the blade in his hands and didn't toss it back to her. "I'll just hold onto this for good measure. Despite you not wanting to kill me, you might still want to get a few good revenge stabs." Will placed the dagger presumably in an inner pocket of his cloak before he crossed his arms over his chest. "Lead the way, Bluebell."

His eyes scanned over her form slowly, and heat swarmed her cheeks. Looking down, she quickly bundled up the dress and covered her front. Without its thin layer of protection, she might as well have been nude due to how soaked she was. Odette picked herself up to her feet and retrieved the wet blanket.

Pretending that Will wasn't present, she ripped off the dress skirt, tossed the thin fabric aside and replaced it with the thicker blanket. She kept on the corset piece of the dress and held it shut with her hands. Odette held her head up high; she wouldn't let the a**hole humiliate her anymore. As her body shivered, she marched past him and headed out of the secluded area.

A chuckle rang behind her, and she almost turned around to slap him. That was until she caught sight of the pale flying creatures in front of her. They gracefully dodged the larger raindrops that filled the air. It would be a spectacle to see if she didn't grow enraged at their presence; they had been watching that entire exchange.

She bottled up her anger, however, and put it into her walking. Odette went right past them and was tempted to hit them to the ground. Resisting the urge to do so, she watched them fly ahead a bit to guide her back to their home. Will's footsteps could be heard behind her, but her attention fell on the soft voice in her head. Tarhuinn was calling her again.

Even though her body was recovering from absolute terror and increasing anger, a small smile graced her lips. She was finally going to see him again. It hadn't even been a week, but the past few days had been a nightmare, and she was ready to leave it. Odette suspected, though, that she wouldn't view a smile upon his lips. No, Tarhuinn would have his gaze focused on Will.

Frankly, she wouldn't mind seeing her husband tear Will to pieces, but she couldn't allow that. She wouldn't let Tarhuinn's rage ruin all of the effort that she put into getting Will to follow her. In the future, though, Tarhuinn could do whatever he pleased. Will would get his bottle of serum if it really did exist, and he would receive the welcoming hand of death also.

Their walk continued through the night, and Will stayed behind her the entire time. Occasionally, he would be closer to her, but he never stepped beside or in front of her. She could feel his eyes scanning over her form, however. The pervert was probably picturing her in only her soaked undergarments or less.

Thankfully, she had some spare undergarments in her pack back at the pixie home. If she was lucky, some spare clothes would be in there too. There was also her cloak. She would be decently covered again. Her eyes traveled to the mark on her right shoulder, however. Will had defiled the mark but made it seem like he hadn't ruined it.

Touching the spot with her left fingers, she wished it to be gone. No longer could she picture Tarhuinn's lips there. Instead, she imagined Will hovering over her in the night. The thought caused a chill to run up her spine. Perhaps, she could ask her husband to kiss the area again. When the idea came to her, her cheeks warmed up. No, she couldn't outright ask that of him. She bit her bottom lip and shook her head. That would be far too embarrassing. It didn't help that he was calling her name.

It seemed like he could read her thoughts in that moment. More heat traveled to her cheeks until a chuckle sounded close by. Glancing to her right, Will had now stepped up beside her. His hands were in his pants' pockets while a grin spread over his lips. "Are you thinking about our future time together? I know that I am."

Disgust rushed over her countenance. "Hardly." She looked forward again and ignored the smirk on his lips. It was unnerving to have him so close to her again, but she didn't wish to tell him to give her some distance. He had agreed to the deal, but she wouldn't put it past him to break it. It would be foolish to think that he was no longer dangerous, so she refrained from possibly provoking him.

Concern did wash over her a little when Tarhuinn's voice stopped. Did something happen? Usually, his voice wouldn't be cut off in the middle of saying her name. Looking to the pixies, she wondered if they knew something about his condition. She kept herself from asking due to Will's presence, though. He didn't need to learn of the entire state of things.

When asking the pixies for directions, she wouldn't mention the authors' names. Hopefully, the pixies would understand and keep to secrecy themselves. They owed her that much after what they had tasked her with. She still desired to damage the wings of the pixies in front of her. The cruel creatures would've watched her innocence be stolen if she hadn't come up with a way to persuade Will. Luckily, she wouldn't have to encounter the creatures again until she made her way back to Tarhuinn's and her home.

~~~~~~~~~~~

As dawn washed over the mountain side, she could see the two streams that surrounded the pixie home. Excitement bubbled up inside of her. Several hours ago, she had thought that she would never see Tarhuinn again, yet he was a now a few moments away from her.
~~~~~~~~~~~

Getting ever nearer to the region, she felt her pace increase. Her body's exhaustion from the night's event and the constant cold seemed to be forgotten. All that mattered was that she could continue her journey with Tarhuinn again.

Traveling down the thin stream and into the home of the pixies, she inhaled deeply before she exhaled. Her brown eyes turned to her left, and she stopped. Tarhuinn was unconscious. That would explain his sudden halt in calling her. It was probably a smart decision. If he was awake, trouble would ensue shortly. She forced her gaze away from him and to the pixie royals. Will came into the home and peered around her to the fallen male.

"Don't tell me that's your husband, Bluebell? You're married to a kelremm?" he asked as amusement was clearly written across his face. He couldn't contain his laughter anymore. "No wonder you want that serum. You'd be dead in a few years anyway, and here I thought that I was shortening your life by a lot."

Will continued to laugh while everyone else stayed rather silent. She wished to punch him in the gut and steal her dagger back. "Maybe, I should let your husband take you back home after your journey. Then, I can sample some kelremm females. I still doubt that they would taste as good as you, though."

Clenching her fists, she kept her gaze locked on the royals and ignored him. "I have fulfilled my part of the bargain. My husband and I should be given passage." Will's laughter continued as the snow pixie queen rose from her chair and flew over.

Dipping her head slightly, she lifted it back up. "You have indeed. We'll have some of our scouts help you escort your husband out of here. We'll leave you with him once he's a safe distance away. You'll see several cuts on him, and that's because he tried to escape on multiple accounts."

The news didn't surprise her. Personally, she was amazed that there had been no pixie casualties while she had been away. "I understand. And after your scouts have left us, which streams do you recommend us to take?"

"Both streams around our home intertwine together before they head more into the thick trees. You'll follow that path. Once you're close to the lake, you'll take a right and head upwards on a nearby stream. From there, you'll reach two streams. The one to your left will lead to a pool but don't go there. There are dangerous creatures in that area. Head up the one to your right, and you'll reach a large lake at the top of the mountains. You'll find your destination there."

"Thank you," she responded, though; her tone was somewhat harsh. The idea of being entirely pleasant to them had long past. She looked over to Will, who was eyeing a couple of female pixies. Rolling her eyes in revulsion, she asked, "Can I have my dagger back before I leave?"

Focusing back on her, he smirked. "Oh, and why would I do that?" He placed his right hand on his hip. "I think that I'll hold onto it. It'll make undressing you easier, and I'll be quite hungry for you when we meet again. Though," he took a few steps forward, "I'll be willing to give it back for another taste of you now."

Scowling at him, she turned on her heel and headed over to Tarhuinn. He chuckled in response but kept his eyes on her. As the pixies helped her lift Tarhuinn, he mentioned, "By the way, I'll want my blanket back at least. You may keep the rest in memory of me until we see each other again, so hand it over, or I'll neglect our deal entirely."

Embarrassment flashed on her cheeks before she glared at him menacingly. She handed Tarhuinn over to the pixies and wrapped her old cloak around her shoulders. Odette proceeded to untie the blanket and toss it his way. He caught it with ease as she hugged her wet cloak to her body. There was no way that she would let him catch another glance of her exposed body. Her focus went to Tarhuinn, and she left the area.

Chapter Thirty Five: Angered Relief

Several hours passed, and they were surrounded by pine trees on both sides of the stream. The pixie scouts dropped their packs at the base of one of the trees before they helped her seat Tarhuinn. They merely dipped their heads before they flew off and left the two of them. She figured that they had several more hours until they reached the cabin or at least were close to it.

Thankfully, Will wouldn't be there unless he broke his promise and turned on the pixies. If such a thing happened, she wouldn't be surprised, but it would mean that she would have a cannibalistic and sadistic mage on her tail as well as an army of pixies if they survived Will's attack. Hopefully, things would go accordingly.

To give her legs a rest and to receive some warmth, she sat down beside Tarhuinn after she cleared away the snow from the spot. She wrapped her cloak tight around her and moved her feet out of the water. Unfortunately, the thick amount of pine trees had prevented her from walking on drier ground. Odette leaned her head against his left shoulder and reached into his one pocket. Pulling out her wedding ring, she slipped it back onto her proper finger. During their walk, she had felt the metal hit her in the side lightly on a few occasions.

As he remained asleep, she grabbed her pack and searched through it. Luckily, she had spare undergarments tucked away as well as one last pair of clothing. There was also the fact that they were dry. Looking to Tarhuinn, she saw that he still appeared to be in a deep sleep, so she got back to her feet. When they returned home, however, she would need to invest in some new boots.

Performing a double check, she saw that he was asleep. Swiftly, she went to work and removed her cloak before she placed it on him for the time being. The underclothes and dress corset from Will had dried some, but the fabric was far too thin for her liking. She slipped out of them and tossed them aside before she changed into new undergarments, a loose grey shirt and some blue pants.

Decent coverage on, she seated herself once more and wringed her cloak out some. Regarding the other undergarments, she did the same. She would hold onto them until they had a fire. From there, she would burn the wretched things.

Bringing her knees up to her chest, she managed to get her feet out of the water again, but her attention focused on Tarhuinn. She hoped that he would wake soon, yet, at the same time, she didn't want him to. His reaction might be to run back to the pixie camp and murder the mage that was there. That fact alone made her nervous. How was she to hold him back? He was over a head taller than her. Not to mention that he was also more skilled with a blade. Odette didn't even have the dagger anymore.

Trying not to go down the endless pit of possible negative outcomes, she moved closer to him and examined him for the wounds that the pixie queen had mentioned. His clothes were torn up, and his cloak was missing. She managed to push him forward a bit. Tarhuinn's back had multiple cuts all along it that were healing. Odette set him back against the tree and looked over the ones on his arms and shoulder. It seemed like the pixies had tended to all of them, but it hurt to know that he had suffered them all to try and reach her. Honestly, he was far too overprotective.

That brought a small smile to her lips, though. With Will alive and waiting for her return, she wouldn't want anyone else by her side. If she could find another mage, that would be useful, but she felt that Tarhuinn had a fair shot at killing Will. Besides, she would stab the man in the back the moment that she received the opportunity. He deserved no mercy from her. His only hope was that the pixies needed him presently, and she required the pixies' good graces.

Delicately, she pushed back some strands of his hair from his face. His hair was rather disorderly, and she noted that his hair tie was nowhere in sight. While she waited for him to wake up, she brought forward some of his strands and started to comb through them with her fingers. Whenever a knot came across her fingers, she did her best to get rid of it without tugging too harshly.

The main trouble, though, was keeping herself from falling asleep. She had stayed up throughout the entire evening, and her body was recovering from Will's treatment of her. When she had been changing, she had already noted several bruises forming on her.

Her arms fell slightly as exhaustion started to consume her more. She needed to stay awake, though. If she fell asleep, she could easily picture Tarhuinn taking off to settle things with Will. Hearing her stomach growl, she reached over to their packs and grabbed a dried apricot to chew on for a bit.

Facing him again, she saw him shift before his eyes began to open. His brows furrowed as he blinked a few times. A puzzled expression greeted his countenance before he sat up suddenly. In an instant, arms wrapped around her, and she was brought into a tight hug. The piece of fruit fell from her hands and onto his lap. Heat graced her cheeks as she felt him nuzzle his face into the right side of her neck. He said something, but it was muffled by her skin.

Before she could return the hug, he pulled away and looked her over. His dark blue eyes fell upon the small cut on her chest. A low growl exited his lips. "What else did this man do to you? And, where are we?" he asked, looking around quickly.

Odette picked up the piece of fruit and stared at it to avoid his harsh gaze. She was happy to see him awake, but she had to face the clear fury that was bubbling up in his eyes. "It's not important, Tarhuinn," she muttered before she met his eyes once more. It seemed like he was about to argue, so she stuck the apricot into his mouth.

Taking his hands in hers, she squeezed them lightly. "Nothing of that nature occurred between us. I made sure that he didn't touch me there." A bit more heat consumed her cheeks. "That's only for you. Please, let's just continue on our journey and forget about him for the time being. He's no longer our concern." That was a slight lie, but she needed to calm him down before he committed something rash.

Breaking her hold on him, he finished the fruit in two quick bites. He picked himself up to his feet and glanced down at her. "He is my concern. He harmed you, and he'll pay the price for that. Besides, how can I trust your words? You broke our agreement when not even a full day had passed. That was a mistake. Instead of coming back and apologizing, you had put yourself in harm's way. You may want to take this journey to extend your life and our future family's time together, but your need to prove that you can handle things on your own is taking things too far.

"It's as if you were hoping for the pixies to give you some bizarre task so that you could go off on your own. You thankfully came back in one piece to me, but the odds of that were incredibly low. I heard the reports coming in. I heard the pixies say that he had you cornered last night and that you would most likely die after he had his way with you, yet you try to hide that from me. Is that so you can seem stronger before my eyes? If anything, it demonstrates to me that you still have little faith in me."

Reaching around her, he snatched up her pack and opened it. He pulled out the undergarments and corseted top before he dropped her pack. "The pixies also mentioned that you were in revealing clothes. You thought to change and hide them from me too. This man clearly did horrible things to you, yet you say that he's none of our concern?!" Enraged, he tore the clothing to shreds before he dropped the pieces into the stream. "Fortunately, you somehow managed to convince him to stop. Just what agreement did you make with him?"

"I simply told him that I would bring him back some serum of eternal life. We don't know if it exists, but it got him to agree to help the pixies."

"Then, he's even more of a concern to us. A man like that will make sure that you uphold such a bargain." He turned on his heel and combed his fingers through his hair. "You'll stay here. I'm going to go deal with him." Before he could take another step, Odette stood up and grabbed his left wrist.

"No, I'm not going to let you make a foolish decision. I told you to calm down with the pixies, and you didn't. Look where that led us. This time, please listen to me."

Peering over his left shoulder and down at her, he raised an eyebrow while a scowl graced his lips. "Why are you protecting him? Let me kill him. Or, are you hiding something else from me? You probably are given how you broke our agreement like it had meant nothing." Hurt, her grip loosened, and Tarhuinn moved away from her. "Stay here, and I'll be back. When I return, I expect you to follow my word for the rest of this journey."

He didn't understand. His present behavior was why she had tried to hide the other pieces of information from him. Why couldn't he grasp that the pixies' sickening task was the only option to continue forward? She had gone through absolute fear to fulfill that agreement. There had been instances where she nearly had given up her fight for a longer life, yet, in the end, she had persuaded Will; she had seemingly done the impossible, and he was about to jeopardize that.

Odette was happy to see him, but it was painful to receive such an unkind greeting. Not being able to restrain her conflicting emotions, she tugged back on his arm. The moment that he had glanced back at her she raised her right hand and slapped him.

No apology left her lips, and her gaze hardened. Stunned, Tarhuinn brought his left hand up to his cheek before he emitted a near growl. Cautious, she took a step back, but she kept her left hand secured tightly around his wrist. She wasn't going to permit him to charge off and ruin her hard work.

Before he could speak, well more likely yell, she exclaimed, "Just listen to me! Don't take apart what I worked so hard towards!" As he was about to counter, she tugged on him more. "You may have heard reports from the pixies, but you hadn't been there to experience it. You hadn't witnessed with your own eyes what h*ll I had gone through to get to this point. Sure, the first two days had made it seem like I was enjoying myself, but I had been absolutely terrified on the inside.

"I had remained pleasant with him because I had wanted to avoid taking the pixies' suggested route. I may have laughed a few times with him, but it had been nothing more than that. Last night should've proved to you that I have no intention of protecting him once he has aided the pixies. As soon as he deals with the other mage, you may kill him to your heart's content if that's what you want. The sick pervert will receive no more mercy from me. Just for right now, forget about him. Please, Tarhuinn."

Wrenching his wrist from her grip, he crossed his arms and leaned against a nearby tree. "And, what about the information that you were trying to hide from me?"

"I wanted to keep that a secret because I knew that you would erupt into fury. If you really want to protect me, wouldn't your ultimate goal be to get me this possible serum? You would be extending my life that way. Put your anger towards that goal instead of on some wretched mage. He can wait, but we may only have so much time to act before we're discovered by the five authors. Who knows if a spy is reporting to them this instant."

"Did he do anything else to you?" When she looked hesitant, he barked out, "Tell me, or I won't even consider your plea!"

Glancing away from him, she smoothed back her still drying hair. She bit her bottom lip. His previous actions before last night hadn't been nearly as bad, but the fact that he had performed them in secret was what made them so horrifying. Not only that but it was also embarrassing to explain such things. Odette felt that if she were to even utter them she would be dirtying herself.

Bringing her cloak closer around her, she peered back over to him. His patience was almost expired. She forced herself to part her lips and slowly explain what else had occurred. Tarhuinn's countenance remained uneasily calm during her accounts. When she finished, he motioned for her to come over to him. Hesitantly, she did so.

Upon reaching him, he softly pulled back her cloak and right sleeves. His fingers traced over the mark before he met her gaze. “I’ll let this one heal before I place a new one here. That way there will be no traces of his mark left.” Heat dusted itself across her cheeks, and she gave no response to his words.

Picking up her right hand, he upturned her palm to him. Despite the skin being healed, the image of Will sliding a blade across it was all too easy to pictue. Tarhuinn rubbed his thumb in small circles there before he placed a gentle kiss on her skin. The heat in her cheeks grew, but he soon pulled away.

“We’ll go forward. You’re right; we can’t have the authors getting a hold of us. We need to catch them off guard as best we can. Did the pixies tell you the way?”

“Yes, it’s quite simple, but, for tonight, I have a suggestion.” She paused, but he motioned for her to continue. He would probably despise it, but it would keep them from the night’s cold embrace. “Will is staying with the pixies right now, so he won’t be in his cabin. I hate that place, but we can have a warm meal there and a bed.”

“I’d rather burn it down.” He grabbed both of their packs and handed hers to her.

Slipping her arms through the sleeves, she rested it onto her back. “I agree, but if he finds that we set his house on fire, he may come after us. And, we don’t need him hunting us down. I want to avoid him for as long as we can. Still, his house would give us one night of decent shelter. I can grab a bucket and fill it with water so that you can place your feet in it.”

“First, you have me refrain from killing this mage. Now, you’ll have me sleep in his house. You’re really pushing your limits, my chosen.” He placed his pack on his back before he swiftly caught her. “I’ll be carrying you before we get to this cabin. It’s been much too long since I last held you.”

Odette couldn’t protest given how exhausted she was and her legs refused to move. There was also the fact that she desperately wished for sleep. She didn’t want to fall asleep immediately, though. The fear of finding Tarhuinn gone when she woke back up was too strong. As if understanding her dilemma, he muttered, “Rest. I’ll wake you when we reach it.”

His soothing voice lulled her even further into sleep's arms. Resting her head against his chest, she peered up at him before she closed her eyes. She hoped that he would truly listen to her, but the decision was now entirely in his hands.

~ ~ ~ ~ ~ ~ ~ ~ ~ ~ ~

Once night greeted the land, the cabin came into sight. Tarhuinn stopped and looked down to his beloved, who remained fast asleep. He didn't desire to wake her; he wished to pass the cabin and continue on their way. An actual bed did sound tempting, but he wanted it to be their own, not that of a horrendous mage. Even if he desired to carry on, he didn't know where to head. Odette hadn't told him the directions.

Reluctantly, he shook her gently awake. She shifted in his arms while her hands clutched more at his shirt. Gazing upon her peaceful look, he lost himself for a moment. He was so elated to have her back in his arms. It was vexing that she had fought against his wishes, but he still adored her. If someone were to ask him to stop loving her, he would state that it couldn't be done. That was why he couldn't have her going off on her own again. The past three days had been rough enough.

Not removing his eyes from her form, he gently shook her again. "It's time to get up, Odette." That time, she blinked open her eyes. She looked up to him before a small yawn escaped her lips. It was an adorable sight to view. As she gained her bearings, he set her down on the drier ground. "I'll head down into the lake while you enter the cabin." A nod came from her. Before she set off, however, he tugged on her right arm and had her face him. "Be careful. He may not be in there, but you need to be cautious still."

Giving him a reassuring smile, she rested her other hand on top of his. "I will be. You do the same. I never had swum out too far in those waters, and I don't want you to do so either."

"I understand. I'll see you soon," he answered before he pulled away and headed off towards the lake.

When she entered the cabin, a chill ran up her spine, but she reminded herself that Will wasn't there. He wouldn't burst through the door and drag her down to the storage area. She made her feet walk further in. At the fireplace, she grabbed the wood and tossed it in. Striking the fire steel, the wood came to life with flames. Heat greeted her as she placed the fire steel back down.

She retrieved one of the wooden buckets and headed back outside. Tarhuinn was sitting upon the rocks where she had gone fishing with Will. His feet were dipped in the water. He seemed to be lost in thought; he was probably debating on how to murder Will. Shaking her head, she walked over to him. "You'll be able to cross the distance between here and the house, right?" she asked while she filled the bucket.

Gaze examining the distance, he nodded. "I'll be able to, but it'll be close. Carry the bucket inside, and I'll come in once you have it set down."

Nodding, she grabbed a few clinglobs before she headed in with the water. Once the bucket was set down, she stood by the doorway and motioned for him to come inside. He walked up to the shore of the lake. She couldn't see his facial expression in the darkness, but his hesitation was obvious. If only she could dig a path for him from the lake to the house in a short amount of time.

About to urge him forward, she watched him sprint towards her. The action caused her to stumble some as she hadn't expected him to run that fast. It was as though she was watching a charging beast race towards her. His pace, though, slowed considerably when he was close to the door. Tarhuinn's pace grew sluggish, and he looked like he might fall over.

Swiftly, she slung his right arm over her shoulders and went on in with him. She seated him down at the chair by the bucket and placed his feet inside. Relief washed over him as he rested his head in the palm of his right hand.

Odette closed the door to trap the heat in. Giving another glance to Tarhuinn, she saw that his stamina was returning. Relieved herself, she proceeded to make them dinner.

Chapter Thirty Six: Caught at Night

Setting the bowls and spoons down, Odette took a seat and glanced over to Tarhuinn. His face rested against his right knuckles. He peered down to the food before he sat upright. "Did he teach you how to make this?" he questioned as he swirled the spoon around in the soup.

"Yes, but it tastes good." Despite her answer, he continued to stare at it. "I know that this place isn't exactly a relaxing retreat, but it's keeping us warm for the night. And, I understand that you don't want to eat something that he had made in the past, but a warm meal will serve you well."

"I know," he responded, leaving the spoon in the bowl. He leaned forward on his elbows and rested his chin on his intertwined hands. "It's just that I see this place, and I see you with him here. It's frustrating to know that I hadn't reached you. I had been so worried that I would never see you again. If I had just run faster when I had escaped the other night, you would've been spared last night's nightmarish happenings."

Shaking her head, she set down her own spoon. "If your escape had been successful, what would've occurred? You would've tried to deal with Will but would've had a high chance of dying. You coming here any earlier would've exposed me, and I might've failed to think of a solution while you might've died. If that had happened, I would've been dragged down to his storage and probably would never see the light of day again.

"Everything worked out in the end. We got past the pixies, and we can go confront the authors. We're back on our original course. Stop dwelling on the past events; it's not worth it. You're sacrificing your health."

A small smile touched his lips before he sat back up on the chair. "Easier said than done, but I'll take your advice for tonight." He turned to the soup and ate with her. Dinner passed by quietly before she took the dishes and went outside. When she had gone to fill the pot full of water for the soup, Tarhuinn had given her another dagger to protect herself with. Thankfully, she hadn't needed to use it on her trip outside.

Coming back in through the open door since he had ordered to leave it open while she was out, she closed it behind her and put the dishes away. Once she faced him again, she glanced between him and the bedroom. If she removed his feet from the bucket, she could hurry it into the other room. Given the distance that he had crossed earlier that evening, he would most likely be alright with the move.

"Can you remove your feet for a moment?" she asked as she bent over to pick the bucket back up. "I'm going to move the water into the bedroom for you." Nodding, he took his feet out while she hurried to set the bucket by the bed. As soon as it was placed on the ground, Tarhuinn had slipped his feet into the water. He seated himself by the headboard of the bed and leaned against it.

"You didn't share this bed with him, did you?"

Seating herself beside him, she shook her head. "No, of course not. I would never sleep beside that monster. I made sure to stay away from the pixies' idea of persuasion."

Wrapping an arm around her waist, he leaned down and placed a chaste kiss on her left cheek. A light dose of heat flooded her cheeks, and she could feel him smile against her skin. "Good. I can't have you cuddling up to another man." He pulled back from her and lifted her legs onto the bed before he draped the sheets over her. "I still intend to kill him on our way back, though."

She figured that he would be set upon that. Allowing her head to rest on his lap, she tightened her fingers around his right pant leg. "Just be careful and don't attack him directly."

"I know." He drew his right hand across her light blonde locks. "I intend to strike him by surprise. That's the only way that'll probably work against the mage. My ability to throw daggers will come in handy. I'll make sure to kill him before he can attack me. I can't let him take you away from me again."

Odette reached over with her hands and wrapped them around his left. She wasn't tired yet, given her long sleep from earlier, so she massaged his hand to relieve any remaining stress. His right hand stopped its movement across her hair several moments later. Looking up to him, she saw that he had fallen asleep. Her hold on his hand remained, however, while she moved her gaze back to how it was. Relaxed, she continued to massage his hand lightly until she drifted off into sleep herself.

~ ~ ~ ~ ~ ~ ~ ~ ~ ~ ~

Bored, Will stood at the entrance to the pixies' home. He tapped his right foot against the snow. There was the future prospect of his bluebell to consume, but until then, he had to watch over the creatures. As if to make matters worse, the king and queen refused to let him eat one of the female pixies. Normally, he would've ignored them, but he had a bargain in place.

Combing his fingers through his golden locks roughly, he groaned in annoyance. His vexation grew until his eyes caught something in the distance. There were a multitude of pixies surrounding someone. All of their weapons were pointed at the individual. "I work for Tergii and Bimaa! I should be allowed passage!" she kept crying out.

Will didn't know who those individuals were, but he didn't care. He had a possible snack coming towards him. Grinning, he crossed his arms over his chest and waited for them to get closer. The person had a hood over her head, and the rest of her cloak covered the rest of her. He was certain that the figure was a woman due to her voice.

When they finally reached the pixies' home, Will stepped aside and smiled to her. She visibly moved away from him, but the pixies' weapons kept her from going too far. Once the group headed inside, he followed after them. He placed his hands in his pockets and stayed close to the newcomer.

Standing before the pixie royals, the guards shoved the individual forward. Some of the pixies pulled her hood back as she fell to the ground on their knees. Will smirked since his boredom could end for awhile. Matters only became more interesting since she was a kelremm.

Her short and untidy ink-black locks covered her all light blue eyes partially. A scowl coated her lips while the royals looked down upon her like she was nothing. “You’re to let me go! You must obey Tergii and Bimaa. I work for them. I have their stamp upon my right wrist if you want proof. Now, treat me with the respect that I deserve and let me through. I need to deal with those two.”

“By those two, do you mean a human woman and her kelremm husband?” Will asked before the pixies could get in a word.

“Yes, but how do you know about them? And, who are you?” she asked harshly, going to stand, but the pixies forced her to stay on her knees.

“He’s the reason why we no longer have to follow your masters’ commands. The only reason that we went along with their requests was because of the mage with them. Now that we have our own mage, we no longer need to abide by their orders,” the king spoke, and the kelremm widened her eyes.

“That’s preposterous. You do understand that you’re stopping one of their spies?! They’ll learn of my absence, and they’ll come to wipe all of you out. One mage can’t harm them.”

Chuckling, Will stepped closer to her. “I’m afraid that you don’t know of the damage that I can create. I’m someone whose powers you don’t want to insult. A kelremm like you is nothing against a mage like me. With one flick of my wrist, I can blow you out of the water and kill you.” He crouched in front of her and bopped her on the nose. “In fact, I’m going to show you a few of my tricks.”

Instantly, she unsheathed a sword from her back and went to strike. She was blown onto her back just as quickly. Will stood over her and smirked. He knocked the blade from her. “That was a foolish move. Now, I may not be able to hold back for tonight. You nearly ruined my charming face.” Facing the pixies, he asked, “May I take this one as my snack for awhile?”

“We have no issue with that. We’d rather you eat her than risk you eating one of our own,” the king responded. His gaze looked past Will to the female kelremm. “Your threats don’t scare us. We now are able to fight back, and the other spies of theirs should learn to stay away from our territory.”

About to reach for her sword, Will snatched it up and swiped it across her. Her cloak fell from her shoulders before he advanced towards her. “You should last me a good few days. Maybe more if I like you.” When she went to turn and run, he knocked her to her feet once more. Grabbing her by her hair, he ignored her trying to bite him and proceeded to drag her a short distance away from the pixies’ home. He finally had some entertainment again.

Chapter Thirty Seven: Out by the Water

Her hands reached out to locate the warmth that was once near her. When they found no such greeting, Odette's brown eyes opened up steadily. Panic arose, however, upon noticing that Tarhuinn wasn't on the bed at all. Sitting up straight, she looked around in fright. Had returning to the pixies and rejoining her husband all been a dream? She almost expected to see Will walking into the bedroom.

Looking over her clothes, she found herself in her shirt and pants. Her cloak was still on and same with her boots. Both Tarhuinn and her packs were on the ground, so yesterday couldn't have been a mere dream. That was when she saw the tipped over bucket. Worry slammed into her before she flung herself off of the bed.

Her feet pounded against the wood, and she used the bedroom doorframe to propel herself forward. The cabin door was opened, and her eyes caught sight of her husband. He was out by the lake and was sitting on the rocks that she had been fishing on the other day. His feet and legs were dipped in the water. Right hand gripping the doorframe, her head leaned forward a bit, and she caught her breath while she rested her left hand against her chest. "Thank goodness," she muttered to herself.

When she looked back up, his gaze was on her. Closing the cabin door behind her, she made her way over to him. "What happened?" she asked as she took swift steps towards him. "Did you knock the bucket over in your sleep?"

"Yes, I barely made it out here in time."

Next to him, she stood over him. "Why didn't you wake me up?! I could've helped you!" she exclaimed, wishing to hit him on the back of the head. "I was ... I was ..." Her anger started to lessen, and her voice grew softer. "Terrified."

"I didn't have much time to reach water, and my body was already starting to enter panic mode. My mind didn't even consider it to be honest. My only desire at the time was to get to water. I apologize for worrying you, Odette."

Resting her fingers against her forehead, she forced herself to sit and compose herself. "It's ... alright. It was my fault for using the bucket and thinking that there wouldn't be a high chance of you knocking it over in your sleep." Her fingers combed through her locks before she met his gaze. A small, thankful smile touched her lips. "I'm just glad that you're alright. I had thought the worst."

An arm wrapped around her waist and drew her closer. He pressed her against his side before he placed a gentle kiss atop her head. "I'm not going to leave you alone in this world, especially with that mage still on the loose." His lips moved from her head and glided down to her right cheek. Tarhuinn placed a feather-light kiss there before he whispered, "Besides, you still have that promise to fulfill."

Cheeks warming up, she glanced downwards. "I'm going to make us some breakfast. I'll bring it out here." She peeked over to him. "Do you want me to bring out your pack so that you can change into some new clothes?"

"I would appreciate that. I'll take a bath while I wait for you."

Nodding in response, she removed his arm from her before she stood up. On the way inside, she grabbed a few clinglobs. After she placed them on the counter, she grabbed the metal pot to fill with water along with his pack. Tarhuinn was already by the shore of the lake and took his pack once she handed it to him. She grabbed some water swiftly before she made her way back inside.

After she finished making breakfast, she opened the door cautiously and peeked out towards the lake. To her relief, he was dressed. Opening the door fully, she walked out and met him at the water. She seated herself on the dry ground before she handed him his bowl. He took a seat himself and began to eat with her. "Are you planning to take a bath before we head out, Odette?"

Placing a bite of food in her mouth and swallowing, she nodded. "Yes, the water will be warmer down here than when we travel up the mountain. I still wish that it wasn't so cold. You're lucky that you're used to such temperatures."

"That may be the case, but I can't travel as easily as you. If I didn't need to have my feet in water, we could've taken a route around the pixies, and I would've been better able to defend you. It's difficult to see you walk into that cabin, yet I can't follow easily. My limitations are great in this environment, and I now understand why my kind likes to stay in our mountains. The water paths are everywhere for convenience. Out here, I have no other choice but to follow the natural course of the water."

"You're forgetting, though, that you're an excellent fighter, swimmer and teacher even though you don't want to teach me anymore." She looked over to him and smiled. "To me, those limitations are little in comparison to your capabilities."

Smiling softly, he set down his bowl and leaned over to her. He placed both of his hands on her cheeks and glided his thumbs over her skin. Heat enveloped her cheeks, but she didn't remove her gaze from him. "Thank you, Odette." Tarhuinn rested his forehead against hers and closed his eyes. "I have forgotten something important, though."

Distancing his forehead from hers, he opened his eyes, and his hands traveled up to her head. His fingers combed through her hair. "I never explained my reason for what I had done to you. I shouldn't have called for you like that, but I had been so concerned for your life. I had thought that maybe I could slow you down and convince you to come back to me. It had been foolish. I could've seriously injured you, yet I had succumbed to my selfish desire to have you back in my arms.

"But, I don't think that I can apologize. Based on the pixies' report, I know that you suffered from it, yet I had been so happy to hear that you were halted in your advance to this cabin. I hope that something like that never happens again, but if it does, I might do the same thing."

She leaned against one of his hands as it came past her. Odette placed her breakfast aside and held his hand to her cheek. "I understand that you were worried and inflamed. I'm not saying that it's okay to perform that tactic on me again. For this time, though, I forgive you even if you don't apologize. I'm just glad to be done with that awful task."

"Thank you again, then," he answered before he gently pulled his hand back.

They returned to eating, and once they were completed with their meals, Odette washed the dishes in the water and took them back in. She placed them where they had originally been before she entered the bedroom and grabbed her pack. Not heading out of the room immediately, though, she checked the wardrobe. It was possible that another cloak was inside.

Searching through it, she managed to find one. It was a thick tan cloak without a hood on it. Still, it looked quite warm, and Tarhuinn had lost his. She took it, along with some of the blankets in the room, and headed back outside. Tarhuinn gave her a questioning glance as she presented the various items. "They'll help us on the colder nights. Besides, you need a new cloak."

"I would argue, but it's unfortunately true. We'll be heading into colder territory, and we'll need warmer supplies to handle the nights up there." He took the cloak and blankets from her before he packed the blankets away in his pack. "You'll wear the warmer cloak."

"No, you will. I still have mine, and it's small for you. If I need more warmth, I'll," she paused for a moment while her cheeks grew a little bit hot, "huddle up next to you." She placed her hands on his upper arms and started to turn him around. "Now, look the other way while I bathe."

Laughing a little, he faced the other way for her. She removed her hands from him and went to tend to her bath. "I expect you to stay close to me a lot, then," he commented, which made her shake her head. Hers cheeks were still warm, but the water would cool them off soon enough.

Slipping out of her clothes, she set her shirt and pants aside. She had only worn them for a little while, so she wouldn't wash them. There was another pair of undergarments in her pack, so she could clean the ones that she was currently wearing. Odette stepped further into the water and shivered a little. If only she could influence the water to be warmer.

Washing herself, she noted the various bruises from Will last night. When her hands ran over them, she winced slightly. At least, the cold numbed them some. Apparently, though, Tarhuinn had heard her quiet shows of pain. He peered over his shoulder, about to swiftly look the other way again, but he spotted the marks. His dark blue orbs widened, and his rage started to grow. "Did he do that to you?!"

Jumping, Odette went into deeper water to hide herself. She looked back at him. "Tarhuinn, please look the other way. I'll be fine. They'll heal," she tried to reassure. Thankfully, though, he wasn't headed in her direction. Instead, he went over to their packs.

He removed a jar of salve and held it up while his gaze turned onto her; however, his eyes only focused on hers. "When you're finished, let me apply this to you. You know that I won't look at you. Let me do that much. I don't want those things on you. You deserve better than to wear those marks of his."

His gaze demonstrated that he wouldn't let her decline. He was allowing his concern for her to get the best of him again. In the present instance, though, she didn't mind. It would be nice to have the marks heal quicker, and she trusted him not to take advantage of the situation. She gave him a small nod and voiced, "That's fine, and thank you." Odette stared at one and muttered, "I hate them so much."

Glad to have her confirmation, he returned to his original spot and set the jar on ground until she was ready. He looked away from her and crossed his arms over his chest. "Thank you for trusting me." She didn't answer verbally, but she smiled a little bit and went back to her bathing.

Upon completing her bath and washing her other undergarments, Odette grabbed half of her outfit. Tarhuinn had kept his promise and had faced the other way the entire time. If it had been Will, he would've probably peeked within a moment's notice.

She slipped into her lower undergarment along with her pair of pants. Odette rolled up the pants to her upper thighs so that the salve could still be applied on her legs. Personally, she wanted to rub the ointment on herself, but she had already agreed to Tarhuinn's request. Otherwise, he might've exploded on her and stated that she was breaking another promise.

There were bruises, though, along all of her back and parts of her midsection. She could cover herself with her undershirt, but it would get in the way of application. It posed another problem too. Tarhuinn had told her that he wouldn't look at her. By adding a hindrance to the conditions, it would display that she didn't entirely trust his word.

After what had happened at the pixie home, she wished to show no more signs of distrust. It wouldn't exactly be easy given how his emotions overtook him from time to time, but she had to make an attempt at it. He deserved at least that much since he trusted her enough to take her on the so far dangerous journey.

Keeping her back faced to him, she covered her chest with her arms. Quietly and reluctantly, she voiced, "Okay, I'm ready." When he came over, he started with her back and rubbed the soothing gel into her skin. Thankfully, she was already shivering somewhat from the cold. Otherwise, the shiver from his hand upon her bare back would've been rather noticeable.

Occasionally, she would wince a little. He apparently noticed as his touch became gentler even though he was being already quite careful with her. It didn't help with the warmth that stuck to her cheeks. The heat in her cheeks did aid with the surrounding cold, but her attention was becoming more and more focused on his hands. They worked as though they were carving a fragile creation; one wrong move and it would deliver ruin.

Her body tensed, however, when his hands trailed from her back to her midsection. She pressed her arms against her chest more as the heat in her cheeks intensified. The sensitivity there did cause her to let out a soft giggle every now and then, which didn't go unnoticed.

Tarhuinn didn't exploit such vulnerability, but she had a feeling that he might in the future. The way that he would pause and laugh quietly pointed to that possibility. Despite her slightly ticklish nature, she found herself leaning back against him. His actions were soothing, and his laugh sounded like pleasant rain drops on a warm summer's day. Her body practically desired to collapse against his.

His hands left her midsection, much to her displeasure and relief at the same time. Had he continued, she might've transformed into a puddle, yet she wouldn't have entirely minded. He moved around her before he grabbed her undershirt and returned to her. Grabbing her arms, he promised that he wouldn't look, and she gave him her trust once more.

Lifting them up, he slid the shirt onto her form and pulled it down. He motioned for her to sit down on one of the larger rocks so that he could tend to her arms and legs. Once seated, he went to work again. The bruises on those areas were fewer and smaller. It took him less time to treat them, but he spent equal amount of care on them. Her whole body felt relaxed by the end of it.

Throwing on her shirt and tying her cloak, she hopped down from the rock and looked out towards the mountains. They would have to take the stream to the right of the cabin before they headed upwards. Her eyes followed its trail before it disappeared into the pines. The slope of the mountain, though, led quite a ways up. She compared it to the approximate distance from the cabin to the door from the third complex. It was definitely longer or at least steeper.

Climbing uphill was going to be a pain, especially in the cold, so she was rather thankful for the extra blankets and cloak. She looked back to Tarhuinn, who handed her his pack and new cloak. "I don't want to burden you with these, but I'll have to meet you at the head of the stream."

"No, it's alright. Besides, it's the least that I can do after you tended to those marks." She lifted the additional pack onto her right shoulder and hugged the cloak. It was rather soft, and it only tempted her more to stand closer to Tarhuinn on their way up the mountain.

A small smile touched his lips. “I couldn’t leave those untended to.” His smile upturned into smirk. “Besides, you looked to be enjoying yourself.” Heat filling her cheeks, she spun on her heel and started to head off.

“Just be careful,” she remarked in a curt tone. She kept her back to him, but he responded the same before a splash sounded. His tone was more amused and caring, though. He probably understood very well the effect that his actions had on her.

Cuddling into the comfortable cloak, she made her way back towards the stream after she had placed on her boots. It meant setting down the cloak for a bit, but she had hurried in covering her feet.

Reaching the stream didn’t take too long, but the snow was getting thicker. Her boots were becoming worn from all the rough usage too. They kept her feet warm to some degree, but the cold managed to seep in a little bit. She would have to bear with them for the time being, though. When they returned home if things went well, she would trade for new ones. That seemed like a long way off, however.

Easily, her mind imagined every obstacle that might be ahead of them. The thoughts swirled around in her head, and she had to remind herself that she had already succeeded over an excruciating task. She had handled Will, so she could deal with the five authors unless they all turned out to be cannibalistic mages too. Then, there would be a major issue.

Splashes of water were heard behind her. Tarhuinn soon stood beside her, and she handed him the cloak. He was reluctant to take it, but she insisted on him doing so. After he tied it around his neck, it draped down to his calves. The water would only occasionally splash up against it. Hopefully, it would stay that way since it would serve as one of their blankets.

As the day pressed on, nothing of interest occurred. They saw a few pixies a few times. Occasionally, a small animal ran by, but it was too quick for them to notice what it was. It was worrying, though, since it might’ve been something that wished to harm them. Fortunately, no hostile encounters sprung up from those times.

Stopping for the night, they both set down their packs and cleared away some of the snow. Her hands grew cold only after a few swipes, but she continued to help Tarhuinn. Despite her body's protest, she reminded it that it would have suitable blankets over it soon enough. Her eyes caught sight of something pale moving a little ways off. It seemed like it was coming towards them. Even though she kept a close eye on it, it went behind a tree and never came back out into the open. She wondered if the being climbed the pine.

Noting her stare, Tarhuinn rested a hand on her left shoulder and squeezed gently. "It was a haasna. You have nothing to fear, Odette. If anything, it might ask for some hair. Other than that, it'll leave us alone." He lowered his hand before he cleared away more snow. "We'll need to be extra careful on our watches, though. Even if we have some time before Tergii, Bimaa and their mage come down this way, they may decide to head back early."

Having his reassurance about that creature, she aided him with the snow again. "I know. Our best chance at finding this supposed extension of life is to find their home without their knowledge of us doing so. It sounds like we might have to swim across a lake or travel underwater. Hopefully, we don't have to do either." A nod of agreement was received from him.

Finally, they both had the snow pushed away. A bed of twigs and pine needles lay underneath. The blankets and their cloaks would provide enough cushioning so that the needles probably wouldn't be felt. If they didn't, they would have to deal with the nuisance.

Laying down the pieces, they rested upon the blankets while the cloak was draped over them. Odette took first watch since she wasn't entirely tired yet. As Tarhuinn hugged her close, she was glad for the heat. To keep tiredness away for longer, she grabbed some dried fish and ate a small dinner. She nibbled on the food slowly while she tuned her ears into the sounds around them.

There was the flow of the stream, and some movement back where that haasna had been. She managed to glance back, and she spotted the creature going in the direction of the cabin. It was pleasant to know that neither of their hair would be requested that night. Her defenses remained on, however, in case something dangerous traveled into their vicinity.

Chapter Thirty Eight: Falling Stars

Odette's watch so far was uneventful. The haasna never traveled back, and no unexpected visitors revealed themselves. She rolled from her left side to her right. Tarhuinn was fast asleep. His chest's steady rise and fall almost lulled her to sleep. Her body wouldn't permit her too much more time to stay awake, so she called out his name quietly a few times.

That produced the desired result, and he steadily began to awake. His dark blue eyes met her brown orbs before he gave her a simple nod. Taking the signal, it wasn't long before her eyelids closed. It barely took a blink of the eyes before she drifted into sleep's embrace. If she could be awake at the same time, she would've surprised herself with how truly exhausted she was.

Switching to rest on his back, he positioned her so that his chest could serve as her pillow. She snuggled into him almost immediately before she settled down again. He made sure that the cloak was secured around them, more her than him. A content sigh escaped her lips while her hands gripped at his shirt lightly.

His right fingers brushed across her forehead softly. Her smooth skin was chilled with the cool night air, and her parted lips gave away her breath. She turned her head so that she could hide her face more in his shirt. Bringing his fingers back, he ran them over her silken locks. He twirled a couple of strands around his index finger. The strands slid off gracefully like a lone petal drifting to the ground.

Most of his attention was on her while some was partitioned to their surroundings. That was the case until the area grew somewhat brighter. A gap had opened up in the clouds. The moon's light shone down on the region while stars twinkled beside it. He was partially tempted to wake her up so that she could observe the spectacular sight. On other nights, he had viewed something similar, but it seemed all the brighter now that he had her back.

The clouds didn't withhold, however. Droplets of rain started to fall a little distance off. Moonlight and starlight caused the beads of water to sparkle some, giving away the exact location of the wall of rain. They were under decent enough cover, and they would probably only receive a few droplets on them. If the rain grew heavier in its fall, then they could get quite wet, but he appreciated the scene before them. It was peaceful and beautiful. To its soothing tune, he found himself lightly humming. The notes were quiet enough that they wouldn't wake Odette, but they were clear otherwise.

As the falling water progressed towards them, he didn't realize that his voice had increased in volume to be heard alongside the drip-dropping of the rain. The tune began to tug at the ears of Odette. She shifted a little, which alerted him. He lowered his voice, but the strings had already been played.

Vision of the world returning to her, she kept herself still. Her ears picked up the sweet sound. They were called to it. It was as though they were listening to a myriad of the most pleasing tunes. Maybe, it was just Tarhuinn's voice's effect on her. His humming most likely was different to other ears, but she didn't mind. She was enchanted by it.

Gaze moving to the rain, she spotted it nearing them. Soon enough, it fell upon them. It was only a few drops, but the feel of the icy water made his voice seem to meld with the rain, yet it contrasted the coldness of it. If they could dance upon the stars and be warm among them, that would be a near perfect description of what greeted her ears.

Sleep kept its arms around her, however. The beautiful humming had tempted her to wake up, but it was now doing the opposite. It melted away the fears of the night and replaced them with a loving enfoldment. Her eyes complied with the comforting shroud and closed once more. She returned to a dreamless sleep, and his humming was the last thing that she heard for that evening.

~~~~~~~~~~~
~~~~~~~~~~~

Come morning, the rain passed, but the clouds remained. Any sound of water came from the stream. Sitting up, Tarhuinn gently placed Odette's head on his lap while the cloak still covered most of her form. A small yawn escaped his lips as he stretched his arms. His eyes scanned over the nearby region. He spotted nothing that would bother them, so he decided that he could let her sleep a little longer.

With his left hand, he reached over and fished out a piece of dried meat. His sharp teeth wished to tear through it, but he made himself eat slowly. If he ate at the pace that he wished, their food supply would be diminished by a decent amount. A yawn, though, caught his attention.

Staring downwards, he watched her blink open her eyes. Her hands traveled towards her face before she rubbed the sleep away. Or, she tried to anyway. Tiredness remained in her eyes upon her meeting his gaze. A gentle smile graced his lips. "Good morning, Odette."

A chuckle parted from her. She proceeded to sit in an upright position. The cloak covered her legs as it did his some. Supporting her weight with her right hand, she covered her mouth with her other hand while her quiet laughter continued. In response, he raised an eyebrow. "I'm not sure what's amusing, Odette."

Hand descending some, her left index finger pointed to her lips. She parted them and tapped the space between her left front teeth. A grin upon her lips, she stated, "You have something there."

Embarrassment washed over his countenance. He looked away from her before he quickly removed the piece of meat from between his teeth. His reaction only caused her to laugh more. It was cute to view him in such a light, especially over a simple matter. She knew that he wasn't a disorderly eater, but there were things that he couldn't prevent all of the time.

"Maybe, that's telling you that you shouldn't eat breakfast without me," she joked as her laughing started to die down a bit.

"If I were to follow that, it would defeat the purpose of me getting most of the food," he countered while he now wore his own smile. "Besides, I liked having you cuddle up next to me. During our travels today, you should stay close and under my cloak. That'll keep us both warmer."

"Yes, and it'll prevent me from eating breakfast since I suspect that you would be carrying me in that scenario," she pointed out, jabbing her left index finger at his chest accusingly. "That, I'm not going to allow. I made you breakfast yesterday, so I expect a fair share of breakfast today in payment." Before she could reach over to one of their packs and pull out some food for herself, Tarhuinn grabbed her wrist and tugged her to him.

"I do suppose that you're right. I should treat you to breakfast," he voiced, his face several inches from hers. It was only moving closer, and he stopped when his lips hovered over hers. Contact between their lips never occurred, though. He placed his hands on her hips and lifted her up. She cried out in surprise before she found herself seated on his lap.

Back to his chest, he wrapped his right arm around her waist. He hadn't pressed her back to him too hard, which was considerate given that the bruises were still somewhat sore despite the salve. His left hand reached over to his pack and retrieved a piece of dried meat for her. Holding it to her lips, he asked, "Well, aren't you hungry?"

"It'd be nice to eat on my own, but if you wish to make me lazy, so be it." She pushed back the heat which rose to her cheeks and parted her lips. Biting off a piece, she smiled in delight at having food. It wasn't warm fish soup, but it did aid a hungry stomach. Odette continued to partake of the meat until it was finished. Tarhuinn retrieved some dried cherries and fed them to her individually. No complaint left her.

Rather, she managed to steal some from him and hold them up to his mouth. "I thought that I was meant to spoil you this morning?" he questioned, and she assumed that there was a smirk upon his lips.

"Yes, but I'm increasing your payment to me. When we return to our home, I expect you to make me a grand feast. Then, we'll be even."

After taking a cherry, eating it and swallowing, he moved her once more. She stayed on his lap but now faced him. Before he took another cherry, he commented, "I had planned that anyway. On the night that we return home, I intend to make sure that you fulfill your promise to me. It's going to be quite a special evening." He bit into the cherry and stole it from her fingers before she could accidentally drop it.

Heat erupted in her cheeks. "Well, aren't you going to feed me the rest of those? Or, do I have to do so myself?" Pursing her lips, she took the remaining amount and pressed her whole hand to his mouth. His eyes shone with clear amusement, and he looked like he wished to say something.

Pushing her hand against his face, she got up from his lap. She took her hand away and stood to her feet as she held onto the cloak. Odette kept it around her shoulders before she picked up her pack. After she slipped it onto her shoulders and draped the cloak over it, she looked down to him. He was eating the dried fruits while a smug expression coated his countenance. "At least, you can't say anything more for the moment," she muttered with a roll of her eyes.

Chapter Thirty Nine: Snow Pixies' Trouble

Bare, medium blue feet hurried through water. Water splashing could be heard, but it didn't bother the others in the room. Where one was worried, the others were calm. They reflected the smooth and soothing nature of the water that ran across the entirety of the room. The peaceful flow descended from the raised grounds to the lower ones, highlighting the natural waterfalls of the room.

Reaching the end of the deeper water, the concerned kelremm went to one knee and bowed his head respectfully before he stood back up. He pulled down his cloak hood and glanced up to the table and five chairs. Only two of the chairs were occupied, however. "My masters, I have discovered terrible news from the region of the pixie home."

Disinterested, the female of the two peered over and down. She rested her chin in the palm of her right hand while her left directed him to go on. Bowing his head respectfully again, he disclosed, "They have broken your agreement and have found a mage of their own. We're not aware of how the mage came to their aid, but, with your deal broken, it's safe to assume that the inquiring kelremm and his wife are still on their way here."

The female kelremm glanced over to the male kelremm. "Well, that's unexpected. What did you want to do? I don't care either way," she mentioned, sounding as though the news had been about some trifle matter.

Flipping over another piece of parchment, he fixed his eyes on the spy. "I want to know why he looks so terrified." He didn't have to ask the spy to answer, for his statement was clear enough. The spy would respond one way or another.

Dipping his head lower, the spy pushed back his nerves. He tried to appear more presentable, but the sights that he had seen were too gruesome not to react to. "When a few others and I had learned of the situation, we had found one of our own in a ... disturbing state."

The spy paused and met his male master's sharp gaze. "She was alive, but it would've been better for her to be dead. We had tried to end her misery, but this mage had been too swift and powerful. It hadn't help that the pixies had sneaked up on us and warned the mage after they had told us to leave and we had refused."

"I'm assuming that the other spies are dead now. Or, they're in a similar state to how you found that female spy. How did you escape, though?" the male kelremm questioned, turning another page of parchment over.

"I had been the last to leave our location, which had been a small stream off to the left of the pixie home. When I saw the mage easily kill my companions, I figured that it would be best to run and to report to you what had occurred. I believe that the female spy had been kept alive."

Getting up from his chair, the male kelremm walked towards the other end of the table. He stood in front of the nearest chair to the spy and rested his hands on the back of it. "You didn't only leave to come inform us of this news. You ran because you were afraid. You didn't want to die, yet you know that you must die for us if it comes to that."

"Should I dispose of him?" inquired the female kelremm as she examined her sharpened nails.

"No, I wish to hear more of his report. Besides, this is rather important. We can't have the pixies killing off all of our spies with this mage. The less that we have to mess with the complexes' populations is better. How many of your companions did you lose to this mage, not including the captured female?"

"Two, master."

"That's not too many. We'll have to replace them, though, to keep our spy population in healthy order. Here's what I'll have you do, spy. Find three spy kelremm that wish to have another partner. Find three willing humans next. That'll be your task after I release you.

"Before that, though, I want you to tell me every detail of what you saw. I wish to know what the mage is capable of before we deal with him and deliver a proper punishment. Second, you're to notify the other spies that if a pixie holds them back they're to kill them. Our agreement has been broken, so none of their lives will be spared if they get in the way. Come and take a seat with us."

Pulling out the chair, the male kelremm stepped aside while the spy ascended the stairs. He took his seat before his one master returned back to his chair. With a subtle wave of his right hand, he motioned the spy to tell them the entirety of the story. Before he could begin, they all heard, "Byda! What's the meaning of this?! Get in here and release me from these chains?!"

Letting out a heavy sigh, she stood up from her chair. "I'll have to miss this conversation. Inform me of the details later, Phyon. My lover apparently doesn't understand why he's in that state." She received a chuckle from the male kelremm before she left the area to attend to the matter.

Phyon focused back on the kelremm spy, indicating for him to begin. Blood drained from the spy's face somewhat before he relayed everything that he had witnessed. As the discussion continued, his master maintained a neutral expression, but, inwardly, he couldn't help but wonder how the pixies had managed to obtain such a man. There was an important piece missing, and he wished to discover it.

~ ~ ~ ~ ~ ~ ~ ~ ~ ~

Several days had passed since they had set out from the cabin. They hadn't run into any real trouble. Only a few haasna had crossed their path and requested a few strands of hair before they had gone on their way. There had been an occasional snowy owl that had hooted at night or had flown overhead. Other than that, their travel had concerned mainly their own banter.

Even at the moment, one was teasing the other. "Once we have a child, I'll have to make sure to secure the window in the garden. I can't have them taking after you and your sense of adventure. Otherwise, they may try to exit through the window and escape on us. There's also the water passage. I'm going to have to monitor what you teach them," Tarhuinn commented casually.

"And, I'll have to make sure that you don't bore our child to an early death. Knowing you, you'll be shoving books in their face immediately after their born. Not only that but also you'll make the child hate reading."

"If I'm so boring, why do you seem so happy by my presence?"

"I'm sorry. I didn't mean to give that impression. I just tolerate you," she answered, shrugging her shoulders and shaking her head. "I just tune you out and pay attention to the scenery around us. I'm happy about that, not you. Really, you should've noticed that."

His footsteps halted. Before she could even turn around, she was pulled backwards. Her back arched while her feet did their best to stay out of the water. She looked up to him while he peered down. Left hand supporting her up, his right gripped her chin. "And, what scenery do you view now?"

Tarhuinn's head blocked the view of the sky as well, so she couldn't utilize that as an excuse. Well, she could lie, but she had a better idea. She closed her eyes and remarked, "I see darkness. It's not as beautiful as the trees and snow, but it'll have to do until you release me."

Due to her current state, she couldn't spot his appearing smirk. "You may view darkness, but I think that you'll feel something else." His hold on her vanished before he pushed her forward. She didn't impact the snow covered ground. Rather, she was spun around and held by him again. Her eyelids opened as his lips neared. Before any contact could occur, they both heard splashes of water a little ways off.

Their lighthearted and intimate atmosphere faded away rapidly. Alertness took over. Tarhuinn swiftly picked her up bridal style before he advanced forward as quietly as he could. Up ahead was the split in the stream. They weren't supposed to take the one going left, but they were left little choice. Those sounds were coming from the right path.

Odette directed her gaze to the right stream. She couldn't remove her eyes from it; she was worried that the owners of the sounds would come upon them soon or that they would hear Tarhuinn and her. Since they were coming from that direction, it could be Tergii, Bimaa and the mage. If they encountered them now, they wouldn't be ready and probably wouldn't have the upper hand.

Thankfully, Tarhuinn made the split before they caught sight of anyone. The trees were currently providing them much needed cover from the higher ground. Heading down the left stream, they followed the wavy path of it. Multiple rock formations were up ahead, but the rocks would hide them even more. What worried her were the threatening creatures that the pixies had mentioned.

Hopefully, they wouldn't have to encounter them until after the unexpected travelers went by. If they were even luckier, they wouldn't interact with those beings at all. Reaching the rocks, Tarhuinn hid behind one of the ones furthest from the split. He set Odette down, but he kept his left arm wrapped around her waist.

Pressed to him, her hands gripped his shirt, but she was tempted, out of curiosity, to peek around the rock. She wished to confirm her suspicion that it was the authors and the mage. Understanding that such an idea was unwise, she held onto him tighter to ease her inquisitiveness.

The splashes grew louder as the newcomers neared. Tarhuinn and Odette remained where they were. Both made sure that the other wasn't peeking out from behind the rock. Their extra precaution was probably unnecessary since the unknown individuals wouldn't have been able to see them unless they traveled down the left path some. Hopefully, they had had no intention of coming down that way. If the left path was their objective, both of them would have to face an encounter.

When the splashes seemed to reach their loudest, both hiders tensed. Her grip somehow tightened more on his shirt while his hands gripped her upper arms. Tarhuinn's hold lessened, however, due to her wincing from the bruises there.

Both continued to listen intently. To their relief, the splashes began to grow quieter. Even when they became faint, they remained as still as possible. It wasn't until the splashes could no longer be heard that they both relaxed a little bit. Before they could take in a moment of peace, Odette jumped. A splash sounded behind them. The noise was much louder than the footsteps and signaled that something larger than feet was behind them.

Quickly, she turned around, but Tarhuinn swiftly moved her behind him; however, she was able to peer around him. Before them was a good sized pool. Ripples glided across the shadowy water and towards them. Stepping back a little, Tarhuinn kept his feet as near to the edge of the pool as possible. Odette ended up pressed tightly between the rock and him.

More of the rocks were towards the opposite side of the pool, and there seemed to be a gap behind them, but they mainly hid whatever was back there. A couple of laughs sounded from behind those rocks, and they were quite melodic. They weren't nearly as enchanting as Tarhuinn's voice, but she supposed that if she had never met her husband, then those voices would be the most beautiful in the world.

As the laughs and possibly whispers continued, Tarhuinn started to move back towards the path. Evident apprehension was written across his countenance while his eyes never left the spot from where the ripples had originated. His feet made light splashes in the water as hers went onto solid ground. She walked quietly beside him as she noted that the noises continued. The source of those sounds was most likely the creatures that the pixies had warned of.

They reached the curves of the stream again, but their sense of unease grew. The sounds of laughter and quiet chattering had grown nonexistent. Their own breathing was the loudest noise in the vicinity. Tarhuinn rested a hand on her back and ushered her forward, but his hand soon vanished from her. Instantly, a yell and splash met her ears.

Rapidly, she turned on her heel. She couldn't see Tarhuinn. Ripples traveled across the water, colliding with each other. The water's surface was chaotic. Internal alarms rising, she glanced over the water and hoped that he would come back up. When he didn't, she tossed her pack far from the water and took out the dagger in her boot. Hurriedly, she removed her boots and cloak before she held the dagger in a reverse grip.

Taking a deep breath, she charged towards the deeper water and dived in. Illumination under the surface was poor, and the cloud cover wasn't aiding in the slightest. She did manage to spot Tarhuinn being dragged deeper. Hands, the same color as him, tugged at his arms and feet. Some undid the dagger belt around his hips and tossed it aside while others removed his cloak and pack. There had to be ten of the creatures around him, and she could only see him through small gaps.

Urgency dominating, she swam downwards. The creatures hadn't noticed her yet. It was clear that they were speaking to him, but every word was obstructed by the water. Their hair, the same color as their bodies, fanned out around them, which only made her view of him worse. They were swimming too fast for her to catch up, but, luckily, the floor of the pool was in sight.

Her fear grew when she saw a few come out from an opening towards the back of the pool. Spears were in their hands. Cursing, she tried to move her legs quicker. Already, though, she could feel her own breath fading. Dirt and rocks started to be thrown around on the base. Tarhuinn was still struggling. Odette caught a glimpse of hands holding his jaw shut.

Kicking her legs faster, she neared the bottom. As one reached out to help in restraining him, she extended out her free hand and tugged harshly on their hair. A loud cry resonated under the water. She forced herself not to cover her ears so that she could hold onto the dagger and attack. Odette made her strike as strong as she could.

Realistically, she stood no chance against the swarm of merfolk, but she couldn't let them skewer Tarhuinn. She had to do her best to free him. Her attack did little to stop the other mermaids and mermen. It only caused the one that she had gained the attention of to reveal its razor sharp teeth while its completely cerulean eyes shone with amusement.

Vision of that particular mermaid vanished as a force collided with her right side. It knocked the remaining breath from her and her dagger for that matter. The blade sank to the floor while her attacker swam by. A merman and mermaid gripped her arms, but their efforts to detain her meant little. Her air was gone. She was beginning to drown.

Her arms thrashed, her side ached, and her vision faded. She called out to Tarhuinn or tried to at least. Her struggling grew weaker until it halted completely. From amidst the throng of merfolk, Tarhuinn saw the condition of his wife. His attention no longer focused on the creatures around him. When his view of her disappeared, his fury grew. A thunderous cry exited his lips, and the water reverberated.

For a split moment, it loosened the grips on him. He forced his way through the merfolk and darted for her. Spears instantly pointed at him and some were thrown. Dodging the attacks, he knocked some of the weapons aside and clashed against Odette. The two of them tumbled through the water. Her head was pressed to his chest when the next impact occurred. His head struck one of the larger rocks under the water, sending his own vision into despair. Merfolk surrounded them as things receded from sight.

Spear tips were pointed at them while discussions broke out among the species. Some attempted to pull the couple apart, but they received no luck. Tarhuinn wasn't unconscious yet, and he wouldn't let them touch her again. He needed to get her air, but darkness was encroaching upon his vision. His grip on her was already growing weaker.

With a few more harsh tugs, they were separated. He wished to cry out, but his voice fell flat. His limbs hung beside him, and the world left him. He only hoped that at least she would make it out of the present chaos alive. Everything remained a mystery to him until cold stone greeted him.

His breathing was rough. He could tell that his feet were barely touching water. The entirety of his body felt immensely exhausted. It was as though he were breathing in the dirt. Moving his fingers slightly, his skin rubbed against stone. Tarhuinn wished to push himself up and examine his surroundings better, but he had no stamina to execute such a simple action.

Even opening his eyes was strenuous. It was as though he was pushing against a great boulder. Vision returned to him steadily, but no sound greeted his ears. Slowly, he lifted his head up. Immediately, it fell back to the rock.

A groan of pain left his lips, but he hadn't lost consciousness again. In that moment, he saw that he was in a cave. His feet were barely touching the miniature pool in the area. To make matters worse, he noted that there were several merfolk in the larger pool. Spears were in all of their hands.

Why had they kept him alive, though? He thought that they had wished to kill him back there. They could've easily succeeded, but he was grateful that he was still breathing. Odette had to be alive, and he needed to reach her since she wasn't in the space with him. Due to his condition, he wasn't able to summon the ability to even ask where she was or if she was alive.

Several days ago, he had gotten her back from that mage. Now, she was gone again. Presently, he wished that he had never agreed to take her on the journey. He never suspected that they would face so many great dangers. Truly, he had thought that only the authors and later their mage would be their only concerns. A part of him voiced that such thoughts were foolish and that their journey was worth the risk. They merely had to crush their current obstacle. Then, he would be able to spend a longer life with his beloved.

Focusing on the more positive notes, he managed to turn his head towards the guards. Their gazes were pinned to him before they whispered among themselves. One of them went under the water and presumably left. He attempted to inquire about Odette's location even though he knew that it was pointless. His lips moved gradually, but no sound left him.

One of the guards, however, responded, "The human's alive. Whether you see her again or not will be decided soon enough. You, kelremm, should've stayed far away from here. This territory isn't for the likes of your abhorring kind."

Chapter Forty: Dreadful Awakening

Limbs sore, Odette felt smooth and cold stone beneath her. Her body shivered from the ice-like rock, but there was nothing to alleviate it. Odette's hands grasped for something, and her mind played the trick on her that Tarhuinn was nearby. When still nothing met her fingers, she opened her eyes. Groaning from the aching of her body, she steadily pushed herself into a sitting position while she regained her vision.

She turned away from the stone wall in front of her and shifted to look the other way. To her fright, she was met with several pairs of eyes. Merfolk watched her, and some whispered some things betwixt themselves. Odette doubted that their words were in her favor, but she was alive so that was a positive. Where was Tarhuinn, though? Had they killed him?

Panic beginning to bubble up, she scanned the space. There was only the small stone area that she was on and the surrounding merfolk-filled water. Her stomach was starting to feel sick. What if they really had ended his life? She would never get to enjoy his warm embrace again or the teasing that they had with each other. It was as though a void was slowly creating itself within her heart and mind. Was that how he had felt when she had left for the cabin? If so, she was gradually beginning to understand why he had wished for her to return so badly.

Meeting the gaze of a mermaid, she managed to ask without stuttering, "Where's my husband?" The mermaid in response looked to another one. They spoke a few quiet words, but that only increased her distress. "Please, tell me ..." She nearly couldn't form the next question. "I-is ... he d-dead?"

Before the mermaid that she had previously made eye contact with could answer, the one next to her took her place. "He's near to dying, but we're keeping him alive for now. His fate will be decided soon as will yours. Hopefully, we'll be able to take back what was stolen from us."

Despite being perplexed by the mermaid's last statement, Odette was relieved to hear that her husband was breathing. There was a chance for them after all, but the odds were stacked against them. If Tarhuinn wasn't fighting or even calling out to her, he was most likely in a less than satisfactory position. For all she knew, the merfolk could be torturing him, and his cries were merely muted by the water.

Those thoughts made her inner torment all the worse. She needed to find a way to him, but she wasn't near the swimming capabilities of the creatures before her. Her eyes looked over the room once more. Odette kept doing so to find a way out if there was one. It didn't help that the merfolk were growing more accustomed to whispering among her.

All of them seemed to have some opinion about her fate. Some desired to eat her, stating that she would be a feast. Others simply wanted to drown her and toss her body into the snow. There were a few that wished to keep her as a pet of sorts. In general, the remarks were only increasing her want to escape. The creatures would most likely not let Tarhuinn or her out without a few scratches. Their injuries would probably be worse than that, though.

A conversation between two of the merfolk caught her attention. She didn't try to pinpoint them among the crowd; she needed to keep her gaze on the more important matter at hand, but she did listen. "I think that we should at least let her see her husband before he dies. That would be the proper thing to do. She deserves that much. Her husband is the one that we despise, not her."

"Yes, but she still loves him. A human not in love wouldn't have dived into a pool of merfolk and tried to attack them. For loving that wretched kelremm, she deserves no decent treatment from us, but I do agree that she should see him before he dies. The council will probably decide for him to be tortured before he's killed. We can let her watch the whole display."

"No, that's taking things too far. That would bring more pain to her than to him. He's our focus, not her. Her seeing the end result of his treatment will be enough for her. You're acting crueler than that kelremm." A low growl emitted from the other speaker, but it was returned by the most recent one. It was most likely a warning sign to back down.

The heightening tension between them didn't go unnoticed by the other merfolk. Whisperings among others began to quiet down as heads turned towards them. Noting the newfound attention that they were receiving, they halted their wordless threats. Of the two, the one that was planning a worse fate for her stared at her and grinned.

"Don't you desire to view the methods that'll kill your husband? I can guarantee you that it'll be quite a show. You'll get to witness ..." Before the merman could even continue, the other merman attempted to hit the male with the shaft of a spear. The attack triggered several merfolk to hold back the one with the weapon. The other laughed it off before he returned to describing the various atrocities that would be performed upon Tarhuinn. None of the other merfolk tried to stop him.

Odette pushed herself to keep searching for an exit, but his descriptions were piercing her heart and mind. Each felt like they were being done to her. Nausea formed, and her arms hugged her body. She felt that she might collapse into the water and sink to the bottom, never to return. Tears threatened to escape her eyes; some were able to. It didn't only take her strength to keep looking but also to prevent herself from striking out at the merman.

Brushing her few tears away, she gave her inspection one last chance, but it resulted in a fruitless outcome. She could hear his remarks still, but her ears were growing numb to them. There were enough images in her mind already, and they were stealing her energy. Odette collapsed to her knees. Her head hung down. Tears arrived quicker while sobs were aching to escape past her lips.

They had made it past the pixies and Will only to wake up in a lair of merfolk, and most were intent on killing them. Their only hope was the merman who had acted out against the one speaking presently. He seemed like he could be reasoned with. Unfortunately, he was restrained, and she could only think of one thing to ask. "C-can I go se-see hi-him? Please, I ju-just w-want t-to see hi-him," she spoke between sobs.

"Oh, so you want to witness his punishment?" the one merman chuckled out.

"I'll take her, then. You might try to torture her on the way there," stated the one who was currently being held back. The two merfolk restraining him shared a glance before they nodded their heads and released him. They stayed at the ready in case he tried something again.

"We'll accompany you two there, but we'll have to wait outside of his room until we're given the signal that we may travel inside. The council still hasn't decided upon either of your fates," one of the two merfolk voiced. Her eyes turned to Odette. "And, the moment that you try something, we'll bring you back here and break your legs. Do you understand?"

Giving a weak nod, she heard movement coming towards her. Almost instantly, she was pulled into the water. She let out a cry, but it fell deaf due to the water. Roughly, she was tugged up above the surface and passed over to the merman. He didn't give his name; he merely moved her in front of him. His left arm wrapped around her waist and pressed her to his chest. Before she could protest, they were back under the water.

Like lightning, they sped through it. It reminded her of when Tarhuinn took her to his home. He wasn't as fast as the merman, but he was near to it. Due to the quickness, she gripped the male's upper arms to hang on better. Darkness raced by them, and she couldn't see anything around them anymore. The merman probably had a similar capability of vision to that of her husband.

Lack of vision was the least of her worries, though. Her lungs were beginning to demand for air. Despite their present speed, she loosened her grip on his left arm and patted it. Hopefully, he would understand the meaning behind it. Or, maybe, his behavior was all a ruse. It could be a trip to her death, and she would never get to see Tarhuinn again. If only she could hear his voice one last time.

As her hope depleted, the water around them became illuminated to some degree. She could barely view her surroundings, but there was some light. They broke the surface of the water. Around them was a large domed room. Torches were on the walls, and the flames flickered, but she was glad to have air once more. Odette took a deep breath in and exhaled. Her lungs were celebrating, though; the air didn't cure her mind.

She could once again feel the tears running down her cheeks, and she was incredibly vulnerable to the merman in front of her. He could kill her within a heartbeat, yet she couldn't help it. Remembering what she had gone through with Will only made things worse. The two other merfolk surfaced but paid her no mind. If anything, they looked annoyed at her constant crying.

Feeling something rest on top of her head, she peered up at the merman. He didn't wear a smile or have a reassuring gaze. The gesture of his hand was all. "You'll be able to see him before he dies. I know that the council will offer you that much. I'm sorry that you caught the attention of a kelremm. If you hadn't, you wouldn't be in this mess."

If the merman's words were meant to be comforting, they were anything but. She knew very well what she would have and wouldn't have if she hadn't stared out at the ruins and caught Tarhuinn's attention. His words only caused her to dislike him. He was being nice enough to bring her to her husband, and she was grateful for that, but his unexplainable hatred for Tarhuinn was beginning to irk her.

They had never encountered the merfolk before, and they wouldn't have if it hadn't been for probably the authors and mage coming down early. Truthfully, they most likely would've still been teasing each other or maybe even sleeping. What else was frustrating was that she had no concept of time in the water-filled caves.

Her attention looked to her right, however, as four more merfolk were surfacing. The merman lowered his hand and nodded his head to the four. Both of the merfolk that guided her to the space performed the same action. Odette gave no sign of respect since the merfolk hardly deserved it. She wouldn't dip her head towards the ones that were going to possibly send Tarhuinn to his death.

"We didn't expect to find the human so near to the kelremm's location. Why is she here?" asked one of the mermen of the group.

"She wished to see her husband, and I agreed to bring her to him. I believe that it's only fair given that he'll most likely die."

The four glanced over to the merman beside her. "We may come to the conclusion that he'll be spared. It depends on what he tells us," one of the mermaids responded. Her gaze moved to Odette, and she swam close. Odette backed away in the water but not too far, for the merman placed his hand behind her back and kept her nearby. "You've been shedding quite a number of tears, human. That's expected, though. You look like you may crumble and melt away into the water."

Odette was tempted to reply with a rude remark, but her gaze focused on the mermaid's approaching hands. She tried to lean back. Unfortunately, the merman continued to keep her in place. Her fingers glided up gently along her cheeks before her thumbs wiped away the tears there.

"You really would be lost without him; wouldn't you? Such a strong devotion that you have for him. It makes me a little envious of you. I find that I can feel no such emotion. I try to, but I only find myself in a void."

Frankly, Odette didn't wish to listen to what emotions the mermaid did and didn't experience. She desired to push her away. As if someone actually cared about her discomfort, one of the mermen cut in. "Aqua, you can discuss your own emotions later with the girl. We have business with the kelremm that needs tending to."

"Be patient, Cetar. I wish to ask her some questions first. Not only her husband will have words about their reason for being in our territory. Two perspectives are better than one. Or, are you still angered by the fact that the kelremm caught us off guard with that call of his?"

An annoyed grunt left his lips. "Fine, do what you want but make it quick. If we intend to have the kelremm tortured, I'd rather start sooner than later. I think that Piscina and Lacus would agree with me."

"Whether we torture, kill or free him, I have no care whether that's today, tomorrow or a week from now," Piscina spoke. She took her hair out of her braided bun and started to create a new one on her head. "And, frankly, this is about the most excitement that any of us have had for quite some time. You should enjoy it more. Or, are you worried that the kelremm will find a way out before we can decree his fate?"

"You know that's the reason," answered the last council member. "Cetar has always underestimated our abilities. He thinks that only he can control the situation. It's because his father filled his head with too many ideas of how to lead."

"And, here I thought that I could count on you two for once," mumbled Cetar. He rubbed the bridge of his nose, becoming obviously more irritated. "Just hurry up with this business, Aqua. Otherwise, I may cause Lacus to become unconscious for his intolerable comment."

Lacus rolled his eyes and signaled for Aqua to continue. She nodded and drew her hands back from Odette. "Tell me why you two decided to travel this way. Were you not aware of our presence here? Or, did you wish to fulfill your curiosity on whether merfolk exist or not? Perhaps, it's another reason altogether."

“My information may free my husband, correct?” Aqua gave a nod and motioned for the merman to let go of her. Without his support, she did have to put in more effort to keep afloat. That was hardly a major concern for her, though. Wiping away the last of her tears, she collected herself even though she was close to breaking down again.

“The snow pixies had warned us that there were dangerous creatures here. We had intended to avoid coming into your territory, but we were forced in this direction due to unexpected visitors. All of you clearly know of kelremm, and we were about to encounter three that we’d rather avoid until the proper time. Are you familiar with the names of Tergii and Bimaa?”

Immediately, looks of hatred gathered in the room. Even Aqua seemed to have gained some emotion, and her voice dripped with venom. “How do you know of those two? Do you know of the other three: Amtoma, Rocean and Alpontus?”

“Yes,” she answered, pausing, as she finally registered how cold the water was since she was no longer focused on crying. She shivered, and she at last noticed that her teeth were beginning to chatter. Odette rubbed her upper arms, but that barely did anything.

“That’ll be all for now, then. You’ll come with us as we interview your husband. We need to get you out of the water. We have no dry clothes to offer you, but there’ll be torches in the place where your husband is at. Warm yourself by one.” Aqua flicked her right hand to the merman beside her before she went back under with the other three council members.

No time to respond was given to Odette. She was back under the water with the merman again. There was some hope for Tarhuinn and her. The merfolk seemed to detest the five authors.

Tarhuinn and she were going to the authors. Maybe, they could promise to bring back one of the authors to get out of the merfolk’s lair. That author would be submitted to a horrible end, but the authors had made multiple attempts on both of their lives indirectly.

Not only that but also they had threatened everyone in the third complex, and they were a hidden menace to the other two complexes. Those five and their spies had probably committed atrocities that were still a secret. She doubted that they were as bad as Will, but she knew better than to underestimate them.

When they resurfaced, she wiped the water from her eyes. Her breath caught in her throat. Odette had never seen Tarhuinn look so weak. There had been the time when he was running to the cabin, but even then it wasn't as bad as the present. His feet were barely touching the water. He was clearly suffering.

She pushed against the merman so that she could go over to him, but he lifted her out of the water and set her on the piece of stone across from her husband. There were three new merfolk in the room, and one of them moved over to her. He held his spear close to her. Odette was tempted to grab the weapon and turn on the merfolk, but that would most likely end in death for her or some grave wounds. Still, she was happy to see her husband alive.

Hearing the movement, Tarhuinn opened his eyes. Steadily, he lifted his head up. Relief flooded over him upon spotting Odette. If he were in better condition, he would've raced towards her.

His joy was replaced by fury, however. He saw how red and puffy her eyes were, and there was a spear pointed at her. The desire to rip apart that merman grew indefinitely. How dare he threaten his wife.

Pressing his hands against the stone, he tried to get up so that he could reach her. His attempt failed, and his head fell back down. He wished to raise his fists and smash the stone beneath him in vexation. She was right there, yet he couldn't go to her. Tarhuinn had caught sight of her mouthing something to him. *We'll make it out of here.*

Her phrase had been chosen over another since the other seemed to be final. Odette didn't wish to speak it under such circumstances unless things became even direr. She would rather wait until they were gone from the merfolk's lair. Then, only his ears would hear it. The merfolk didn't deserve to listen to those three words.

Swimming up to the edge of the larger pool, Aqua lifted herself out of the water and sat on the edge. She kept her distance from Tarhuinn despite his weakened state. The other council members remained close to her while one of the merfolk with a spear stayed next to the higher authorities.

"Your wife has mentioned the five names that create great loathing among my kind. Now, what do you say on this matter? She mentioned that you two wish to avoid them until the right moment. What did she mean by that?

"Answer carefully, and you may be spared. If we dislike your responses, you'll be killed. Whether you're tortured or not beforehand will depend on the opinions of the rest of the council. Remember to answer truthfully. No lies will be accepted here."

Chapter Forty One: Something Disclosed

A raspy breath escaped his lips while his head still felt like it was fastened to the stone below it. "M-m ... my ..." he tried to speak but even saying that one word was like scratching gravel against his throat. Aqua leaned in a little bit to better hear him, but no other word left his mouth. He required water. His body was far too weak to have any conversation.

"Put his feet entirely in the water already!" he heard Odette cry out. He hated to hear the pain in her voice; he detested how he couldn't rush over to her and wrap his arms around her. "How do you expect him to talk when he's like that?!"

"He'll be able to handle whatever suffering he's experiencing. It's nowhere near what my kind have gone through," Cetar retorted.

"That may be true, Cetar, but his wife does have a point. We'll be here for hours if we keep him up there," Aqua voiced. She signaled for two of the guards to come and lift him off.

"I hope that you know what you're doing, Aqua. Once his feet fully touch the water, he may try to attack us again. This time, we might not be fortunate enough to escape with no wounds," Cetar responded, crossing his arms over his chest and keeping a firm gaze on Tarhuinn.

Before the guards could bring Tarhuinn up or before Aqua could answer, Odette interrupted once more. "Let me bring him into the water. None of you will have to come near him that way. His feet will be in the smaller pool still so that there's a decent amount of distance between all of you. I haven't tried to attack any of you since I've woken up. Please, take that into consideration and let me help him."

The council members shared a glance before they grouped together and conversed on the matter. A spear remained pointed at her, but her attention was mainly focused on the four authorities. She wished to bring her husband to better health and be able to hear his voice again. When the four merfolk broke apart, Aqua halted the two guards. "She can bring him further into the miniature pool. She knows the consequence if she tries to cross us."

Relief flooded her countenance before she pushed herself to her feet. She was a shivering mess, but she could warm herself by one of the torches after Tarhuinn was taken care of. Odette rubbed her upper arms and walked around the pool before she reached him. His head turned to her. Dark blues met brown ones, and his lips steadily upturned into a small smile. The fingers on his right hand twitched as he attempted to lift his hand up to her.

Returning the smile, she clasped his hand with her own. Warmth greeted her touch as she pulled upwards on him. Given their weight difference and the fact that he was practically dead weight, she struggled in the effort, but, eventually, she had him sitting up. Immediately, his body went to fall backwards. Quickly, she rested her other arm behind him and held him up.

His left hand raised itself to rest over their intertwined hands, but, in the process, he slumped forward. The weight of him drove them both into the small pool. Water splashed upwards. All of the guards instantly had their spears pointed at the pair but kept the weapons far enough away that neither could reach out and grab one of them.

Water being wiped from her eyes, she felt herself moved into a sitting position. Thumbs glided over her cheeks gently. She brought her hands up and placed them over his right. Odette leaned into his warm and comforting touch. “I’m so happy that you’re alright. I was ... w-was ...” The words wouldn’t leave past her lips.

Taking her hands in his now, he brought them to his lips. He kissed her fingers caringly. “I’m here before you, Odette. You don’t need to worry about my safety now.” Tarhuinn locked his eyes with hers and moved her closer. After he connected his lips with her forehead, he whispered, “Like you told me, we’ll make it out of here. I’m not going to let them separate or harm us again.”

“Just please answer their questions. I don’t want you to attack unless it’s absolutely necessary,” she whispered as she leaned her head against his chest.

"I understand." A relieved smile overtook her lips while his arms wrapped around her and brought them both to their feet. He set her back on the stone before he took a seat on the edge of it nearest to her. It was also the section furthest from the merfolk. Tarhuinn kept his distance intentionally for both his beloved's safety and to prevent himself from killing one of the nearby guards.

While Odette warmed herself by a close torch, he looked to the merfolk. "As my wife told you, we know of the five authors. We've read of their work, and my wife found something odd in their writing. We wish to ask them about that. In the process of searching for them, we've discovered that they don't desire to be found and that they're willing to kill us to keep themselves hidden. That is why we wish to avoid them until the proper time."

"And, why would you risk your lives to ask them a mere question?" Cetar inquired while he narrowed his eyes in suspicion.

"Their writing differs from the writing of one of our main history texts. The reason for the difference could have a life changing impact on kelremm and their partners. My wife encouraged me to help her seek out why the discrepancy between the texts existed. I decided to agree to her wish."

"You're remaining vague on what this difference is. What are you hiding from us?" Cetar asked, his tone growing impatient.

"This dissimilarity could mean that my wife and I may be able to spend more time together with our future child. My wife was kept from me for twelve years, and I'd like to claim that time back. Even if I only get one year extra with her and our child, all of this trouble will have been worth it."

"I'd rather you two never to have a child, and your kind to go extinct." Cetar looked away from him and to Aqua. "This is a waste of time. We should proceed with torturing him. His wife can watch if she wishes."

Teeth bared, Tarhuinn almost lunged forward at the merman, who was now discussing his opinion in more detail with the others. Odette rested her hands on his shoulders and pulled him back into his sitting position. Seating herself on the stone, she wrapped her arms around his torso. Her head pressed against his back to comfort him. "He's only one of the council members. The other three haven't decided upon anything yet."

"I know, but I never want you to view me that way. I didn't even want you to see me when I was lying on that rock near to death. I couldn't come over to you and comfort you." His hands went up to hers and lied over them. "It reminded me of how I couldn't help you when you were alone with that detestable mage."

"Tarhuinn, that doesn't matter." Heat developed in her cheeks. It wasn't the time or place for it, but she couldn't help it. "I just want to remain by your side. I understand how you felt when I left for the cabin. When I woke up, it was painful not to know where you were or if you were alive. It seemed like a void was slowly consuming me, and I couldn't escape. I don't want to experience that again or for you to either."

Tarhuinn squeezed her hands. "Thank you."

Increasing her hold on him, she replied softly, "You're welcome."

All of the council members turned back to them. Aqua spoke before Cetar could. "I'm sure that you two understand Cetar's position. He's unwilling to change it. The rest of us are still undecided." Both Tarhuinn and Odette looked to them, and Odette moved herself out from behind him to sit beside him. "We have decided to tell both of you where our hatred comes from, though. We owe you no explanation, but you share our dislike of the five authors.

"I can tell that you, kelremm, intend to show them no mercy even if they answer your inquiry. For that, both of you will have a reason."

Tarhuinn and she nodded, but they readied themselves for a fight. They stayed close to one another even though it probably would've been better for her to warm herself up more by the fire. She had him, though, and she preferred his nearness over the fire's warmth.

"We have lived in these mountain pools for as long as any of us can remember. Few had known of our existence, and few had made it back out of our home if they had entered. One of the few that had lived after their encounter with us was a mage. He had insisted on living with our kind for a duration of a month. Our ancestors had allowed him to, but they had made no promise on letting him out alive.

"During that time, he had charmed and fascinated a few mermaids. A few mermen were even impressed with his magic capabilities. When the month expired, he had convinced those five to guide him out of our home in secret. The moment that he was outside of our home, he had caught them off guard and had murdered them. One of Cetar's past relatives had witnessed the event since they were going to view the moon with their lover. Before either could act, the mage had the five merfolk out of the water and had made his escape."

Aqua glanced around the room once. "This had been where the mage had stayed. He had slept on that very stone where you were lying, kelremm." Her fingers ran along the edge of it before they tightened their hold. The stone appeared as though it would crack, but she eased her hand and drew it back to beside her. "When the situation was reported to our ancestors, all of them had hurried back here. Nothing of his had been left behind. They had checked the rooms of the five, and, in one of them, they had found a message, which had been made of the plants that grow at the bottom of these pools.

"This note had belonged to one of the mermaids, and she had explained how she was leaving with the mage to help him with his experiment of creating a new being. She had written that she intended to marry him. Obviously, he had shared no such sentiment. Unfortunately, she had disclosed no more facts on the process of the experiment, but our ancestors had made the connections.

"Those five that had been killed and had been combined with several other species. Our ancestors had learned of such a fact when they had encountered the mage's creations later on. From the day of the mage leaving, they had placed guards out by the entrance to our home. Every day, they had waited for the mage's return so that they could exact proper punishment. The mage had fulfilled that wish two years later.

"Performing their duty, four guards had waited. They had heard footsteps down the main stream and had gone to investigate. The guards had kept themselves hidden, but they had nearly struck out immediately. Before them had been the mage, but he hadn't been alone. With him had been five children. From the reports that had been given, they had looked to be of different ages. It had been clear, though, where they had received some of their characteristics."

Her cerulean eyes had glanced over Tarhuinn. "Similar blue skin, eyes all one color, sharpened teeth, it was as though someone had taken merfolk and had turned them partially human. In actuality, those guards' report hadn't been too far from the truth."

Odette noticed that Tarhuinn had tensed. She was aware of the connection that was already beginning to form, and it wasn't only the fact that his kind was probably part merfolk. "And, these five children hadn't been killed that day?" she questioned, resting a hand on Tarhuinn's upper right arm to comfort him.

"No, they hadn't," answered Lacus. "In fact, those five children had nearly killed the guards. They had the assistance of the mage, but they had utilized a similar yell as your husband had emitted. They had stunned the guards for long enough and had permitted the mage to attack with ease. Those guards had barely escaped that day. Most likely, they would've been killed had the mage decided not to be generous." He rolled his eyes at the end of his statement, clearly thinking that no kindness had existed in the situation at all.

"Then, those five are the five authors?" Odette inquired further.

"Yes," Piscina responded. "It makes you wonder how they have managed to survive for so long. I'd even say that you two have a good chance of extending your lives if you make it out of here," she added as her eyes gleamed with interest. "It's exciting to think of a prolonging life serum. I'd love to see it."

Tarhuinn moved Odette closer to him and wrapped an arm protectively around her waist. Before either of them could remark on her comment, Cetar intervened. "You know well enough Piscina that even if such a serum exists we want nothing to do with it. It had been most likely created by that mage, and we won't drink anything that had belonged to him. We don't even know how it would truly affect our kind."

"I know, Cetar. There's no reason to snap at me. It's merely thrilling to picture something of that nature."

"Regardless," cut in Aqua, "the fact of the matter is that those five authors had been turned into what they are now. We don't know what the procedure of the experiment had been, but we have come to the conclusion that the five authors had been originally human children. That would also explain the reason for them being different ages. We don't know what other species they had been combined with, but we have our theories.

"The voice of a kelremm gives clue to one. It's more powerful than any of ours could ever be. The sirens that live out on the rocks of the sea possess such voices too. The important matter here, though, is that those five authors are the ones who extended out your kind. All kelremm that have come after them are related to one of them."

"How could there be so many of us, then? A kelremm kills themselves once their human partner dies except in rare cases. The authors may have cast that aside, but what about the others?" Tarhuinn spoke, fury starting to become more evident in his eyes.

"That hadn't always been the case. We don't know what the circumstances had been, but, back when your kind had been created, each kelremm had moved onto a new human partner once the old one had died. Guards had reported seeing the same kelremm with a new human every few years or so," Lacus voiced and shrugged. "And, the five authors supposedly haven't been seen with a human partner since the mage had passed away."

"How are you certain of all of this?" asked Tarhuinn, his voice becoming harsher.

Cetar looked as though he would lash out at him, but Aqua held her right arm out in front of him. "It's fine to question our facts. We really only have what has been seen and told, and that information might've changed with age."

She turned her attention from the merman to Tarhuinn. "The answer is that we're not. Again, this is just what has been passed down to us. The mage might still be alive, and the five authors might still be taking human partners. There may have been more than just those five as the original kelremm. Or, there might have been some before them.

"It's uncertain, but the facts about you being part merfolk are right in front of us. Not only are you similar in appearance to us but also you're a skilled swimmer. You move nearly as fast as us when in water. There's also the fact that you possess a powerful jaw for latching onto your prey. You may not eat like that regularly, but you know very well that you could catch a fish with your mouth and end it in a bite."

"You're thinking of torturing and killing my husband, then, because of what this mage had done to those five merfolk a long time ago?" Odette questioned, heat beginning to take over her own voice. She received no immediate response, but a collective yes was soon her answer. "That's ridiculous! He had nothing to do with that mage's choices!"

No longer holding onto Tarhuinn, she got to her feet. She held out her left hand to signal for him not to stop her. Odette kept her gaze locked onto the four council members. "He may have been brought into existence at the cost of those five merfolk, but that isn't his fault. That fault only falls on the mage. He's the one who had killed those five, not my husband!

"Yet you cast the blame on him because he's a kelremm. He reminds you of that mage, and you wish to seek revenge for those murdered merfolk, but you're no better than the mage, then. How dare you attack him, bring him to near death, insult him and plan to torture and/or kill him over such petty reasons. You'll solve no revenge by injuring my husband.

"All of you are just too scared to admit that you're too late to exact revenge if the mage is already dead. Your time is up. Move on and spend your energy on your own kind, rather than expending it on this over expired hate!"

Fists clenched, she caught her breath. Perhaps, that hadn't been the best tactic to leave the merfolk's lair, but she couldn't sit back quietly. They had put them through horrible suffering all over a preposterous reason. She could've had a peaceful night with Tarhuinn, but instead she had been submitted to their torment. "Well, what do you have to say for yourselves?!"

"I'd say that you bring a different perspective to us," Aqua replied calmly. "No matter what you say to us, though, he does remind us of our fallen, and we cannot rid those images from our minds. We won't forgive him, but we can make a deal. Cetar won't agree to it, but Piscina and Lacus may. If they do, we'll ask both of you if you accept. We'll be gone momentarily."

The four merfolk descended into the water and disappeared from sight. All of the guards remained. Odette seated herself on her knees. She clenched the fabric of her pants and bit her lip in frustration. Taking a deep breath and exhaling, she relaxed herself and met his gaze. "I'm sorry that I couldn't do more. You shouldn't be hated for such reasons. It's absurd."

"You don't have to apologize, Odette. You did enough, and I appreciate you defending me." He glided his fingers along her left cheek and brushed some loose strands of hair back behind her ear. Leaning closer to her, he whispered, "Should this deal be a poor one, however, I want you to get as far back from the pools as possible, and I wish for you to close your eyes."

"But, I..."

"I understand that you don't mind how you view me, but recall that nightmare that you had. I might look like that if things go sour for us. Will you be able to come to terms with that image if it becomes a reality?" he asked while his fingers glided away from her light blonde locks.

Remembering his teeth stained with red, she gulped. He had a fair point. Her stomach was already turning at such a possibility occurring before her, and she would be lying if she said that she wasn't fearful of him in that light.

She had to trust him, however. If she closed her eyes, she would be sending the message that she didn't trust him completely. Yes, she could easily picture him going against her when he was in that state, but she needed to push that image aside. It wasn't a reality; it was merely fear trying to control her.

"I understand ..."

She cut him off. "No, I won't close my eyes. If that happens, you'll be protecting me. You won't be harming me. I won't stay in the back and cower in terror." Keeping her voice low so that the guards wouldn't hear, she added, "I'll help you fight against them. If one manages to sneak on you, I'll strike them down. If too many surround you, I'll draw some to me and finish them off. I'll be your daggers." Her hands wrapped around his. "I won't take no for an answer."

Before he could utter a word, she pressed her lips to his. The action caught him off guard, but he returned the gesture nevertheless. Their kiss remained short, but it was enough to allow the other's feelings to get across. Both were saying that they had the other's back.

When the kiss ended, they remained close to each other. Odette's forehead rested against his chest while his arms were encircled around her. She only wished that their intimate moment didn't have to be shared with the guards in the room. It would've been easier to ignore them had they not been shifting in the water occasionally. At least, she didn't have to look at them.

A feminine cough, though, drew her attention towards the larger pool. She drew her head back and peeked around Tarhuinn. The four council members had returned. Cetar seemed less than pleased while the other three wore expressions that weren't easy to read. Aqua swam closer to the edge of the pool. All of the guards kept near to her, and their spears remained pointing at Tarhuinn and her.

"We have come up with a proposal, and all three of us have agreed to it. You two are traveling towards the authors' home. In payment for letting you both continue to head there, you'll bring us back the five authors. They'll most likely try to kill you on sight, so we won't ask you to bring them back alive, but we do want their bodies. They had been made from those five merfolk, and we wish to give our ancestors a proper burial by stripping the authors of the pieces that make them part merfolk."

"I have no issue with that," Tarhuinn answered swiftly. "I was planning on killing them regardless."

"That's if you can kill them," Cetar cut in. "They have at least one mage on their side, and that mage is no apprentice in magic. Guards have reported some of the terrifying things that this mage can perform, and those were merely things to entertain herself on her travels. There's also the more simple issue; you two will be severely outnumbered. Spies are most likely around and in their home as well, and they'll be the ones that you'll encounter first. Making it through them won't be a mere swim in the pond."

"I'm sure that they're both aware of that," Lacus commented, crossing his arms over his chest. "Besides, it's their only option. They either agree to bring us them, dead or alive, or they don't leave our home." He moved his gaze to both of them, and he had to peer up some since they were standing now. "And if you do kill them but don't bring them here, you better be careful of any water. Merfolk will come after you, and, eventually, no water will be safe for you."

"It would be foolish of us not to pay our end of the bargain," Odette answered, though; she had no intention of going back with Will once she gave him the supposed serum of eternal life. Thankfully, the council's deal didn't involve a sadistic, cannibalistic mage.

"It would be, though; I wish that I could see this fight," Piscina remarked as excitement laced her cerulean eyes. "It would certainly make the blood pump in one's body. Just thinking about it is making my heart beat faster. Perhaps, you could also tell us the details of the fight when you return."

Lacus chuckled. "I doubt that they wish to spend a long time here when they return, Piscina. They'll most likely drop off the bodies and leave immediately after."

"Not if we add it to be part of the deal," she argued back, a small grin tugging at her lips.

"That wasn't part of the deal," Aqua mentioned as she kept her gaze on Tarhuinn and Odette. "Since you have accepted, we'll guide you out of our home, and some merfolk will bring your belongings shortly after."

The two of them nodded, and, shortly after, they were back in the water. Tarhuinn kept a firm grip on Odette. One of the guards offered to take her since she couldn't breathe under water and they could swim faster, but he refused as did she. If the deal hadn't been reached, the guards would probably be attempting to kill both of them. Such a thought caused her to grip all the harder on his shirt.

Holding onto him tightly, they went under. Darkness enveloped them both. She didn't focus on her decreasing air. Rather, she paid attention to the fact that they were going to get out of the merfolk's lair alive. Their journey could continue, and they were near to their destination. The authors wouldn't be able to hide their ways in secret for much longer, but Cetar was right. Even if their intent had been to still only ask a question, they would've found themselves in a dangerous situation.

Odette did find it difficult to think, however, when her air supply was nearing its end. She shut her eyes and gripped Tarhuinn's shirt more. Her lungs were beginning to cry for air, but she had seen previously that the waters remained dark. How much longer did they have until they reached the surface again?

No answer being given to her, she nearly wished to bang her fists against Tarhuinn in a panic. She refrained from doing so, but she noted that her consciousness would fade soon. Air didn't greet them shortly. Her grip on him weakened. The last thing that she thought of was how thankful she would be for solid ground. Feeling Odette go limp in his arms, Tarhuinn swam all the quicker.

Warmth greeted her upon waking up. It came from whatever she was laying upon and from the few beams of sunlight that broke through the clouds. Dry fabric was draped over her shoulders and around her form partially, but she was pressed against something firm. Her fingers traced over skin, and her brown eyes were met with medium blue. Blinking a few times to confirm the truthfulness of her vision, she found herself using Tarhuinn as a makeshift bed.

Heat dominated her cheeks. Why didn't he have a shirt on? Noting her exposed arms, she soon realized that she was lacking a shirt also. She only had her underclothes on, and the same applied to him. Her cloak was over the two of them, mostly her though.

Sitting up, she kept the cloak wrapped around her form. She saw that he had his eyes closed, but he was most likely awake. He was probably enjoying her confusion. What had happened after she had lost consciousness? No question left her lips, for she was tugged down.

Laying on him once more, she felt his hands secure themselves around her waist and slip under her undershirt slightly. The heat in her cheeks increased. He beat her words again. "You should keep close. Our clothes, blankets and my cloak are all drying. This is our best way to stay warm for the time being. You were freezing when we left the water."

Doing her best to rid her mind of the image of him undressing her partially, she inquired, "Did the merfolk say anything before they brought us back out here?"

"Only to keep our end of the deal." An annoyed, "tch," left his lips. "I'm happy to be out of there, but part of me wishes to go back. I want to slay a few of them so that they understand that we're not to be trifled with and to pay them back for the harm that they had caused you."

“We have nothing to prove to them. They injured and insulted us. We shouldn’t waste any more time than we have to on them. If anything, it makes me want to complete this journey already. That way, we can deliver the authors to them and be on our way. We can be finished with Will and relax at home.”

Chuckling a little, a smirk tugged at his lips. “I don’t think that’ll be the case on the first night back, Odette.” Heat traveled to her ears. In retaliation, she huffed and slapped his left upper arm playfully. She mumbled something under her breath, which only caused him to become more amused. Odette was about to hit him again, but the smell of rain caught her nose. They were under no cover and were just beginning to get dry.

“We should find some shelter. We don’t need to be poured on.” Hearing his agreement, she sat up with him. His arms stayed around her as he lifted her up and headed towards some of the pines.

Chapter Forty Two: Future Circumstance

Underneath one of the larger pine trees, the snow was cleared away. The bed of twigs and needles was still wet but not to the point where they would be soaked from sitting upon it. Odette stayed there with the cloak wrapped tightly around her form. Her eyes were averted from Tarhuinn, given his current dress state as he went out and retrieved their drying items.

He swiftly returned and placed the items underneath the tree before he took a seat beside her. She wished that she could tolerate the cold like he could. It would make their traveling easier. If she was a kelremm, though, she wouldn't probably have ever married him or have had any of their other interactions. Those facts made her sensitivity to the chilly air more bearable.

Their clothes were still drying, however, and she desperately wished to wrap herself in his cloak. Unfortunately, that was the item that would most likely take the longest to dry off completely. Noting her staring at the article of clothing, Tarhuinn moved her over to him. He spread his legs apart and seated her between them. His arms wrapped around her waist as a light does of heat dusted across her cheeks.

Head lying against his chest, some of his long, ink-black locks fell over her form. Her fingers reached over and twirled around some of the soft strands. They glided over her fingers like the water from a gentle waterfall. She almost got lost in them due to the soothing action, but something that Cetar had mentioned disturbed her peaceful state. "Can we really fight off the five authors, their mage and their spies?"

The smell of rain grew stronger, and the first drops began to descend from the sky. "We'll be able to," Tarhuinn answered, his grip tightening by a little bit. "We fight, or we die. Those are our two options, and I refuse to have you be killed by any of them."

A small smile rested on her lips. "You always refuse to let anyone kill me," she chuckled out softly. She moved her feet closer to her as a few drops of rain hit her skin. "I'm glad, though. That declaration of yours has worked so far. I don't think that I could ask for a better protector."

"And, I the same," he responded, placing a gentle kiss on her right cheek. His lips lingered there. "You've been keeping a watch on me ever since we left our home." Left hand going over to his daggers, he picked up the one that wasn't sheathed. He held it before her and twirled it between his fingers. "You even drew a blade on a mermaid to protect me." The dagger was placed in her left hand. "You've truly earned this."

His hand clasped hers. They both held the blade as he lifted their hands to her chest. "For the rest of our lives, we'll protect the other. When we enter the authors' home, we'll be swift, and we'll come out alive." Hand moving from hers, he wrapped his left arm back around her waist. "I'll show them no mercy. They've tried to take you from me. In return for their gesture, I'll take away their lives from them. Their bodies will be left for the merfolk but not after ..."

Setting the blade aside, she turned around in his hold. She sat on her knees. Her hands rested on the sides of his face. Odette shook her head. "Don't lose yourself, Tarhuinn. Not right now, save that hate for when we encounter them. Don't let it control you but guide it so that our trip to their home is truly quick." A few drops of rain managed to fall upon them. "If we're lucky, we'll be able to sneak through their home and take them by surprise one by one."

"Odette, you know that such a possibility will be unlikely." Her hands fell from his face and rested on his chest. "We'll have to fight them. They're skilled at secrecy and acquiring information. We'll probably only go unnoticed for a short while.

"Before even going into their home, we should stay in that general area for awhile and see if we can learn any valuable information. We know that two of the authors and the mage have probably left. They won't be back for some time. That'll make things easier, but there may always be another mage or mages on their side. If there are any more, we should take them out first."

"Are we going to fight Tergii, Bimaa and the one mage on the way back, then?"

"Yes, but they're going up against that wretched mage. He'll probably keep them occupied for awhile as will the pixies. He might even successfully kill the three of them for us. Whether he defeats them or not, we'll have to fight someone on the way back unless they all kill each other in their encounter."

"If we have to fight any of them, I hope that it's Tergii or Bimaa. I'll even take both of them over either of the mages, especially over Will." Just recalling the time that she had spent with him, her hands pressed more into Tarhuinn's chest.

"You shouldn't even utter his name, Odette. He doesn't deserve to have his name said by you." Leaning his forehead against hers, his lips hovered over hers. His gaze stayed locked with hers, however. "I wish for you to forget the nightmare that was him. That time in your life is past."

Her eyes averted away from his stare. "That's hard to do when he left those terrible memories in my mind. I want only to remember that I beat the obstacle that was him, but, sadly, that includes everything that led up to that event."

"It doesn't have to. You only have to recall that you conquered a terrible mage. Everything else about him can fade away." His lips ghosted over hers, and her breath hitched in her throat. Slowly, he started to lean back. "You can forget his hair, eyes, nose and mouth. His whole appearance can evaporate from your mind." The tips of his right fingers slid under her chin. "Abandon the thoughts of his words. They were deceptions utilized to lure you in and to frighten you."

Another few raindrops fell upon them. One ran down her lips. His thumb wiped it away. "That may not be simple, but I can help. I can fill your head with memories that you'll cherish." Lingering on her lips, his thumb slid down them steadily. A shiver traveled up her spine, and her eyes closed for a moment. When she opened them again, his face was nearer. "Will you let me take one away and replace it with a better one?"

Odette laughed, and it was like a delicate snowflake coming into contact with the snowy earth below. She moved his hand from her head before she kissed his thumb lightly. Meeting his gaze once more, she smiled. "Silly, you're already creating a better one." Moving closer to him, she chuckled. "You should pay more attention. Besides, you missed a drop."

Not permitting him to say a word, she leaned forward and pressed her lips to a raindrop falling down his left cheek. Her lips pulled back, and she caught his stare once more. "And, you forgot something else. Perhaps, I might wish to form that better memory with you."

"I think that I can grant that request, but," he turned her head to face him completely, "I overlooked another raindrop." That time, he didn't let her speak. His lips met hers as his hands glided under her chin. Her hands traveled up from his chest to his shoulders to better support herself. Their lips harmonized in movement like the raindrops around them.

Some pixies on patrol in the area were flying by, but they halted their return to their home. They sped behind a nearby tree and peeked around the trunk at the two. A quiet chuckle left one of them, for they hadn't seen such a scene since the wedding of their queen and king. The other pixie merely smiled, glad to view something of such a nature. It was a pleasant change from the scenes back at their home. Witnessing the actions of the mage upon that female kelremm had been enough to leave anyone more than unsettled.

Both of the pixies soon left, however. They decided to leave the couple in peace. Having gone unnoticed by the two, Tarhuinn and Odette finally parted their lips from the others. Catching her breath, Odette rested her head against his chest. There was some heat present in her cheeks, but she didn't mind it with the cold around them. She could still feel his lips against hers. Her eyes closed while her right hand kept her cloak wrapped around her.

She was quite happy that they didn't have merfolk watching them. They could enjoy the other's presence without interruption or harsh stares. Had she known about the pixies, the moment would've ended already. Not having that knowledge, though, she kept enjoying it. To her, it was only the two of them. It was indeed becoming a beloved memory.

There was something that she had forgotten, though. Her lips upturned, and she glanced back up at him. Recalling the phrase that she had mouthed to him, her smile grew. They had managed to find a way out of that situation, and they had their lives still, but there was something missing. "Back in the merfolk's lair, I never had told you something. I hadn't wanted them to hear; they hadn't been warranted to hear."

"And, what would this be?" he asked, a small smirk forming on his lips.

Most likely, he already knew what would leave her lips, but she liked to think that it remained a mystery to him. Sitting up straight and bearing a large smile, she disclosed, "It's simple. I love you." She kissed him once more and pulled away shortly after.

Chuckling, he replied, "That I already knew." He returned her kiss and moved her back closer to him.

Chapter Forty Three: Inspecting

A couple of days had faded away since they had left that spot under the pine tree. Tarhuinn and Odette had traveled up the right stream, but they had walked slower on the second than the first day. The uphill climb had only grown steeper, and it had reminded her of the walkway back on their way to the third complex. At least, there hadn't been a ledge for them to fall off of.

When they reached the end of the path, a large lake was before them just as the pixie queen had mentioned. Around the edge, there was a narrow path that led around the entirety of it. Up above the path, rocks jutted out of the mountain, and small streams of water trickled downwards. Some of the rocks could easily cut into one's skin if they weren't careful, but if they climbed up a little, they could use them to hide behind. That would allow them to listen in on any individuals passing to and from the authors' home.

The problem would be getting from behind their current cover of pines to some of the rocks. It wouldn't be a surprise if some of the authors' spies were waiting for intruders to step out into the open. Tarhuinn, though, was already analyzing the area for any sign of someone else. He did have his daggers, and she had seen him throw them before. There was the possibility that he would be able to kill any hostile kelremm without them even seeing the two of them.

"Do you spot anyone?" she whispered, her eyes still on the lake.

"No, I haven't noted any movement, but I don't think that we should head out there yet. We may want to remain here for the time being and wait for someone to come out of hiding or switch watches."

"Won't someone find us, then? You have to stay in the stream, and we're only covered right now because of the pine branches in front of us. We need to find a better place to hide."

"I agree, Odette, but I can't think of any. Walking out there isn't an option. If there are spies, we'll be attacked within moments, and everyone inside of the authors' home will be alerted."

"I understand that," she responded quietly, scanning over their surroundings. To both her right and left, she noticed that there were the mountain walls. There weren't too many pine branches that she would have to push out of the way to get to either, which meant that her movement wouldn't create too much noise.

Hugging her cloak tighter around her, she pointed to her left. "Let me head over to the wall there. I'll try to climb it. If I can, I'll look out for spies and see if there is water up there. If there is, you should be able to make it in time and meet me up there."

Hesitation was clear on his countenance, but she could tell that he was near to complying. Crossing his arms over his chest, his gaze hardened. "You have the dagger that I gave you. I expect you to utilize it the moment that you see another kelremm. I don't care if they try to persuade you that they're not going to hurt you. I want you to give them no opportunity to talk. Strike and move along. Do you understand?"

"Yes," she simply answered. "I'll be careful, and you'll see me again soon enough."

He nodded, and she was off. Due to the thicker snow, it took longer to reach the wall, but she made it nonetheless. She hadn't glanced back once; she told herself to hurry so that Tarhuinn could be behind better cover. It was also important that they weren't separated for long. They had no idea how many spies there were, and they could be trapped swiftly if they weren't careful.

Peering upwards, she noted that there were some rocks that would allow her to ascend the wall. She would need to be careful and not grab hold of one of the sharper ones. It didn't help that there was ice. The likelihood of one of her hands or feet slipping was quite too high for her liking, but she had to press on.

Extending out her right hand first, she gripped one of the rocks before she grabbed another with her left hand. She climbed, but she did so slowly. Her ascent was realistically at the pace of a snail. At times, one of her feet slipped, and she nearly fell into the snow below, but she hung onto the rocks like her life depended on it. Odette wasn't too high up from the ground, but she didn't wish to start over. Time wasn't on their side.

Hands beginning to become numb, she tried to increase her pace. The tip of her nose was growing too cold also. Beforehand, she had been able to cover it with her cloak somewhat. Now, it felt like it might freeze completely. How she wished to summon a fire to her hands. If she could've been born a mage, things would've been simpler, but she wouldn't have been on their journey, then.

She grasped another rock and pulled herself up. Peering over the rock in front of her, she noticed a small space where she could lie down. It was high enough that it would be a good lookout spot. Odette climbed a bit higher before she rested her feet on the flat area.

On her stomach, she stared through the gap between the two rocks in front of her. She caught sight of no kelremm, but she was happy that there was a small stream behind her. It was large enough that Tarhuinn could keep his feet there and remain in fighting condition. When she saw no other individual, she carefully looked back to him.

His head was turned towards the lake, but he glanced her way a few moments later. She waved her left hand but made sure that it wasn't too high in the air. He seemed to understand the message since he nodded his head and faced her way completely. The snow would slow him down, but he could climb up the section where the stream trickled down. That amount of water might not prevent him from being weakened, but he wouldn't die.

That fact didn't stop her breath from being caught in her throat, though. Her body tensed when he started racing towards her location. It wasn't his normal quick run, but it was still frightening to watch. A charging kelremm in a fight was something that she wasn't looking forward to, but she knew that it would happen at some point. How she would be able to match a skilled spy's speed was beyond her. She only knew that she would have to, or she would be kidnapped, killed or both.

By the time that he stood before the wall, he was almost out of breath. He appeared as though he might collapse into the snow, but he grabbed the rocks and let the water from the stream run over him. Some of it touched his feet, and a little bit of relief painted his face. Still, he made the climb steadily. Given his present condition, it didn't shock her that he was slower than her.

Once he stood on the top, he laid himself down and kept his feet in the water. His eyes closed for a bit while he caught his breath. Odette found herself breathing normally again. She placed her left hand on his right upper arm in comfort. "We should be fine up here."

"Yes, and if someone tries to attack us, we'll have plenty of time to strike before they reach us. It looks like the only way to get up here is to take the route that we took. If we stay here for the night, we should learn enough information to find the entrance to their home. If we don't, we'll unfortunately have to choose the riskier option and explore all of that terrain until we discover the way inside."

Her hand moved back in front of her. She rested her chin on her forearms. "Let's hope that doesn't happen. I don't desire to be worn out from exploring and possible fights before we reach at least one of the authors." Closing her eyes, she let out a sigh. "But, we have tonight to rest at the very least. Would you like me to take first watch?"

Opening his eyes, he voiced, "Yes, I'll take second, though; my eyesight is better at night and in the early morning. Perhaps, I should stay up the whole time."

Shaking her head, she opened her eyes back up. “No, I’ll be able to handle a watch. You need your sleep. Even if I can’t see as well, I can still hear, but can we share your cloak? These rocks are freezing, and I can barely feel my hands and nose.”

“Of course,” he chuckled out softly. He untied the cloak, but he didn’t motion for her to come closer. The small, flat space already had them right next to the other. Tarhuinn draped it over them after he removed his pack, and he proceeded to take out the blankets afterwards. Both of them adjusted their positions until they managed to lay one of the blankets under them. As for the second blanket, they placed it in front of them so that it could be utilized as a makeshift pillow.

Beginning to become warmer, a smile fell upon Odette’s lips. She could fall asleep right then and there. Tarhuinn draped his right arm over her back and hugged her closer, which didn’t aid her, but she forced her eyes to stay open. To help keep herself up, she removed her pack and retrieved some dried pears. Odette nibbled on one and offered another to Tarhuinn. He took it gratefully, and they both continued their watch.

Chapter Forty Four: A Spy's Spy

Vision poor, Odette relied on her ears for the first watch. The sky was thick with clouds, and she could barely see past the two rocks in front of her. Beyond the gap between the two rocks, it was pitch black to her. There was no rainfall, which she was grateful for, but there was a slight breeze. She could hear it travel between the pine branches. Its soft sound didn't hide the movement on the forest floor, however.

She noted that it wasn't footsteps, and she was quite certain that it belonged to a haasna. A bird flapped its wings occasionally, and she figured, at another point in time, that some birds had flown overhead. Besides those noises, there was the sound of Tarhuinn's steady breathing. He was fast asleep, and she had to remove his arm from around her. If she hadn't, she would've been pulled to his chest, and her vision would really be useless at that point. Were they not in a dangerous situation, she would've happily accepted his embrace.

Odette did glance over to him, though. There were still no signs of any movement down by the lake or around it, so she figured that she could admire him. She couldn't look over all of the details of his face, but she could gently glide her fingers over them. It was a soothing action, and it was even more so when she pushed back some of his long strands of hair.

Their water-like flow eased her mind. She remained worried about someone spotting them, but her nerves weren't screaming at her to run back and return to the first complex. Her fingers halted, however, when her ears picked up something. It sounded like small stones hitting the stone path around the lake, and she heard splashes of water.

Her hand drew back, and she grew still. She heard a female voice state, "Thanks for relieving me."

"Did you find anything on your watch? Was anyone foolish enough to come up here?"

"No. I honestly don't even know why our masters are so worried about that male kelremm and his wife. They'll most likely be killed before they even make it to the split streams, and the only reason that they managed to get past the pixies was because of that mage."

"From the sounds of it, though, that mage is incredibly deadly. And, for that reason, Alpontus is wondering how the pixies acquired him. Recently, he developed a theory that the mage was brought to the pixies by that male kelremm and his wife. He's certain that the pixies wouldn't have been able to convince him to help otherwise. He says that those two must've done something."

"Well, based on the account of the mage's actions, why would he let that kelremm and his wife go? It's more likely that he would've killed the kelremm and taken the wife for his own amusement."

"That's why it's so troubling. Master Alpontus is considering that he may have underestimated those two. And, he's given new orders on what to do with them. We're not to kill them anymore. If we find them, we're to bring them back alive. He wishes to learn whether they really had a hand in the mage's arrival."

"Did he tell you what he intends to do to them if they had acquired the mage for the pixies?"

"No. I received these new orders and this information through word of mouth. Apparently, though, the spy that had reported the pixies' betrayal fainted when he was asked that very same question. It would seem, however, that Master Alpontus has planned a punishment equal to that of what he intends to give the mage. Of course, they'll be quickly disposed of if their answer is that they hadn't participated in the act."

"Well, we'll catch them soon enough." Odette heard a yawn before a chuckle escaped the other speaker, who she assumed to be female based on their voice. "I'm looking forward to that moment. I want to see these two foolish individuals. These two were married right before leaving the first complex, though, right?"

"Yes, that's the information that the spies in the area informed our masters of."

"I wonder if they were daft enough to create a child before setting out."

"If that's the case, our masters might keep the human around until the child is two. They like maintaining the general kelremm population where it's at. The human will just have to undergo extensive training to do everything that our masters tell her to do so that the child will go back to the first complex without ever asking any questions."

"Master Rocean will probably try to see to her care, then."

"You shouldn't say such things. You know how jealous Master Amtoma becomes, and she still hasn't recovered from his last human partner, which was supposedly over several generations ago."

"So what? It's clear that Master Rocean is still interested in taking another human partner. I've seen how his eyes have stayed fixed on some of our fellow spies' partners. No matter how committed he says that he is to Master Amtoma, he'll always want some human girl fawning over him since Master Amtoma doesn't give him the compliments that he desires. Regardless, you're just worried that some other spy will report on us talking about our masters in such a way.

"Lighten up, will you? I'll make sure that no one says a word about this, and you better do the same. Otherwise, you might lose your stellar reputation with Master Amtoma. I know that you desire to bed her. Wouldn't want to ruin that, now would you?"

While the female spy continued her teasing of the male spy, she quietly shook Tarhuinn awake. A moan of discomfort left his lips. Instantly, she placed her right hand over his mouth. The two spies continued their conversation, much to her relief, but that had been close. The sound hadn't been exactly quiet.

His eyelids blinked open, and she drew her hand back steadily. She placed her index finger over her lips to indicate for him to keep quiet. He nodded in reply, and his attention went towards the two spies. Most likely, he could probably see every detail of them or most of them at least.

They were still discussing who the other wished to have relations with. Despite the awkwardness of the conversation, they were giving the two of them vital information. Already, they had learned some of the layout of the authors' home as well as the personalities of some of them.

Apparently, they were so confident in their abilities that they didn't care that anyone in the nearby vicinity could hear them. Were they the only spies in the area around the lake? It seemed like it, but she was surprised that they didn't even consider that trespassers could be listening to them. Odette hoped that those two weren't some of the tougher spies and that they just weren't that bright when it came to the task of performing their job.

The two stopped talking, and they could hear the spies say their goodbyes to each other. Odette glanced over to Tarhuinn, but his gaze remained fixed forwards. He was most likely waiting for the one spy to enter the home.

Hearing a rock scraping against another, she peered out towards the lake once more. It was frustrating that she couldn't see what was happening, but she was pleased at the same time. The entrance to the home was probably being revealed, and it didn't involve diving into the lake. The noise halted for a few moments before it returned and stopped again.

"Could you see how she entered?" Odette questioned in a hushed voice.

"Yes, the way in is at the opposite side of the lake from us. She pushed a decently sized rock aside and crawled through a space. She put the rock back into position afterwards, but I could see a pool of water just beyond the rock. We might not have to swim, though, if the ceiling beyond the rock is higher."

"Let's hope that's the case. I'm already at a disadvantage against a kelremm. If I'm shivering, I'll only be more so," she muttered, cuddling into the blankets more. "And, the author, Alpontus, sounds like he has something dreadful in store for us. He knows about the mage back with the pixies, and he's quite certain that it was us who had brought the mage there."

"Then, they were talking before you woke me up."

"Yes, and I think that we should try and take out Alpontus first. It sounds like he's the one who guides the actions of the other four, or they at least look to him for making the final calls. If he's gone, chaos may ensue, and we can use that disorder to our advantage."

Chapter Forty Five: Strike and Fly

Even though she wished to keep some of the details secret from Tarhuinn so that he wouldn't worry, Odette ended up disclosing them to him. If it wasn't a necessity that they remain quiet, he probably would've shouted in anger and took off to kill both of the spy kelremm. Instead, he took the approach of calling her by that convenient nickname that he had for her. The result was her falling asleep shortly after. She cuddled into him to be warmer while she maintained her tight hold on the blankets and cloaks.

Awaking later on, she draped the cloak over her head. The morning sun shone through a gap in the clouds, and its brightness wasn't welcomed by her eyes. Her discomfort, however, was soon replaced by panic and worry. She didn't feel Tarhuinn next to her. Despite her increased heartbeat, she reminded herself not to shoot up from her spot and call out for him.

She forced herself to raise herself slowly. Her head didn't go past the rocks, and she remained hidden. Alarm dissipated in the process. He had simply moved away from her and was crouching towards the back of the flat space.

Water from the small stream ran down the back of him, but he didn't seem to notice in the slightest. He didn't even greet her with a good morning. His attention was trained directly ahead. Most likely, he was observing the hidden spy, so she didn't disturb him. She followed his gaze and lowered herself once more.

Out ahead, she spotted a head of ink-black hair. Short and curly locks rested atop the male's head, and she could see the right side of his face. His features were somewhat childlike, but when he turned his head to the right some more, his light blue eyes were anything but that. He stared out towards the stream that trailed off from the lake, but she moved her head even lower.

It might've been out of terror. Those eyes of his spoke that he would complete his mission even if it meant going to extreme measures. To her, his eyes looked more like those of a trained assassin, yet there was a tinge of madness to them. She considered that the trait might be there because of his supposed devotion to the author Amtoma. Whatever the case, he didn't fit the voice of the male that she had heard last night.

Whispering, she asked, "Was there another swap of positions after I had fallen asleep?"

"No. That's the same male from last night. After observing him through the night and morning, I can tell that he's very skilled with the blade in his left hand, but he doesn't know how to hide like the female kelremm that hid before him. I'll need to take him out without a close-range encounter. I'll only have one shot to throw one of my daggers and hit him. If it doesn't kill him, I have a feeling that he'll call out for others and/or charge towards us."

Her hands clutched at the blankets a little more. "I believe that you can hit him. You struck those gnashers with only one hit to each of them."

"Yes, but I'm not fond of the present angle. I could easily miss and hit a rock instead. And, I've tried to aim from other angles, but they were no better. In fact, some were much worse." His eyes narrowed a bit as if he was testing a scenario out in his head. He shifted his dark blue orbs over to her for a moment.

"If I miss, hold your dagger tightly and stay low to the ground. You'll only attack if he makes it to the wall and starts climbing up here. If more kelremm reveal themselves and some have bows and arrows, press yourself up against the rock and hold your pack over your head. I'll try to hit any away, but if they come in a great quantity, I can only do so much unfortunately."

"I understand, but you'll need to take cover too. I won't let you act like a target for practice."

"Don't worry, I won't let a few arrows kill me, but that scenario is one of the worst case ones," he responded, shifting the dagger a bit in his hand. His focus returned entirely to the spy. She didn't say another word and continued to believe in him. He would hit the target, and they would continue towards the authors.

He raised his hand, and her gaze didn't leave him. Her breath caught in her throat when the blade took flight. It raced past her and through the gap. The dagger charged towards its target, and the spy looked the other way. He halted his movement midway before he swiftly turned towards the flying blade. Shock overtook his eyes while his left hand lifted itself.

"Don't block, don't block," she found herself muttering. If her fingernails were sharper, they would've torn through the blankets. She bit her bottom lip in anticipation. The spy's blade just missed Tarhuinn's.

Falling backwards, the spy impacted the stone floor behind him. The blade rested in the spy's head. Her attention didn't stay on the spy, though. Instead, her eyes darted over the rest of the area. If there were any other spies, they most likely would've seen what had just occurred. Her heart pounded loudly in her chest, but she spotted no movement.

"Let's move Odette. We have no time to stall," Tarhuinn announced, his voice still hushed.

After a quick nod of the head, she was climbing down the wall with him. She had to be careful on her descent, but she didn't slow down too much. They couldn't stay in one spot for too long even if there was no other spy in the area. Another one would show up eventually, and they had to run to the other side of the lake.

Once at the bottom, she sheathed her dagger in her right boot and took off with Tarhuinn. He was dashing out ahead. She couldn't keep up with him, but she didn't yell for him to stop. His need for water was more important, and they were under no attack at the moment, so for them to be apart for a little bit would be alright.

Running at her fastest, she maintained her balance despite the layers of snow trying to send her downwards. There was no option to decrease her pace. She needed to keep going. Up ahead, Tarhuinn halted and rested his feet in one of the streams until his energy regained itself. About to catch up to him, she watched him take off again.

By that point, her legs begged for her to stop while her mind finally registered some of the scrapes upon her skin from the pine branches. None of them were serious, but a few had broken her skin. The thin trails of red didn't bother her, though. Her shirt would soak them up. All that mattered was reaching the entrance before they were spotted.

Jumping over a small stream, she landed back on her feet. She propelled herself forward, but she could only push her body so much. Her pace began to slow, yet Tarhuinn kept bolting forward. He would stop in a small stream every now and then, but she couldn't match his speed. Her heart seemed to stop for a moment. If she were to lose him, she imagined it feeling like the present image before her; his back turned towards her while he faded out of her sight.

The urge to call out to him was rising. If she weren't becoming out of breath, she probably would've cried out his name. Her lips parted, but nothing exited them except labored breaths. Another foot forward and another kept her going. She was getting closer to the entrance, and he was even nearer. Soon, they would reach their destination.

No matter how much the odds were stacked against them, she couldn't imagine losing him. She couldn't think about it. If she worried too much, she might miss the strike of a blade towards him or herself. He depended on her to watch his back, and she counted on the same. When they were in the authors' home, she wouldn't see his back; she would be beside him or their backs would be together as they defended the other.

Like she had told Tarhuinn to guide his fury, she had to control her fear. Her opponents in there would feel her terror. If she didn't make the first move, they would, and she had no intention of experiencing what Alpontus had in store for them. Both of them had dealt with enough.

Relief rushed through her, and her legs stopped their run. She rested her hands on her knees, catching her breath. Tarhuinn stood in front of her, and he was already moving the rock out of the way. Its movement was loud and would most likely draw attention. Currently, she had a chance to regain her energy, but she would have to rush forward soon after they entered.

Stone pushed aside, Tarhuinn motioned her to go on in. She gave no protest. Hurrying, she crawled through the space. Behind her, she heard the stone shift again. Its movement ended as Tarhuin caught up to her. When he was beside her, she instantly felt better.

Rising, the ceiling gave them more room, and they were able to stand up. Her pants and cloak were partially soaked. She could feel the cold embrace her, but she saw a land path beside the water trail. There was water in her boots, but she would deal with that later. At least, there was no more to enter them. They had a straight path before them, so they couldn't stop. Until they found another decent hiding place, they would need to keep moving.

After awhile, the path split into four ways. They had been running for quite some time, but they had encountered no one. Moving the rock had caused no alarm it seemed. Perhaps, the authors were too confident on their security, and they didn't bother with checking on who entered. Whatever the case, it was to their advantage. Tarhuinn and she only needed to decide on which way to head.

They heard splashes of water down the far left and center right paths, so they avoided those, but they had learned from the spies that the authors were at the center of the home. All of them were in one large room while five doors branched off to each of their own private rooms. Apparently, they rarely left the area, with the exception of Tergii and Bimaa. If they were lucky, all of the paths would eventually lead to the center.

With neither the far right nor center left looking better than the other, they picked randomly the center left. A few ceiling windows illuminated the path with morning light and permitted them to note that the path dropped off up ahead. She hoped that they hadn't chosen a dead end since splashes of water sounded back where they had left. Luckily, those splashes weren't coming their way.

They proceeded carefully, however, since they didn't desire to alert anyone. When they reached the drop, they both crouched down and stayed near to the stone walls. No window was above them, but the last one cast shadows over them. Remaining within them, they peered out ahead.

Water cascaded off of the drop and into a large pool below. A large window permitted light to shine down on the pool, illuminating several figures there. All of the ones swimming were kelremm. They were most likely spies since none of them fit the descriptions of the authors that the spies from last night had disclosed. Casual conversation existed between them, but Odette noted something odd, and it wasn't just the fact that kelremm were swimming together when such a thing apparently never happened in the three complexes.

Off to the side, there were two humans: a male and a female. They were hiding behind some rocks and watching the five kelremm. Presently, they seemed to be whispering to each other. The only explanation for the humans being in the authors' home was that they were partners to two of the kelremm in the group. Most likely, they probably weren't supposed to leave the rooms of their partners.

"Should we do anything right now?" Odette asked in a whisper.

"No, we'll watch for a little longer. We'll see what those humans down there have planned. They might create a distraction for us, and we can sneak around the five spies."

"How? The only way is straight down."

"It isn't. There's a thin path along the wall to my left. No water runs down it, but I think that I can make it down to the waterfall behind those rocks over there." He pointed with his right index finger to the path and then to the waterfall. "It'll be a risk, but it's better than fighting through those five and possibly the two humans."

"I don't like it. You can't run down that path. It's too narrow. You'll fall off if you try, and if you walk, you won't make it in time, but I agree that taking them head on would be a bad idea. We should save as much energy as we can for the authors."

"Yes, I have a greater urge to kill them than any of the spies here, though; I would love to kill the kelremm down there too, but that might put you in unnecessary danger, which I'd rather avoid. That leaves us with the thin trail."

A visible frown made itself known on her lips. It just wasn't possible for him to make that distance at the slow pace that the path required. Her eyes peered down to her boots. His feet were larger than hers, but he could fit part of his feet into her boots.

Sitting down on the dry ground, she untied the laces and worked on taking them off. They were soaked with water anyway. Her feet were shivering, and she didn't need water like Tarhuinn. The boots would deliver him better use than her.

Puzzled, Tarhuinn focused some of his attention on her. The rest remained on the seven individuals below them. He finally understood once he saw her dip the shoes into the water. When she removed them, the bottoms were filled with water. She held them out to him. "These should help you somewhat. You may be walking awkwardly, but you won't grow weak. I can continue on barefoot. My feet need to dry off anyway."

"Thank you, Odette. I'll make sure to replace them when we get back home."

"You better. I prefer warm boots to cold stone," she remarked, though; she had a playful smile on her lips. In truth, she did wish for new boots, but she would be happy enough if they made it home.

Lightly laughing, Tarhuinn set the shoes aside for the time being. Their lighthearted moment quickly ended, however, as they both gave their full attention to the kelremm and humans down below. The kelremm were still joking around, but four of the five soon swam deep below the water's surface. Dark green grass grew at the base and hid their forms from sight.

Standing up on one of the rocks by the pool, the one remaining kelremm stretched before she combed her fingers through her messy, short hair. The wavy locks covered her dark blue eyes partially, and a yawn escaped her lips.

"That's the female spy from last night," Tarhuinn commented before his gaze shifted to the pile of weapons by the pool. "We should avoid her. Like the spy that I killed outside of this place, she's skilled at close range, and I didn't see a weapon on her last night."

"Couldn't it have been hidden?"

"Yes, but I have a feeling that she doesn't need one. Even now, look at that pile of weapons. There are two swords, a spear and several small daggers. They most likely belong to the other four. She hasn't even glanced at them once, but the other four have. And if you examine the rock that she's on, you'll notice pieces of rock at the base of it. They fell from the areas where her hands had been at."

"If we do have to fight her, we'll avoid her hands, then."

"Exactly. If her objective were to kill us, she would most likely go for our necks first. Since she's been ordered to capture us, though, she may aim for our legs and/or arms and break them if we don't allow her to knock us unconscious or if we don't come willingly."

"Well, we intend to do neither of those, but you've already found a way around her. We'll need to create a distraction, though, if the two humans remain behind those rocks."

"I don't think that we need to concern ourselves with that scenario."

She was about to ask why, but he merely pointed over to the pair. Both were huddled closer together, and their whispering had grown a little louder. It didn't help that the woman started to cry while the male slammed his right fist against the rock in front of them. Those sounds combined drew the female kelremm's attention. A smirk formed on her lips before she placed her hands behind her head, chuckled and took a few steps forward. "Why don't you two come out already? I'd love to hear how you got out of your rooms."

Each of the humans froze, but the girl's sobs continued. She remained sitting behind the rock while the man stood to his feet and revealed himself. "You don't need to know that information. What's more important is that our partners are down there," he stressed and pointed to the pool, "probably committing adulterous behavior."

Another chuckle left the kelremm's lips. "Oh, do you have proof? It's not like you're down there with them. You should go back to your room and take that human girl with you. Besides, both of you promised your partners that you would never leave their rooms, yet here you are. You're quite the liars. I wouldn't blame them if they sought out other company." She shook her head a few times. "Really, you're only creating more trouble for yourselves."

Clenching his fists more, the male took a step forward, and his eyes for a moment looked to the weapons' pile. An amused grin crossed the kelremm's lips. "Oh, do you intend to fight me? If so, I'd suggest that you really think about that." To taunt him further, she tapped her right index finger against the side of her head.

Growling, he went for one of the swords. By then, Tarhuinn had the boots on and was heading towards the path. He signaled for Odette to quickly follow. They had their distraction, but it probably wouldn't last too long. Like before, time wasn't on their side.

Their backs were pressed to the wall as they made their way slowly across. The boots made it even more difficult for Tarhuinn, but their benefit was more than their cost. She only wished that they could go faster since they were quite vulnerable to the spy below. If she were to turn around or if the human were to give away their position, they would have a hard time dodging any attacks. It didn't help that they were high above solid ground. Were they to jump, they would be killed.

Thankfully, they hadn't been spotted yet. The spy was merely dodging the human's attacks while he swung one of the swords at her. His strikes were clumsy, and he clearly was no skilled swordsman. He could be killed probably within moments or less if the spy chose to actually take him seriously.

Meanwhile, the woman remained sitting. Odette couldn't see her form well from her current position, but she knew that the woman hadn't moved. Her sobs could still be heard, and, in all honesty, she felt bad for the woman. Who knew what she had given up to be a partner with a kelremm. Maybe, she had been forced to be the kelremm's partner, but she had grown to like him.

It wasn't a surprise that the man had taken up a sword. He was probably in just as much emotional pain as the woman, and the female kelremm was only aggravating that hurt. In some respects, she wished to call out to the kelremm and draw her attention away from the male. That slight distraction might allow the human male enough time to strike her down, but it was far too risky. If that didn't permit enough time and the kelremm dodged, she would most likely deal with the man swiftly before coming after Tarhuinn and her.

"You're a really poor fighter. You should put down that sword before you kill yourself," the kelremm chuckled out, spinning on her right heel. She stood behind the man and crossed her arms over her chest. "No wonder Galvi selected you. She has always loved weak men."

The man turned around and swung the sword at her. She simply stepped back as another laugh left her lips. “How pathetic. Are you sure that you’re aiming?” A growl left his mouth, and he charged once more at her. Stepping to her left, he missed her again, which caused him to lose his footing. He fell forward and impacted the stone.

Groaning, he went to pick himself back up. The kelremm, however, stepped on his right hand before she removed the sword from his grip. She twirled it in her right hand as she took a couple steps back from him. “I really don’t see the point in these. You would’ve been better off using your hands,” she stated before she pointed the tip of the sword to his neck. “If you had, you wouldn’t have a sword near your neck.”

He dragged his fingers across the rock, frustrated. The man looked to his right and up at her. “Maybe, but that doesn’t matter. I knew that I couldn’t beat you.” Moving his neck back some, he managed to sit up. She kept the blade at his neck while amusement painted her countenance. It looked as though she would burst out laughing.

“Is that so? You really aren’t that bright, then,” she responded, resting her left land on her hip. “I’ll really need to have a talk with Galvi on her choice of human partners. She’s only damaging herself with men like you.”

“Yes, she is,” he agreed, but a smirk started to form on his lips, “though, not in the way that you think.” The kelremm raised one of her eyebrows, and she stood up straighter. During her insults, she hadn’t noticed that the crying in the background had ceased. “Today, she’ll lose one of her friends, and I’ll be a part of the reason why.”

“Oh? You think that you can frighten me since that weak woman moved her location?” she questioned, a smirk on her own lips. “Well, guess again. I can’t be scared so easily. I’ll be able to hear her coming towards me, and if she attacks, this sword will end your life in one swipe.”

"Are you so sure about that? You're far too arrogant. Not only have you allowed her to slip by, but you also haven't noticed the other two intruders in this room. Looks like you're actually a terrible spy." His brown eyes glanced over to Tarhuinn and her. Odette froze for a moment before Tarhuinn motioned for her to keep going. She nodded, but her heart started to beat faster.

Fear began to consume her as she watched the spy look over to them. Her dark blue eyes widened before a large grin dominated her lips. "Well, would you look at that. Master Alpontus will be so pleased with me that I brought him the inquiring kelremm and his wife." The sword's tip stayed pointed at the man's neck, but her attention was mostly on them now. "That's who you both are, right? You both fit the descriptions." She didn't wait for them to answer. "My, my, I can't wait to see what Master Alpontus has in store for you two."

Her grip on the sword lessened as she took a couple of steps their way. Tarhuinn didn't pay her any mind, though. Instead, he kept urging Odette forward. Odette did notice that he had his right hand over a sheathed dagger, though. If the female kelremm was to come too close, he would attack, and Odette prepared herself to grab the dagger from her boot. Hopefully, she would be able to push aside her fright if she had to fight the female kelremm.

"Ignoring me?" she asked before she shook her head in the direction of Tarhuinn. "How rude." Her eyes turned to meet Odette's own orbs. The grin on her face widened. "You seem quite terrified. You shouldn't have walked into my masters' home. You're making this too easy, but I do have a question for you. Do..."

Dropping from her hand, the sound of the sword hitting the stone floor rang throughout the area. Red decorated the kelremm's blue lips, and a trail ran down her chin. Drops fell to the floor while her blue, short-sleeved shirt became stained with the color. Her eyes peered down to the metal in her chest, and her hands reached up to the weapon. Before they could grab it, she fell forward and collided with the ground.

Motionless, the second sword, from the weapons' pile, rested in her back. Standing above the kelremm's fallen form, the woman stared down at her. Her intertwined fingers were clutched to her chest. She shook her head some before she directed her gaze to Tarhuinn and Odette.

Both of them were continuing on their way down, and they weren't letting their guard falter. The two humans could decide to attack either of them. They hadn't helped them with the female kelremm, and they might be rather angered about that. For the moment, it was a silent exchange of stares between the four until the woman and man walked towards Tarhuinn and Odette.

Tarhuinn's hand moved closer to the dagger while Odette's heart continued to pound in her chest, but the pace had slowed down some from before. She believed that she could take out at least one of them if they tried to attack, but she went over the dagger grips in her head. Scenarios began to form, and she played through each one.

Nearing the bottom, Tarhuinn and her noted that the pair had stopped a little distance away from them, but neither of them had grabbed the swords from before. They were quite defenseless unless they had hidden weapons, but Odette doubted it. Both of them didn't seem the sort to carry such defenses since they had risked going for the swords.

Once at the bottom, Tarhuinn and she stopped. They maintained their distance from the pair of humans, and she moved a bit closer to Tarhuinn. "What do you two want?" Tarhuinn questioned in a threatening tone.

"You're here for our partners' masters, correct?" the woman inquired.

"Yes, we intend to kill them. If you plan to get in our way, we'll show you no mercy. My wife and I don't have time to be standing around here."

"We won't get in your way. Besides, we'll be killed after the body of Phiinae is discovered," the man answered, a sigh leaving his mouth afterwards.

"Then, why don't you two run and get out of here?" Odette questioned, though; she only moved nearer to Tarhuinn. At any moment, the pair could turn on them despite their words.

"You tell us the way out, and we'll tell you the best route to their masters." The man glanced between the two of them. He held out his right hand. "Do we have a deal? If not, we should both keep moving on ahead before the others resurface. I'd rather not die today."

"How can we trust your word?" Tarhuinn questioned, doubt clear in his tone.

"Simple, we have to trust your word on the way out of here, and it wouldn't make sense for us to lie to both of you. Even if we turned you into their masters, we would still be killed. A human here is sentenced to death the moment that they end the life of a kelremm. There are no exceptions made."

"If I discover that you two misled us, I'll hunt you down and show you no mercy. You'll be killed the moment that I see either of you, and my wife can validate my claim. Do you two understand?" Tarhuinn emphasized as his eyes narrowed and a threatening aura dominated his being.

"We understand. We just wish to get out of here before they resurface, so do we have a deal?" the man asked, his right foot tapping a bit in impatience. The woman kept glancing between them and the pool, clearly nervous about the other four spies. She had every right to be, though. There was no telling how long they would be down there.

"Yes, tell us the short route," Tarhuinn responded, glancing to the male's tapping foot. It seemed like he would tackle the man if he continued, but her husband maintained his present position. It probably also helped that she now had her hands resting on his right upper arm.

"From here, you'll want to head to the far back of this space. There, you'll enter the next path, and there will only be a few torches to light your way. I doubt that you'll have trouble seeing, though. Afterwards, you'll be met with two paths. Take the right one and continue straight. There will be constant turns down that path but always go straight.

"At the end of the path, you'll be met with a large pool of water. On the other end, there will be another path. Don't go down that way. It leads directly to the spies' main sitting room. You'll both need to swim down to the bottom of the pool, but it isn't too deep. At the bottom, you'll both see a path to your left. Take it, and you'll find yourselves in a hallway overlooking their masters' main space.

"There will be two or three spies guarding that area. Two will be facing their masters' room, and one will be facing the pool. If you two have made it this far, you shouldn't have too much of a problem disposing of them before they sound an alarm."

"And, is there a way into their masters' main room directly without being seen by those two spies?" Odette asked since a problem could arise on the way to the lookout spot.

"Not that I'm aware of. The moment that you enter that space, someone will be alerted of your presence immediately."

"Then, you have saved us from a terrible outcome," Tarhuinn admitted, though; his tone hadn't softened. To complete the deal, Tarhuinn narrated to the pair the path that they had taken to reach the current space and explained that there was some movement on that path, so they would probably have to stop a few times and wait until it was clear for them to move ahead again.

When Tarhuinn finished his explanation, the four of them thanked the others for the information before they took off in their respective directions. As Tarhuinn and she left the space, the two humans were still walking along the narrow path. Turning their backs to the two humans, they started down the poorly lit way. Odette could see torchlight far down the path, but it barely illuminated the ground. She allowed Tarhuinn to guide her until they drew closer to the light, but she did still hold onto his upper arm even when she could view her surroundings better.

With how severe their situation was, his arm was a sense of comfort for her, especially in the darker parts. She knew that he was there and that she shouldn't worry if she heard water splashes off in the distance. Even now, they could hear individuals up ahead. It sounded like there were at least five, and, from their encounter with the two humans, they were probably all kelremm.

It wasn't much of a surprise that they would keep their human partners locked up. Such a case would've applied to her had she not managed to convince Tarhuinn otherwise. The part that concerned her was that the humans in the authors' home seemed to have no defense, and the spies took advantage of that. That coupled with what she had heard last night only produced more worry. If they were caught, she would probably be treated only as breeding stock if not tortured and then killed.

Her grip on him increased. As for Tarhuinn, he would be given the treatment that the merfolk had planned for him if not worse. Things would become forever a nightmare until she died. She could barely describe the feelings that were bubbling up in her, yet she knew that she had to keep pressing on. No matter what, she had to defeat the authors and gain her possibly extended life with Tarhuinn and their child.

Were it not for those facts, she probably would've collapsed where she stood and broken down into tears. She turned her gaze up to her husband when they passed by another torch. His expression was neutral, but there were hate and rage in his eyes. They gave off the image of dark blue waters alight with flame. Odette could only imagine what was going through his mind, and if they were successful in their task, the authors would be the fearful ones.

His gaze eased her mind some and allowed her to look forward again. The movement ahead grew louder, but there were no voices. She only hoped that those individuals were coming up the right path to go down the left. If they were to come down the path that Tarhuinn and she were on, they would have to fight and make it swift.

Heartbeat quickening, she carried on. She hoped that they couldn't hear the light splashes of water that Tarhuinn made or her quiet footfalls. Both of them tried to be more silent in their steps, but they could only do so much. Neither of them were trained spies, which was part of the reason why she was shocked at how the spies walked about.

All of them moved so that they could clearly be heard. The amount of confidence that they had in their abilities must've grown to a harmful quantity over the years since there were most likely few intruders in their masters' home. Still, she would've thought that the authors would've said something about that to their spies. In the end, though, it only proved a benefit to Tarhuinn and her. They knew where their opponents were, and they could change their plans if they needed to do so.

Before they reached the split in the ways, both of them halted. They remained in the shadows and watched five kelremm exit the left path and head down the right one. She cursed mentally. "We'll follow them at a distance, but we should keep them in sight in case they're already aware of our presence. That way, we won't get caught off guard," he told her in a hushed voice.

Agreeing, they both waited a little more before trailing the five. They kept as quiet as they could, and the spies' loud splashes of water seemed to drown out Tarhuinn's and her movement. Neither of them dropped their guard, though.

One of the spies branched off from the other four and took a left turn. The others continued on straight ahead. Finding that odd, they slowed down. Reaching the spot where the one had separated from the others, they cautiously paused and peered down that way. They could just see the spy's back facing them. Thankfully, the spy didn't look back but kept going forward.

At the end of the hallway, there was a wooden door. The spy opened it and revealed for a moment what was behind it. For a glimpse in time, she saw horrid looking tools. She couldn't help but gulp as blood drained from her face. Her hands squeezed Tarhuinn's arm, and he rested a hand reassuringly over hers. "We'll never have to go in there, Odette," he whispered while his gaze softened. "Let's keep moving."

"Rig-right," she simply answered, her voice somewhat shaky.

Gazing away from the wooden door, they proceeded straight down the main path. By that point, the other spies were out of sight, but they could still hear them. Even though they wished for the spies to be in view, they didn't increase their speed. Doing so could alert the four spies of their presence.

Coming upon the room with the pool, they could see the four spies at the other end. All of them headed towards the spies' main sitting room, which left Tarhuinn and her the ability to dive into the pool without trouble. Due to past times, she instinctively went to take off her boots.

Seeing and recalling that they weren't there, she looked over to Tarhuinn. They were no longer on his feet, and they weren't in his hands either. Confused, she glanced up to him. "Where did my boots go?"

"They're in my pack. I emptied the water and placed them in there during our time in that dimly lit hallway. I may have to carry you all the way back home since they're quite ruined now."

"I don't think that I would mind that after everything that we've been through and will be through. I might have to wait on that offer, though, since we have to carry the authors back to the merfolk."

"Yes, unfortunately, they'll have to be carried before you. I'd rather let them rot here, but the merfolk wouldn't take kindly to a broken deal."

"I just hope that we have no more deals ahead of us."

"We won't, Odette. The authors and the spies will get none. Unlike those two humans, I'll spare them no time to even propose one. Now, I want you to hold onto my hand. We're very close."

Chapter Forty Six: Gazing

Like the human male had stated, the pool wasn't deep, but the water was piercing cold. Odette's teeth chattered while she kept her mouth shut. She needed to preserve as much oxygen as she could since the man had never disclosed how long the distance was to the lookout spot. How he had even discovered to get to such a place was curious, but she didn't question it too much. After all, he had little reason to lie to them unless he liked to make others suffer.

The important matter was dealing with the three spies in the near future. They made no plan to take them out, for they couldn't stand around in one area for too long. Tarhuinn seemed confident in disposing of them, though; her thoughts soon only went to her lack of oxygen. Her eyes were already shut, but she closed them tighter as if that would help solve her problem.

When air greeted her lungs, she felt Tarhuinn's grip on her disappear completely. Her eyelids shot open, and she spotted three stunned expressions. The looks quickly changed to ones of glee, but Tarhuinn already leaped out of the water and attacked the one facing the pool.

She just caught him plunging one of his daggers into the neck of the spy. They both fell to the ground, but he was back on his feet instantly. He went after the one to his left, but the other spy looked over to her way. The grin never left the spy's lips as he charged towards Odette. Instantly, she went to reach for her dagger, but she realized that she no longer had it on her. It was in Tarhuinn's pack.

Cursing, she didn't know what to do. Fighting a kelremm in the water would be near impossible, but she couldn't get out in time. Tarhuinn was busy dodging the attacks of the other, but his gaze did turn her way for a moment. Realization struck him, and he dealt a blow to the one spy's right arm.

Odette had to look away from him; the one spy had reached her. She swam farther back into the pool, not having anywhere else to go. The spy dived in, and she prepared herself. Both the spy and she knew her obvious disadvantage, and Tarhuinn wasn't there to defeat him.

Luckily, the spy hadn't drawn the daggers at his side, but his mouth full of sharp teeth was intimidating. The spy parted his lips to presumably make some remark, but she didn't allow a word to leave his mouth. She pushed her feet off of the stone wall behind her and shot towards him. He wasn't expecting that and had no time to dodge.

Colliding with the kelremm, she clasped her hands around his throat. Odette was shivering from the cold, but she forced herself to push the feeling aside. She tightened her hold as much as she could, but it had barely any effect. The kelremm brought up one of his knees and impacted it against her midsection. Her grip vanished, and she felt the air leave her. Almost, she thought that blood would come up.

Pushing her under, the kelremm held her there as she regained her senses. She struggled and tried to get away, but things weren't in her favor. Her eyes directed themselves over to the dagger that was on the left hip of the spy. In a last effort to escape, her right hand grasped the weapon. Odette managed to unsheathe it before the spy could do anything. Instead of trying to aim for anything in particular, she stabbed the blade into the spy's left side. A clear cry of pain exited the spy's mouth, but she barely heard it and only saw bubbles rise to the surface of the water.

Wasting no time, she pulled out the blade and plunged it into the spy again. She never saw where she hit on the second strike, for the spy was knocked to his right. Long, ink-black locks flew by her before she saw the spy and Tarhuinn collide with the stone wall. Her need for air, though, drove her to the surface.

Breaking it, she gasped and wiped the water from her face. She pushed back wet locks of hair. Before her, she saw the body of the first fallen spy while the second one was in a worse condition. The second spy shouldn't have kept Tarhuinn from getting to her. Otherwise, she might've had a quicker death.

Her fingers grasped the stone, and she pulled herself up from the water, but she was mindful not to touch the crimson, which was slowly covering the whole floor of the lookout area. Once on her feet, she walked over to the first fallen spy and removed his dagger belt. The belt sheathed four daggers, and they were somewhat similar to Tarhuinn's.

As she tied the belt, Tarhuinn surfaced while the third spy floated up. Getting out of the water, he sheathed his one dagger and walked over to her. "Are you alright? Did that kelremm seriously injure you anywhere?"

"No, I'm fine, Tarhuinn. Thank you, though." Her eyes darted over the corpses again. She was tempted to ask him if he really had needed to kill them in such ways, but she remained silent. To him, it was necessary, and she probably wouldn't be able to convince him otherwise.

Directing her gaze to the window in the space, she headed over there cautiously. Tarhuinn placed a hand on her right shoulder and pulled her back a little. He motioned for her to stay close to the wall and not stand directly in front of the window. She already knew not to do that, but she assumed that Tarhuinn was using that as an excuse to care for her more. The gesture caused a small smile to fall upon her lips. Honestly, he needed to make sure that he had no injuries as well, but his body heat was welcome.

Next to the wall, she peered out through the window. Down below, the entirety of the floor had water running over it. It cascaded down the multiple stones steps, which led up to a stone table and five chairs. It looked like in the past there had been room for a sixth chair. Currently, no one occupied any of them. No one was even in the space.

Unsettled, she looked over her left shoulder even though she knew that no one was behind them. She heard a door open, however. Her attention turned back towards the room, and her eyes widened. Of course, she knew that an author would eventually enter the space and that she would see at least one of them with her own eyes, but it was still a shock actually to view one.

Mind processing the information, her eyes took in everything about the author. She recalled the information that she had learned the night before. The straight, shoulder-length hair and sky blue eyes gave away the author. Before them, Rocean stood.

His hands were on his hips, and he was shirtless. Only some grey pants were on his legs while his countenance displayed irritation. He glanced over the room before he turned on his heel and headed towards one of the doors in the space. Raising his right fist, he pounded on the object. “Byda, I know that you’re in there! Get up and open this door, will you! You promised that you would meet me in my room around this time. Hurry up and come already!”

The male received no answer. A growl left his lips before he frustratingly combed his fingers through his hair. He pulled it back and grabbed something from his right pants’ pocket. It was a purple ribbon, which he used to tie his hair back. Banging his fist against the door again, he yelled out the same commands. Again, no answer was given. “Fine! I’ll just go enjoy the company of a woman. I’m sure that one of the spies wouldn’t mind sharing their partner.” He started down the steps, skipping one every now and then. Almost at the bottom, the door that he had been hitting swung open.

“Don’t you dare! Get back up here, Thy!” a female kelremm shouted. Based off of her hair being tied up in a bun and her ocean blue eyes, Odette assumed her to be Amtoma. “How dare you threaten me with such information!”

Smirking, Rocean glanced over his left shoulder and up at her. “I knew that you would come around, darling. You should know that I’ll just go off if you ignore me. You already give me so little attention; it’s hard not to walk off on you on a daily basis.”

“Oh, so you’ve been seeing someone else, then? Just who have you been visiting?” she asked, taking some steps forward. The female kelremm looked like she would strangle him, but he only kept grinning. It was obvious that he wanted to provoke her more, and she was falling right into his desire.

“I wonder. Maybe if you give me some more affection, you can get me to tell you. Otherwise, I’ll just have to keep her name a secret. What do you say, love? Want to play a little?”

Instead of answering him, she marched down the stairs. She stopped on the one above his before she leaned towards his right ear. Amtoma whispered something to him, but her next action was anything but intimate. Bringing up her right foot, she kicked him in the midsection, which caused him to fall backwards. Water splashed upwards as he fell into the pool at the base of the steps. He propped himself up on his hands and laughed loudly. “You must’ve been in quite a deep sleep. Did I really anger you that much?”

Stepping into the pool, she grabbed him by his bangs and tugged him towards her. Several groans of discomfort left his mouth, but he never lost his smirk. “You have no idea.” Her hand traveled to his right arm, and she lifted him up before she dragged him back up the stairs. Soon enough, his room door slammed behind the two.

Despite having two of the authors presumably preoccupied, Odette wondered why Tarhuinn hadn’t taken them out. The window probably didn’t allow the best of throwing angles, but knowing him, he could’ve made both shots. “Is something wrong?” she asked, though; her eyes never diverted themselves from the authors’ room.

“Yes, that room is too well guarded. We may be hidden now, but if I had attacked either of those two, several spies would’ve seen, and Alpontus would’ve been alerted. Not to mention that we know nothing about their fighting abilities. They’ve possibly lived for centuries, so their experience in combat might be well above mine.”

“Are you saying that you don’t think that we have a chance at all at beating them?” she questioned, her voice displaying evident distress.

“No, but we should take out those spies first. There’s no way to get around them. With two of the three authors busy, we can go after Alpontus next. They shouldn’t even notice judging by how their conversation just went, but we have no idea what Alpontus is doing right now. If we open his room door and he’s staring right at us, we might have some trouble.”

“I still don’t see these spies that you’re referring to. Where are they?”

Carefully, he moved her to stand in front of him. His right hand rested on her right shoulder while his left index finger pointed towards the ceiling of the space. Even though the windows in the ceiling illuminated the area well, she could barely spot the four spies. There were tiny spaces in the stone close to the ceiling, and the spaces were designed to merely look like a decorative wall pattern. Within four of them, though, were the spies.

The shadows of the spaces concealed them nearly to perfection, and if Tarhuinn had never pointed them out to her, she would've never noticed. It was relief that he had such stellar eyesight. "How do you plan to take them out? Is there anything that you would like me to do?"

"I want you to stay close for now. From here, I can't hit them. This room is much too low. We need to get to higher ground. To our right, there is a path. It might lead upwards towards them. We'll take that slowly, and when we reach them, be ready for a fight. We don't need another situation like the one in the water, but you had performed well."

A small smile graced her lips at the compliment, but she pouted in a playful way afterwards. She crossed her arms over her chest and met his gaze. "May I suggest that you don't run off with my only weapon next time, though?"

Realizing what he had accidentally done, he looked like he might fall over and faint. If they weren't in such a hostile environment, she would've laughed. It was truly a hilarious expression that had befallen his countenance. To correct his past mistake, he reached into his pack and removed her dagger.

Holding it out to her, he apologized. "I could've gotten you killed. I'm so sorry, Odette."

She smiled just a bit more and shook her head before she signaled to the blades around her waist. "I'll be fine now. And, you were thinking about taking out the spies in this area quickly. You didn't want them to sound an alarm, which would've ended badly for both of us. Your actions had probably been the best to take given our situation at the time.

"Besides, we both had forgotten about my dagger. If it had been anyone's fault, it had been both of ours. For now, let's keep that blade hidden." She received a nod from him before he put it away once more.

"Thank you." He leaned down and placed a soft kiss on her forehead. With his lips still ghosting over her skin, he mentioned, "Let's continue forward." As he pulled back, she nodded and started down the right path with him.

The path was narrow, like the path where the five kelremm had been. Thankfully, there were walls on both sides of them. They had to advance slowly and walk sideways, but it was better than the possibility of falling off a ledge and impacting stone below. There was a clear downside, though. If they did meet a hostile while on the path, they would be nearly defenseless. Their daggers wouldn't be able to deflect too many blows.

Luckily, none came their way. Instead, at the end of the path, they were greeted by a stairwell, which traveled upwards. It wound itself around a stone pillar, and they could only guess that it went to where the spies were. If it didn't lead there, they would have to find another path to take.

Cautiously, they made their ascent. Odette had to be even more careful since water traveled down every step. Slipping would be rather easy, but Tarhuinn remained close and had his right fingers intertwined with her left. That made the water-covered steps more travelable.

As they continued upwards, she constantly would search the higher steps for a spy. She was worried that one was waiting for them. It didn't help that there were light splashes of water every time that they took another step. If the spies were already alerted of their presence, she wouldn't be surprised, so she increased her grip on one of the daggers in her belt.

Tarhuinn seemed to have similar thoughts as he unsheathed one of his daggers and held onto it tightly. His gaze indicated that he would strike at anything coming down the stairs. When they reached the top, they pressed themselves to the wall next to the opening.

Steadily, Tarhuinn peeked out. He motioned for her to stay back before he took a slow step out into the open. His fingers left hers, and she was tempted to latch her hand back onto his. She resisted the urge, but she did look around the corner herself.

Tarhuinn was advancing towards a spy, which had her back turned to him. To keep his movement quiet, he stepped out of the water. The spy was close enough that he would make it, but Odette felt nervous about the situation regardless. He would need to kill the spy in one hit; otherwise, the spy would have the clear advantage.

Right behind the spy, Tarhuinn spun the blade in his hand so that it was a modified saber grip. Before the spy could react, he held the blade to her neck and sliced. The spy dead, he walked back into the water as silently as he could. A quiet sigh of relief left his lips before he motioned for her to come out. Maintaining her slow pace, she eventually reached him.

Once she was next to him, he pointed towards the next two spies. Both of them were close to each other, and one of them was starting to face their direction. Tarhuinn and she ducked and hid behind the rocks that were in front of them. Due to his height, he had to practically submerge himself entirely into the water to hide. His long hair began to fan out around him. Swiftly, she reached over and grabbed it to prevent it from being seen.

She received a nod of thanks from him to which she gave him a small smile. Their focus shifted back to the two spies. They both peered out from behind the rocks. The one spy's attention was directed a bit above them, but his gaze remained towards them. Thankfully, the deceased spy was out of the new spies' field of vision. Going back behind the rock, they waited some more. No conversation occurred between the two spies, which was most likely because they were the ones most responsible for guarding their masters.

Moments later, they checked again. This time, the one spy was facing the other way. Tarhuinn submerged himself completely in the deeper water and swam out towards the spy. She quietly started to head out on the dry land to attack the other one.

Silently, Tarhuinn rose from the water. Like before, he brought the blade to the spy's neck. That time, however, someone else noticed his action. The second spy was about to shout, but she darted out and tackled him. She raised her dagger and brought it down. Blocking her attack with his left hand, he pulled his hand back and went to punch her with his uninjured hand.

Odette ducked, but the kelremm suspected that. He went to bite into her left shoulder, and she had nowhere to go. Cursing, she went to bring her dagger down again on him, but his injured hand gripped her wrist hard and prevented the action. His grip wouldn't last for long due to the blood there, but it would be enough for him to bite her.

Before his teeth could sink into her skin, Tarhuinn came and stabbed his dagger through the spy's heart. The spy's grip left her completely, and she thanked her husband. That had been too close for her liking. Looking back, she saw that the other spy was in a similar condition to the first one.

There was one problem, though. Tarhuinn was soaked from head to toe, and water was dripping from his form. The drip-drop sound echoed in the space. He noticed the issue as well and went back into the water, but the last spy's attention had already been caught. Not only had the water drawn the spy's attention but also the previous struggle had done so. Both of them heard splashes of water coming their way. Odette hid herself behind some rocks while Tarhuinn remained low in the water.

Closer and nearer, the spy came. Tarhuinn and she remained in their positions, not moving at all. They kept silent, and the steps slowed. When the splashes finally came to a stop, the spy's shadow stretched across the stone wall. Light flickered and changed the shadow's shape occasionally. They both noticed the shadow of a short sword extending over the stone.

Odette darted her eyes over to Tarhuinn. He had one of his daggers at the ready. The spy moved a few steps closer, and the spy's bare feet were seen. She stayed hidden, and she would do so until the spy came closer to the rocks or until Tarhuinn drew the spy's attention. Their enemy was so close. Her hands tightened even more around two of her daggers.

The spy's eyes fell upon Tarhuinn, and she immediately went to shout. As she turned, Tarhuinn leaped out of the water. The spy turned her back to Odette, and the woman darted out from the rocks. Dodging Tarhuinn's attack, the spy spun on her heel and right into one of Odette's blades. Metal plunged into her chest, and her eyes widened as the life faded from her.

After the spy collided to the floor, Tarhuinn walked over to Odette. They gave each other a congratulatory smile, but they were hardly done with their mission. There were still five authors for them to bring back to the mermaids. Two of them, they wouldn't have to encounter currently, but the three below weren't easy prey.

Both of them, though, headed down the way where the last spy had been. They kept their attention to the room below and saw that no other kelremm entered the space. No human made themselves known either. The authors were on their own unless there were guards in their rooms.

When they reached the end of the path, there was a stairwell leading downwards. Cautiously, they made their descent. They kept their pace even slower because of the water since Odette had nearly slipped several times. If it wasn't for Tarhuinn, her face would've impacted the hard stone.

At the bottom, they carefully peeked out from behind one of the stone walls. They were at the top of the space where the room doors were. Their focus directed itself to the door in the middle. According to what they had heard last night, that door led to Alpontus's room.

Quietly, they traveled across the floor. Light splashes of water sounded, but they hoped that no one would notice. Besides, Rocean and Amtoma were rather preoccupied at the moment. Once at the door, Tarhuinn rested his hands over the metal doorknob. He took a deep breath in before he exhaled. Steadily, he turned the knob. The door opened and made a slight creaking sound.

Gulping, Odette peered around him and into the room. The space was domed, and a circular, ceiling window allowed light in. It illuminated the main water path of the room. As for the furniture, it was similar to their home back in the first complex but more spread out, larger and cushioned with regards to the bed. Pillows and sheets were piled on top, and some were near to dipping into the water. Torches were around the space as well but were unlit for the moment.

Stepping into the area, Tarhuinn closed the door behind them. Movement could be seen under the sheets. Quietly, they advanced towards the bed. Sheets slipped down some to reveal long, ink-black locks in a thick braid. They were near in length to Tarhuinn's but just a little shorter. Alpontus turned his head towards her, and she froze. His eyes remained closed, but she took a worried step back. Jaw-length bangs brushed against the kelremm's forehead and hid most of it while they fanned out over the rest of his face.

Tarhuinn took several steps more towards the male. He moved his right hand to rest the blade against the male's neck. In the blink of an eye, another blade revealed itself. Not thinking, she jumped forward and pushed Tarhuinn back. There was little time for anything else, and he wouldn't have been able to dodge.

A loud splash of water echoed throughout the space while a cry of pain exited her mouth. The dagger sliced through her pack, cloak and clothes to her back. While her supplies spilled out from the pack, she could feel the blood already running down her skin as she hit the cushioned bed.

Instantly, she felt weight on her back. Another scream departed from her when pressure was applied to the large but not deep cut. Hair being clutched, her head was pulled up, and she saw Tarhuinn stand to his feet. His teeth were bared, and his dagger was at the ready. Eyes filled with rage and hate, he snarled out, "Let her go! You have no right to touch her!"

More weight was applied to her lower back and away from the cut, much to her relief, but she wanted the male off of her. She was about to fight back until she felt cool metal rest up against her neck. “You’re in no place to be making demands. I have your wife, and I’ll kill her the moment that you try to attack me. You should get on your knees and beg me to release her rather than order me around in my own home.”

“You’ll never hear me beg to any of you.” A growl left Tarhuinn, but he didn’t attack. He remained fixed in the same place and kept his gaze on the author. Alpontus laughed for a brief moment while the blade stayed to her neck.

Pressing his free hand against her cut, he elicited another shout of agony from her. “Fine, but I don’t intend to let her go or you for that matter. You both invaded our home without our permission, so you’ll pay the consequences soon enough. For now, however, I wish to have a quick chat with you two before my friends join us.”

Alpontus shifted his weight from her back to the bed. He pulled her up and seated her between his legs. Her back was to his chest, and the blade continued to reside by her neck. His free hand slipped around her waist to keep her more secure. Tarhuinn continued to stand in an attack-ready position, and his dark blue eyes never lost their wrathful gaze.

“Given how you appear, you would think that I was the one invading your home,” the author remarked, chuckling a bit. The blade tapped against Odette’s neck, and beads of sweat formed on her forehead. If he hit the blade any harder, it would cut her skin.

“The other authors and you were the first ones to attack. We only wanted to ask all of you a simple question, but then you tried to have us killed on multiple occasions. We thought that we would return the favor and learn the answer to our question before we killed all of you,” Odette retorted, reaching for one of her own daggers steadily.

"Speaking of favors, I might need to return one as well to both of you. My chat pertains to that matter actually, for ..." he paused, and his free hand slapped her left hand away from her nearest dagger. Swiftly, he untied the dagger belt from her and tossed it aside. It sank to the bottom of the water path, and the only near weapon now was the blade against her neck. His arm returned to being wrapped around her waist, and his grip on her increased.

"Continuing from what I was saying, I discovered that the snow pixies, which we had an agreement with, betrayed us. They attacked our own spies with a human mage. How they attained this mage is rather confusing. Perhaps, one or both of you could clear this up for me. It would be appreciated." Neither of them answered. "I see. Well, let me rephrase this. Did one or both of you persuade this mage to help the pixies? If I don't receive the truthful answer, I'll kill one of you slowly."

Standing up a bit straighter, Tarhuinn chuckled bitterly. "Even if we answered truthfully and didn't convince the mage to aid the pixies, you would still kill us gradually, or one of the other authors would. After this chat, they'll probably have a say in our fates too."

"Yes, that's true, but my word always is the deciding factor. I can guarantee you both a quick death if you had nothing to do with the mage, but I think that I already have my answer. You wanted nothing to do with the mage, am I correct? It was your wife's decision, and she went against you to bring him to the pixies. A husband as protective as you wouldn't have allowed her near such a vile man otherwise."

Choosing silence, Tarhuinn looked as though he was ready to pounce. She wouldn't be surprised if the handle of the dagger was crushed by his fingers. Her attention was forced away from him, though, as Alpontus gripped her chin roughly. The author's indigo-colored eyes stared into her own brown orbs while a menacing smile coated his lips. "Did I get that assumption right, human?"

Instead of answering him, she spit onto his face. The action stunned him for just enough time. He had pulled back on the blade a little, giving her the chance to punch him in the midsection. His grip on the dagger didn't loosen anymore, but she was able to roll away from him and off of the bed. Tarhuinn swiftly moved her over to and behind him before he charged at the author.

Alpontus wiped the spit from his face and blocked Tarhuinn's blade. A chuckle left the author's lips, and he shook his head. "I assume that you were the responsible one, then," he remarked, keeping his gaze locked with hers. Tarhuinn struck at him again, and Alpontus had to look away while he defended himself, but a terrifying grin painted the author's mouth.

Each of the males' attacks matched the others, and they were moving too quick for her to step in and help. She had to view the fight on the side, but she could battle anyone who stepped through the door. Most likely, someone else had heard the commotion in Alpontus's room.

Chapter Forty Seven: Flight

Brown orbs left the fight and looked to the closed door. Or, it should've been closed. Several spies had opened it and were now guarding it. Some of them looked rather pleased to be blocking her way while others seemed as though they wanted to kill her then and there. Odette stepped closer to the stone wall, but her eyes shifted over to her dagger belt.

It was closer to the spies, but she needed something to defend herself with. Tarhuinn was still fighting Alpontus, and he couldn't handle any others at the moment. She made swift eye contact with the spies once more before she darted towards her daggers. The action set two of the spies in motion.

They ran towards her, and she dived for the blades. She hoped that she wasn't distracting Tarhuinn from his fight, for he needed to give it all of his focus. He couldn't concern himself with her now. Water splashed up around her, and blue feet soon came into close view. Odette couldn't stop herself, though; she was sliding through the water too fast.

In the process of reaching her left hand out for the belt, she collided with one of the spies. The spy was knocked over, but she was able to grab the weapons. Hurriedly, she unsheathed one of the blades and looked to the fallen spy. The other one was nearing her, but she wasted no time. She leaned over the recovering spy and ended the spy's life with one slice to the throat.

"You d*mned human!" she heard, and she looked up to see a spy reaching for her. Shifting the blade in her hand messily, both from the water and her fear at being captured, she didn't know what hold she put it into; she just struck with the blade. It slashed across the spy's torso as a cry of pain left him. He took a step back, which gave her enough time to get to her feet.

She noted the other two spies charging towards her, and she only had a few moments to finish off the one. Utilizing the spy's last moment of being stunned, she darted to him and finished him like the last spy. As he fell, she turned back to the other two. Her eyes glanced to Tarhuinn for a brief moment, and she saw that he was still battling Alpontus. His movements had become more rushed, however.

He must've seen her run off, and he probably knew of her current state. His attacks were suffering from that knowledge, though. She needed to end her fight quickly, but, now, she wasn't working with one opponent at a time.

Cursing, she watched one of the spies dart around her to her back while the other kept coming at her front. She had to create distance between at least one of them. Odette clenched her fists and ran at the one racing towards her front. The spy was momentarily puzzled by her action, but she kept coming regardless.

Instead of aiming for her heart, neck or head, Odette leaped forward and aimed for her legs. She watched as the spy's blade rose. Unfortunately for the spy, she couldn't kill the human, which gave Odette a clear advantage. Before the spy's blade could strike, they both impacted the water. Odette's blade now rested in the spy's right thigh.

On her feet, Odette grabbed the spy's ankles in the process. Odette lifted the spy's feet out of the water. A loud gasp parted from the spy before she tried to struggle out of Odette's grip. The other spy had reached them now, but Odette couldn't let go of the one. Little options presented to her, Odette held onto the one while she reached the dresser behind her. She threw open one of the drawers and rested the spy's feet in there.

While the spy continued to try and get her feet back in the water, Odette retrieved her dagger and managed to avoid the spy's attempts at grabbing her. The other spy's blade was now traveling towards her right shoulder. Her eyes widened, and she swiftly jumped to her left.

Footing lost, she slid across the stone floor while water obscured her vision. She felt the stone cut her skin along her arms and legs, but she couldn't dwell on it too much. Odette went to unsheathe another dagger, but her hair was grabbed roughly. The action caused her to emit a yelp as she was pulled up out of the water.

The spy lifted her high enough so that her feet weren't touching the ground or water. A smirk covered the spy's lips, and she took note of the other spy recovering since her feet were back in the water. Odette's gaze focused on the one holding her, and a glare covered her expression. She speedily reached for her daggers, but the spy holding her stopped her. His free hand had retrieved the belt and tossed it aside once more. "For a human, you're not too bad of a fighter, but you should've remained still. Now, their deaths will be added to your punishment."

Turning around and moving her with him, he displayed her clearly to Tarhuinn and his master. That resulted in the fight between the two kelremm coming to a halt. Both had a blade at the other's throat. Tarhuinn looked to be more out of breath than Alpontus, but his grip on his blade didn't lessen from it.

"Well, what do you intend to do? Your wife seems to be caught once more," Alpontus remarked in a far too casual voice as though he was expecting it all along. "Why don't you let me kill you swiftly? You're not responsible for the mage; she is. I just want to punish her. You can die and not worry about a thing. Is your wife really worth the pain of a slow death for you?"

Lowering his blade, Tarhuinn took a step back and relaxed his position. He appeared defeated. The recovering spy was now back on her feet, and Odette's dagger had been removed. The female spy stood next to her and chuckled. "Looks like your husband has finally realized his mistake in letting you leave your home." Her desire to plunge her dagger back into the spy's thigh grew tenfold. Odette remained quiet, though, since she wondered what Tarhuinn was planning; he wouldn't give up so easily.

Doubt was tugging at her, however. They were both in a less than satisfactory position, but he always grew furious if anyone threatened her life, yet it appeared as though he had lost all hope. It seemed that he was abandoning their quest. Everything that they had worked for seemed to mean nothing to him presently. She forced herself not to think of that possibility.

"You choose to die swiftly, then?" Alpontus asked, amused. "I don't blame you. No human is worth a horrendous death. Remove your pack and drop your blade."

Tarhuinn gave a simple nod. His free hand took off the pack from his back. He bent down to set it in the water, but she noticed his fingers unlatch it. They slipped into the pack rapidly. She blinked before she saw a blade flying towards them. It lodged itself into the chest of the spy holding her. The male spy's grip slackened, and the other went to take his place, but another dagger took residence in the female spy's chest.

Before she could even process what had exactly happened, she was grabbed and thrown over Tarhuinn's left shoulder. A pained gasp left her lips due to the wound on her back, but her attention turned to an enraged Alpontus chasing after them. If she were a master of daggers, she would've removed one from Tarhuinn's belt and thrown it at the author, but her skills were nowhere near that. It would be better not to attack and save the weapon for later. She had no idea where Tarhuinn was going, though.

Entering the main room, they noticed Rocean's door opening. They only saw Amtoma for a moment before Tarhuinn rushed into another one of the rooms. Instantly, he slammed the door behind them. He set her down before he ran over to a nearby dresser and moved it to be in front of the door. Once it was secure, he turned to her and frowned at the scrapes on her. "We need to bandage those," he commented worryingly.

About to grab her, she stopped him. "We don't have time, Tarhuinn. Besides, you're exhausted, and we're about to have three skilled fighters banging at that door. We need to hide somewhere or get out of here for now. It's too dangerous. I can tolerate these wounds for a little longer. They're not deep."

When he was about to argue, a groan was heard from across the room. They both froze. Tergii and Bimaa weren't supposed to be in there, and the mage should've been gone too. Had they miscalculated that information? The authors' yells could be heard from the other side, which only caused the individual to shift more in their sleep. "We need to find a place quick," she whispered, her eyes already darting around the room for some location.

There were several windows in the space, and they seemed to share a similar idea. Tarhuinn grabbed her left hand and ran with her over to one. He undid the latch with his free hand and motioned her out first. She was about to protest, but they didn't have time for that. She climbed through the window and fell into a pile of snow. When she recovered herself, she noticed Tarhuinn outside as well and closing the window. Once it was shut, he picked her up and carried her before he went over to the water path in the area.

The path ran out from under a closed door and towards an opening on the other side. Around the path were the tall stone walls of the mountain. Sharp peaks were at the top but were occasionally hidden by the clouds. The climb upwards would be impossible given the smooth walls, so they headed for the opening. Soon enough, the authors and the previously sleeping individual would learn of where they had gone, so there was no time for trying the closed door.

Tarhuinn hurried to find some end to the present path. She couldn't see a thing given the lack of torches, but Tarhuinn wasn't slowing down at all. Beneficially, they hadn't been met with a dead end yet, but that was a severe concern. They would be cornered, and that fate was grim.

No splashes of water sounded behind them yet, but, perhaps, that's because they were only focused on getting out of there for now. The splashes that Tarhuinn was making created enough noise for her ears. There was also the fact that her heart was pounding in her chest. She had managed to fight off some of those spies, but she had barely been able to defend herself against more than one at a time. Even then, she had been captured.

That fact was incredibly frustrating. If it hadn't been for Tarhuinn's actions, he would've been killed, and she would be in that horrendous room that she had seen earlier. It wasn't the time for tears, but she could feel them forming. They weren't out of fear or worry but only irritation at herself.

She didn't desire to lose Tarhuinn because of her poor fighting capabilities. It was unrealistic to think that he could defend against all of the spies and the authors, and it was near impossible if not entirely for her to fight multiple kelremm at once. The reality of their situation was crippling.

Not being to help herself, she leaned her head more against his chest and permitted a couple of tears to glide down her face. They would've been more noticeable had the both of them not already been soaked. A gentle squeeze on her form did indicate that Tarhuinn had seen them. He remained silent for now, though, and she appreciated that. Right now, she needed the silence. The present darkness only aided that. All she wished for in that moment was to know that he was there and that they were momentarily alright, and that's what she received.

When light did greet her eyes, she peered towards it and squinted. Presently, she could barely see due to her eyes adjusting to the light, but she did note the icy-blue hue to it. Not only that but also it felt warm. It was as though she was wrapped in the soft blankets back at their home. Her clothes were drying as well while the warmth continued to enfold around her.

Once she was used to the light, her lips parted a bit in awe. The water path continued on its way, but it soon surrounded a glowing, icy-blue tree. Its branches stretched to the top of the cave, and small, icy-blue leaves grew upon its branches. Around its base, the water appeared shimmery.

Wishing to be set down, she tapped him lightly on the chest. "I want to swim and walk the rest of the way," she spoke softly as though yelling didn't exist in the current space, and the danger behind them seemed to fade from her mind.

Obliging her, he placed her feet into the water. Her toes curled a bit at the warmth in delight. She moved forward with him until they reached the tree. Curious, she extended out her right hand and pressed her palm to the trunk. Warmth seeped through her fingers and up her arms. It felt like it was mixing with the blood in her veins and traveling through her entire body. "Do you think that this is the energy source that the authors have been using?"

Reaching his left hand up to one of the higher branches, he ran his fingers gently across one of the leaves. "Yes, it has to be. I've never felt such a feeling before. It's like I'm gaining life that I never had before, and I can feel it coursing through my body ... It's incredible."

"We'll need a container to bottle it and to bring some back home with us. I lost my things back in Alpontus's room."

"We can use one of the containers in my pack and empty it out. Still, the tree's effects seem to only extend out a little distance from it. Otherwise, it would be in all of the water supply. Then, we wouldn't have had to come all the way up here." A sigh escaped him, but a peaceful smile remained on his lips. The tree was too comforting to be around.

"Do you think that the authors will attack us in here?" she questioned, but she couldn't feel concern at the present time. Tarhuinn pulled out a medium-sized, metal container and handed some of the dried cherries to her. He took the rest of them, and they aided their hunger for a bit. "Surely, you've noticed, Tarhuinn, the obvious effects of this tree. I don't think that a fight would be possible in here."

"Agreed, but we should be on guard even though that seems so ridiculous right now." He crouched down and filled the container. "If they weren't presumably nearby, I'd ask you to take a bath with me."

Heat dominated her cheeks, and she had to glance away for a moment. Honestly, it didn't sound like a bad idea, and she was tempted to accept the offer regardless of how close the authors were. It was hard to hold onto reason with the soothing effects of the tree. Her right hand wrapped around her left wrist as she bit her lower lip. Quietly, she commented, "We can take a bath when we get back home."

Sealing the container and standing, he stored the valuable water away in his pack before he looked to her. He stepped closer to her as his right fingers glided under her chin. Tarhuinn turned her gaze to his and met her lips with his. It was a short kiss, but when it ended, his lips remained near to hers. "I would like that."

It was evident that he wanted to add that nickname to the end, but he resisted. She couldn't be useless in fighting even with the tree's effects urging them to continue their affections. Odette desired to have him say it for once, and she nearly asked him to do so. Her hands clenched his shirt as she forced herself to mutter, "We should leave now. Otherwise, I don't think that we'll be able to do so."

His lips pressed to her forehead. "You're right, but I'll carry you out. You look like you're about to collapse, and I didn't even call you by that name." A light chuckle left his lips, and his breath tickled her skin a little.

Out of embarrassment, a pout formed on her lips, but she couldn't deny it. Nor, did she mind him carrying her. "Let's go, Tarhuinn. You're making it worse." Another chuckle left his lips before he lifted her up and started to head away from the tree. He walked slowly away, and she couldn't blame him. She desired to stay longer too, but they had to face what was back out there. Unfortunately, the tree was a dead end but a pleasant one. They had some time to themselves before having to face the authors again, and they were no longer cold, though; that didn't last long.

They could easily tell when they were out of the tree's range. Worry plagued her mind once more as did fear. The vexation returned also. It didn't help that she felt the chill of the air again. Up ahead, they could hear movement in the water. Tarhuinn stopped and set her down. She could see somewhat since a little bit of light from the tree reached their location. Out ahead of them, though, it was completely dark.

He unsheathed a dagger from his belt and passed it to her. No words were exchanged; no advice was given. She knew what she had to do, and Tarhuinn understood that. It was fight or be killed. Her grip tightened on the blade's handle, and she positioned herself in a fighting stance. Odette took a deep breath in and let it out.

Splashes grew louder, and she could steadily see the outline of an individual. When he came closer, she didn't recognize him, but she instinctively took a step back. He wasn't running but simply walking. Each step was powerful, though, and the kelremm wore a smirk on his lips. No weapons were on him. Sky-blue eyes observed them both while straight, chest-length hair rested upon his head.

"It's been awhile since we've had unwanted guests. And, it's a first to have them invade my father's friend's room and then mine. Still, you should've accepted Phyon's offer," his gaze pinned itself on Tarhuinn. "Now, you're going to die quite steadily. I think that you'll be alive for another week. It might be longer depending on how Phyon feels. He's quite enraged at the moment, though."

About to charge at him, Tarhuinn was pulled back by Odette. "Wait," she whispered to him. She moved him back a bit more with her, and he didn't put up much resistance, but it was clear that he would attack as soon as she let go.

The enemy kelremm stopped and placed his hands in his pants' pockets. His gaze shifted over to her. "As for you, you're in for quite a time. Phyon has no intention of letting you die any time soon, but I won't spoil his plans. He probably wishes to tell you them himself."

He removed his hands from his pockets and looked to them both. "Since I can't kill either of you, I'll have to hold myself back a little, but it'll hurt still." When the kelremm opened the palm of his right hand, Odette released her grip on Tarhuinn, and the gleam of a blade was all she saw before the weapon flew past.

Chapter Forty Eight: Dancing Waves

Metal hovered in the air. Water surrounded it, forcing the blade to keep its distance. The sphere bounced up and down a little before a hand rested underneath it. Odette took a step back, and Tarhuinn pulled her closer. His right hand wrapped around her left wrist tightly, and he began to move back.

"Ah, you two look rather frightened. Did you only think that there was one mage here? If so, you miscalculated. My cousin is the mage that's recognized for her talent in fire. I prefer water. It's much more suitable for a kelremm." He let the ball collapse against his hand before his fingers wrapped around the handle. "You should know, though, that this weapon will do nothing against me unless you get close enough to stab me. I won't let that happen, however."

As he had been talking, the two of them had been advancing backwards steadily. If they could get back to the tree, its effects might soothe the mage into not attacking them with magic. They would be affected too, but they would have a better chance at battling him there if they could.

While they were backing up, though, she felt something hard and cool behind her. She wasn't able to move back anymore. Confused, Odette glanced behind herself for a moment. An ice wall blocked their path. "You didn't think that I would let you get back to the tree, did you? Both of you have no right to that water or its calming effects."

Neither obliged to answer him, they remained quiet. She held onto her dagger with a firmer grip while Tarhuinn took a step forward. He had little choice to go elsewhere. That was what it seemed like anyway. With a dagger, he slammed his other hand into the ice wall. Much to her surprise, it shattered upon impact. Instantly, he darted back towards the tree with her.

"Looks like I'll have to make the next one stronger," they heard as they ran. Another wall started to form, but Tarhuinn jumped over it. She was about to do the same, but an ice spike shot out from the water. Instead of letting her go, Tarhuinn tugged her over to him and into his arms. His speed increased, and she clung to him to hold on.

The mage cursed in irritation, and no more ice rose from the water. That gave no reason to celebrate, however. Rather, it was a cause for severe concern. Tarhuinn was about to run into the area of the tree, but a wall of water blocked their path. There was nowhere to turn. They couldn't even run back, for it was coming down upon them too fast.

Pressing her to his chest, he braced them for the impact. Cold water showered and covered them. It pushed Tarhuinn back for the first moments before he started to swim forward, yet that didn't even work. He tried to swim towards the tree, but he was moving back instead. She peered around his left upper arm and noted that the water was pulling them back towards the mage.

When the water level began to lower, she glanced back to him worryingly. The dagger was still clutched in her hands, and she wondered if he wished for her to attack the mage. His lips parted, and he mouthed, "I'll find a way to get back to you."

Brown eyes widening, Odette shook her head furiously, but the water continued to tug him back. He said no more on the subject, released her and shoved her through the water. Odette was about to swim back to him but the water level would reveal both of them soon. There was no time to think on the decision, and, unfortunately, she would have to agree with his.

Painfully, she turned her back to her husband and swam in the opposite direction as swiftly as she could. As she found deeper water, she lowered herself more so that she would remain hidden. By then, Tarhuinn had probably already been captured, but he wouldn't be killed. She kept reassuring herself about that fact.

There was no possibility of her winning against the mage head-on. To make matters worse, the mage was part kelremm. She struggled enough with non-mage kelremm. Her best hope against that male was to attack him by surprise. In order to get back to Tarhuinn, she would have to use stealth. If she was caught, her chances of escape with Tarhuinn would be little if not nonexistent.

Needing air, she carefully rose from the water near a wall. She peeked out from behind it and back towards where she had come from. The mage was still standing there, but he now had Tarhuinn wrapped up in water bonds. Odette could feel some of the effects of the tree, but they weren't enough to cloud her mind. Rather, they merely eased her racing heart to a steady beat.

"Human, I can move the water to bring you back to me. There's no point in hiding. Besides, there's no other way out of this room. You have to come back to me eventually. Or, should I torture your husband here and now while I wait for you?"

Tarhuinn was about to speak, but water speedily covered his mouth. The mage's eyes peered over her way, and she moved farther along the wall. Her attention focused on something out in the water. It was heading directly for her and at a fast pace. She needed to find dry land. Eyes searching the room, she found a small ledge several feet away, but she couldn't dart to it, or her location would be given away.

Being as silent and swift as she could, she swam through the water as the thing raced towards her. The dagger was in her right hand, and she hoped that it would be able to stall the thing for a bit if it reached her. About a foot away from the ledge, she felt a tug on both her ankles. An instant replay of the moment back with the tenlites occurred in her mind, but she had a blade unlike back then.

Submerging herself, Odette found herself staring at a water-formed fish. It had two arms and hands rather than fins. Both were clasped around her, and it was swimming backwards. She readied the blade and struck at its wrists. The dagger cut through both and broke contact for a mere moment. That was enough for her to create the needed distance.

Breaking the surface of the water, she reached for the ledge and gripped it. The fish had her once more, but she held on. Her fingers scraped against the rock, and she knew that they would become bloodied soon. When that happened, her hold would vanish.

A horrid cry rang throughout the space while blood drained from her face. It seemed as though her heart stopped. Desperately, she wished to dart back towards Tarhuinn. Just what had that mage done to him? Another one followed, and she thought that she would be sick.

Her ankles were tugged on again, and she was nearly pulled under. She bit her lower lip and attempted to focus on that rather than the screams as more came. Utilizing her strength, she managed to wrench her ankles free and climb onto the ledge. The fish swam around the land while she pressed herself against the wall.

Hands covering her ears, she attempted to block out the screams, but she still heard them. Even though they were painful to listen to, she had to endure them. Otherwise, she would be caught, and she wouldn't be able to free her husband, but she hated sitting there. The thought of somehow bringing the mermaids to the authors' home passed through her mind. Odette disliked those creatures, but she wouldn't mind them killing the authors, their spies and mages. They could probably fight against the authors while a group worked on taking out the mage, but they weren't there. There was no one to help him but herself.

A sharp cry penetrated her covered ears and drew her from her thoughts. She pressed her hands to her ears more, but she heard another one. Her whole body shook, and she desired to sob. "I'm so sorry, Tarhuinn," she muttered to herself. Another met her ears, and she curled up into a ball. "Please hang on for me." Water dripped down from her and quietly hit the stone, but it felt like she was being drenched in tears.

"You're still not coming out? Well, you're tougher than I thought. Your husband is rather weak, though. I've only begun, and he's already close to passing out. Maybe, my estimation of a week was a little bit too much. Should I tell you what I did to him?

"Afterwards, I'll draw you out with another wave. I'm surprised that my minion hasn't brought you back yet, but I have enjoyed this extended time with you two. I might even get you both for a long while in the future."

"Icniss! What's taking you so long?! Phyon is growing impatient. So, am I. I've already had to deal with your father today, and, now, I have to deal with you! Honestly, I just wanted to sleep in peace." Loud splashes of water continued, and a displeased groan from the mage followed.

"Byda, you need to learn to calm down. What my father does isn't my problem. He's your issue. And, I was about to retrieve the human. You can take her husband back to Phyon to calm him down."

"You can take her husband back with me. The human will have to come out eventually, and you released one of your minions on her already I presume. She won't be able to escape the area. We'll place several guards at the entrance as well, but you can't wash her out. She's too far in, and we can't risk damaging the tree."

"Fine," she heard last before footsteps sounded again. A sigh of relief left her lips, but such a feeling didn't last long. She needed to discover a way around the fish and free her husband before anything else was done to him. There would also be the issue of the guards and the fact that she wouldn't be able to see in part of the passage.

Shifting her eyes back to the tree, she looked to the leaves. If she could pick a few, they might light her way through the tunnel. With the idea in mind, she peered down to the fish.

Back and forth, back and forth, the fish continued the pattern. Its hands would occasionally reach out and try to grab her, but she stayed huddled to the wall. She could feel the sharp pieces of stone press against her skin, but she was glad that the effects of the water had soothed her injuries some before. The cuts were still there, but the bleeding had stopped. Perhaps if she stood next to the tree for long enough, her wounds would be completely healed, but she didn't exactly have the time to test it out.

Somehow, she had to evade the fish. She could jump over it and into the water, but it would catch up to her rapidly. That would also give away her location. Thankfully, the fish was rather quiet with its movements. Odette took in her surroundings once more to spot a possible hidden way out, but it continued to appear closed off except for the one entrance and exit.

Standing, she pushed back some strands of light blonde hair and kept her fingers in her locks before she paced back and forth. Tarhuinn's screams played back in her mind, and her chest tightened. He was probably being tortured again. She despised being so weak, yet she also wanted to break down and cry. Odette wished to pour out her emotions and relieve her mind entirely of them.

She froze completely before she felt a sob form in the back of her throat. Leaning against the wall, she covered her mouth with her hands. Odette closed her eyes. He had called her name, but it had sounded so faint. Tarhuinn was probably in no condition to expend his energy on speaking her name. His own health was more important, yet he had ... he had spoken to her. Another sob threatened to escape, but she forced it down. Her hands lowered, she whispered, "I'm co-coming."

Odette glanced back down to the fish. There was no other way out, and she couldn't out swim the fish. She did have a dagger, but it would only break the fish's contact for a mere moment. With the fish around, she wouldn't be able to sneak up on the guards if that were even possible. No matter what, the fish had to be dealt with before she could do anything else.

It jumped up and reached for her. She took a step back and dodged before it merged with the water again. Its movements continued, and its back fin was seen by her every now and then. The fish's hands were the main problem. If she could secure them, she could possibly ride the fish. That would surprise the guards awaiting her, but she didn't know how to secure water.

At times, the fish would harden itself, like it had done when it had grabbed hold of her ankles, but it could immediately go back to its complete liquid state. The only way to capture the fish might be to have it catch her. If she surrendered herself, she would have more control of the situation.

First, though, she required some of those leaves. She still wished to view her captors as she had no intention of going with them willingly. Odette waited for the fish to grab for her again; she would have to time it right. Dagger at the ready, she held it in a modified saber grip.

The fish leaped up and came towards her. She waited until it reached its highest point. There, she slashed it. Water split apart and fell back down. Odette dived into the water and zipped through it to the best of her ability. It grew warmer as she went nearer to the tree, and she was tempted to slow down, but she kicked regardless. Soon, though, her efforts at forcing her movement became fruitless. Already, she could hear the fish coming up behind her.

Shimmery water encircled her and clouded her vision some. Her pace was leisurely as though she was taking a casual afternoon stroll. What was odd, though, was that the fish stopped. Its gaze was pinned on her, but it didn't come any closer.

Breaking the surface, she took in a breath of needed air and swam closer to the tree. She saw the top half of the fish at the edge of the sparkling liquid. Amtoma had mentioned that they couldn't risk injuring the tree so that might've been why the fish was keeping its distance. Whatever the reason, it gave her a safety zone.

Standing up, she peered out towards the entrance and exit. She noticed no guards in the illuminated area. Beyond that, though, she couldn't tell. No one was emerging from the dark so that gave her some comfort. Attention on the tree again, she reached up and removed a few leaves. They continued to glow in her hand, and she would make sure to maintain a firm grip on them.

She allowed herself a deep breath before her gaze met the fish. Steadily, she walked to the edge of the glimmering water. Odette secured the dagger at the back of her pants and made sure that it wouldn't fall out. Once she was certain of that, she returned the fish's gaze again. "I surrender. Take me back to your master."

In response, the fish moved closer and turned its back to her. Thankfully, it didn't seem to mind that she had a blade or the leaves. Hesitantly, she climbed onto its back. It took off, slowly, and kept her above the surface. Its watery hands pushed the water aside, and ripples dominated the water around them.

Effects of the tree ebbed away. Doubt in her decision crept up on her, but she couldn't back down. She was in control, and she would keep it that way. The guards ahead would be defeated, or she would never return home with Tarhuinn. To her, that wasn't an option. They had worked so hard to get where they were at, and she wouldn't let the authors stand in their way.

Darkness rolled in. She loosened her hold on the leaves a little bit and held up her hand. They illuminated the space some and revealed that no guards were currently in sight. There was a corner up ahead that blocked some of her view, but something seemed odd in the distance. Odette lifted the leaves up more, and the light caused something to glint.

Squinting, she noted that it was the tip of an arrow. More of it revealed itself, and a guard soon came into her field of vision. The arrow was pointed at her right side, and she quickly held up her hands. "I surrendered. I've realized that I can't win; I've accepted my fate."

Lowering the arrow, the guard relaxed. "Hand over the leaves," he ordered when she was right next to him. She gave a simple nod while they moved forward. The guard matched the pace of the fish and held out his left hand to her.

Swiftly, she switched hands so that she could draw her dagger. The guard reacted almost immediately, but she already had the blade swiping across his midsection. A pained gasp left him as he leaned forward. She slashed the blade again but across his neck. He fell forward and into the water behind the fish, but the water was too low in the area for it to wash him away. Odette put the dagger away and snatched the guard's bow and arrows before she lost them.

Surprisingly, the fish had paid no mind to whole encounter. It merely kept going forward; it seemed to only care about getting her to its master and that she had surrendered to it. Apparently, the authors had overlooked that detail, which she was grateful for.

Her brown eyes shot towards the next guard. She hid the blade before the guard made eye contact with her, and she held the leaves behind her back. It appeared as though her hands were bound. The guard caught on quickly, however, since she saw fresh blood on Odette as well as the bow and arrows. The guard called out an alarm, and two more guards rounded another corner.

Pressing her legs more into the sides of the fish, Odette made sure that she wouldn't fall off. She would need complete balance to handle the situation, but that might not even be enough. All three charged, and she aimed. Her aim wouldn't be that great, but her goal was to stun them for a bit. The first arrow flew and struck the one guard square in the chest. A victory smirk painted her lips as the guard collapsed into the water, but she didn't cheer yet; the other two were near to being on top of her.

Shooting another, the next guard dodged and rolled through the water towards her. He rose right next to her as she was about to string another arrow. Hurriedly, she grasped the arrow and slashed at his face. His cry rang out, but she felt the other guard pull on her right arm. She refused to be taken, so she stabbed the arrowhead into that guard's left forearm, but the other guard now secured her other arm. The fish, however, noted that it was losing its catch.

All of a sudden, the fish sprung out of the water. She was thrown off while the guards were pulled down with her. Their grips loosened, and she wrenched her arms free. Odette released her dagger and rolled on top of the one guard. The blade flew downwards and into his chest. He died shortly after while a growl of fury left the other guard.

Before either could attack, the fish swam up under her and started to carry her once more. Her back was to the front of the fish, and she nearly fell off again, but she had managed to grab the bow and an arrow. Aiming, she made the shot. The guard had been too slow to react, and the arrow lodged itself in his head. He fell back, and a loud splash echoed throughout the area.

Throughout the fight, though, she had lost the leaves. Fortunately, they were floating down the water. They didn't move as quickly as the fish, but they allowed a little illumination to exist in the dark tunnel. Hopefully, there would be no more guards.

Chapter Forty Nine: Covered View

Light flowed in from outside. She could see the closed door from before, but she wouldn't stay on the fish long enough to find out whether the fish could open it or not. The other issue was the two guards standing by it. Her dagger had been lost in the previous fight, and she had no arrows left to string. All she had was the bow.

Currently, the guards were having a conversation with each other. It didn't take her long to figure out that they were discussing her fate. They hadn't seen her yet, and if she had arrows, it would've been the perfect moment to strike. She couldn't make up some story about the other guards either. Blood painted her clothes and skin.

There wasn't anything to hide behind; there was only snow, but there was no possibility of surprise if she stayed on the fish. Deciding on a plan, she leaped off of the fish and to her left. Snow puffed up into the air as it surrounded her. She rolled onto her back and quickly pushed snow out of the way to create some distance between the water and her. The fish tried to retrieve her, but she was out of range. Unfortunately, the guards witnessed her action.

They darted towards her. She grabbed a fistful of snow and formed it into a ball swiftly. Odette threw it at the one's face and stunned her for a moment, but the other guard reached for her. Dodging his hands in time, Odette stood to her feet.

Extending out her right foot, she tripped the one and turned back to the other. As the female guard went to grab her, Odette stepped to the side before she stood behind her. With the bow, she placed it around the guard's neck and pulled. The string pressed against her neck, and she was already starting to become weak from being out of the water. She reached up to try and break the string, but she didn't succeed; however, the male guard recovered.

Closing the distance, he grasped Odette's upper arms and tugged her back. She lost her grip on the bow, but she managed to elbow the male guard in the midsection. A gasp escaped his mouth while Odette wrenched her arms free and pushed him down. Odette noted that the other one was about to remove the bow, but she grabbed it once more and tugged towards herself again.

Slowly, the guard on the ground began to get to his feet again, but his balance was poor. He almost fell again while the other could only hold onto the bowstring. The female guard's life soon vanished from her, and Odette pushed the guard away from her. Odette looked back to the other one. The male guard was directly in front of her, but he could barely stand. Before his hands reached her, she kicked him in the midsection.

It appeared as though he was trying to call for help in the process, but his voice was too hoarse. Figuring that he wouldn't be a problem for much longer, she went over to the other one and searched her for anything. Surprisingly, there were no weapons on the female guard. Thankfully, she had avoided the guard's hands.

Peering back at the male guard, she noticed that he stopped breathing. Cautiously, she went over and examined him. Like the other guard, he lacked weapons. Annoyed, she combed her fingers through her hair. A chill took over her, though, as she calmed down from the fighting.

With the day beginning to fade away and becoming colder, she needed to get inside. The tree and the fighting had kept her warm, but she required a fire to dry off. She was soaked, and she didn't want to be shivering when she was freeing Tarhuinn if he hadn't managed to escape already. Finding a fire, though, wouldn't be easy, and it was probably too much of a luxury in her present situation.

She directed her gaze over to the windows. They would lead into that mage's room, but all of the windows were closed once more. Breaking one was out of the question; it would draw too much attention. Odette saw the fish waiting for her by the edge of the water. It would seem that she would have to go through the closed door.

Odette picked up the bow again and readied herself. "You're not going to accept another surrender, are you?" she asked quietly. In response, the fish only continued to reach its arms out towards her. Steadily, she walked towards the door while she kept her eyes on Icniss's minion. If the door was locked, that would create another issue, but she would solve it if it came to that. She wouldn't accept failure.

The cold bit at her skin, reminding her to hurry, but she would only rush once near to the door. Step by step, her heartbeat quickened. She started a countdown in her head. After one, she charged and jumped into the water. Odette grasped the handle and pulled. It opened! Instantly, she closed it behind her as quickly and quietly as she could. Water splashed against the other side, but she was still standing in water.

To her right, there was a land path. Hopping onto it, she walked speedily along it. The fish could grab her easily if it caught up, but she didn't glance behind her. Sadly, though, she couldn't run. Her feet were wet, and slipping would only give the fish more time to reach her.

Up ahead, she saw another door. Water splashed behind her, and it only grew louder. Cursing, she wished that her feet were dry, and she decided to risk moving a little bit faster. When she reached the door, she pulled it back hard and went into the next area. Again, she closed it behind her. Like before, the fish crashed into it.

Before her, there was a large pool, and bath supplies rested on shelves. There was a small room off to her left, and there was a door ahead of her. She traveled on the dry land around the pool and stayed close to the wall. The fish luckily couldn't reach her if she remained pressed up against it, but it matched her pace.

Close to the door, she wanted to shout in frustration. The fish blocked it. She watched its hand movements and timed them. When she thought that she had the pattern down, she moved closer and brought down the bowstring. It severed the fish's hands, and water splashed all around.

That giving her the time that she required, she opened the door and shut it afterwards. To her surprise, she was back in Alpontus's room. It was possible that her daggers remained inside, but the fish would be a problem again soon. The next door, she couldn't charge through either. If she was going to avoid capture, the fish would have to be dealt with.

Thinking on what she could do, her attention turned to the bed. Swiftly, she went over and grabbed the sheets. She returned to the door that led to the bathroom. Already, the fish was forming in the area. Odette stepped back a little and held the sheet out. Once the fish was fully formed, it raced towards her. It hardened itself to grab hold of her.

Using that to her advantage, she draped the sheet over it and wrapped it around the creature. She lifted it up and tied it off. The fish struggled inside, but the soaked blanket was beginning to drip. Odette went back to the bed and secured the other sheets around it before she set the mass on the stone. It would escape eventually, but she had bought herself more time.

Rubbing her hands against her upper arms, she traveled to the next door. Her eyes landed on the dresser, though. She didn't wish to wear Alpontus's attire, but it was dry. If she changed rapidly, it wouldn't delay her too much. Besides, it would keep her warmer.

She opened the drawers and pulled out things that might fit. Getting out of her soaked, outer clothing, she shoved it into the drawer. She changed into some black pants and tied the drawstring at the waist tight. Odette slipped on a long-sleeved, black shirt too. The clothes were quite big for her, so she rolled up the sleeves and pant legs before she headed over to the door.

Odette pressed her right ear to it and listened. No voices sounded on the other side, but she remained cautious. Had they already taken Tarhuinn to that dreadful room? She hoped not, but she would have to advance to find out. Slowly, she opened the door and peeked out into the main space. It was empty.

After she checked the above area also and noted that it was clear, she headed out into the open. She closed the door softly after her and made her way for the upper space. Once up the stairs, she hid in the shadows and overlooked the space once more. Amtoma's room door opened, and the three authors walked out. Icniss made himself known as well, and he was dragging out Tarhuinn by his hair.

His clothes were torn, and long red marks covered his exposed skin. Some were bleeding as they were deeper. Burn marks were on his wrists and ankles. Her hands covered her mouth as a sob threatened to expose her, but she could feel tears at the corners of her eyes. It felt like her heart was being shredded.

Icniss lifted him up and roughly set him down on one of the chairs. The mage held him up against the chair by his hair while Amtoma walked up to Tarhuinn. Odette was tempted to call out and warn her not to go closer. In her shock, though, Odette collapsed to her knees and leaned against the wall for support. She was about to lower her hands, but she held them there when a shout nearly left her lips as the sound of skin impacting skin resonated throughout the area.

Pain raced through his right cheek. Tarhuinn groaned in discomfort, and, steadily, he opened his eyes. As he awoke, he felt how badly the rest of his body hurt. The burns on his wrists and ankles made his skin there far too sensitive for his liking. It was as though he was still being burned by the watery restraints.

He shifted himself a bit to try and be more comfortable, but that only caused the stone chair to rub against his wounds. His breath caught in his throat as he held onto a sharp gasp of pain. A rough tug on his hair caused him to emit it. Behind him, he heard a chuckle. "I'm surprised that you woke up so quickly. I thought that you would've been out for a lot longer given how pathetic you are," Icniss taunted, moving around the chair and releasing his hair.

Tarhuinn's head fell forward from the sudden release. A glare rested upon his face as he looked up to the mage through his disarrayed hair. Before he could respond, his chin was grabbed roughly. He met the ocean blue eyes of Amtoma. There was a small smile on her lips while she dug her sharp nails into his skin. Already, he could feel a warm substance run down his cheek from the slap, and more added itself as she held his gaze.

"Don't listen to the boy. You lasted long enough for a first time, but I do expect you to stay awake longer on our next session. After all, you disturbed me while I was dealing with my disgraceful partner. I can't let you get away with that."

An amused smile fell upon Tarhuinn's lips. "What makes you think that you'll be disturbed only once? You've already failed to capture my wife, and I doubt that you'll catch her. She's not an easy individual to restrain.You're all laughable excuses for a threat. You hide behind your spies and have them do your dirty work. The merfolk are more dangerous than any of you will ever be."

"Why you!" she shouted, gripping his face harder. Red pooled around her fingertips, but Tarhuinn continued to smile while his eyes shone with a bloodthirsty gleam. "How dare you compare us to those creatures! We're better than them, and they bow before us. We're the ones controlling everything in these parts, and you'll learn that I'll be your worst nightmare!"

Plopping himself onto one of the chairs, Rocean crossed his arms over his chest and placed his feet on the table. "You're making me jealous with the way that you're talking to him," he chuckled out, closing his eyes some as though he was about to take a nap.

Dropping her grip on Tarhuinn, she roughly faced her partner. "Now, you know how I feel every day, yet you continue to jest about sleeping around!"

"Byda, you need to get over it. So, I slept with one of Cian's daughters. I don't even remember her name. She could've lived years, with the serum, after Icniss turned two, but I let you kill her on his second birthday. Still, though, you remain so jealous."

"It's because you act so flippant about it! We both know that you would sleep with another human if you were given the chance. Obviously, I need to be rougher with you. I'll ..."

"That's enough you two!" Alpontus slammed his hands on the table. "You can save your arguments for later. We have more important matters to take care of." His eyes turned to Tarhuinn, who leaned back in his chair and scowled to the head author. The author looked back to the arguing lovers, who did quiet down. Amtoma took a seat across from Rocean while Icniss leaned back against a nearby wall.

Relieved, Alpontus seated himself again and pushed his braid from his right shoulder. He rested his right knuckles against his cheek. His left fingers tapped against the tabletop while he looked over Tarhuinn's various injuries. "You'll be tied up for the rest of the day. I want those cuts to heal before we continue with any more punishments. I desire to have you around for a week or two. And once we have your wife, she can listen to some of the sessions. I have other plans for her after all. She'll suffer a treatment as excruciating as that mage inflicted upon our spies."

Tightening his fists, Tarhuinn darkened his gaze considerably. His smile fell while his teeth began to show. "None of you will catch her. If one of you so much..."

"Making threats won't frighten us. You can't stop all of us, and you know that quite well. We're all at equal strength, except for Icniss, who is stronger, and there are four of us. There's only one of you, and we'll have her in our clutches soon. She can't outrun Icniss's minion, nor can she get past all of the guards and spies in this place on her own. She is but a human. Even if she does manage to do the impossible, she'll come to us on her own.

"You're with us, and you'll draw her to us. I doubt that she would abandon you when the two of you seem to have such a tight bond. And, that's why I intend to use that bond to my advantage. It'll bring both of you immense misery," Alpontus remarked casually. He only grew more entertained by the murderous countenance of Tarhuinn.

"If she does come here, it'll be to end all of your lives. You'll be dead before you can execute any of your plans on her, and I'll make sure of that."

"You're really just a foolish boy. You can believe in your wife all you want, but that belief won't make it a reality. She's a human. Enough said." Amtoma examined her nails and wiped the blood from them on her black dress. "Why you let a human girl entrance you so will forever puzzle me." Her eyes darted to Rocean for a moment, and he rolled his eyes before he grinned to himself.

"Like Byda stated, your belief will not change the outcome. She'll suffer and at my hands. My friends have already agreed with me on this since I haven't had a human partner in so long." Immediately, Tarhuinn went to leap out of his chair, but the water restraints held him back. A shrill cry left him as they burned his already damaged skin. He fell back into the chair and had to catch his breath.

Pleased at the scene, Alpontus sat straighter and intertwined his fingers. "I would've paired her with Icniss, but, unfortunately, his mother managed to cast a spell on him before she died. It left him infertile, and the spell could only be reversed by the caster. We hadn't discovered that until she had been already dead." An irritated glance was shot in Rocean's direction. He held up his hands, but it was clear that he felt no guilt on the matter.

Looking back to Tarhuinn, the head author continued. "No matter, I think that taking your only child with her from the both of you will be repayment enough for her bringing the mage to the pixies and for you not abandoning her when you had the chance. Of course, I'll add a few more things to her suffering, but I'll leave those to your imagination. I wouldn't want to spoil everything for you."

Something clicked off in his head. Not a single emotion could be seen on him. Tarhuinn's dark blue eyes appeared void of life; they were like blue abysses. His fingers scraped across the stone chair, and more crimson decorated him. No reaction to the pain displayed itself. The long, ink-black locks upon his head made it seem like he would melt into the shadows.

Witnessing the display, all four captors paused. Even they couldn't act as though it wasn't terrifying. They all held their breath, and the water running down the steps sounded louder than before. Rocean removed his feet from the table, but the action caught the dark blue eyes.

They snapped towards the author, and he remained motionless once more. The two stared for a time that felt like years but was only a few moments. Dark blues moved gradually over to Alpontus. Steadily, lips were pulled back into a smile. Teeth revealed themselves as fingers twitched. Keeping still in his seat, Alpontus spoke softly to Icniss, "Knock him unconscious now."

Those words set him off. The water burned him, but he didn't care anymore. He forced his wrists and ankles free as Icniss shot more water at him; however, Tarhuinn moved faster. Going straight for Alpontus, he jumped onto the table and darted across it. Before any could restrain him, he collided against the head author and toppled to the ground with him.

Teeth sank into the head author's right shoulder, though; they had tried to go for the neck. Tarhuinn pinned the male's wrists to the ground and didn't remove his teeth. Rather, he bit down harder and tried to reach deeper flesh. A loud cry of agony escaped the author's mouth.

Amtoma was the first to reach the pair. As she went to stop Tarhuinn, he ripped back and struck at her. Her right hand became caught in his mouth, and she screamed in response.

Rocean attacked as Icniss's water reached Tarhuinn. The pair managed to knock him unconscious before anymore damage was committed. Collective sighs of relief rang out as Amtoma freed her hand and grumbled, "I'll be taking him to the room first. He needs to be taught a lesson."

Picking himself up, Alpontus agreed along with the other two. "Just keep him alive and be careful. If he wakes up in that state, he could be capable of anything. And, see to your hand first. I need to tend to my shoulder." The head author walked off, and, soon, he closed his room door behind him. A smirk did grace his lips, though, when he saw the sight before him.

Chapter Fifty: Careful Steps

Almost as soon as he closed the door, Alpontus reopened it. Grin painting his lips, he announced, "It would seem that his wife has already made it through my room and past Icniss's minion."

Shock and anger covered Icniss's countenance as he burst out, "What?! That's impossible!" To prove his statement further, the head author stepped aside and revealed the tied up fish on his bed. About a dozen curses left the mage's lips. "Where is she, then?!"

Amtoma was more enraged than the mage. Walking over to the younger kelremm, she lifted her hand, but Rocean held her back. "Byda, calm yourself. I do like this side of you, but this merely means that she'll be coming for her husband. If even one of us stays with him, we'll have her." For once, she didn't retort. Rather, she wrenched her wrist from him and glanced over to Alpontus.

"He's right. We have nothing to worry about. She may have done the impossible so far, but she was dealing with mere spies. We now know that she can handle several of them on her own. I'm not sure how, but all we need to do is give her tougher opponents. We'll be those, and we know that she'll probably try to sneak up on us. If we take that advantage away from her, she won't win against us," the head author spoke, his indigo eyes scanning over the area.

Odette hid herself fully behind the one wall. She calmed herself as best as she could, but he was correct. The authors were no simple kelremm. They had countless years of fighting experience, and Tarhuinn could barely handle Alpontus in one-on-one combat, but her husband's rage might change that as his previous display had demonstrated.

"For now, we'll keep to our plan. We have no need to find her; she'll show herself soon enough." Alpontus turned and headed into his room again. The sound of the door closing hit her ears, and she heard splashes of water. Tarhuinn would soon be under even worse conditions, but if he woke up in that state, he could possibly escape on his own. Odette wished for that to be the case, but she had been frightened by him.

In that moment, he had looked like nothing but a deadly killer. Chills had run up her whole body. She had to remind herself that he was still her husband and that his particular state then had been caused by Alpontus's statement. He had been merely trying to protect her from that awful fate. Just recalling what Alpontus had declared made her sick.

Her hands covered her midsection, and she brought her knees to her chest. "I'm not going to let that happen," she mumbled before she bit her bottom lip to calm her growing nerves.

Carefully, she peeked around the corner. Tarhuinn was still unconscious on the ground while Amtoma was sitting at the table. Icniss was gone, and she had noted hearing a few other doors opening and closing a few moments ago. Rocean was absent from the room as well, but he soon returned with bandages. Amtoma snatched them from him and tended to her wound. He seemed to have no problem with her nonexistent gratitude. Rather, he waited for her to finish before he took the leftovers and headed back into his own room.

Glancing towards Tarhuinn, Amtoma stood up and walked over to him. She kicked him in the side to test his unconscious state. When she was satisfied, she grabbed his hair and began to drag him off. That was enough to spring Odette into action. Odette quietly headed back down the stairs since she couldn't go back the way that Tarhuinn and she had come into the main room. The water passage would be too much of a risk for her.

Once at the bottom, she peered out from behind the wall and watched Amtoma disappear down another passage. As softly as she could, she traversed into the main room and followed after her. She never did look back; she only listened. Keeping the female author in sight was more important; she couldn't lose her in the unfamiliar home.

Luckily, she heard no movement behind her, but she spotted spies ahead of her. The two greeted their master, but Amtoma simply walked past them, not paying them any mind. As the author created distance between the guards and her, Odette noted that the guards started laughing quietly, and they began to place bets on how long Tarhuinn would last.

Fists clenched, Odette reminded herself that she couldn't storm up to them. Instead, she advanced slowly. There was a hallway off to her right, and she took it. Thankfully, there were no spies down it. Already, she was losing the author, but it looked like she would have to find another way to the torture chamber. She could try and take out those guards, but she wished to draw as little attention to herself as possible.

Quietly, she traveled down the hall and took a left turn. Up ahead, she noted a spy. Their back was turned to her, but she didn't how long that would remain the case. Cautiously, she carried on. She did her best to match her steps with the quick moving spy, but her steps would probably be noticed soon. The spy stopped and stretched. Odette slowed her steps immediately, but they gave her away.

Turning, the spy gasped before he leaped into action. That gasp, though, had cost him a blade. Odette had utilized that moment to grab one of his daggers. She collided with the spy and crashed against him into the wall. In the process, the spy's stolen dagger plunged into his chest. The noise from the brief encounter had probably caught someone's attention, though.

Spotting a nearby room, Odette dragged the body and opened the door. It happened to be a storage area. Odette dragged him over to some crates and dumped his body behind them. She grabbed the remaining daggers, went back to the door and peeked out into the hallway. There were no new spies, so she closed the door behind her and continued down the path.

Making another left turn, she immediately took a step back. She pressed herself to the wall and worked on steadying her breathing. Almost, she had walked right into Amtoma, but, thankfully, the author's gaze had been elsewhere. The author neared, and her heartbeat couldn't remain steady. Beads of sweat began to form on her forehead, and her hands gripped the stone wall firmly.

Footsteps stopped too close for comfort before they continued. The sound of another door opening and closing soon hit her ears. Rounding the corner, she took another left and made her way softly to the door. She pressed herself to it and listened. Water splashing and metal moving, her mind started to form dreadful scenarios, but it seemed like Tarhuinn wasn't awake yet. More metal clanged. She took the opportunity and opened the door.

Slipping inside, she closed it quietly afterwards. Amtoma took no notice due to the chains that she was handling. Odette hid behind one of the pillars in the room and scanned over her husband's state. His wrists were bound in metal, and he was hung up. Only his toes were in the water, but his ankles were restricted too. His wounds were still healing, but he would lose probably too much blood if he received any more lacerations any time soon.

Securing the chains that were holding him up, Amtoma walked up to him and tapped her left index finger against her lips. Torchlight flickered off of her sharpened nails as she circled him. Odette remained hidden and reminded herself that Alpontus had given the order to wait until Tarhuinn's cuts were healed. The author's steps halted, and Odette looked out from behind the stone. Amtoma rested her hands on his shoulders.

"I know that I shouldn't injure you right now, but you owe me for the hand wound. I want you to cry in agony and call out to your wife. Bring her here and call her your chosen. Then, you can receive your whole punishment," she spoke, her thumbs just below his eyes. She dug her nails into his skin. "Cry for her and make your misery worse."

About to step out, Odette froze as his eyes snapped open. They locked onto Amtoma, and that frightening grin graced his lips even with his energy evidently depleted. Eyes mirrors of blue voids, he opened his jaws and snapped at her. Immediately, she ripped her hands back and created some distance. She scoffed at his action, but the fear in her eyes was clear. "You d*mned beast. How can you lower yourself into such a state for a mere human girl?"

No answer was given to her. His eyes shifted from her momentarily and, in the process, spotted Odette. She instantly pressed her right index finger to her lips. As if he hadn't seen her, he fixed his gaze to the author once more. Smile widening, an amused appearance took over him. It was as though he was silently laughing at the female kelremm.

"What's so funny?! I'll not have you laugh at me." She went to raise her hand, but she put it back down. He quirked a brow, and her temper only grew. Furious, she rushed over to a table of tools and picked up a pair of pliers. Amtoma hurried back to him and lifted them into the air.

During her inflamed display, she hadn't considered the other splashes of water in the room, nor did she notice the figure now standing by the chain roller. Seeing Odette too late, Amtoma couldn't react in time to her releasing the device's hold on Tarhuinn. Chains plummeted to the water. Tarhuinn's feet landed in the water, and he freed his wrists from the chains.

Amtoma swung the pliers at him, but he knocked them aside; however, he lost balance due to his bound feet, and he fell against the author. Water splashed up around the two. Odette retrieved the pliers and ran over to his feet, but a sudden, massive amount of crimson began to fill the area around the two kelremm.

As the red spread out further, Odette froze for a split moment. Tarhuinn's hair fanned out around them, and Odette couldn't tell who had been injured. Her heart beat quickly, and she regained her focus before she snapped the lock on the chains. Her husband's feet moved, and that steadied her heart a little, but Amtoma's legs did the same. Bubbles rose up to the surface as though one of them was screaming.

Hands shot up from the water and gripped Tarhuinn's arms. They were forced off of him, however, when Tarhuinn started to lift himself up. Odette was tempted to rush forward and help him, but a violent splash of water halted her. She covered her eyes and kept her mouth shut tight.

When she removed her arm, she noted that beads of bloody water dripped down her, but she didn't spend time in wiping them off. Her eyes fixed themselves back on the two kelremm. Tarhuinn didn't even look to her; he simply snatched the pliers from her hand. Amtoma's hands were wrapped around his neck, and they were both sitting up.

The author's eyes widened at the sight of the tool. She released her grip on him, but the tool was already swinging towards her. It impacted her head and sent her flying to Tarhuinn's left. Her sharp nails left scratches along his neck, but they weren't fatal. Amtoma's body twitched, and Tarhuinn got to his feet. He stood over her body and jabbed the pliers into her neck.

Odette took a step forward, but she instantly turned her head away. He ripped the pliers apart. Once the gruesome sound of the action ended, she hesitantly stared over. Amtoma's head bobbed a bit in the water and started to float through it before her head hit the closed the door and stayed there.

Carefully, she advanced towards her husband. Lightly, she rested her hands on his right upper arm. He released the pliers, and they crashed into the water, but he didn't move. Odette peered around him and down. She noted the deep bite marks in Amtoma's left shoulder. It was a surprise that she hadn't died immediately from them, but the author was now dead, and they had one less enemy to worry about.

That relief was short-lived. Tarhuinn faced her and locked his gaze with hers. His eyes continued to display dark-blue voids. He stood to his full height, and she almost stepped back, but she forced herself to keep her ground. She reminded herself that he wouldn't hurt her; she had to trust him. Gently, she raised her hands and rested them on his cheeks. "I'm sorry that I couldn't get to you sooner," she spoke softly as her eyes glanced over his various wounds briefly.

His hands covered hers, and he leaned into her left one. Tarhuinn's gaze began to return to its normal state while his lips took on a caring smile. "You have nothing to be sorry about. You performed splendidly, and I have you back with me. That's what matters." He moved his head away but kept his hold on her hands while he looked her over. "Where did you get those clothes, though?"

"I think that's the least of our concerns, but I stole them from Alpontus. I was cold and wet; these were dry. I'll get better clothes when we have the chance."

"Yes, you will. Those clothes aren't fitting for you, but you're right. We have the other authors to worry about." He dropped her hands and gathered Amtoma. Tarhuinn tied her wrists to the chains before he undid the bun in her hair. Long locks draped down, and he used them to secure her head to her left arm. Odette only glanced to the scene a few times, but she couldn't observe the sight for long.

Tarhuinn hoisted her up high into the room. After he secured the chain roller, he headed over to the tools' table. "We'll leave her there until we kill the others. We'll come back and retrieve her afterwards."

Picking up some knives and one of the belts, he added the items to his person. "Tarhuinn, I know that we can't sit around forever, but shouldn't you let your wounds heal for a little bit longer? Some of those aren't small cuts. Alpontus mentioned that you wouldn't be tortured until they were healed, so we should have some time to wait in here."

"Then, you heard what he plans to do to you if he captures you? You were there for all of it?"

"Y-yes," she stuttered, hearing the slight growl in his voice. She wouldn't change her mind on the suggestion, though. "But, that's why we should stay in here for a little while. You need to heal, and I can't battle them all on my own. I somehow made it here by myself, but I was lucky. I don't know how far that luck will extend out. I'd rather not test it anymore than I have to."

He gave the belt a tug, and it was fastened. Facing her, he leaned back against the table. His hands squeezed the tabletop, and she could hear the stone crack some. "As much as I wish to break them all now, you're right. If I receive too many more wounds like these, I won't survive, and I can't have them taking you." More stone broke, and small pieces fell off into the water. "Just the thought of that author ..." No more words came out, but rage dominated his expression.

She walked over to him and rested her hands on his shoulders. "I'm right here with you. Like you mentioned, that's what matters. You shouldn't think of him taking our future child away from us because it won't happen. I'll never let that monster touch me." Her eyes peered over to the door before she looked back to him. "Let's seal the door and rest. We both need it after everything that we've been through today. I only wish that we had better accommodations."

A light chuckle left his lips. He walked over to the door and placed one of the tables in front of it before he locked it too. "Yes, I suppose so, but we're probably the safest that we can be. I'm assuming that the other authors expect Amtoma to be in here for awhile. And, I don't think that any of the spies will disturb her session."

"I suppose that's true, and we have an arsenal of weapons should someone try coming in." Looking to her once more, he nodded in agreement, closed the distance between them and took her right hand in his left. She allowed him to guide her away from the body and towards the far, right-side of the room.

There, a small waterfall flowed downwards from a high opening in the wall. Odette moved herself over to one of the torches in the area to warm herself some. She seated herself on a small space of dry stone and rolled up the pant legs that had fallen. Cold, she rubbed her upper arms. Her gaze fell back on her husband, only for her to look the other way.

Heat touched her cheeks lightly, but her embarrassment was met by something soft hitting her head. Taking it off of her head, she found a clean, wet towel in her hands. Confused, she almost peered over to him again but, immediately, recalled his current state. "There's a stack of them over here. They must use this area to clean the tools if they need to do so."

"That would make sense, though; it makes me wonder how disgusting the water in here could become at times." She heard a hum of agreement before she looked over herself and her stained pant legs. Odette unsheathed a dagger and, instantly, cut off the ruined fabric. It would only serve to trip her later on, and she'd rather not walk around with Amtoma's blood on her.

Once finished, she tossed the fabric aside. She removed some fabric from her sleeves also. They were much too long and would only hinder her in combat. Completed with that, she worked on wiping the blood from her. "You're welcome to join me, Odette. I'm sure that I can keep us warm."

Heat rushed to her cheeks again. "I'll be fine over here. And, you should know that this isn't the time or place for that," she remarked, grumbling towards the end. The fact that he was teasing her when there was a hanging body in the room was somewhat disorienting. "How you can go from being utterly frightening to being like this in a matter of minutes will forever puzzle me."

"We're resting now. That's why. Regardless of what's surrounding us, we need to enjoy this small break. We might not get another for awhile, Odette." She heard splashes of water before her chin was lifted. Flames danced in her cheeks as she swiftly made eye contact. His eyes displayed a troubled expression. "Did I terrify you that much?"

"Y-y-yes." She couldn't help but stutter. Constantly, she had to remind herself not to glance down. Odette forced her chin away and turned her back to him. It wasn't to be rude, but she couldn't answer him seriously given his current state of dress.

Bringing her knees to her chest, she placed the towel to the left side of her. "When I saw you like that, I reminded myself that you were still Tarhuinn; you were still my husband, but ... I thought that for a moment I might lose you. I thought that your anger would forever consume you and that I wouldn't get to interact with you like this again. You truly appeared as though you were only meant for killing."

Hands squeezed her shoulders. "I apologize. I only ..."

"You only did it to save me from Alpontus's plans," she answered, cutting him off. A small smile returned to her lips. "And, I appreciate that." She moved her hands up to his and intertwined her fingers with his. "You may have scared me, but you did the same to them. After witnessing them like that, I understand that we can overcome them. We've already dealt with one, and we can finish the others."

Odette turned around and wrapped her arms around his neck. She closed her eyes and leaned her forehead against his chest. Her fingertips glided over some of the cuts on his back, so she made sure to be careful. "I trust that we'll make it out of here and return home, but even if that doesn't happen, I won't let them separate me from you again; I won't let you separate me from you. We're in this together."

Arms wrapping around her, he held her to him. A kiss was placed on top of her head while a gentle laugh escaped his lips. The sound soothed her and reminded her of a pleasant rain on a warm day. "You're starting to sound a little like me, Odette. Perhaps, you'll be the next one to frighten them, though; you're up against some tough competition."

Returning a laugh, she drew back and peered up to his dark blue orbs. "Well, they should know not to mess with the wife of an overprotective husband like you. I'm starting to learn some of your tricks after all." She winked before she placed a light kiss on his left cheek.

"It would seem so since you're learning to enjoy this break like me." She rolled her eyes and pushed against his chest. Her eyes directed themselves to her right. He closed the distance again, though, and whispered, "And, it would seem that I solved your problem of being cold." A kiss was placed on her left cheek, and he pulled back before she could react.

Despite him being back by the waterfall, she splashed a handful of water in his direction. Her cheeks were on fire, and she threw the towel at him. "I need a new one," she remarked roughly as her arms crossed over her chest. A small smile painted her lips, however, and Tarhuinn noted it. He was just happy to see her smile even in such a dreadful place.

Chapter Fifty One: Caught

Bang! Bang! Startled, Odette jolted from her sleep. She didn't go flying off into the water due to Tarhuinn's secure grip around her waist. They had both finished cleaning themselves up and had decided to rest their eyes for a short time, but it seemed that their sleep would be cut short. Tarhuinn's dark blues snapped open, and, instantly, he became alerted.

They stared to the door and quietly stood to their feet. "Byda, are you really going to stay in there until the kelremm heals completely?! I know that you're furious about your hand, but why don't you come join me? You're probably only glaring at him right now, and you could be doing something so much better with your time." The two remained as silent as they could since one wrong move would sound an alarm.

There was a pause in Rocean's persistence. Perhaps, he had given up, but they couldn't hear any movement from his end either, and they couldn't remain still forever. If they allowed him in, they would be able to corner him. She glanced up to Tarhuinn, and his gaze stayed on the door. Maybe, he had a similar idea. He needed to be careful, though, because of his wounds.

A loud laugh reached their ears. "Don't tell me that you ignored Phyon's directives?" Again, they allowed no words past their lips. "You did, didn't you?! Now, you have to let me in!" The lock kept him out, and his laugh grew in volume. "Are you torturing him, right now? If so, I could always tell Phyon; I'm sure that he wouldn't appreciate your behavior."

Leaning down, Tarhuinn whispered, "Hide." His arm slipped from around her waist before he created loud steps toward the door. She complied and made herself scarce from sight. Tarhuinn pushed the table aside and unlocked the door. Slowly, he pulled back and remained behind the door. Rocean stepped in and examined the area.

Confused, he paused. "Byda ..." His sky-blue eyes spotted the drops of blood coming from the ceiling. Hesitantly, he stepped forward some more and gazed upwards. From her hiding spot, Odette saw the blood drain from his face. "Wh-what? N-no ... m-my lo-love." He backed up in disbelief as the door slammed shut behind him, and the lock clicked once more.

"I'm surprised. You're acting as if you actually cared for her deeply." Tarhuinn leaned back against the door, and he nearly appeared amused. Swiftly spinning, Rocean's shocked expression morphed into one of hatred, rage and possibly elation.

"You managed to escape from her? I'm surprised. Byda lets no one go once she's in such a fired up mood." His lips curled up into a grin. "Don't tell me that your little wife is in here also? Then again, she couldn't inflict a miniscule cut on Byda. No matter, I'll take up Byda's task and make sure that you suffer in here for a long time." Deftly, he reached down and pulled out two daggers, one each from around his calves.

Unimpressed, Tarhuinn pushed himself off of the door. He appeared nonchalant in the whole affair. That didn't last very long, however. "You disgust me." Unsheathing a knife, he twirled it between his right fingers and held it in a hammer grip. "You act as if you're honoring that female kelremm by your plans to torture me. You're doing no such thing. You're too late to honor her. You made it that way by your constant desire to bed others."

Coming closer, Rocean chuckled and shook his head. "You're criticizing me because I wasn't overprotective of my partner? That I wasn't faithful to her? Please," he shrugged and smirked, "I'm just a kelremm who likes a little variety. Nothing wrong with that."

"And, to think that you're one of the individuals who helped to write the history and principles of the kelremm population. Disgraceful."

"I'd have to disagree." He charged forward. "You're the disgrace in thinking that you can tear my lifestyle from me all so that you can keep your human for longer." Blades clashed, and dark blues narrowed as a snarl escaped Tarhuinn.

“She’s not my human; she’s my wife.” He spun on his heel and moved behind Rocean. His knife changed into an edge-in position, and it swung down upon his target. The knife scraped the author’s right shoulder, but he had reacted in time to avoid a more serious blow. Tarhuinn dropped the knife before it could come back and strike him. Quickly, he caught it and maneuvered it into a modified saber. Slashing, the blade struck Rocean’s, and they continued in the fast-paced struggle.

Odette stayed behind the pillar and inspected the fight from there. She would only come out if things were looking poor for her husband. Right now, she would only get in the way; she could barely keep up with the movements, but she could tell that Rocean wasn’t as skilled a fighter as Alpontus. That tilted things in favor of Tarhuinn.

Already, she noted that Rocean was having difficulty keeping up. His growing irritation wasn’t aiding him either. It was beginning to control him, not the other way around; however, Tarhuinn’s injuries were starting to affect him. They had healed some more over their brief rest, but they required more time. If the fight didn’t end soon, Tarhuinn would end up on the defensive only.

Her hands slid down to her daggers. She would be prepared to strike if she was required to do so. Clips unlatched, her hands gripped the handles. A dagger went flying from Rocean’s left hand as he made a miscalculation. Crimson decorated the air before drops collided with the water and surroundings. A scream would’ve been emitted if it weren’t for Tarhuinn kneeing the male in the midsection. He went for the final blow, but Rocean’s remaining hand blocked it.

The author’s jaw was clenched, and he was out of breath, but he kept the blade up regardless. His left foot kicked out, and Tarhuinn nearly dodged. Balance lost, Tarhuinn fell backwards as Rocean threw himself against the taller male. Both impacted a nearby pillar while the knife fell from Tarhuinn’s hand. Rocean made the move to stab his opponent in the neck.

Deciding it time to act, Odette ran out from behind the pillar. Her pace wasn't too quick due to the water, but it was fast enough for her to slip. Eyes widened as she cursed loudly in her head, but her fall had created the needed distraction. Rocean looked behind him slightly, and a grin painted his lips, but his other dagger was lost in the process. Before Tarhuinn could do anymore damage and unsheathe another knife, the author kneed him in the groin and used the male's weakened state to throw him aside.

Rocean hurried over to Odette and snatched up one of her daggers. The other was kicked aside, and her back was pressed to his chest. Holding his knife to her, a larger smile plastered itself on the author's lips. "So, you were in here. How splendid, but you should've hid for longer, human. I wonder what will be added to your punishment once Phyon learns that Byda is dead."

Tarhuinn picked himself up, and a knife was in his right hand once more. "You still intend to attack me?" Rocean questioned, chuckling a bit. He pressed the knife more into her neck, and a bead of blood formed at the tip. "I'd be careful where you aim that knife. My dagger might just slip across her delicate skin." Her fingers dug into his arm, but the author didn't flinch. Rather, he seemed to be enjoying it.

Lips coming down to her right ear and ghosting her helix, he remarked casually, "I wonder if Phyon ..." His words never came to a finish. All she heard was the sound of metal zipping through the air. She could see a knife handle out of the corners of her eyes.

"Never take a hostage that you can't kill," Tarhuinn commented as the author's grip on her disappeared. The blade fell down, but she caught it in time before it could commit any more damage to her. She gave a grateful smile to him and had no desire to look behind her. "I'm sick of these authors disrespecting you. They should learn to keep silent." His tone reminded her of hot water burning skin. There was no pleasant quality about it; every single, harsh note was highlighted.

He walked past her and retrieved the knife. The blade was cleaned in the water before it was sheathed again. "He'll be hung next to his partner." Tarhuinn gripped the back of the author's shirt and proceeded to drag the body through the water. "In death, he can remain loyal to her."

No comment left her lips; she was merely relieved that another author was gone from their lives and that they were still breathing. Their main difficulty would be the last two in the area. The mage could be caught off guard, but once they revealed their presence, they could be snuffed out easily by him.

Chains rattled, and she leaned back against a nearby pillar. She sheathed her weapons and held her arms across her stomach. The pang of hunger was starting to get to her. They had been fighting ever since they had entered, and their food was gone. All of their possessions had been lost, and Tarhuinn's pack, wherever it was, had been most likely emptied before the items had been discarded. "Hold on a little longer, Odette." He must've heard her stomach growl.

She would've been embarrassed had she not been so exhausted from everything, but her mind turned back to that storage area. They could head there on the way back to the authors' main room. Tarhuinn was probably hungry too. Peering over to him, she disclosed, "I know a place."

Chapter Fifty Two: Going to the Main

They checked carefully before they left the torture room behind. No spies, author or mage were in the nearby halls. Carefully, they traveled to the storage room, but they examined every path before going down or crossing it. Fortunately, the room wasn't too far. Odette only hoped that there was food in the crates.

Coming up to the room, Tarhuinn cracked open the door slightly and peeked inside. He closed it silently afterwards. Two of his fingers were held up. She listened closely and heard two quiet voices on the other side of the door. "Could you see what they were doing?" she whispered as she backed away from the door a little bit.

"They're only talking."

"Well, we need to deal with them quickly. There's a dead kelremm hidden in there."

"You're becoming quite the fighter, Odette. I'm impressed."

She couldn't help but smile some. "Looks like I didn't need your training after all," she remarked, her smile forming into a smirk.

"We'll see about that later." She wondered if that meant that he would teach her how to fight even better when they returned home. Or, was there some other message behind his words? Odette pushed the thought aside as Tarhuinn reached out his hand. His fingers went to grab the handle, but it was pulled back from him. They both stood face to face with two spies.

Immediately, weapons were unsheathed, and metal clashed. She could barely hold against the one spy since his strength outnumbered her own. His short sword neared her neck, and, in turn, it was pushing her own dagger towards her throat. Tarhuinn, noting that, managed to trip the other spy and slash the spy's neck in the process.

Realizing that his partner had been killed, the second spy kicked Odette back. Her breath got caught in her throat, and the spy faced her husband. The spy had been too slow, though, and Tarhuinn wasted no time in defeating the male, but he didn't give him a slow death either. She looked away as metal met the spy's midsection, and she covered her ears to dull the sounds of the grisly death. His cries of anguish were muffled most likely by Tarhuinn covering his mouth, but she didn't peer over to check.

A loud splash signaled that it was over. She uncovered her ears and faced Tarhuinn again. Refusing to look down, she moved the first spy and ignored the second. He dragged the other one into the room, and they stored them behind the crates like the other one. "Someone might notice the blood flowing out of here," she commented, quite worried at an alarm being sounded.

"Yes, we don't have much time to eat something." With that in mind, they washed their hands of the blood by using a nearby, small waterfall in the room. Once done, they began to open the crates. Some stored daggers and knifes while other contained spare linens and bath supplies. Beneficially, there were also crates with food.

Partaking of some dried fish and fresh fruit, they hurried along so that they could get to better ground. Someone could easily walk in on them and alert another before they could stop them. Amtoma and Rocean were no longer issues, but the mage could subdue them in a heartbeat. They would be wrapped in water bonds and would have to face a terrible fate if they couldn't escape again, and Odette had no desire in visiting Alpontus's room again unless it was to end him.

Finished with eating, they left the room as quietly and carefully as they had exited the torture room. Tarhuinn shut the door behind them and had to follow behind Odette as she knew the way through that part of the tunnels. That wasn't to say that he didn't walk right on her tail. He nearly stepped on her several times, but he wouldn't let her go too far ahead. Any distance between them could be begging the enemy for more to be created.

Before they made the last turn, Odette looked to see if the two guards from before were still there. They were. Tarhuinn and she could try moving along the wall, but the guards probably would spot them since they weren't chatting with each other nor did they have a distraction. As she thought about what to do, she didn't notice that Tarhuinn had already headed out into their line of sight. Odette couldn't do anything; he took off and dealt with them swiftly. Her eyes weren't able to keep up with Tarhuinn's fast strikes. The other two had no chance against him, and they were killed moments later.

It was near frightening how efficient he was when attacking. The authors should've trained better spies, but the authors' arrogance in their abilities was serving to aid Tarhuinn and her. Their past mistakes couldn't be fixed now. Two had already paid the price, and three more would follow.

Going into the hallway, she stepped beside him, and they reached the entrance to the main room shortly after. There was no one in the space, but they could spot spies back in the high section of the area. Both of them hid behind some rocks jutting out from the wall. "Should we come back in the other way and take them out like the previous ones?" she questioned in a hushed voice.

"We might ..."

"Or, you might want to check your surroundings better." Both of them spun around, only to be ripped back from their hiding spots. They were thrown into the main room. Odette slid through the water, and the same happened to Tarhuinn. Water splashed all around, and a door could be heard opening behind them. "I'm curious how you, kelremm, managed to escape Byda. And, what about my father? He was going to check up on her. Then, there's the human. How did you get past those guards and trap my minion?"

Coughing up water, Odette went to pick herself up, but water forced her back down. Her head was above it, but she was pinned. She glanced Tarhuinn's way to find him in a similar condition. "Do explain these things to me; I want to know." His tone was commanding and growing lower. It was clear that he was becoming furious.

"They can tell us both, Icniss, but it might be faster for you to go to the torture room. Please restrain them to two of the chairs first. I'd like to have a small chat with them while you go there." A grumble escaped him, but he did as asked. Roughly, the mage lifted them out of the water, removed their weapons and placed them each on a chair. Water wrapped around their wrists and ankles before the mage stormed off back down the hallway.

Alpontus took a seat at the head of the table. His indigo eyes glanced between them, and a smirk formed on his lips. He intertwined his fingers before he leaned back in his seat. "I must say that I'm astounded by your ability to reach your husband, human. It simply was unexpected, but I do wonder if you were here when I told your husband of my plans for you. Were you?"

Noting the expression of hate and disgust on her countenance, he nodded. "So, you were. Good, that saves me the time of explaining myself again." He chuckled in amusement. "And, you seem to be acclimating to your fate already. I do wish, though, that you hadn't ruined my clothes, but they do look nice on you. Of course, after today, you won't be getting to wear my clothes again until I feel like you've earned the right to do so. No, I have much better attire in store for you."

Odette struggled in her seat, and a sharp cry was heard. The water burned her skin, but her scream caused Tarhuinn to completely lose it. He had already been fading back into that pure-killer state of his during Alpontus's words. Now, he wore a murderous grin. "You'll not lay a hand on her, but I'll lay a hand on you!" he laughed out. Immediately, he went to wrench himself free, but a deafening screech was the result.

"Tarhuinn!" She forgot about the water's effects and went to run over to him, but a shriek exited from her.

Entertained, Alpontus shook his head. "Do you really think that Icniss wouldn't make the bonds stronger after your last display? I won't have you biting into my shoulder again." His gaze directed itself over to her, and a heavy glare set on her face. "You, on the other hand ..."

"I'd rather bite off your tongue!" she yelled, cutting him off.

"That would imply that you would have to kiss me. Whether I should give you that luxury or not is another matter. This is a punishment for you after all, but I do wish for it to be pleasurable for me in more ways than one. As you know, you'll be my first partner in quite some time. Why ..." Again, he was cut off but by Icniss.

"They murdered them! They're hanging by the chains, dead!"

His hands spread out over the armrests of the chair, and his indigo eyes stared at the mage kelremm. Stone broke under Alpontus's fingertips, and he slowly rose from his seat. Icniss appeared as though he might rip off the heads of Tarhuinn and her, but Odette didn't care. What mattered was that they had two less authors to concern themselves with. "Take a seat, Icniss. They'll be punished properly for this crime, and you can administer it to her husband. I'm sure that you can keep him better secured."

Reluctantly, the mage did so, and a sickening grin spread over his lips as he met Tarhuinn's gaze. To spite him, Tarhuinn looked away and rolled his eyes. Immediately, water slammed against the side of his face and forced him to stare at the mage. "You'll learn to respect me. You killed my father, and I intend to make you suffer for it."

"You shouldn't make promises that you can't keep." Another wave of water met him, and Odette was tempted to signal Tarhuinn to stop antagonizing him, but she found that she couldn't. Tarhuinn was right in not showing the mage any form of respect; he didn't deserve it, nor was he worthy of an apology.

"Icniss, enough," Alpontus ordered, starting to walk towards her. "You'll have plenty of time later." She visibly tensed in her seat, and Tarhuinn's eyes followed his every move. A smirk rested on Icniss's lips. The head author's hands rested on her shoulders, and low growl could be heard from her husband. "Did I ever tell you why the rest of the kelremm population began the tradition of killing themselves after their first partner? Not only was it having to go through the suffering of losing a loved one but also it was because their children were being killed off too. Everything from their previous partners was wiped out from existence."

Squeezing her shoulders some, he lowered his lips to her left ear. "I intend to do the same to you. You'll experience years of suffering by means of using the tree's life-giving ability."

"And, just how were their children killed off? Were you behind that? It wouldn't surprise me if you committed such an atrocity," she barked back, spitting on his face in the process.

A look of disgust swept across his countenance, and he wiped it off using the back of his right hand. Skin collided with skin, and she knew that a bruise would form on her left cheek. Tarhuinn tried to get out of his chair, but water slammed him back down completely. "You're lucky that I know how to restrain myself. Otherwise, you would've lost a few teeth, human, but I need to keep you pleasing to the eye."

Moving away from her, he leaned back against the table to her left. He deliberately kept his back to Tarhuinn as a way to demonstrate that he wasn't important for the moment. "I didn't kill them. Some of those were my own grandchildren. My children were spared by the graces of Cian, our lovely father if you will." His sarcastic tone said otherwise. "All of my children but one, however, killed themselves later or went off with the rest of the kelremm when the policy had ended and are dead now."

"And, just what was this policy?" she asked, not that she cared. It was more to buy time for them. She was in no rush to be tortured, nor did she desire to have Tarhuinn in that room again.

"The wizard, Cian, had made a long-term agreement with a nearby kingdom. They would provide him with resources, and he would create them a weapon for battle. The kingdom happens to have shores on all sides of it but one, but on that side there are massive mountains that an enemy would have to traverse, and the passages aren't large enough for an army to cross efficiently. Most of an army would die as well from the cold weather of those peaks. Naturally, it makes more sense to attack from the sea, then.

"As you've seen, kelremm are quite the fighters and perfect for shoreline battles. So once we were created, he had raised us and, at the age of eighteen, he had started to have us breed. That's when he had discovered that kelremm could only produce a child with a human and that human life energy was needed to keep the child healthy and alive. Despite us being part human ourselves, it hadn't been enough, and that remains the same today.

"We had children with our human partners, and the humans would pass on. Our children had done the same, and their children had been used as the first fighters for that kingdom. They had performed marvelously in battle, but the kingdom had demanded more and more. That's when kelremm had begun to grow weary and furious. We only had children so that they could be killed in battle eventually.

"Even Cian had noticed the ill treatment of us, his creations, and he had put a stop to it. He had cut off his agreement with the kingdom, but they hadn't accepted that. They had refused to give back the still living kelremm. So, he had taken the five of us to the kingdom, and we had devastated them before we had guided the other kelremm back to this place. Frankly, his late response, though, left a tear in his relationship with us. It also had left a separation in the kelremm."

Pushing himself off of the table, he glanced back to Tarhuinn. "He's one of the results of the other side. Most of the returning kelremm had wished to have only one human partner and end their life afterwards to save themselves from the pain of loss. This group had happened to be a majority of the kelremm at the time, so the five of us hadn't been able to stop them. We had looked to Cian, but he instead had offered to help them build a new home in the mountains while the rest of us had stayed here.

"We had found it much more beneficial to us to end having relationships with human partners or if we did have one not to treat it as serious. They were to be used if we needed more kelremm to watch the other group. This way, there wouldn't be any unneeded heartbreak. It's still terrible to lose a human partner, but you find yourself growing numb after so many."

"Your treatment of humans is deplorable. No wonder Cian didn't support you," she commented, her voice harsh and strong.

"It had been his mistake. He had left his angered children behind, and we had formed our vast spy network in his absence. We had studied his research, we had found the tree that he had thought that he had hid so well, and we had captivated his daughters. When he had returned after several years, we had paid him his dues.

"His daughters had helped us to kill him, but they were more true to their father than us; they had wished him a quick end. We had promised him a swift death if they had agreed to give us two mages. The bargain had been struck, and we had executed our plan. Cian's body had been disposed of, and two years later his daughters had joined him."

Head falling forward, Odette couldn't believe what she was hearing. If the authors had been dreadful before, they were now the definition of despicable and cruel beings. Their hatred consumed them to a point beyond the edge of reason. "You make me sick. You killed those who helped you also."

"They were only humans. They're only good for children and, maybe, some entertainment; they're worthless otherwise. Besides, his daughters had supported our views. They had been willing to be brainwashed into our ideas even though they had been contradictory to their own well being. It's not our fault that they had been foolish."

"Maybe, but it had been your fault for killing them. You still had murdered those who had trusted you. You had broken their trust, like Cian had broken yours."

Laughing, Alpontus closed the distance between them and rested his hands on her left arm. "You compare us to him? That's childish. He could've prevented so much death if he had distributed the energy from the tree beforehand, but he had kept it to himself and had allowed many to die. Then, he had acted as though he had cared for all kelremm."

"Why, you just showed that you're similar to him," Tarhuinn chuckled out. Water slammed against him, but he kept laughing. "Apparently, your hatred also made you the fool." Narrowing his eyes, Alpontus made to stride over to him.

"He's right. All this time, you have kept the serum to yourselves; it sounds like you haven't even given it to your spies. You've allowed countless kelremm to die with their partners over the years, rather than give a small dose to each kelremm family to allow them even a few more years of life with their partner. Not only this but also you kill any suspecting kelremm or human that tries to search for you, and you've committed a whole complex to absolute fear of your presence.

"If anyone's worthless, you are," she declared, looking to both Alpontus and Icniss. "You're deliberately demeaning and snuffing out life. If you support such polices, commit them upon yourselves; you have no right to force them upon others."

Alpontus shared a look with Icniss, and a scream left her. Her ankles and wrists burned, and she could feel tears prick at the corners of her eyes. Tarhuinn nearly wrenched one of his wrists free, but Icniss strengthened the bond. "And, you'll learn your place, human," the head author ordered.

"I know my place, and it's not as your breeding stock!"

"Knowing isn't understanding. Knowing is merely thinking or believing, but you don't comprehend your situation. I could care less about your beliefs, human. What matters to me is that you pay for your crimes against us."

"The only crime that's been committed is that we haven't killed you yet," Tarhuinn remarked snidely. His head was thrown back against the chair with more water, and a grunt of pain left her husband's lips. Her fists tightened, and she only wished to get out of the blasted chair so that she could set him free and deal fatal blows to their captors.

"Surprisingly, I'd have to agree with you." Everyone in the room fell silent. She recognized that voice, and fear gripped at her. Nausea formed in the pit of her stomach. Her legs moved closer together, but the restraints kept them apart some still. Blood drained from her face, and she desired to dart from the room with Tarhuinn. Perhaps, she was losing her mind due to everything that had happened in the authors' home, but she was too terrified to confirm that.

Alpontus quickly unsheathed a dagger from his left thigh, but Icniss motioned for him to stop. "He's a mage," Icniss warned, getting out of his chair and standing to face him. That fact only made things worse for Odette. It had to be him. Slowly, she turned her head to her right. She tried to scoot back into her chair more as if that would hide her from his view, but Will's green orbs met her own brown ones. A grin covered his lips as his hands rested on his hips.

Tarhuinn struggled more with his bonds, but Icniss kept them strong. A growl left him, and he was beginning to get more agitated. The head author understood that the human mage was the one that had killed his spies, but he was confused about the human girl's reaction. "I thought that you had convinced him to aid the pixies?"

"Oh, she did by promising me the serum of eternal life. I take it that you two have it. I couldn't get a confirmed answer from that other mage kelremm and the other two, but I did manage to get some directions to this place. I didn't think that I would have to go so far, though, to get such details. That female mage certainly was an unexpected treat." Will licked his lips and stepped forward, but water wrapped around him. Both Alpontus and Icniss were enraged, but Alpontus kept his distance.

With a flick of his right wrist, the water was sent flying outwards. "Please, don't underestimate me. Bluebell already made that mistake, but she's paying me back nicely for it. So if you won't mind, I'll be taking my serum and her. Her husband can be killed for all I care."

Not being able to maintain her gaze with him, she broke it and glanced to her husband. Her horror was clear to spot, and Tarhuinn returned a reassuring, small smile. His eyes were still filled with the intent to brutally kill the three other men in the room, but concern for her was there too. If they were lucky, the three might kill each other, and they could go free.

Laughing, Alpontus shook his head. “I’ll be holding onto her, and you’re going to be killed. You owe us your life for what you did to our spies, our friends and my daughter. I intend to make you suffer just like this girl here.”

Crossing his arms over his chest, Will glanced between Alpontus and Icniss skeptically. He raised an eyebrow in amusement. “I don’t think that you understand who you’re dealing with here. And, which one was your daughter, the mage or the other female?”

Walking around her chair, Alpontus stepped up closer to the mage. Icniss eyed Phyon out of the corners of his eyes. “That doesn’t concern you. I’ll have you screaming to the point where you can’t even ask questions.”

“Wow,” Will whistled out. “Now, you’re acting like the overprotective and jealous husband over there.” Neither the head author or Tarhuinn were amused, but Tarhuinn said nothing back. He was using the distraction to his benefit and trying to work his way steadily out of the restraints. Odette decided to follow his example but more slowly. Will still had his eyes somewhat on her after all, or, at least, she assumed that he did. “So, it was the mage, then?”

Without thought, Alpontus squeezed his dagger a little bit more. “Ah, so it was. I can tell you the details of what she went through.” Water grasped his ankles and pulled Will onto his back. A loud splash sounded, and the male was covered in water soon after.

“Phyon, let me deal with him until he’s knocked out. You can torture him later. You’re stepping right into his trap. Deal with the human girl, and I’ll take care of him. Otherwise, we might lose all three of them.”

Relaxing, Alpontus agreed. “You’re right. Thank you, Icniss.” He sheathed his dagger and faced Odette once more. Instantly, she stopped her wrists’ movement. Her countenance morphed back into one of pure hate, and she dropped any evidence of fear despite the fact that the head author had noticed her frightened expression beforehand. In her mind, Will would always be more terrifying than Alpontus.

“You’re coming with me. We’ll begin our business in my room now.” He grabbed the back of her shirt and lifted her out of the seat. The water bonds detached from the chair and surrounded her skin completely. Tarhuinn halted his efforts to get free until Alpontus passed with her. Staring back to him, she noticed that he continued subtlety. She told herself that she could stall long enough for Tarhuinn to get to her and help.

Presently, she tried to drag her feet across the floor, but Alpontus tore her from the ground and into his arms. “Your efforts are useless. You’re only hurting yourself more.”

“I’ll be injuring myself when I stop fighting you, you disgusting fish!” The insult did cause him to pause. His indigo eyes met hers, and she could hear water crashing and being thrown around in the background. He dropped her, but before she hit the ground, he grasped her again, though; her view was of the ground.

His knee came up and impacted her midsection. Her breath caught in her throat, and she tasted blood. A few droplets mixed into the water at their feet. Tarhuinn made no noise, but she knew not to bring that up. She had to handle the situation on her own for now, and she didn’t even want to consider what was occurring between Will and Icniss. If both of them didn’t die in the fight, one of them would quickly become a problem again.

Alpontus continued to carry her in the same position until he opened his room door and took her inside. Despite her hurting midsection, she continued to struggle, and she even managed to grab the dagger on his thigh. His knee met her again, though, for it. More crimson spilled out of her mouth, and she thought for a moment that her internals would be forever damaged due to the pain.

They neared the bed, and she noted that the fish minion was no longer present. His bed was soaked, however, and only made it more undesirable. To her shock and relief, he walked right past the bed, but she had a feeling that things would still be horrible. The man had promised her horrendous suffering, but the moment that he let her go, she would act. Right now, she would just be kneed again.

He opened the next door and stepped into the bathroom. Alpontus shut the door behind them and spun her over in his arms. She only saw him for a split moment before she was dropped into the pool of water. Cold enveloped her, and she quickly swam back up to the surface. Her hair was grasped, and she was lifted out of the water. A cry of pain shot through her as it felt like he ripped her hair from her head.

The position didn't last long as she was tossed to the side. Stone scraped her skin and reopened some of her previous wounds. Her whole body ached, and her plan to act was slowly fading. She did have distance between them, though. Picking herself up, she grabbed a nearby bottle of washing soap and broke it against the wall. Glass spread over the floor while she held onto the weapon firmly.

"You're going to try and attack me?" He closed some of the distance between them but remained in the water, and he stared at her like she was a mere child holding a wooden sword. "You wish for me to humiliate you more, then? I suppose that today will be a very harsh lesson for you."

Standing up straighter, she smirked. "Are you sure that the lesson won't be for you? You're the only author left, and your underestimation of your enemies has bitten you more than once recently. I think that you should be the one to learn." She kept her stance and remained in position. He would come to her, and she would strike him. Her feet were bare, and she didn't need pieces of glass stuck in them.

Despite her reply, though, she couldn't help but shiver. She needed warmth, but her adrenaline would keep her standing for a little while longer. "You're mistaken. I've seen your abilities, and I know that you should receive no mercy from me. No ounce of kindness will be shown to you." He stepped forward more and out of the water.

Rapidly, he stepped through the glass. Instantly, she swiped the broken bottle. The head author leaned back and dodged before he caught her wrist. His hold tightened, and she thought that he would snap it. Agony displayed itself on her, and the bottle dropped. More glass scattered, and he caught her other hand before it could strike him. "Time to stop this delay, human," he voiced before he tugged them both back into the water and into a shallow section of the pool.

Chapter Fifty Three: Dual Dislike

Watching the abhorrent author take her away, Tarhuinn nearly yelled for him to put her down. He had no right to carry or touch her. When the author kneed her, he almost gave himself away again. His thoughts were starting to lose control of themselves, and the desire to kill beat rapidly in his mind, though; his heart rate remained steady. If he succumbed completely to his own desires, he wouldn't be able to focus and free himself from the bonds. Odette needed him, and when the door closed behind the two of them, the sense for urgency increased.

At the same time to his left, there was a battle of magic occurring. Water, flames and air struck against each other, and fire nearly scorched him on several accounts. The benefit, though, was that it heated the water bonds, and the water began to evaporate more quickly. His healing burn marks weren't too appreciative of the heat, but getting to his wife was more vital than his damaged skin.

He needed to escape the restraints before either one of the mages was killed. Once their fight was over, he would either be tortured or killed, and Odette would have to fend for herself. That wasn't an option to him. Alpontus was just too skilled a fighter in comparison to her even though she had improved tremendously in her combat abilities. The best that she could do would be to stall him. Unfortunately, that wouldn't probably last too long either.

Whatever words were exchanged between the two mages, he didn't pay too much attention to them. It was mainly insults and the human taunting the kelremm to no end. Clearly, Icniss was falling right into the trap as he would hurl yells of pure rage back. As the fight progressed, Icniss's control over his bonds weakened. Tarhuinn was near to slipping his hands free.

A loud impact alerted him. Briefly, he peered over and noted that Icniss had been thrown into one of the walls. The human advanced towards him and continued to gibe him. The bonds became more forgiving. His hands were free. Instantly, he went to work on his ankles. It didn't take as long due to Icniss's condition and the aid from his hands.

Glancing back to the two mages, he noted that Icniss had picked himself back up and was defending himself from an onslaught of fire and air attacks. The kelremm mage's attention being elsewhere, Tarhuinn stood from his seat. His eyes caught sight of the bodies of four kelremm spies up above. Given their hand positions, it looked as though they had been strangled. It was most likely the work of the human mage since there was no rope, chain, fabric or other items nearby.

Glad that he wouldn't have to worry about them, he darted towards Alpontus's room. Before Icniss could spot and stop him, he opened the door and closed it behind him. He barely even registered that they weren't in the bedroom when he heard Odette's scream. Several yells followed. Racing ahead, he threw open the next door and barreled through.

His dark blues caught sight of the scene before him. Odette was pinned to one of the walls in the pool. Hands clenching tightly, he thought that he might break his own bones. Alpontus glanced over, and his eyes narrowed considerably. Puzzlement wrote itself across his countenance as did utmost vexation. The author's grip increased on her wrists, and Odette yelped in pain. "I'm getting very tired of seeing you free. I didn't wish to be disturbed."

Odette attempted to use Tarhuinn's distraction to wrench herself free, but a loud snap caught all of her focus. Another scream left her, and she couldn't help the tears that formed. She bit her bottom lip while her whole right arm began to tremble with shock from the pain. At least, the cold stone finally served a positive purpose against her skin.

Her watery eyes saw a flash of blue before it made contact with her captor. Alpontus didn't let go of her, however, and she went crashing towards the water and stone base as well on her right side. A piercing cry echoed throughout the room as already damaged bone only became more ruined. Thankfully, the author lost his grip when Tarhuinn snatched up his arms and pulled him away. Both of them went tumbling into a deeper section of the pool.

Part of her wished to jump into that section, but she would be near to useless there. Besides, she was a shivering, shaking mess. She removed herself steadily from the pool, cradled her wrist to her chest and curled up into a small ball, rocking herself back and forth as she dealt with the pain. It was excruciating, not just from the injury but from the fact that she was so defenseless. Her improving strength had been taken away from her so easily, and she couldn't even focus on the fight in the water; her wrist kept demanding her attention.

Several moments passed, and she could finally take a steady breath. Forcing herself, she sat herself upright. Her wrist remained close to her chest. She utilized her other hand to fix her outer clothes. Thankfully, Tarhuinn had intervened before Alpontus could cut her underclothes. The pants were ripped beyond repair and useless, but the shirt could still act as a very loose, long jacket. Her left hand clutched it close so that it would cover her torso and thighs.

Taking another deep breath and exhaling, she finally was able to view what was going on in the pool. The color red dulled her view, and her heartbeat quickened, but spotting Tarhuinn swimming swiftly, she relaxed a little. His speed didn't slow, but Alpontus was achieving the same results. They were both matched, and no progress happened. Each one had a dagger, and Tarhuinn must've stolen one of Alpontus's.

Blades clashed, and she saw one go flying through the water. Alpontus had lost his, and he swam quickly towards it. Letting go of her ripped shirt, she thrust her hand into the cold water. Just as speedily, she pulled it out before he could reach it. She couldn't move back from the water fast enough, however.

Alpontus leaped out from the water. She threw herself to her left, but he was ripped back. Odette heard a shout of rage before the water silenced it to her ears. Due to her poor landing, though, the blade was lost to her grip. It slid across the stone and towards the door of the room. Cursing, she pushed herself up with her left hand. With time, she managed to get onto her feet.

From the ongoing fight, water had splashed up onto the stone. Her right foot stepped into the puddle a little too quickly. Slipping, she fell back. Water splashed up from her collision with it. Something slammed into her back and took the breath from her. Bubbles floated upwards as her vision was poor.

There was a braid in her line of sight. The blurred, long locks were replaced by malevolent, indigo eyes. Terror grasped at her as there was nothing that she could do against him. She was far too weak presently. His hands reached out to snatch her, but they stopped midway. His lips parted while more bubbles filled the surrounding area.

Surprise controlled him before he regained himself. Rapidly, he turned and latched his jaws onto his attacker. A muted howl traveled through the water. Metal, however, met the head author's back. The ancient male released his hold on her husband. His body slackened, but her vision of the deceased author ended when Tarhuinn gently grabbed her left wrist and swam upwards with her. They broke the surface before he sheathed his blade.

Barely able to handle the cold anymore, she wasted no time in huddling to him. "We'll leave Icniss to that human mage. We need to get to the tree. The cold could kill you soon, and my injuries aren't light." She gave no argument; she merely kept near. Odette would've moved closer had it not been for her wrist.

Tarhuinn swam across the pool hurriedly and instantly stood when he could do so. He lifted her up into his arms carefully, being mindful of her broken wrist. The door was left open behind them, but he didn't care. If one of the mages caught up with them, it would be at the tree. There, the chance of an all out fight would be lessened significantly, and both of them were in no fighting condition.

Annoyingly, that would be taken advantage of. They had barely entered the cave when two spies made themselves known. Both had crossbows. Weapons were pointed, but Tarhuinn stopped only momentarily. He glanced between the two. His hold on her grew, causing her to wince a bit, but she made no complaint to him. She trusted that he knew what he was doing.

Charging forward, Tarhuinn ducked. Arrows swept overhead while he stood back up to his full height. He spun on his right foot and impacted his left against the face of one of them. She clutched onto him with her left hand and swallowed back some slight pain that shot through her from the movement. The spy was knocked down. Before the other could react, he latched his teeth into the spy's throat and killed him instantly.

Recovering from his fall, the remaining spy went to shoot the crossbow. Tarhuinn kicked the weapon upwards. He managed to still hold onto her and catch the bow. Once his finger was on the trigger, the arrow zipped towards the spy. The spy nearly dodged, but the arrow found its home in the right side of his forehead.

Dropping the weapon since retrieving the arrows would take too long since they had started to run with the stream of water, Tarhuinn continued on his way towards the tree with her. They heard loud splashes of water behind them. With no desire to face someone else, he took off sprinting.

Chapter Fifty Four: Interrupted

It was as though a blanket of warmth swept over them as they neared the tree again. She kept close to Tarhuinn, however, since her wrist was in a comfortable position. The warmth began to wrap its tendrils around her broken wrist, and a small sigh of comfort escaped her lips. Hopefully, the tree would heal her wrist completely if they stayed by it for a decent span of time. If it could keep one young, broken bones wouldn't be too much trouble.

In the distance, they could still hear the noisy splashes of water. Most likely, they belonged either to Icniss or Will. Personally, though, she was rather pleased that they no longer had to worry about the head author, and she was keeping that thought in her mind. Otherwise, a torrent of negative thoughts would flood her head. The tree also aided in maintaining her positivity. Her worry was fading, and the temptation to fall asleep in Tarhuinn's arms grew.

When they finally reached the tree, he seated himself down in the water with her. Her back and head lied against his chest while she sat between his legs. His arms were around her waist, and his head was against the trunk of the tree. Despite the calming abilities of the stunning plant, her cheeks were warm on their own.

The water caused the torn shirt and undershirt to pool around her. Tarhuinn's arms rested underneath the pieces of fabric, and she felt him shift them across her skin. A shiver would've run up her spine, but, in the shimmering water, she only felt the pleasing sensation from the contact.

Her breath caught in her throat momentarily, and it was released as a faint moan. Instinctively, she brought her knees closer to her before she turned onto her left side. She brought her hands up to her chest and was mindful of her wrist, though; it was beginning to feel better.

His arms adjusted to the new position, but his fingers glided delicately over her skin. Another near inaudible moan left her, and she closed her eyes. She didn't care that a threat was bearing down upon them; she was merely enjoying her husband's presence. The splashes of water grew, and she heard someone whistle. Easily, she recognized the owner.

Her eyes remained closed as Tarhuinn tightened his grip only slightly. He probably had a similar mindset to her at the moment, and she hoped that Will would follow in step. Otherwise, the very water around them would become their enemy.

"So, this is where the serum of youth comes from. Spectacular!" His green eyes latched themselves onto the couple, mainly Odette though. He only cast a quick glance to the male, who presently couldn't form a glare. "And, I have my other prize here too." At the pace of a snail, he looked her over. Tarhuinn wrapped his legs around her more while his hair pooled around her. Losing his view, Will pouted but chuckled regardless. "And, you're in such better attire. It makes me want you right now, but this tree is causing my urge to kill your husband to disappear. I don't even have the desire to summon a simple spell."

Making another few steps forward, Will could've reached out and grabbed her, but he refrained from doing so. Tarhuinn wanted the tree's effects to wear off; he wanted to attack the mage. He fought against the effects or tried to, but he could only bring Odette closer to him. There was also her wrist to consider, and the memory of such an event would've usually fueled his anger enough.

Presently, it only caused him to frown slightly. "Take the serum and leave us," Tarhuinn demanded, but his tone wasn't threatening in the slightest. "You can find yourself another woman, and you can have many with the serum."

Never did Odette expect her husband to negotiate with the male before them. She suspected that he would have his hands around Will's throat or his teeth in it if it weren't for the tree. Odette wasn't too hopeful on Will being persuaded. The mage's following laugh proved her to be correct.

"I don't think so. I want my bluebell back. You've had enough time with her." Will extended out his right hand towards her, and Tarhuinn couldn't pull her any closer. He tried to open his jaw and bite the male, but his will to commit to the action was lacking, so he repositioned himself and moved Odette behind him.

She opened her eyes and, reluctantly, met the mage's gaze. His hand withdrew itself, but he didn't take a step back. A grin was plastered on his lips. "I told you that I would be taking you back with me, Bluebell. Don't tell me that you intend to refuse me?"

"I'm not going back there with you. I'm never going to enter that storage space."

"That's unfortunate. If you came with me, you would get to see the rest of the authors and that mage. I'd even let you stab their remains a few times. Isn't that consideration at its highest point?" He held out his hands as though he was offering her the platter of her greatest wishes. His deal was anything but that. Her only wish was to return home with Tarhuinn with some of the serum in hand.

Not even going to entertain him with a response, she remained quiet and managed to bring herself to her feet. The tree kept her terror of Will suppressed. Her right hand rested loosely on her husband's left shoulder. It was still healing, and it shook a little bit from the small amount of applied pressure, but she didn't move it. "He's my husband, and I love him, not you. I'll never let you touch me. You'll be killed if you don't leave us, and I'll feel no sympathy for you. I'll feel no guilt that you died by my hands. You'll be forgotten, and everything of yours will be burned until even the ash vanishes."

"Such harsh words for a flower." He crossed his arms across his chest while his eyes directed themselves to her right hand. "And, a broken one too. I'm supposed to be the one to damage you. I should've come sooner. Then, that author wouldn't have laid a hand on you. How unfortunate." Finally, a threatening growl emitted from Tarhuinn. Will gave him an uninterested glance but maintained his typical grin. His eyes looked back to Odette. "And, did I hear that you intend to kill me?"

“Yes, I don’t want you in my life, and I’ll end your life if I have to.”

Standing to his feet, Tarhuinn gently removed her hand from him. He leaned down and whispered, “Odette ...” Before he could utter anything else, she pressed her lips to his. Her cheeks burned some, but she continued the kiss. She didn’t care that Will was watching. To her, he wasn’t even there in that moment. When she pulled away, she didn’t let Tarhuinn finish his thought.

Lips still close to his, she whispered, “I know what I’m doing.” That wasn’t the case at all, but her fear was absent. Its lack of presence was dangerous, but she couldn’t stop herself. Her mind had committed itself to the next task. Reason was probably gone from her as well; she couldn’t take on a mage by herself, but, in the present environment, logic didn’t necessarily play a role.

Stepping back, she avoided her husband’s right hand when it reached out for her. She created distance between herself and the two males before she faced Will directly. “Are you going to disappear, or are you forcing my hand?”

“I don’t know what you intend to do in this place,” he answered, spreading his arms out to indicate to the whole area, “but let’s see this oh so deadly side of you.”

Everything was against her. She had no weapons on her except her hands, but one of them wouldn’t be able to form a strong grip. Despite that, she took a step towards him. Part of her wished to fall asleep, but that overwhelming sense of relaxation prevented her from thinking about the possibility of dying. Tarhuinn, though, wouldn’t stand for it. The kelremm went to stand between the two, but Odette instantly locked her gaze with him.

“No,” she managed to speak in a strong voice. It took some energy, but she felt that it was worth it. He needed to understand that she had the situation in her hands. The task was hers, not his. To fully get rid of the nightmare of Will, she had to deal with him herself; she had to know that he was dead.

"She's correct. Don't ruin the show, fish. You're tiring me," Will remarked, yawning for emphasis. Tarhuinn ignored him completely and paused only because of Odette. Shortly after, he continued his advance but towards her. She didn't speak the word again, and she stayed in her present place.

Walking up to stand right beside her, he faced the opposite direction. His right hand placed itself on her right shoulder. "No, I'll kill him with you. We both have more than a quarrel with him, but you deserve the final blow." He increased his grip on her. "Even you said that we'll stand side by side."

Focus remaining on Will, she clenched her left fingers softly. That was true, but she wished to finish him on her own. She had set her mind to doing so, yet that was being taken from her. Tarhuinn had good intentions; he didn't wish to lose her, and if she was in his position, she would be behaving in the same fashion. She forced herself to see some reason. A slight nod came from her. "Just make sure that I receive the killing strike."

"Don't worry. I have no intention of stealing that from you. Now, let's go under," he replied in a hushed tone. At first, she didn't quite understand him. When she felt him press against her shoulder, she knew exactly what he had meant. They were in water, and Will wasn't a kelremm. As she became submerged, she smiled; they could have the upper hand after all.

Chapter Fifty Five: Water Run

Cool, comforting hands seemed to wash over her while her eyesight was somewhat compromised by the shimmery waters. They almost made her forget about her present plan; they nearly lulled her to sleep in their soft embrace. Tarhuinn was still as well, most likely undergoing a similar experience. Everything above the water almost faded away into a distant memory, but she could just barely spot Will's calves and feet. Those kept her mind from disappearing into a dreamland.

Will started to move, however, out of the enchanting waters. She darted her brown eyes over to her husband, and he was already on the move but slower than usual. Odette could only move so fast herself. The invisible hands kept aching for her to swim back. It was like someone forcing her out of an amazing dream; she didn't wish to leave, but she had to. Will, under no circumstances, would be allowed to escape.

Pushing the waters aside, she kept her mouth shut tight. She would drink some of the water when they returned home. If the effects of the waters were strong outwardly, she didn't wish to discover their influence inwardly presently.

Tarhuinn was a little ways ahead of her, but she knew that he wouldn't kill Will. He had made her a promise, and he would keep it. Grabbing hold of Will's left ankle, Tarhuinn tugged him under before he could exit the glimmering section. Her husband went to bite the mage's left shoulder, but Will managed to force him back. The water threw Tarhuinn back and forced her somewhat towards the tree. His green eyes looked her way. As quickly as she could, she swam in another direction. The water, however, shoved her towards him.

It didn't help that she needed to get some air. When she went to breach the surface, the water pushed her down. Cursing mentally, she wished that her body wasn't acting so relaxed about her situation. Since Will was a mage, it was probably easier to break out of the tree's effects for him. They needed to get him closer to the plant again.

That could only happen if she remained conscious. If she passed out, all of his attention would direct itself to her husband. No element of surprise would be permitted that way, which begged the question of where Tarhuinn had gone. Even with her poor perspective, she had been able to see him before. Now, she couldn't even spot an outline.

When the water's hold on her broke, she burst up for air. She caught sight of Will being pulled under again. Regaining herself, she noticed that both Will and Tarhuinn were zipping through the water. They both left the shimmery parts of it and went flying quite some distance away. Tarhuinn slammed against a rock to her left, but he recovered almost immediately after the impact. Will, on the other hand, stood to his feet to the right of her. Water formed around his feet in the shape of shoes while he tested some of his wind magic in his hands.

A satisfied grin overtook his lips. "Now, things will be how they should be." Wind shot from his hands, and water rose into large, charging waves. Tarhuinn dived into the water and disappeared while she did the same. Unluckily, the waves were much stronger on her side.

Tarhuinn hadn't been able to reach her in time. Even under water, she was tossed back. She rolled through the water and slammed against the trunk of the tree. Her breath was lost, but she didn't feel much pain. Thankfully, her wrist didn't return to its previous damaged state, but it had almost collided with the tree.

Leaves fell from the branches and drifted off in the water. Using her left hand, she pushed herself up against the tree and noticed that Will was keeping his distance. Tarhuinn was still gone from sight. Will pushed water back to try and locate him, but she knew that the mage would attack her again soon. That disgusting smile of his said so.

Somehow she needed to near him and attain a weapon. Since he wasn't attacking her yet, she searched the room for some method of defense. His violent treatment of the water had caused some of the rocks from the walls to break off. If she was lucky, she would find one that was sharp, but searching would consume too much time.

Glancing up to the tree, she looked over the branches. The points of some were rather sharp, and the branches themselves looked sturdy. She could possibly fight with one, but she would wait until Tarhuinn's next attack to break one off. Water snatched her ankles once more. Her back slid down the tree before water took over her form.

Instantly, she threw out her arms and gripped the trunk. Her fingers dug into it. They scraped across, and skin broke. Crimson and the tree's effects weakened her hold, but she refused to let go. Thankfully, the pain in her wrist was barely noticeable, but she was tempted to call out for Tarhuinn to strike Will already. Desperately, she required a distraction. Where was he?!

Violently, the water tore her from the tree. A scream of frustration left her, but it was barely audible as the tree soothed her once more. Across the surface of the water, she slid. Her eyes widened, though. Tarhuinn leaped straight out of the water and took Will's left hand in his mouth. Due to the speed of his ascent, the kelremm removed the mage's hand. It was Will's turn to cry out in absolute agony.

Released, she swam back towards the tree. Before she turned completely, she saw Tarhuinn spit the hand out and come back down on the mage. Still in shock from the loss, Will didn't block in time. The kelremm slammed against the mage. Both went under, giving her some time.

Making it back to the tree, she brought herself to her feet. She grasped the closest and strongest looking branch. Her fingers weren't healed, but they were being soothed during her action. Odette tugged downwards, but the branch wouldn't budge, so she jumped up, grabbed it and pulled. That didn't work either. No matter what she tried, nothing resulted in success. Her eyes looked to the point again, and she confirmed once more that it was fatal enough. If she couldn't bring the branch to Will, he would come to it.

Inspecting the water for the two males, she spotted them close to the entrance of the cave. Tarhuinn shot up into the air, but he twirled himself around so that his feet would hit the ceiling. He pushed himself off and flew back towards the mage. Will smirked and lifted his only hand.

"Will! Did I ever tell you that I saw Patricia in my old village?!" Of course, that had been a lie, but the question worked. He turned to look at her, but his locked gaze with hers was short-lived. Water enveloped both males once more. Immediately, Tarhuinn was sent back down the tunnel leading to the room. Will rose up from the water, and a glare covered his expression. To her surprise, there was no insanity in his intense stare; only anger and hope resided there.

The mage probably understood that she was lying, but there was a shred of hope in his eyes. He didn't know every detail of her background. Even though he had seen Patricia die, they were in a room with a tree that extended one's life indefinitely. There existed the smallest of possibilities that she was still alive. She kept her expression neutral and allowed the tree's effects to calm her completely. He needed to head closer to her.

His left wrist rose before he dropped it again. Skin had been pulled over the once exposed innards of his wrist. Raising his right hand, he flicked his middle and index fingers. Her feet were pulled out from under her. Tarhuinn was coming up from behind, but Will kicked his left foot back. The kelremm's movement halted while a wall of water blocked him.

Odette reached the mage. He grabbed her shirt and lifted her up. In an instant, he hardened the water wall and slammed her up against it. A cry left her as they were some distance from the tree. "What do you mean? You were just lying to me, weren't you? I never told you her description! How could you have known her?!"

Keeping up the fabrication, she answered, "She told me her name was Patricia; she was incredibly nice. She said how she missed a good friend of hers but couldn't return to him. She stated that she was thought dead." Her hands circled around his wrist to try to loosen his hold on her.

"What did she look like?" His voice grew calmer, but his tone remained threatening.

"She had red, short hair and light brown eyes. She stated that she had her appearance changed as a precaution." Amusement crossed his expression, and she understood that she had made a mistake in describing her, but she could only keep the act up for so long. After all, it had been meant only as a distraction. Otherwise, Tarhuinn would've probably been dead.

"I knew that she was dead. Her eyes were a dark blue, and she wouldn't have gone through the trouble of changing them. The hair I can believe but nothing else. Besides, she knew how much I loved her eyes. She wouldn't have changed them no matter the situation." Insanity washed over him, and he began to laugh. "I think that it's time." He slammed her harshly against the wall before he dropped her.

Her vision became incredibly blurry, and she could hear Tarhuinn banging against the wall. The back of her shirt was grabbed, and Will dragged her through the water to the tree. "We'll be having a lot of fun shortly, Bluebell. And, I'll even add something extra in for your lovely falsification."

Chapter Fifty Six: Final Opportunity

Her back against the trunk of the tree, she heard banging. Tarhuinn called out her name in her head. Will spoke something next to her, but it was far too quiet for her to understand it. Her vision remained lacking, but before she panicked, she realized that it was only due to her eyelids being closed. For a brief time, she must've lost consciousness, but the effects of the tree brought her back to her senses probably quicker than Will had anticipated.

She closed her left eyelid again and kept her right eye open only a little bit. Peering upwards, she noticed that Will was dropping a few leaves into a small glass jar. He capped it and placed it into presumably a shirt pocket. Another tiny container was removed from his person before he filled it with some water from the base of the tree. Once finished with that one, he continued with his muttering. His right foot tapped in the water as he examined the tree.

His back turned to her slightly before he crouched and pushed some of the water aside. A few of the tree's roots revealed themselves. Having an idea of what he was debating, she waited until he lowered himself closer. Will's back completely faced her. It helped further that he shoved the water around since it drowned out her movement somewhat. While she changed positions, she briefly analyzed him for a weapon, but she, unfortunately, didn't see one.

Odette stood behind him and waited for him to stand. Time passed slowly, and it felt like ages passed before he stood back up. His gaze looked to his right, but she mainly focused on the fact that his height put him directly in front of some branches. Wasting no time, she threw her hands out and shoved them against his back.

Caught off guard, he lost his balance for a split moment, but that was enough. The branch pierced through his chest, and crimson was coughed up from his throat. His hand reached up to the branch, but she pushed him forward more.

More red decorated the area. The next time, his hand aimed towards her. His already slow ability to fight becoming even more so, she managed to grab hold of him beforehand, but nothing happened due to the tree's effects.

His breathing became slower. His hand reached down to hers, but she pulled them back before he could cause any damage to them. She rammed herself into his back again, and she thought that she killed him that time; however, she noticed that he was losing too little of blood given the circumstance.

Looking to the wound, she saw that the tree was stopping the bleeding. It couldn't completely heal him, though, since it was in the way of itself. It gave Will somewhat of a fighting chance, so she hit him again as hard as she could. Red ran down the branch and dripped into the pool. "Bl-bluebell, ... y-you surpr-ise me ... I didn't th-think y-ou capa-ble ... of su-such a d-eath." She ignored him and knew that the branch was close to his heart.

As she was about to shove him again, he reached behind himself and grabbed her left wrist. Utilizing the last of his physical strength, he tugged her around him until his left arm wrapped around her waist. Her wrist was pressed against his chest, and a grin painted his lips. "Bu-but, you st ... -ill fai-led."

Forcibly, he pressed his lips to hers, and she could hear Tarhuinn shout out her name. None of her offered any attention to the kiss; she had other things to worry about. Will needed to die. He went to take a step back, but she secured her free arm around his waist and pushed him forward.

What she assumed to be blood ran down her lips, and she wanted to instantly wipe her mouth clean. Will, however, persisted and didn't break the kiss. Teeth snapped down on her bottom lip, and a yelp exited her before the taste of metal swept through her mouth. Disgusted completely, she retaliated and bit down on his tongue hard, and a cry left from him. The kiss broke as she wrenched herself away.

Despite that, his green eyes gleamed with malevolent amusement. His lips curled up more. The bloodied, wide grin caused him to become utterly terrifying. If she weren't by the tree, she probably would've run. She did miss a step, though. His lips parted as if he wished to speak but no words came out. It would probably be a few more moments before his tongue would be back to normal.

Expectorating the blood from her mouth, she wiped the remaining from her lips and returned his maddening smile with a forbidding scowl. Eyes lit up, he extended out his right hand to the tree. "Die soon, Bluebell," he mouthed, and her eyes widened. Somehow, he had managed to break past the tree's effects.

"No!" she screamed but knew better than to run towards him. A heated, large blast thundered throughout the area, and she was thrown back. Water splashed up around her as waves came crashing down. Darkness enveloped the area while the shimmery waters receded. Her mind entered a panic as the tree's effects withered. She could feel them lightly, but they weren't enough to do much.

Realizing that she was sinking, she composed herself and swam to the surface. Cold began to ensnare her as her teeth chattered. Arms wrapped around her, and she nearly thought for a moment that Will had survived, but she recognized Tarhuinn's firm, yet comforting hold. She could feel his warmth, and she cuddled into him.

Air greeted her lungs as she took a deep breath and exhaled. Her sight was poor as the tree's light was close to being nonexistent. Where the tree had once stood, though, she was just able to spot things bobbing in the water, and they didn't belong to the tree. The sight would've made her sick had she not seen countless other horrors that day.

Turning away, she lightly clutched Tarhuinn's shirt. "What ... d-do we do?" Her voice no longer could remain calm. The tree had been destroyed. Even the leaves were blown to dust from the blast.

Arms remained around her comfortingly. "It's not completely dark in here."

"I know, but it'll be soon." She rested her head against his chest. "It wa-was all f-for no-nothing," she choked up, sobs of frustration beginning to break free. Her grip grew tighter, and she was glad that her wrist had been healed enough before the tragic incident. "I'm s-s-s-so sor-sorr..."

"Odette, it won't fade away. We still have what we came for." Steadily, she looked up to him. She noticed his reassuring smile, but before she could ask what he meant, she was scooped up out of the water and into his arms. Being out of the frigid liquid was welcome, and her tears dried up at what she saw.

Tarhuinn was right. Beneath the surface of the water, a miniscule pool of shimmery water remained. Some of the roots survived. He directed her eyes to two small bottles some ways away from the roots. Leaves and the water remained intact inside. Will must've used some magic to strengthen the glass. Otherwise, those would've been obliterated.

Walking through the water, he voiced, "We'll keep the bottles for ourselves. After all of this, I'll not have you die when our child turns two. As for the roots, we'll transport them back to the first complex and have the tree grow back to its former glory. Until then, everyone should still be able to extend their lives somewhat. If possible, we can grow a second and third for the other complexes, but that's not important right now."

Stopping, he leaned down and kissed her. It was short, but it contained all of the passion from their previous ones. "We need to get you some warmer clothes. I'm sure that the authors won't mind us taking some of their things. We'll burn them and those books after we return home."

She nodded and rested her head against his chest. She was utterly exhausted, and she wanted a warm meal, but she didn't desire to stay any longer than necessary in the authors' home. There were still spies around, and they would have to be wary of them. With the spies' masters gone, they had no idea what to expect. Some of the spies might've left already, but some would most likely try to kill them.

Even with that in mind, she could feel a smile forming on her lips. The authors were gone, Will was dead and they could return home. They had to give the bodies of the authors to the mermaids, and that involved entering Will's storage room, but that was nothing in comparison to what they had accomplished.

Several weights were lifted off of her shoulders at once, and she had been the one technically to deal the final blow to Will. She ended the possibility of that nightmare ever coming true. That was enough to make her giddy for a year if not longer. Tarhuinn would never hear the end of it, and if he were lucky, he might get some credit attributed to Will's death.

Setting her down in the water, Tarhuinn removed the roots from the ground. She maintained her small, victory smile as she bent down and helped him. It aided in keeping her mind off of the biting cold. His dark blues glanced to her momentarily. "I think that I've decided to train you."

Surprised, she asked, "You mean it?!" The excitement in her voice was hard to contain.

"Yes." His gaze grew a little serious. "I grew jealous with how you were fighting the authors and that mage." She caught his eyes doing another take of her current state. There was an evident frown on his lips, and an immense wave of heat overtook her cheeks. Now really looking at herself, she hadn't noticed before how bad things were. Her soaked clothes clung to her so much that she was practically on display. Instantly, she wrapped the ruined shirt around her as if that would help.

"Thank you for the opportunity," she meekly replied as she clutched the cloth more, "but, please, let's just hurry up here." She couldn't meet his gaze anymore even though she had been running around in her present condition for some time, but it was embarrassing given how he had pointed out his opinion so honestly. Had that been why his fighting had sometimes been slower when he had been away from the tree's effects? Had he been watching more than just her combat skills? Shaking her head, she was swooped up again.

"For our fighting, you'll be wearing something that'll keep you warmer," he reassured, pressing a light kiss to the top of her head. Odette could tell, though, that he was smirking somewhat, but she let it slide. She would just make sure to beat him in the first fight. That thought caused a smirk of her own to form.

Chapter Fifty Seven: Return

Getting out of the authors' home had been simpler than expected. Unfortunately, they probably had Will to thank for that as they had found countless dead kelremm on their way out. The state of some of the females had been terrifying, and she had been quite happy that he was no more. With the lack of spies, it had been easy also to take supplies from the authors' home. Both Tarhuinn and her had been clothed in dry articles, and they had two packs full of supplies. To top it off, they each had their own winter cloak. For once, she hadn't been freezing.

Despite those benefits, they still had to collect the bodies of the authors. Alpontus, Amtoma and Rocean hadn't been too much trouble, but Tergii and Bimaa had been a different story. The main issue with the first three had been carrying/dragging their bodies across the cold, snowy land. She had been tempted at one point to let the bodies simply flow down the river and let the merfolk catch them, but she had a feeling that such a plan wouldn't turn out so ideally.

When they had been finally able to drop off the three to two of the merfolk, she had to explain that the remaining two authors would be there soon. The guards hadn't been exactly too accepting, so she had ended up having to discuss the matter with Aqua. She had been agreeable and permitted it, which had been an immense relief. Odette had been rather happy that Cetar wasn't the one that they had spoken with. That conversation would've most likely resulted in a completely different outcome.

For Tergii and Bimaa, their retrieval had been less than pleasant. Tarhuinn had offered to enter the storage room and bring them out, but she had known that was unreasonable. He wouldn't have made it there and back in time, so she had to enter the dreadful place twice since she hadn't been able to carry both of them at once.

The process had consumed quite a significant amount of time. It had taken her several moments to even open the door. Her hand had been shaking the entire time. When she had opened the door, she had nearly fainted. She had thought that she had seen enough horror back at the authors' home to numb her of such things, but she had been far from right.

Frozen bodies that were beginning to unthaw with the death of Will had been spread throughout the entirety of the place. Some had been hanging, and others had been in large bins. Pieces had been scattered throughout while his latest victims had been set on stone tables. Alpontus's daughter nearly had made her vomit. She had to turn instantly away from the scene, but it would forever be imprinted in her memory.

Bimaa had been in terrible shape too, but, in comparison to the female mage, she had looked as if she had never been touched by Will. Concerning Tergii, he had been in two pieces since he had been decapitated. The rest of him had been left alone. Once she had finished with that ordeal, she had needed a moment to rest her mind from the sights of that room. Tarhuinn had comforted her throughout all of it and had reassured her that they would never need to return to the cabin. To them, it would become a distant memory.

The moment that they had dropped off the bodies to the merfolk she had practically skipped off. They had finished it all. On their way back home, she had seen multiples snow pixies, but they hadn't bothered either of them. Even though Will had left them before the two of them had returned, Tarhuinn and she had fulfilled their end of the bargain, and Will had killed the mage that had been threatening the pixies.

There had been one problem with them, but it had been settled with her holding Tarhuinn back. He had still been infuriated about the pixies' treatment of them. It hadn't surprised her that he would never forgive them. To him, they had sent his wife on a suicide mission, and that would always be unforgivable. If any of the creatures had gotten too close, he had unsheathed a dagger. On one occasion, he had been about to slash it through the air, but she had luckily deflected it in time before it had made contact with the pixie in question.

From there, there hadn't been too many issues. Traveling through the third and second complexes had progressed smoothly. Those in the third complex had even gone to celebrate with the news that the authors were dead. There remained the threat of the spies, but none of them were a mage and none of them were excellent fighters either.

They hadn't said anything about the authors in the second complex, only that the books needed to be adjusted as a solution to their human partners dying had been discovered. The news had struck up conversation, but Tarhuinn and she had mentioned to the residents that they would have to wait until they had reached the first complex. Arrangements needed to be made before anyone could partake of the solution.

Now sailing through the large span of water that separated the first and second complexes, Odette was met with the darkness once more, but she knew what to expect. The water pixies flew around her and whispered things into her ears, but they weren't commenting about Tarhuinn's violent and overprotective nature. Rather, they were stating that he had calmed some and was more respectful of her. They noted that she had grown strong and gained her own protective nature of him. She felt pride in herself that her strength was being recognized, but her cheeks did warm somewhat at the second remark; she couldn't deny it, though.

Passing through the area, she nearly leaped out of the boat and onto the steps. A chuckle escaped Tarhuinn as he followed behind her. She couldn't contain her excitement at coming home even though it was the reverse of what she had done before. Frankly, she had enough traveling for a good few years. Odette was ready to collapse upon her bed and cuddle into the sheets.

Some kelremm looked up from their stalls to see her practically running through. Their stares moved from her to Tarhuinn, who gave them a respectful nod and a smile. As he passed, he told stall owners to spread the news that they had solved an ancient problem of theirs and that in the next few days they would explain the solution.

Curiosity arose, but he withheld the details, stating that his wife and he required some rest. Thankfully, they understood. He walked back to Odette's side before he climbed up the ladders, which had water running down them and flat rather than circular rungs for better grip, after her.

At the doors to their home, Tarhuinn stepped up and unlocked it. Inside, he called out to Nyclaya, who made herself present a few moments later. She looked the same as when they had left, though; her outfit was all blue leather. The female kelremm looked them both over and grinned. "I see that the two of you picked up some souvenirs while you were away. Bring anything back for me?" she asked, looking over to Tarhuinn. "Or, did you forget about that little conversation of ours?"

"Of course," he answered, maintaining a neutral expression. He reached into his pack and removed a fine, silver bracelet. His eyes glanced to Odette momentarily, and she gave a silent approval.

Analyzing it after he handed it over, she placed it onto her right wrist and held it up. "Amazing." She whistled and twisted her wrist some. "It's feather-light and shimmers in the right angle of lighting. Where did you find this?"

"That can be saved for another time. We're having a meeting called for the whole complex later tomorrow. You'll learn the answer, then. Right now, I can't thank you enough for watching over our home for us."

Glancing between the two of them, she chuckled and held up her hands. "Alright, I have my item to add to my collection. I'll leave you two be now." Her hands returned to her sides before she walked by Tarhuinn and whispered something to him. He rolled his eyes and made a shooing motion with his right hand. Another laugh left her, and she exited the house but not before winking to Odette.

Even though she didn't know the context of what had transpired, she could guess it, and heat tickled her cheeks. The doors closed, and Tarhuinn locked them once more. "Well, let's change and get out of these awful clothes. We can leave the packs by the door; we'll be trading the items later on anyway." Nodding in agreement, she dropped her pack and started down the path.

Stretching, she remarked, "We can finally relax." She heard a second pack hit the ground before splashes of water proceeded afterwards. Soon enough, Tarhuinn was walking beside her.

"Odette, did you forget about what I had told you before?" Glancing over to him, she raised an eyebrow. He took that as a yes. Personally, her mind was settling on the fact of taking a soothing rest. "Just what makes you think that you'll be able to relax all of today?"

Memories coming back, her face filled with heat. In a stuttering manner, she responded, "I ... I-I don't w-want to ta-talk about i-it." She quickened her pace and rubbed the sides of her cheeks. Swiftly, he caught up to her and wrapped his right hand around her left wrist. He pulled her to him, and she would've fallen into the water if she hadn't been supported by his chest.

Hands against him, she cautiously peered up. Almost, she jumped back. His lips were dangerously close. He tugged her nearer but in a gentle manner. Mere centimeters from her own, his lips parted. "Then, let's not discuss it. We both could use a delightful bath after all." She gazed sideways while her cheeks burned. Recalling the conversation back at the tree, she remembered herself mentioning them taking a bath when they were back home. In truth, it did sound ... nice if that was the right term. Her blood was much too hot for her to think of a more descriptive word.

Returning her gaze to him, she stood up on her tippy-toes and kissed him. He picked her up, and her legs wrapped around his waist while her arms found themselves around his neck. The kiss progressed from gentle to heated within a matter of moments. A door opened behind her before it closed again. Soon enough, she was seated on the edge of the bathtub.

Water soaked her cloak, but it slipped from her shoulders after Tarhuinn untied it. Odette kicked her boots off as she removed his cloak from his shoulders. Tarhuinn placed his hands against her shoulders and pushed her back until they both fell into the tub. Splashing up, water surrounded them both, and they had a brief break from the kiss before it continued.

Bringing her up into a sitting position, she straddled his lap, and her hands slipped the loose shirt from his shoulders. His fingers ran up her torso before they rested at the top of her shirt. They tore at the fabric and ripped the shirt in half. It fell from her form, and he cast it out from the bathtub. Tarhuinn moved his lips from hers as she caught her breath, but that didn't last long. He trailed kisses down her neck. Each left her breathless as they switched between being feather-light and passionately rough.

Taking her hands in his, he directed them to his midsection and glided her fingers up his shirt. His muscles rippled under her delicate touch. He found and nipped at her soft spot, but no blood was drawn. Rather, a quiet moan parted from her. Her hands slipped up his chest as she nearly collapsed against him. Tarhuinn continued to hold onto her hands until he released them. With understanding, she ripped the fabric and allowed it to flow out of the bath.

She couldn't help but glance over his toned form. Her fingers ran along his skin, but her attention on his torso was broken when he lifted up her chin. His lips ghosted over hers before he held them to the right corner of hers. Left hand sliding up her undershirt and drifting over her bare back, she shivered at his touch. "Your warm breath against my skin is intoxicating, Odette," he whispered before he pressed a kiss to her jaw.

His other hand slipped down from her chin to her midsection. Fingers trailed up under her undershirt, and she tensed. Her breath got caught in her throat again when they slid through the middle of her chest. The hand at her back pressed against her, and her back arched while her chest moved closer into his other hand. Tarhuinn's lips traveled down to her neck once more. Lips caressing her skin, he glided them down her skin. Near to his hand on her chest, he peered up at her and softly asked, "Do you accept me, my chosen?"

Legs growing weak, she fell into him more. Her head hung down, her arms wrapped around him and her hands rested loosely against his bare back. Lips to his right shoulder, she moved them into his neck. She wished to melt against him. Words almost lost, she managed to answer, "Yes, my chosen." His lips smiled softly against her skin before fabric ripped and fell around her. Water encircled them more as their devotion to each other molded together.

Epilogue:

Face snuggled into a pillow; Odette wrapped her arms around the soft, delightful object as she continued to enjoy her sleep. Her fingers and arms twitched a little at the odd sensation, though. Something was off with her cushiony item. Eyes closed tighter while her body tried to comprehend it. She brought it closer to her only to receive an alarming, "Squawk!"

Jumping up in bed, she threw the thing away from her. The chicken flapped its wings before it collided with Tarhuinn, who had awoken at the sound. Instantly, he grabbed the bird and held onto it tightly until it calmed down. He blew a few feathers from his face before he looked around the area.

Odette knew exactly who he was looking for. The little three-year-old was hiding somewhere in the vicinity. Another squawk, quieter than the last, came from the chicken. A groan sounded from her husband before he stood to his feet. He glanced over to her, and she nodded. "I'll find her," Odette answered before he left to place the traumatized chicken back in its pen.

Despite kelremm children maturing mentally at a rather quick rate, her child never grew out of pranks. Her daughter would spend hours reading, or she would ask for another story from either Tarhuinn or her, and she would act like a young adult at those times. Ten minutes later, she would be running around the house and plotting her next scheme.

Pushing back some strands of light blonde hair, Odette climbed out of bed and onto the dry area of the room before she headed into the small, water room that they had made for their daughter. It had taken a year and quite a bit of trading, but the end result gave their daughter her own space and privacy for Tarhuinn and her. She crossed her arms over her chest and examined the places that her daughter could be hiding in, behind or under. Mentally, she smiled upon seeing locks of ink-black hair in the water behind the child's bed.

As silently as she could, she advanced through the water. She heard slight movement behind the bed. Odette shook her head a little when she noted her daughter trying to sneak around the object and back out the door. “And, where do you think you’re going?” she asked, raising an eyebrow. The girl froze and glanced up at her mother before her dark blue eyes darted to the door.

Knowing exactly what her daughter intended to do, Odette sprinted into action before the girl could take off. She grabbed the back of her daughter’s blue dress and lifted her up. “Set me down, mother! The chicken got out of the pen on its own. I swear!”

Skeptically, she looked to her child. “Do you swear on your silver headband?” No answer came from the young girl as she looked to her left and mumbled something under her breath. The headband didn’t look like too important of an object, but, to her daughter, it was her favorite possession. The young girl hated having her hair fall over her face while reading or doing anything really, so she kept her hair just below her ears and wore the headband as an extra precaution. “I’m sorry; I couldn’t quite hear that, Delphi.”

She pouted and somewhat glared at her mother. “No.” Keeping her child’s stare, Odette gave her the look to continue. “... But, it was just a prank!” Her serious expression faded, and worry set in. “Besides, you liked cuddling with the chicken!”

“I’m waiting, Delphi.”

“But, you didn’t deny it!”

“I don’t have to. You’re just saying things to try and get me off topic. Now, what do you say? I’ll keep holding you until you answer properly.”

A childish groan left her lips before she reluctantly replied, “I’m sorry for putting a chicken in father’s and your room, mother.”

"Thank you. Now, go apologize to your father. I'm not the only the one who might take that headband away." Instantly, she pressed against Odette's arms, and Odette released her so that she could race to Tarhuinn. Shaking her head in amusement, Odette watched the child scurry off and out of the room. It sounded like she didn't have to run far as a loud splash sounded in the next room.

Walking back out into her bedroom, Odette noted Delphi quickly apologizing to her father while her small hands held onto her headband like it was her lifeline. Tarhuinn glanced over to her, and Odette shook her head as if to say that they could let it go. A sigh left him before he signaled her off. "Meet us in the kitchen, Delphi. We'll be eating some breakfast before heading out to the market."

Wasting no time in standing around, she ran off, and the sound of tiny splashes of water grew faint soon after. Tarhuinn closed the door after she had left before he closed the distance between the two of them. His right fingers glided smoothly over her left cheek, and she moved her face more into the palm of his hand. "How are you feeling today?" A light laugh left her before she met his gaze.

"You don't need to ask me that question every day, Tarhuinn. It's been a year and a half since her second birthday. I'm doing marvelous. Everyone else is experiencing the same results with their human partners. The tree is only growing more with each year, and we should be able to plant a second and third one in the other complexes soon. Stop worrying about me. You need to be more concerned about Delphi and what prank she intends to pull next."

It was his turn to laugh. He removed his hand and placed a light kiss on top of her head. "I think that the blame falls on you for that one. You're the one who keeps insisting that you killed a powerful mage completely on your own. She has your sense of adventure, Odette. And, these pranks are her way of trying to get that out."

Rolling her eyes, it was her turn to pout before she turned on her heel and headed over to her dresser to change for the day. "You're not going to want to take a morning bath?" she heard him ask. Heat filled her cheeks, and she shook her head. After that one day, it was hard for her to think of a bath as simply a bath. He chuckled before he commented, "Suit yourself ... my chosen."

Falling forward some, she supported herself on the dresser before she glared to him. "Let me guess; you're going to carry me on your back through the market again." She received a simple shrug from him. Delphi thought that it was comical, and she could only imagine what her partner would have to endure.

"I do intend to wear that cloak that you really like, though: the incredibly soft one," he mentioned, a small smirk on his lips.

Hearing that, she couldn't help but smile. "Or, I could just steal your cloak and cuddle in it. You're going to have a hard time carrying me that way."

"That's if you can get to the cloak first, Odette. In your condition, do you really think that's possible?"

"Try me." Silence took over and thickened before she pushed herself off of the dresser and forced her legs somewhat to run. In reality, her sprint was more like a poor representation of a bunny hop. Unfortunately, Tarhuinn reached the cloak first and held it high. That didn't mean that she had given up, though.

When she finally stood before him, she grabbed onto his shoulders and lifted herself onto her tippy-toes to attempt to attain the article of clothing. He watched amused as he merely raised it more into the air. "You might as well fall into me and accept the situation."

"Like I'm going to do that." She did stop using him as a support and fell to her knees, but, in the process, she grabbed his ankles and tugged him down swiftly. Caught off guard, he fell into the water with a loud splash as the cloak flew down. It never touched the water, however, due to small, blue hands grabbing it and running off with it.

Both parents were shocked when they saw their daughter dash off with the object. She was giggling the entire time, and she called back, “You two were taking too long! Come to breakfast if you want it back!” While they had been fighting if it could be called that over the cloak, she must’ve slipped in and waited for the right moment. Delphi was taking after her in the fact that she observed Tarhuinn’s fighting closely. At times if the girl focused enough, she could move almost as quietly as one of them, but it probably had helped that they were both too preoccupied with the cloak.

“It looks like we’re being summoned,” Tarhuinn joked, glancing over to her. He stood to his feet and held out his left hand. She took it, and he helped her up before he lifted her into his arms. The action didn’t surprise her, and it was more convenient since her legs were wobbly.

“Yes, but I think that you’re just happy because you get to carry me sooner.” She crossed her arms over her chest and gave him an accusatory glance but in a playful manner.

“Maybe, but you’re enjoying this. That I know.”

Looking away for a moment, she laughed softly. “Well, I can’t necessarily disagree. Besides when I’m like this, it means that you’re on breakfast duty.” A smirk tugged at her lips, and she looked to him victoriously. “I think that I won this fight in the end, Tarhuinn.”

“We still have the rest of the day, Odette.” Challenging stares were shared between them before each broke out into their own laughter, and they headed off to the kitchen. It helped as well that Delphi was now threatening to give the cloak to the chickens. That made both parents curse loudly before Tarhuinn hurried the rest of the way. Children of the water did tend to be quite persuasive.

Made in the USA
Columbia, SC
10 July 2020

13546630R00264